ONCE A PIRATE ...

Isabella looked at the handsome pirate captain who was standing with arms crossed in the center of his cabin. This had to be a dream. Pirates lived in clouds, not on earth. Her mind couldn't take the collision between her rich imagination and her fear of the real world.

"Am I your captive?" she asked softly. She could feel waves flowing beneath the ship; it was in motion.

"I prefer to call you my ... guest," he said, emptying wine into two silver goblets.

"Are you going to ravish me?"

"Of course not." He touched her pink lips with a hard thumb. *Poor thing,* he thought, *scared out of her mind. That's very good. They fall more easily when they are frightened. For then, lovemaking comes as a comfort.* "On the contrary," he went on, "I wish to pleasure you. We don't ravish women." He took her hand. "All women secretly yearn for a pirate, Isabella. For we are free. Let me be your fantasy."

Isabella gasped as his hand crept up her thigh. It was obscene and exciting and terrifying. Then he bent his lips to hers for a deep seductive kiss.

"I ask only one thing," Isabella said, between kisses. "Please cut my throat when you have finished. Then bury my body at sea."

"I'm happy to indulge a woman's fantasies," he replied, "but I'm afraid you've pushed my limit. Let me ask you one thing ..."

"Yes?"

"What do you want from a man?"

Her answer came surprisingly quickly. "Love," she said. "Passionate, deep, true love."

"Oh, you're one of those," he replied. It all made sense now.

"No," she corrected him. "I'm not one of anything. I am entirely unique, and there is no one else quite like me."

"I'll agree with that," he said. "But I shall win you," he whispered.

It would be three weeks before they reached their next destination. By the time this voyage ended, he vowed, she would be his.

BOOK YOUR PLACE ON OUR WEBSITE AND MAKE THE READING CONNECTION!

We've created a customized website just for our very special readers, where you can get the inside scoop on everything that's going on with Zebra, Pinnacle and Kensington books.

When you come online, you'll have the exciting opportunity to:

- View covers of upcoming books
- Read sample chapters
- Learn about our future publishing schedule (listed by publication month *and author*)
- Find out when your favorite authors will be visiting a city near you
- Search for and order backlist books from our online catalog
- Check out author bios and background information
- Send e-mail to your favorite authors
- Meet the Kensington staff online
- Join us in weekly chats with authors, readers and other guests
- Get writing guidelines
- AND MUCH MORE!

**Visit our website at
http://www.zebrabooks.com**

MY LADY PIRATE

Elizabeth Doyle

ZEBRA BOOKS

KENSINGTON PUBLISHING CORP.

http://www.zebrabooks.com

ZEBRA BOOKS are published by

Kensington Publishing Corp.
850 Third Avenue
New York, NY 10022

All Kensington titles, imprints and distributed lines are avail-
able at special quantity discounts for bulk purchases for sales
promotion, premiums, fund raising, educational or institutional
use.

Special book excerpts or customized printings can also be created to fit specific needs. For details, write or phone the office of
the Kensington Special Sales Manager: Kensington Publishing
Corp., 850 Third Avenue, New York, NY, 10022. Attn. Special
Sales Department. Phone: 1-800-221-2647.

First Printing: March, 2001
10 9 8 7 6 5 4 3 2 1

Printed in the United States of America

Chapter One

He was too cheerful for a man who hated so much. His face was too handsome for his angry soul. "Have you looked at this rubbish?" he asked, blue eyes sparkling through a fashionably bearded face.

"No, and I don't care to," replied the old quartermaster, lowering himself into a seat with care, worrying over his aging, unsteady legs.

"Hired to hunt us down," the young captain informed him. "Can you believe that? Governments are hiring men to hunt us down? Ha!" He rose to his full height, and paced before the desk, the excitement of rage illuminating his golden face. "I thought they hated us because we are hunters, because we are practical men who seek compensation for our troubles. And now look what they have done. Hired mercenaries to kill us."

" 'Tis the way with those men," grumbled the quartermaster. "Which country is it that's seeking our heads?"

"I don't know," the captain said. "They're all the same. They're all the enemy. Would you just look at this nonsense they've written about us?'' He tapped the paper with his callused knuckles and read, '' 'It is time to take action against the bandits who terrorize our seas.' Well, all right,'' he admitted, ''that part's fair. But listen to this. 'Pirates are stinking, murderous demons without souls.' Now personally, I take offense at that.''

''As do I,'' agreed the quartermaster.

''I, for one, take baths regularly,'' smiled his captain. ''Call me what you like, but not stinking!''

''Not me. I never bathe.''

''I've noticed that. But let me read on.'' He cleared his throat. '' 'Pirates attack innocent merchant ships.' Did you catch that? Innocent? Have you ever known a merchant ship that was innocent? Innocent of what? Innocent of flogging its crewmen? No. Innocent of starving its crew? No. Innocent of paying its crew a barmaid's wage while the captain retires to his glamorous plantation after a couple of years? Makes me ill. All right, now listen to this. 'Attack innocent ships, and murder all its crew in the most torturous fashion imaginable.' ''

''Oh, now that's outrageous!'' cried the quartermaster, who was not usually as passionate as his young captain. ''Kill the crew? Are they joking? Every time we've stopped a ship, the crew has begged us to let them join! They hate working aboard those merchant ships. Half of them were abducted in the first place. We're rescuing them, not killing them!''

''And listen to this,'' added the captain with a furious raise of his dark eyebrow. ''And the women aboard are forced to suffer a fate worse than death.''

The quartermaster chewed upon his cheek thoughtfully.

''Oh, come now!'' cried the captain. ''Surely you take offense at that! I certainly do. Being bedded by a lot of handsome gentlemen like ourselves? A fate worse than death? How insulting!'' He chuckled brightly, for he had never ravished a woman in his life.

"I've heard some pirates do that sort of thing," the quartermaster said after a moment's pause, "but I know that you are not the only pirate captain who does not tolerate the mistreatment of feminine captives."

"Most of us don't," grumbled the captain. "What the men do with mercenary ladies at port is their own business. But aboard my ship, they'll behave as gentleman. Not so much can be said of honest sailors, I daresay."

"I agree with you wholeheartedly," said the quartermaster. "But it makes no difference. They will say whatever they must in order to get those anti-pirating laws passed. And we've no way to silence them."

"Listen to this," continued the captain, unable to stop his rampage. " 'We propose that any merchant convicted of conducting business with a known pirate be sentenced to death, for as an accomplice, he is no less guilty of piracy.' "

"That should hurt business," the old man agreed.

"Hurt business?" cried the outraged captain. "Hurt business? Who cares about business? It's the principal of the matter which troubles me. Imagine hanging a man simply for buying bounty! And they call us murderers?"

"Sir," warned the quartermaster, concerned that his captain was suffering in his youthful rage, "we cannot control this. They will say what they will, and we are unable to reply. I suggest we simply ignore them."

"Ignore them when they are hiring sailors to hunt and kill us?"

"What else can we do? You knew when you signed your life to this ship that pirates are hated. Why do you seek the approval of a world you reject?"

"I reject the dry world, it is true. But I ask that land people leave me be in my chosen life away from them, at sea."

"But you're robbing their ships."

"Why must you be so argumentative? Men of dry land have

no business sailing ships. Pirates own the sea, and anything which travels on its waves is rightfully ours."

"You're an idealist, Captain. But your men and I are not. We are happy to be hated, for our own hate is just as deep."

"Well, I am sick of being hated," stormed the captain, his blue eyes flaming bright. "I am an honorable man running a business as honest as any merchant's. What I take is mine, and I share it with my crew, as they are my equals. It is the governments, the 'honest' businessmen, the land creatures who are criminals. They don't want to kill me because I steal their loot. They want to kill me because I am free, and they fear that others will follow me."

"I'm not sure that's true," said the old man with caring eyes. "Why don't we go below and toss some dice with the men? I'm sure they're wanting us to join them. Come. It will take your mind off your troubles."

The handsome captain sighed. "I suppose you're right. I am a bit wound up today."

"You need a woman is all," observed the quartermaster.

"Do you think?" The thought of something soft to hold at night gave the captain's face a sudden and strange glow. "Are we nearing New Providence anytime soon?"

"I don't think so, Captain. We shan't see dry land for some time."

"Hmm, that is a bother. Oh well, we'll just have to invite some comely maidens aboard after our next capture."

"And we'll afford them every courtesy?"

"Absolutely! I insist upon it. In fact, I plan to invite at least one of them to sleep in our most honored quarters—mine."

"You aren't forgetting your principles now, are you, Captain?"

"Absolutely not! I wouldn't dream of harming the poor thing. Nor," he shrugged, "would I dream of allowing her to sleep in the heavily cumbersome undergarments that men of dry land so savagely inflict upon her. And naturally, should she be frightened by a passing storm, I would feel that as her host and captain it was my duty to comfort her.''

"And lock the door against suspicious intruders?"

"Naturally."

"You are a true gentleman, Captain."

"Well, I am a pirate after all."

Chapter Two

Costa Verde, 1720

Isabella had a Spanish name because her parents had never cared about propriety. They liked the name "Isabella," and so they bestowed it upon their daughter. Portuguese or not, it was a pretty name. That was the problem with her parents—they were always failing to notice what everyone else thought. And most likely, it was why they died.

They gave birth to a daughter who was a perfect reflection of their strengths and their follies. She was as romantic as the wind, and just as unpredictable. She was an unearthly beauty, and yet she had no idea why anyone would want to be so. She had long, yellow locks which the Mother Superior had thrice shorn in order to control her vanity. She had misty gray eyes which reflected the smoke of her soul. She had naturally pink lips, straight and vulnerable, never quite closed. And her figure, though too slim for some men's liking, was nevertheless padded in all of the most feminine places, and cloaked in a cloudy, white skin that did much to enhance the ethereal feeling she gave to those who met her.

All of her life, she had been called lovely, and this gift had brought her many things. It had brought her flattery from adults. It had brought her shame as she trounced through the narrow, cobblestone roads of her village, dodging the rudeness of men she had never met. It had brought her into the fantasies of many a boy too shy to approach her. And it had brought her many a scornful eye from those who thought beauty on women was in itself, seductive and a sin. But it had never brought her love. No man had ever sworn his devotion to her, nor even looked at her in that way men reserve for only the most lovable of women. Isabella understood the problem. The world thought her lovely, but not beloved. And being the romantic sort that she was, she would have preferred to be the plainest woman in all of Portugal, and have one man pledge his love to her, than be the beauty she was, and have nobody care.

Isabella, it was commonly thought, was better left in the fantasies of men, and kept far away from their scrutinizing mothers. No one had quite forgiven her parents for being what they were. And nobody trusted a girl who spent so much time daydreaming. Yet Isabella had hoped wildly that one of the village boys would come sweep her off her feet, rescue her from the convent, and pledge his undying love from on top of a mountain. To someone more sensible, this might have seemed unlikely from the start. Shouting devotion from mountaintops was not particularly in fashion, as mountains were difficult things to climb, and it would be hard for a maiden down below to hear what was being shouted at her. No, the boys in Costa Verde were more likely to ask a woman's father for her hand, and then lock her in a kitchen somewhere. But Isabella had hoped. And now that she had been passed over by every boy in her village, all of her hopes were gone. She would grow old and be a spinster. Now, she would need her imagination more than ever to keep from falling into despair.

Of course, there were advantages to her foggy way of life.

Had she been concerned with practical matters and decency, she would never have found herself staring into the green hills on that fateful afternoon. Costa Verde was beautiful at this time of year. The vineyards were ripe, promising a good season of port wine. The rivers were crisp and ran swiftly in loops around the bright hills. Concrete houses in the distance were small, but brilliantly silver in the sunlight, and positively dripping with grapevines of their own. There would be a beautiful sunset, Isabella knew. She closed her eyes to the heat of the sun as though in prayer. The convent was so cold all around her, yet through this open window, she could feel scorching heat. With a sigh, she opened her eyes and looked at her favorite patch of pine forest, directly to the west of this echoing building. She believed that werewolves lived there, and rather than scaring her, this thought entranced her. How wonderful it would be to meet a werewolf!

It was that thought which made her realize it was time to leave this place. She was a grown woman now, no longer a captive of the nuns. They had let her remain as a housekeeper, but everyone knew she was hopeless at polishing and dusting. She could not see the spots she missed, because to do so, she would have to break free of her daydreams and look around. No, she was becoming a burden to the nuns, and she knew it. They would try to stop her from leaving, but they would be glad to see her go. And besides, if she stayed here, she would never find a husband. And she would certainly never meet a werewolf.

She did not care to say goodbye to anyone, for no one at the convent had ever really liked her. The other girls had always been friends with one another, but never with her. Fortunately, they had never been cruel to the strange orphan who had shared their massive bedroom, but they had not been kind either. She had never been asked to join in their games or their gossip, but had been left to wonder where everyone had gone as they raced around the convent playing. She decided it would be best just to slip away. She had just gained hope of achieving her quiet departure, when she was stopped by shuffling footsteps, made loud by the echoes of the stone ceiling. It was Sister Josefa. Isabella knew that before she even saw those round brown eyes glowing within a youthful face, before she saw the slim black habit. She was a person who hated to hear footsteps, and so she had memorized everyone's.

"Isabella!" cried Sister Josefa, "Where are you going?" She observed the packed trunk with astonishment.

"Going?" asked Isabella frantically, having hoped so hard for an invisible exit that she had not prepared an explanation. "I'm . . . I'm going to Madeira."

"What?" Sister Josefa looked shocked in that way that people often did when Isabella said what she considered to be the simplest things. "What's in Madeira?"

"Nothing," Isabella shrugged, her eyes evasive. "I overheard some of the girls say that it's a beautiful island, that it has purple mountains as high as you can see, and that the stars twinkle on the ocean all night long." And that there are lots of handsome men, she added silently.

"So you thought you would just pack and leave? With no one to take you in?"

Isabella was wounded by Josefa's anger. She hadn't expected her to take it this badly. People were always so unpredictable to her. She just couldn't understand them. "Well, I'm sure someone will take me in once I find work. And I . . ."

"Even if," Josefa snapped, "we were to let you just walk out of here . . ."

"Let me?" cried Isabella with more bewilderment than anger. "I am not a nun! You know Mother Superior has always said I am unfit. I am nothing but an employee now, and not a very good one."

"You cannot leave without so much as bidding farewell to Mother Superior!" Josefa cried. "She took you in, fed you, raised you, despite . . ." Josefa could not finish. She could not blame the child for the tragedy which had befallen her parents. She could not bring herself to say what should always remain unspoken. "If you would just visit her before you go," she pleaded more gently. "Just let her help you plan for your future. Perhaps together, you can find a path."

"There is no path for me," said Isabella. "You know that as well as I."

"But . . ."

"I don't want to die here!" she cried, clutching the handle of her trunk.

Something about that touched Josefa and changed her expression from one of scorn to one of pity. She suddenly imagined Isabella in twenty or thirty years, still at the convent, still scrubbing floors, never a nun, but no longer a beauty. It troubled her.

"I know I can find work," continued Isabella hotly, "and if I can't, then I will come back. But you must let me try!" she pleaded as though her very life were at stake. "At least, give me a chance!" She pushed past the young nun while she still seemed to be thinking, and then hurried outside.

Several minutes passed before Isabella heard rapid footsteps hurrying behind her on the grassy hills. She turned, prepared to face more resistance, but was greeted by the cheerful face of a friend who wished only to bid her farewell.

"Take this," said Josefa, handing her a pouch filled with coins. "It isn't much, but it should help." Isabella embraced the slender nun, tears filling her eyes. "May God be with you," blessed the nun.

Isabella nodded reverently, though she had never understood such talk.

"And cover your face more carefully," she scolded, pulling the girl's hood to her brow. "Sailors are brutal men, and will be even more so when they see you are traveling alone. At the very least, you must cover your beauty."

"I will," Isabella promised through clenched teeth. How many times had she been told to do this?

"We shall think of you," promised Josefa, then required no more formalities of the ethereal girl.

She watched the fair-haired creature disappear gradually into the bright sunlight. The open space of the rolling green hills suited her. Josefa could see that. And she could remember the very night that flaxen-haired bundle had been brought to the convent. Crying more wildly than any child should be made to cry, she had been a kicking and screaming captive of their kindness. The look of horror on the girl's face had been beyond what stirs pity in people's hearts. Just as there was sometimes more sympathy for one who scraped her knee than for one whose leg was sawn away, so it was with this traumatized child. No one quite wanted to hear her story, for they knew enough to feel repelled by its horror.

Sister Josefa watched the grown child, only seventeen years of age, retreat deeper and deeper into the sunset, disappearing just as strangely as she had once come. Perhaps it really was her time to go. Yet surely a girl like that would never survive in the real world. Sister Josefa sighed worriedly. "Oh Isabella," she whispered with a shaking head. "Whatever it is you've been searching for all of these years, may God help you to find it."

Chapter Three

The docks were crowded that day. Fishermen were always cheerful, for nowhere were there greater catches to be found than off the coast of Portugal. But sailors were always crude. Many of them were retired navy men, miserable that Portugal, finally free of Spanish rule, was now at war with no one. Men who had hoped to become war heroes were doomed to a life of shipping cargo from the mainland to the islands. Some of the luckiest of them got to take those long, arduous trips to Brazil, bringing home silver, gold, and jewels. But most of them had ships which were not equipped to face the high seas, and so they trekked from the Madeira Archipelago back home, over and over again, like the most bored and frustrated of daily commuters.

They cursed and spat as they hauled their bounty from their tiny ships to the brilliantly sunlit rocky shore. Most of the sailors seemed to know one another, having found themselves unloading cargo side by side at the very same hour of another day. Parents awaiting passage to the islands covered their children's ears with passionately appalled roundness in their eyes.

Some of the local fishermen, looking forward to the day's end when they could return to the wives and children they adored, tried not to listen to the filthy language of the bachelor merchants. They hauled their nets of fish to shore with heads bent down and a nervous set in the mouth.

Isabella thought the docks looked wonderfully romantic. The sky was so much paler than the sapphire sea which sparkled below. The sun shone so brightly upon the moist boulders of the shore. Anchored boats of every size rocked nervously, engaged in a complicated balancing act, trying to stay upright against the waves. All around her, men wore powdered gray wigs, tied neatly with bows. Knee-length breeches showed off white stockings and shiny, black shoes with buckles. Women's skirts made stiff circles all around them. And while many wore hooded capes, nowhere did Isabella see a cape so miserably concealing as the one she had on.

She felt horribly out of place. Her hair hung loosely beneath her black hood. And while no one could see her free locks, she knew that if a gust of wind should bare her head, everyone would think her a horribly unclean girl. Her gray skirt was round, but in one place, the framework had been crushed and not repaired, causing a strange dent in the side of her hoop. Worst of all, her hood, as low as it had been tugged, did not hide her lovely, fine-boned face. All of the sailors, both young and old, stared at her. She began to breathe rapidly. She almost turned and fled. But then she thought of how it would feel to return so quickly to the convent, so easily defeated. And she remembered what was at stake.

"You want passage to Madeira, pretty thing?"

"Yes please," she whispered, head bent low, eyes in another world.

"All alone?" he asked suggestively.

She nodded.

"I'll tell you what," he said, eyes twinkling, "I'll let you ride for free if you'll slide over here and let me look under your dress." Both he and a nearby companion laughed uproariously.

"Please," she murmured. "Just let me buy my passage."

"What's in it for me?" he teased.

Isabella didn't know what to say. Her heart was pounding.

"Hey, I know how she can pay for her passage!" called an overhearing sailor, carrying a heavy load.

"Yeah, me too," chuckled another. "Say, sweetheart, we're having a party tonight. Want to come? You'll be the guest of honor." This brought many more laughs.

Isabella looked frantically around her for help. But there was none. Families moved away from her, for in their eyes, she had become soiled by the men's foul mouths.

"No, seriously honey. You want to buy a ticket?" a sailor asked gently. Isabella relaxed with a sigh, nodding vigorously. "Fine," he said gracefully. "Just give us some coins and then dance." He burst into hysterics when he saw the expression of horror he'd caused her to wear. That he'd made her trust him initially made the joke that much funnier.

"May I just purchase my fare with these coins?" Isabella nearly sobbed, lifting the pouch Sister Josefa had given her.

"It depends what you're willing to do with them."

No one quite understood what he'd meant by that sloppy joke, but most of the men laughed anyway. Isabella closed her eyes. "Sell me passage," she said with a trembling voice, "or else I'll be on my way."

The sailor casually accepted her coins, then called to her turned back, "Hey, where are you going? Hey, you frigid— Where are you going?"

Isabella tried to hide among the crowds who were now boarding his vessel. But those who had seen the abuse she'd taken would not let her stand near. Even the gentleman, in their fine silver-buckled shoes, could not respect a lady who had been spat upon. It was another horrendously unfair day in Isabella's life. And she had trouble steering her mind away from it. Even after she had settled herself on deck, cloaked tightly against the wind, even as the ship made its gradual retreat from port, steering directly into a spectacular orange sunset laced with lavender, Isabella could do nothing but replay her embarrassment at the dock over and over in her mind. But as the hours passed, and the sky dimmed to a crisp clean cornflower blue, the first star appearing on the horizon, Isabella at last found relief. She did not know what would happen to her when she arrived, but at least she would arrive. At least, she had made it this far.

Huddled at the stern, she found a family who had not seen her before boarding. They were happy to let her sit near them while she ate the less than scrumptious fare of tripe and warm water served on deck. She did not join them in their sporadic discourse, but took comfort in knowing they were with her, and that no sailor would trouble her while she seemed thus occupied. She relaxed enough even to appreciate the lushness of moving water beneath the boat. Flocks of white seagulls flew gracefully overhead toward the early star. Blissfully strong winds relieved her of the summer heat, and carried droplets of saltwater to refresh her cheeks. She felt anxious once again to follow her new path to freedom.

"Do you think Mother will be the same as always?" asked the woman of her husband. She was busily fanning her face with a lovely pink folding fan, even though the breeze was strong. Her brown hair was tied into a bun, then hidden beneath a puffy white spot of a hat.

"I imagine so," said her tall, slender husband, whose wig was powdered white, rather than the more fashionable gray. "Probably ordering your father about as always, and hating me for taking you to live so far away."

The woman's fanning accelerated in her worry. "I wish she would come to live near us. Madeira is not safe these days."

Isabella had never heard that before, and was startled.

"I'll do what I can to persuade her," the gentleman replied, "but I've never been able to persuade her before."

"Stop that!" the woman scolded her little boy. "Don't play so near the railing. You'll fall in!" She swatted him lightly, then asked her husband, "Shall we buy bananas while we're there?"

"I don't know," he replied unhappily. "It could be that the you-know-whos are draining the banana supply."

"Surely not all of it!" she gasped. "Bananas grow everywhere. How many bananas can a pirate eat?"

"What pirate?" asked the little boy.

The woman realized her blunder, and tossed a hand to her mouth. "Oh dear," she said to her husband apologetically.

But her husband was more of a mind to tell the boy. "Madeira is having a problem with pirates," he explained. "Do you know what a pirate is?"

"Uh . . . I think so," the boy lied.

"A pirate is a bad person," explained the father, just as surely as if the boy had said no. "They rob and hurt people, and that's wrong, isn't it?"

"Yes," said the boy.

"You would never do that, would you?" lectured the father.

"No." The boy fidgeted a bit, then asked confusedly, "So why don't they just put the pirates in jail?"

"They're trying to," the father explained, "but they have to catch them all first."

"I hope they catch them," said the boy.

"So do I."

"I hope they catch all the bad guys, and cut off all of their heads!" grinned the boy excitedly.

"Me, too," the father winked proudly.

Encouraged, the boy made a chopping gesture with his hand. "They'll go bam bam, and slice off their heads, and they'll roll away!"

"It's what they ought to do."

The mother winced. "Oh, stop it, both of you. Let's not discuss this anymore. We aren't going to see any pirates on this journey, so let's just not think about them."

Isabella couldn't help feeling a bit worried. One of the girls from the convent had been born in Madeira. She had told stories of cliffs plummeting into majestic waves, of purple mountains and tropical plants. All of the girls had screeched and yearned to go there for themselves. Even Isabella, isolated from the talking, listening stiffly from her own hard bed, had yearned to see those cliffs and those violet mountaintops. But no one had ever said anything about pirates. Was it possible she should have done more asking before taking off on this voyage? Was it possible that two minutes had not been quite enough time for planning the course of her future?

And why hadn't anyone said something to her *sooner?* Sister Josefa surely could have mentioned it. "Please say goodbye to Mother Superior," she could have said, "And also watch out for those bothersome, cutlass-wielding pirates." Or the girl from the convent. She could have said, "What a beautiful island I come from. Banana trees everywhere, lovely rocky beaches, and one-legged gentlemen with parrots on their shoulders, everywhere you look." Or what about the man who sold her passage! "Have a fine time in Madeira," he might have had the courtesy to say. "And try not to be ravished, then cannibalized on your way." Had it slipped everyone's mind? She was beginning to panic. She was an independent young woman, comfortable living by her own inner guide. But even she could see the danger in arriving alone on a strange shore, with no one there to meet her save a population of strangers, terrorized by the threat of pirates.

The night was not helping her to relax. Its cloak over the sun was driving passengers under the waves, where they huddled into their bunks. Isabella lost the safety of her companions. The slippery black sky also had a way of stirring her imagination. When she was feeling cheerful and safe, the night brought friendly ghosts, imaginary lovers, and well-wishing angels. But when she was scared out of her wits, the night brought angry phantoms and whistling winds of warning. By the time Isabella scurried into her closet-sized, windowless cabin, she was no longer blinking, she was so fearful of the sea's mysterious sounds. She had always wished for the privacy of her own room at the convent. But right now, she would have given anything to hear the whispers and giggles of the convent girls all around her. She felt dangerously alone in the dark of this strange ship, in this tiny room, with strange creaking all around her.

Out of habit, she got on her knees and pretended to say her prayers. Then she sat upright on her hard cot and began to undress. She could not bring herself to extinguish the lantern. Once she did so, her cabin would be completely dark, for there was not a single porthole to let in the gentle moonlight. Wide-eyed, Isabella could hear the distant, heavy sound of water. She could hear the loud obscenities of joking sailors above deck. But most of all, she could hear a thickness in the air. It was a muffled, heavy sound of silence. She didn't know whether it was her wild imagination or a genuine intuition, but she felt that something was about to happen. It was like the stillness before a tornado. The air knew something that no one else did. Isabella's pulse felt heavy and urgent within her wrist.

In one swift motion she rose to her feet and extinguished the lantern. But even when she fell to her hard cot and clenched her eyes shut, the eerie feeling did not go away. "Just sleep," she whispered to herself. "Come on, you can do it. Just sleep." But it didn't work. She was still very awake. And worse yet, her odd feeling was growing more specific. Goosebumps were freckling her arms, and her vision seemed strangely bright in this darkness. She felt watched, as though a pair of wild eyes were fixed on her, gazing at her through a solid wall. She felt a frightened tickle in her belly and a strange warmth in her heart. She had the strangest inkling that she was about to meet a werewolf.

Chapter Four

The lookout was the first to see it. "Captain!"

Several more shouts were needed to bring the dozing captain to the deck. "What is it, Fernando?" asked the grizzly-bearded old man. He was a gentle captain, the dreary years having robbed him of all passion for his job, but not for his crew. "Is something the matter, boy?"

"Sir," replied the competent young man, standing formally before his superior, "there is a double-masted schooner to the north. It carries the flag of pirates."

"Skull and crossbones?"

"Nay, sir. A hanged pirate skeleton. But it is black and red."

"Are you certain?" asked the old man, aghast.

"Yes, sir." He handed the captain his telescope.

The old man peered into the distance with a flutter in his heart. "They couldn't possibly be interested in us," he reasoned. "We are a small vessel, carrying little cargo. Ships are sailing by the dozens from Brazil this time of year. Why would they waste their time on us?"

The young man was silent, his face stiff.

''Well, perhaps they are merely crossing our path by chance. Perhaps they have no interest in us after all.''

''Sir,'' replied the boy cordially.

''Yes?''

He cleared his throat uncomfortably. ''Umm, sir. Pirates don't reveal their flags unless they are going to attack.''

''Perhaps near these islands they do,'' hoped the captain. ''Perhaps they have grown cocky, now that they have nearly overrun Madeira.''

The boy blinked furiously. ''Perhaps, sir.''

There was a long, frightening pause. The captain's pale eyes began to sting and trouble him.

''They are growing nearer, aren't they, Fernando.'' It was a statement, not a question.

''Aye, sir.''

''Fernando,'' he asked gravely, his silver hair glowing in the bright moonlight. ''Would you think less of me if I told you I am scared?''

''No, sir,'' whispered the boy.

''Go awaken the crew, but not the passengers yet.''

''Aye, sir.''

As Fernando went to do his bidding, the old captain sank into a chair. His light blue eyes sparkled with life as he looked about him at the glorious dome of stars. It was so beautiful on deck. Cold, windy, but so very private. So very peaceful. He wanted to remember the world as he was seeing it right now. For well he knew this may be his final hour. ''Sir,'' Fernando interrupted, ''I have awakened the crew.''

''Thank you, lad,'' he replied, rising firmly to his feet.

There was another awkward silence. The two men could hear only the waves, the loud, freezing waves, as dark as the sky above. ''Sir,'' said the young crewman, ''we must make a decision. Shall we attack?''

''We have only two cannons,'' he croaked desperately. ''How many do they have?''

''Eight, sir.''

The old man wrinkled his forehead as though in pain. "Are their gunports open?"

"It appears so, sir."

The old man bowed his head.

"Sir," the youth urged him, "we must decide whether we shall fight, or whether we shall surrender."

"What if they aren't interested in us?" asked the captain desperately. "What if this is all a mistake? Perhaps we could reason with them, tell them that we have no valuable cargo here."

The boy, realizing that his captain was crumbling under fear, cleared his face of all emotion. It was his responsibility to be strong when the captain was weak. "That may be true, sir. But nonetheless, we must decide on a course of action, should they become hostile."

The captain looked the boy steadily in the eye. Fernando could see the child who had once inhabited this old man. "Is it true that pirates always kill the captain?" he asked soberly.

"No, sir." The boy swallowed.

The old man bowed his head. He knew Fernando was lying to him, and he appreciated it. With a long, heavy sigh he tried to regain his composure. "We have no choice but to surrender, do we? You say our weapons are badly outmatched."

"Yes, sir. But we could wait for them to board the ship and then fight them on deck. That would take cannons out of the equation."

With a twinkle in his eye, the captain shook his head. "No. We will try to talk to them, and if they won't talk, then we will surrender."

Fernando became frantic. "Sir!" he cried. "I must tell you! I"—he swallowed—"I lied to you a moment ago. If they capture us, they will kill you. They always ask us crewmen to join them, but they'll kill you."

"I know," smiled the old man, with a strange calmness glowing around his face. "I know that."

"But sir . . ."

"If we fight them on deck, some of you boys will die," he explained. "And I will have no young men die just to save the life of this old geezer."

"But sir!"

"You would likely lose anyway," he explained. "You are sailors, not fighters. And pirates are both."

"But sir, there are innocent passengers aboard!"

"Passengers who will not be any better served by a dead crew than a captured one."

"But sir . . ." A bright ball of fire hurt their nighttime eyes. A crackling made their eardrums sting. An eerie silence followed.

"Fernando," the captain asked, "was that a warning shot?"

"Yes, sir," he confirmed. "It was not aimed at us. They want us to surrender."

"Tell Lorenzo to raise the white flag. Go below and wake the passengers. Tell the men to hide their valuables, and the women to get dressed."

"Yes, sir!"

Hearts throughout the ship were beating with such strength and speed that they were nearly audible. The boat itself seemed to throb with the pulse of a thousand fearful passengers. Every inch the pirate ship gained on its merchant victims made the horror that much more real in the minds of those aboard. Grappling hooks pulled the merchant ship helplessly to the pirates' side, like a maiden being thrust into an assailant's squeeze. Gasps were heard all around as the passengers, many now on deck, awaited to see what would emerge from the ominous pirate vessel. They could scarcely believe that whatever was on that ship would be made of flesh and blood. Pirates were like werewolves or demons. Those who saw them never lived to tell of it. And those who had not seen them did not imagine them to be human.

But humans were what they were. Men with loose-fitting trousers and scarves round their heads leaped jovially from their deck to that of the captured vessel's. Each wore a loose-fitting jacket with wooden buttons to protect him comfortably from the cold. Some wore buckled shoes; others were barefoot. But they all looked outrageously casual, being among the only men of their age who dressed for comfort rather than beauty. They were saddled down in one respect, however. Each man carried an assortment of pistols, cutlasses, and daggers tucked into every part of his body he didn't need. One man carrying a boarding axe went busily to work, slashing the sails and rigging of this poor, ravaged merchant vessel.

Some of the passengers were strangely relieved that the pirates did not take much notice of them. Huddled near the stairway, as though being able to run downstairs would save them, many of the braver men and women had come on deck to see what would be their fate. They tried not to look at the pirates, for fear of catching their attention and being the first victim. But the pirates appeared to be talking among themselves, strangely disinterested in the unimpressive ship they had taken. One of them even yawned, muttering something about not having gotten enough sleep last night. Though badly dressed, they appeared to be just ordinary men.

Then the sea of casual pirates parted, and from their vessel emerged what could only have been their captain. Dressed in the finest purple velvet, fastened tightly to his sleek muscles with brilliant gold buttons, the captain stepped forward like a king among his subjects. He wore a long pistol, strapped to him by a shoulder sash, and a sword glittered at his hip. His eyes were a shockingly bright blue, set within a fine bronze face, adorned with a small, clean beard. He wore his own natural hair, not powdered white, but oil black as the day he was born. With his hair blending into the sky, he seemed to be part of the night itself. He was as bright and striking as the cannonball which had summoned so many to the deck.

"Surrendered so easily?" he asked jovially. "What a shame. You know, we have all these cannons and muskets and such, and you deprive us of the joy of playing with them."

"What do you want with us?" asked the merchant captain sternly. "We have no valuables here."

"Isn't that what they all say?" he asked his men, who laughed in turn.

"We are a small vessel," continued the old captain. "Why would you wish to trouble us?"

"Just bored," sighed the pirate captain, examining his surroundings with disinterest. "All right, men!" he called. "Go find all the valuables they don't have!"

Like a pack of dogs unleashed, the men scurried in every direction, racing to see who would find the best treasures first. Though all bounty would be shared equally at a later date, the man who found the best of it would have reason to show pride. The passengers gasped and cried out as the men crudely stripped them for jewels and hidden coins. "Easy with the women," their captain would warn them from time to time. But he did not stop them from checking their hair and stockings for loot. Many crewmen and passengers alike now ran desperately downstairs, as though they could find safety there. And it was this commotion which finally brought Isabella from her cabin.

The crew had come earlier, pounding on the cabin doors, warning everyone of the danger. But Isabella had frozen. She could not bring herself to rise from the safety of bed or to venture into the open air. A strange, watery feeling had come over her. She felt paralyzed, not from fear, but from feeling somehow that she was about to face something. Something she had always known she would face. She had left her eyes and mouth open wide, listening to the screams and ruckus above deck as though from a great distance. It was not until now, as the cries grew so near that she could no longer pretend they were a dream, that she rose to her feet. She fetched her cloak, and wrapped it over her sleeping gown. Then, for some inexplicable reason, she opened her cabin door and emerged.

Women were being cornered, their gowns being shredded and inspected. Those women's cries were almost as loud as those of the women whose husbands were offering them to the pirates in exchange for letting them keep a prized watch. Men were weeping savagely; women were screaming and running. Strange people with red handkerchiefs on their heads were tearing doors down. But Isabella was not afraid. She felt as though she were sleepwalking. Perhaps she was. She climbed the stairs, and let the wind smack her hard in the face as she ascended into the starry world outside. She was intrigued by the strange costumes around her. Men without wigs. She liked that.

Everyone else seemed to be running away from the deck. People were shoving her to get by. But Isabella was still being summoned by the strange feeling that perhaps, after all of her yearning and all of her dreaming, she was finally going to see a real werewolf. She could feel the magic all around her. Creatures that could bring such terror to the hearts of their victims. Mythical creatures, ominous creatures. Were they werewolves? No, even better. She could see now that they were pirates. Yes, that was what they were.

Pirates. Others feared them, but she was drawn. She was drawn to their legend, their mystique, their fearsomeness, and the fact that they had sprung from the world of ghosts and dreams. She did not even flinch when the pirate captain approached her.

"Hello, strange creature," he greeted her, his voice reaching her amid the clamor. He lifted her chin with a strong finger and looked right into her eyes. She was not afraid of him, and that pleased him. His smile was handsome. But she slapped his hand from her face. He didn't mind. He grinned affectionately, as though she had kissed him. A few strands of his hair came loose from their knot, and flew wildly in the freezing wind. There was intelligence and beauty in his mysterious face.

He turned from her abruptly, and she saw how his velvet costume clung to him, showing her that he was in every way a man. He looked exactly as a man should, she thought. Round in the buttocks, strong in the legs, sleek in the middle, proud in the shoulders. "Javier!" he called, his voice carried on the night wind. "Javier, have the children put on life boats with their mothers!"

"The crew don't wish to join us, sir," came a voice. But Isabella could not see its source, for she saw only this phantom, this werewolf, this handsome, wild man with no wig.

"Why not?" he asked.

"Because they're voluntary merchants," called Javier. "Just small-time sailors. Don't have any gripe. Just want to go home."

"Well, blast it," called the captain, his voice competing and winning against the roar of the night ocean. "Tell them to join anyway or else we'll cut their throats. There aren't enough life boats for those sissies, and we're not going to leave them here!"

Isabella was startled. Cut their throats? She squinted. She was waking from her dream. She jiggled her head a bit, and for the first time, noticed the cold. What was going on here? Were these really pirates? What was she *doing?* Werewolves were all good and well in fantasies, but this was real! She had nearly been entranced by the creatures' magic. She must run! She must flee to safety before they see her, and . . .

"Oh, and Javier," the captain called, grabbing the fleeing Isabella effortlessly by the elbow. "Put this one in my cabin. I like her."

"No!" she screamed in a voice not at all her own.

"Hey, hey," said Javier, accepting the prize as she was handed by her elbow, "Don't struggle now. You're going to have the nicest cabin on board!" He chuckled.

She looked back at the handsome pirate captain who was standing with arms crossed, casually observing the interrogation of a wealthy man. The men were holding burning embers near the poor man's loins, asking him where he put his jewelry. The man wouldn't answer, so the pirates poked his bare buttocks with the hot ember. And the captain chuckled. Chuckled! He was amused. And Isabella was on her way to his . . . his cabin? This had to be a dream. Nothing like this had ever happened to her before. Well, in her fantasies perhaps. But never in real life! Confused between reality and mist, she didn't know whether to scream aloud or will the pirates away with sheer concentration. It was all too much. Pirates lived in clouds, not on earth. Her mind couldn't take the collision between her rich imagination and her fear of the real world. And so she fainted into her captor's arms.

Chapter Five

When she awoke, she felt a moist cloth against her cheek. It was cool and comforting. It made her wish for a swim. Her gray eyes opened to the vision of a man. She knew he was the pirate captain, but he looked different now. Away from battle, away from the open air, he looked like a man displaced. His face was too fresh for the drabness of the wooden cabin. His eyes were brighter than the flickering candles. "Hello, strange thing," he greeted her warmly. But he was a fearsome-looking man, even when he was kind.

"Am I your captive?" she asked softly, with resignation. She could feel waves flowing beneath the cot, and knew that the ship was in motion. The room around her was spacious, but barren. Everything in it was made of rough, brown wood. The only color she could see was in the captain's blue eyes.

"I prefer to call you my guest," he shrugged, rising to his feet. "Would you like some port wine?" He lifted a ruby red decanter temptingly.

"Yes," she heard herself say. Something about the color had drawn her.

"A woman who enjoys life," he smiled. "Very good." He emptied some wine into two silver goblets, each elaborately laced with pictures of fighting pirates. "Madam?" he handed her a goblet with a threateningly intense look in his eye.

Isabella took it, but concentrated on the wine rather than his face. She sipped it cautiously, and found its sweetness pleasing. She suddenly thought to look down at herself, and saw that she was still wearing her sleeping gown, but no longer her cloak. Her stomach tickled from the excitement of having a man see her in such a state. But her hands began to shake, causing her to splash a little wine.

"That's all right," the captain assured her, wiping the spill with an old shirt. "I don't worry about the state of my cabin. It's only a place to sleep."

Isabella could see from his plain decor that this was true. He had never spent a moment decorating.

"I apologize," he said smoothly, "I have failed to introduce myself." He tapped his hard chest with his knuckles. "I am Captain Marques Santana. And who might you be?"

"Isabella," she whispered with a bowed head.

"Ah, a fine name," he praised her, lifting her fingers to his mouth. A gentle kiss was all he gave them this time, but he promised himself he'd be sucking them within the hour.

"Then you are Portuguese as well?" she asked. It was a hard thing to tell. Though he spoke Portuguese, it was well known that pirates spoke in many tongues. And Portuguese could be as dark as he or as fair as she, depending on whether they were descended from Moors or Celts.

"I am nothing," he replied harshly. "I swear allegiance to no kingdom. I follow no man's laws. And there is no country which misses me. However," he added, not wanting to mix lovemaking with politics, "I was born in Madeira." He held her white hand in both of his dark ones, and stroked it, coddled it, studied it.

"Are you going to ravish me?" she asked softly, fearfully.

He did his best to look offended. "Oh, now, of course not."

He planted gentle kisses on her wrist and then her arm. "I would never hurt such a lovely, vulnerable lady." He reached for her, touching her face with course knuckles that excited her and made her shiver. He opened his palm so that her soft cheek could rest against it. "Such a beauty you are," he said softly, seductively. Her smoky gray eyes were bashful and distant, her face so delicate and tender. He touched her pink lips with a hard thumb. He wished she would take it in her mouth. But he knew that the art of seduction was one that required patience, so he did not push. He longed to get a better look at those pretty gray eyes of hers, but they were downcast. *Poor thing,* he thought, *scared out of her mind. That's very good. They fall more easily when they are frightened. For then, lovemaking comes as comfort.*

"Are you going to hurt me?" she asked, her voice a mere squeak.

"Never," he whispered fiercely. "On the contrary, I wish to pleasure you." He moved forward, like a panther who knew when its prey was ready to fall. He captured her lips, holding them securely between his own, rendering them immobile, showing her he was strong. Then he relaxed his mouth and stroked her lips gently and soothingly, showing her he was also kind.

"You are," she whispered despairingly. "You're going to ravish me."

"No," he whispered, gliding his lips against her cheek, letting her feel the slight roughness of his beard and mustache.

"Yes you are," she nearly wept. "For that is what pirates always do. What a fool I was to think you might leave me be."

"No, no," he said in her ear. "We don't ravish women. Women come to us willingly." He took her hand, to encourage that suggestion. "All women secretly yearn for a pirate, Isabella." He smiled at his own gall. "For we are free. And who covets freedom more than a slave? And what are women if not slaves?" He placed her hand on his strong thigh and looked piercingly into her eyes. "Tell me, Isabella. Have you ever longed for a pirate?"

She shook her head, too ashamed to admit the truth.

"Let me be your fantasy," he urged her. "Tell me what I did in your dreams. Did I ravish you? Is that what you want?" He leaned into her until she was lying flat on the cot, helpless and making tiny efforts to struggle. He smiled, in that nearly but not quite kind fashion of his. He threatened her with his nearness, his flashing eyes so close to her evasive ones, his rugged, handsome face looming over her own. But he did not kiss her. He let her wonder. He let her wonder what he would do next, and when. "If it would excite you, I will play the fearsome pirate," he pledged. "But I can also be a gentleman." He allowed himself a daring glance at her soft breasts, stuffed into her gown like pillows in a case. "What do you prefer?" he whispered in her ear, his hot breath blowing her hair.

Isabella struggled weakly beneath him, not pushing with all of her might, but still giving him every signal that she was resisting. "I . . . I want to go home," she whispered absently.

"How adorable," he grinned, lifting her skirt and placing a firm hand upon her bare leg, "but I'm afraid that is one thing which cannot be arranged."

Isabella gasped as his hand crept up her thigh. No man had ever touched her bare leg. It was obscene and exciting and terrifying. "Don't do that!" she cried out, striking at his shoulder, for it was the only part of him she could reach.

"Ouch," he said mildly, glancing at her fist. "That nearly hurt." Then he plunged down for a deep, seductive kiss. He thought he had her. At first, she writhed beneath him, struggling delicately to be free of his command. But the longer his lips rhythmically pushed against hers, opening her, teasing her in all the right ways, the more still she grew beneath him. He eased up, lifting some of his weight off her, granting her the freedom that is earned with trust. He even gave her the opportunity to stop the kiss. He pulled his lips away for a good long pause, allowing her to turn her head in protest. But several breaths later, it was clear that she would not. She was not meeting his eyes, but she was not turning her head. He continued the kiss, this time thinking more and more about the hand on her thigh. Of course, he wanted to lift it. Of course, he wanted to feel her soft bed of hair. But he dared not startle her with any abrupt advances. He let her get used to the idea that his hand was going to remain on her leg. He squeezed her thigh, massaged it, reminding her of the arousing possibility that he might venture further.

But then, the ethereal voice of his captive startled him into stillness. "I ask only one thing," she said proudly, her cloudy eyes meeting his sharp ones at last. "Please cut my throat when you have finished."

"What?" This certainly spoiled his mood, and he showed it with a wrinkling of his forehead.

"Go ahead, ravish me," she urged him. "But do not leave me with my shame. Bury my body at sea." She had been thinking this over very carefully during their last kiss. It would be a romantic way to die. To be captured by pirates, brutally taken against her will, and then thrown out to sea. It was not a happy ending, but it was a glorious one. She felt very brave, being able to face this fate with courage.

Captain Marques groaned. "I'm not going to cut your throat, woman!"

"I beg you," she said, a delicate hand reaching for his angry face. "Let me die here. Or at least leave me a blade, so I may conduct the task myself."

He squinted hard at her, deciding whether this was a joke. He could see it was not. The woman was simply out of her mind. He rose to his feet. He could not look at her. He was too aroused. He needed a moment to calm himself, to forget that he had only a moment ago thought he was on the verge of making love to this beauty. She threw herself at his feet, kneeling before him, tugging at his waistcoat, trying to draw tears to her eyes. "Please," she begged, "I shall be your willing prisoner tonight, your"—she swallowed, head bent—"your mistress, your victim. I shall not resist you. I shall not struggle. But I beg you, if there is kindness in your savage pirate heart, release me when you have made good use of my flesh. Send the rest of me to Heaven, where I may seek forgiveness.''

Marques cut his eyes sharply to the side. "I'm more than happy to entertain a woman's fantasies, but I'm afraid you've pushed my limit.'' He kicked her gently from his calf. "Get up, woman.'' He reached angrily for his glass of port.

"If I have angered you,'' she pleaded, "it was not my intention. Does this . . . does this mean you will not grant my wish?''

"I'm not even going to leave any knives where you can get to them tonight!'' he snapped, swallowing the rest of his drink in one gulp. He took another few moments to collect himself, then stormed toward his trunk. "I'm going to change into my bed gown,'' he announced. "If the sight troubles you, then close your eyes. Otherwise, watch as you please.'' With that, he flung open his trunk, and retrieved a beige, knee-length gown, the customary nightwear for a man. He pulled off one button of his vest at a time while Isabella gasped in horror. "Don't worry,'' he groaned. "I'll not touch you. I'm practically scared of you,'' he added with a smile. It was the first trace of amicability he'd shown since being so painfully rejected.

"You mean,'' gasped Isabella, "that you'll not . . .''

"Please don't make a speech about it,'' he begged her. "Just get under the blankets.''

Isabella did so with a scurry. And she chose to clench her eyes tightly shut while her handsome pirate undressed. She was dangerously curious. At every moment, she wondered how far he had gotten in changing, and what she would see if she opened her eyes right now. His bronzed skin must have looked beautiful in the candlelight. She wondered how much chest hair he had. It wasn't a sin to wonder, she told herself. It was quite natural for a victim to wonder about her brutal captive. But she would learn nothing of his body tonight, for he had already extinguished the candles, and slid beneath the blankets of the other cot in the room. "You can open your eyes now," he assured her.

She did so, and found everything to be dark, save the slight blue of waves slapping a porthole far above. She realized they must be far below deck, for the water's surface was near. Oddly, she felt rather cozy. It was a very nice blanket she had, warm and thick. The cot was more comfortable than the one at the convent. And she could look right out of the porthole from her bed. She liked the smell of wood all around her. "Let me ask you one thing," came her captor's deep voice.

"Yes," she asked shakily.

"How could I have won you tonight? I have never failed so miserably with a woman before, and I want to learn from it." She could not see it, but his arms were crossed pensively behind his head. "What do you want from a man?"

Her answer came surprisingly quickly. "Love," she said naturally. "Passionate, deep, true love." She had always wanted that.

"Oh, you're one of those," he replied, as though it all made sense now.

"No," she corrected him, "I'm not one of anything. Like all people, I am entirely unique, and there is no one else quite like me."

"I'll agree with that," he chuckled. "There's certainly not anyone else like you, strange thing."

Isabella bit her lip in the dark, uncertain whether he had paid her a compliment or tossed her an insult.

"But I shall win you," he whispered beyond her hearing. It would be three weeks before they reached their next destination. That would give him plenty of time to woo her. By the time this voyage ended, he vowed, he would find a willing and docile maiden in his cabin, bare skinned and legs parted, whispering words of devotion and faithfulness.

Chapter Six

In the morning, Isabella learned that her trunk had been lost. Marques could not find it, and explained that it must have been left behind because it did not contain any valuables. Something about that hurt Isabella's feelings. She knew that her dresses were not finely woven, but to think they had been passed over as worthless somehow bruised her tender ego. So the question was now, what should she wear? Marques suggested that she secure an apron over her nightgown. This is what peasant women did when they could not afford dresses. But Isabella said she would feel naked. So he went and fetched her one of the finer gowns that had been carefully removed from a screaming woman's body during the attack, and promised his men they could deduct it from his share of the treasure.

Isabella did not tell Marques that it was by far the finest gown she had ever worn. She thanked him, eyes downcast. Then when he left her alone for dressing, she buried her face in the succulent velvet, and breathed in its scent. She believed she could smell its color, luscious maroon. It was a beautiful color, like red after it had been roasted to perfection. The gown, though far too hot for the season, felt wonderful on her skin. It fitted her perfectly in the waist, flattering her figure like no gown she had ever worn. It made such a smooth and gentle line through her middle. And its wide, low cut was deliciously fashionable. She had asked the Sisters a thousand times to let her sew a dress in this shape, but she had always been refused. Fashion was not for convent girls. But today, Isabella looked like a city woman, her round, white breasts pressed together and peeking boldly from her velvet bodice. Her sleeves were elbow length, and ended with a romantic, bell-like flair. She crossed her arms and rubbed them, letting her fingers relish the thick velvet in which they burrowed.

"Like the dress?" smiled Marques, who had been watching longer than Isabella would care to know.

"Oh!" she cried, startled. Then her gaze lowered dramatically. "Yes, thank you," she said in a coldly polite tone she felt was appropriate for a captive at the mercy of a dangerous villain.

Marques was already rather used to her ways, and did not take offense at being spoken to like the most ruthless of captors. Instead, he merely grinned at her drama, and turned his attention to the beautiful picture of Isabella in pure velvet. He was appropriately impressed. The gown's dark wine color was absolutely breathtaking against her white skin. Her yellow hair looked paler and even more angelic than it had last night. And her figure—he had never seen a more perfect specimen of a female body. Slender but not bony, curvaceous but not obscene. Aye, he was sure she must have received a lot of flattery in her life. So flattery would not be the way to her heart. He took careful note of that.

"I, uh . . . I really should put my hair up," Isabella stammered nervously, "but I'm so terrible at working behind my own head, it usually looks just awful when I finish. I—"

"Leave it down," he ordered gently, brushing a strand from her forehead, a motion that gave Isabella shivers. "There you go. You're fine."

Marques was not dressed in his captain's plumage today. It would be an ordinary day, devoid of conquest, so he dressed casually. Comfortable breeches and an oversized white shirt were his garb. His dark hair was tied into a small ponytail. If anything, he looked more masculine than before, his arm muscles rippling his shirt, his chest hair displayed through an open button. Isabella knew that to be attracted to him would be natural, for evil was always tempting. She did not blame herself for feeling so weakened by his gentle sweep of her hair, but she did wish that her heart would stop fluttering so. "Will I be confined to the cabin?" she asked him shyly.

"Of course not. Just confined to the ship." He winked at her jovially. "If I find you leaping overboard, you'll be in big trouble. Now, come. Breakfast does not wait."

Isabella took his arm, which felt as though it were filled with boulders. She could not believe that no matter how hard she squeezed, there was absolutely no cushion, only solid rock. She found herself clinging to him rather nervously as they stepped out of the cabin. She could hear laughter and foul language in the distance. She'd always been a little afraid of people, and wasn't sure she could face a room full of pirates. If she had trusted Marques, if she had considered him a friend, she would have asked for encouragement. She would have confessed her fear, and let him console her. But he was just another frightening stranger to her. The king of the demons leading her to his chamber of servants.

The Great Cabin was a loud, filthy place. The men ate on a long, three-legged table which occasionally threatened to topple over, dumping all of its culinary delights to the filthy wood floor. Some of the pirates sat in chairs, others sat on the table, and others were so restless, they did not sit at all. They jumped and shouted and joked, feeding themselves from their bare palms between obscenities. None of this surprised Isabella. It was exactly the nerve-racking breakfast she had imagined. But what was surprising was that there were a few women about. Some of them seemed to be pirates, dressed exactly like the men, right down to their breeches. "There are women pirates?" she asked Marques in a whisper.

"Of course there are," he answered in surprise. "Some of the best of us are women."

Isabella was stunned. And she was not at all sure she was ready to dine with those strange women in men's clothes. They were shouting and cursing just as loudly as the men. Somehow, she didn't think they would like her. But she spotted two ordinarily dressed women sitting quietly in a corner of the long table, and thought she might feel comfortable eating with them. "May I sit over there?" she asked, pointing.

"Certainly," he said, bowing low as he backed away. "I shall fetch you at the end of our meal." The men had been waiting vivaciously for their captain's arrival, and now cheered him to the center of the ruckus.

Isabella took a deep breath. She was scared, but worked up the courage to approach the wobbly Great Table and ask, "May I sit here with you?"

One of the ladies turned. Isabella now saw that she was badly scarred, perhaps from smallpox. She had lovely, shiny black hair and dark eyes, but her face was covered with deep indentations. "Of course," replied the woman with ease.

Isabella sat down, but didn't know what to do next. Should she just reach out and grab something to eat? There didn't seem to be any plates.

"Just take what you want before it's all gone," advised the second woman. She appeared to be African. She had a long, graceful neck, a beautiful face with prominent cheekbones, and lots of thick, course, braided hair piled on her head. Her skin positively glowed in its rich darkness. "If you don't grab it," she advised, "you'll go hungry."

Isabella nodded her head in thanks, then reached for . . . well, she wasn't sure. It seemed to be some sort of a withered, leathery slab of something. She brought it nearer, and saw something white crawl over it. She dropped it, causing both of her new companions to chuckle. "I recommend the biscuits," said the African woman. "They're hard as rock, but at least nothing lives in them." Isabella didn't think she could eat, after all. She bowed her head in despair, feeling hungry but not wanting to touch the food. The two women continued their talking. Isabella was about to find herself left out, as usual. She was about to sit out the entire meal with her hands in her lap and nothing to say. But something in her told her no. She would try. She would try not to be the one left out.

"What . . . what are your names?" she asked. It was not an interesting question, she knew. But she was so inexperienced at making friends.

"I am Saada," said the African woman. "And this is Luisa."

Isabella nodded at them both. But she had already run out of things to say.

"What is your name?" asked Luisa, helping the conversation move forward. Luisa kept her head bent down a little while she spoke, and Isabella could guess that she was worried about her pock marks.

"Isabella."

Both of the women nodded kindly, even though they knew what she was. She was the pirate's latest fancy. How many of them had come and gone? They couldn't remember. They didn't usually bother to befriend them, for they never lasted long. He always tired of them within a month or so, and then dropped them off on shore. But this one, they instantly liked. She had a shy approach, a lack of scrutiny in her gaze, the kind of eagerness to accept others which could only come from having been rejected. "I am the sail mender here," Luisa explained. "I fix the sails when they tear." She held up a badly swollen set of fingers, making Saada chuckle. "This is how you can spot a sail mender."

"And I am one of the navigators," Saada explained rather proudly. It was a prestigious position.

"Oh," said Isabella. "Then you're not pirates?"

"We consider ourselves pirates," explained Luisa patiently. "Our duties just don't require us to fight."

"But you don't dress like pirates," Isabella noted. "You don't dress like them." She pointed to the other women pirates, already getting drunk in the early morning.

"They are fighters," said Saada, "but Luisa and I are every bit as much pirate as they are."

Luisa had a wonderfully honest face beneath her scars, and looked at Isabella with warmth, explaining to her gently as though she were a child, "A pirate is a pirate in the heart, you see. We are the unwanted ones. That is what makes us pirates, no matter what our tasks."

"Every person is instrumental in his own way," Saada broke in. "If Luisa here didn't mend the sails, we could run out of them while in midocean. We would all die."

"And if Saada misdirected us, we could be shipwrecked," chimed in Luisa, wanting to return the compliment.

"But why did you become pirates?" asked Isabella.

The reply was dead silence. It lasted for nearly a minute.

Then Saada warned her in a slow, haunting voice, "Whatever you do while on board this ship, do not ever ask a pirate what drove him to it. Trust me. You're not prepared for the answer."

Isabella felt quite scolded, and bowed her head shamefully. But Luisa took her hand. "It's all right. You didn't know." Isabella looked up into the girl's kind, dark eyes and wondered whether, perhaps, she had made her very first friend.

It was now time to go to work. The galley master came in to the Great Cabin, all covered with soot, and ordered all of the men out. The men grunted and groaned, but went to their chores without hesitation, for none were afraid of hard work. Marques caught his lady by the arm, and asked, "Did you eat well?"

She had not eaten a thing. But she did not tell him that. Somehow, she thought it might hurt his feelings to know that she couldn't stand his ship's food. And evil as he may be, she didn't like to hurt anyone's feelings. "It was fine."

Marques smiled knowingly. It always took people of land some time to adjust to the Spartan life at sea. "I fear I must leave you for the morning," he announced apologetically. He lifted her hand and offered it a lingering kiss. "I trust you can amuse yourself?"

She pulled the hand away. "Yes."

His smile broadened. "Somehow, I'd suspected you had the imagination to do so." He lowered his voice and added, "And don't worry about the men," as though he were actually concerned. "They will behave respectfully, so long as you are sleeping in my cabin."

Isabella nodded, though the thought of everyone's knowing where she slept made her swallow.

"If you have any problems, come find me," he said. Then he backed up respectfully, and turned on his heel.

Isabella watched him go with a certain regret, for though she hated him, he was the only man she knew on board. Without him, she felt at the complete mercy of the other pirates. Still, she collected her bravery, and went on deck to get some sweet-smelling sun on her hair. As soon as the ocean's wind struck her cheek, she realized she was overdressed. Everyone else wore baggy clothes and kerchiefs. She was wearing an elegant velvet dress. It looked ridiculous. Worse yet, the fine cloth of her gown was being soiled by a myriad of wild animals brushing by her as they ran about. It was the strangest thing she had ever seen. Goats, chickens, dogs, and cats were everywhere. They were not tied up or caged, but left to stroll about the ship at their own leisure. There seemed to be nearly as many animals as there were pirates. Isabella could not help laughing. She approached a black-and-white spotted mutt. He was eager for affection, and let her stroke him, squeeze him, and even play with his floppy ears. His brown eyes were round and bright. His mouth was opened in a joyous pant. The sea breeze rippled his multicolored coat. Isabella could see that he was happy here.

She felt she should leave the deck, even though, as Marques had promised, the men did not trouble her. It was just that everyone was so busy and she was so self-consciously idle.

She felt ridiculous standing boredly in her lovely new dress while all around her, hardworking, sweaty men excused themselves to pass by. She called to the dog, to see whether he would follow. He did so eagerly. That made her smile and kiss the top of his head. The dog wagged his tail appreciatively. In turn, she walked a ways and called him again, over and over until they were both below deck. She raced him into Marques's cabin with a laugh. The animal and the girl embraced one another, both appreciating the coolness of the wooden walls around them in contrast with the hot sun outside. It was nice to find privacy and to hide from the crowd of strangers. Isabella shut the door firmly, then urged the dog onto her cot. She wrapped her arms about his neck and snuggled.

"Oh dog," she said softly. "Stay with me this afternoon, will you? Keep me company."

The dog did not reply, but Isabella thought it might have.

"You're hungry, are you? So am I." She touched her grumbling belly, wishing she had ventured to eat at least something for breakfast. She rubbed her nose against the dog's shoulder, amazed at its patience in letting her bother it. "I'm so sorry," she said suddenly, "I have not introduced myself. I am Isabella. And who might you be?"

She scratched the dog's ear for a good long minute, causing the animal to lean into her hand, yearning for more. "Perhaps your name is Pedro," she said at last. "Perhaps if you were able to speak in words that I can hear and comprehend with my weak, mortal ears, you would tell me your name is Pedro."

The dog seemed to have no objection.

"Oh Pedro," she moaned, falling on her back. The dog rested his long nose across her belly. "Have you ever been lonely?" She thought hard for the course of a long, eerie silence. "I never have. Isn't that strange?" she asked softly, "Despite all of the times I have been alone, I have never been lonely." She squinted as her thoughts continued to move. "Perhaps it is because I wish so desperately to be alone. Oh, how I wish there were no one on this ship but you and me, Pedro." She paused one more time, then asked, "Is there an opposite to loneliness?"

Marques, in the meantime, was making himself busy in the crew space, where last night's treasures had been divided in his absence. He trusted his crew enough to allow them to figure out his portion for him. Could such a thing be said of any "law-abiding" captain? he thought proudly. The crew space was where all of the men slept, save himself and a few others of high rank. A private cabin was the only luxury he stole from his men, for it was tradition. And he was thankful for it, as women could not be seduced so easily while being stared at by a hundred others. The crew space was filled with hammocks at night, all hung so closely together that walking through them was like entering a maze. But in the morning, the hammocks were rolled up and stored. So it was quite an empty, dusty room at present.

Marques was delighted to find a fiery ruby bracelet among the remaining loot. The men had left it for him, and it was perfect. Why hadn't he thought of it before? What does a romantic lady want? A gift, of course! That had been his error all along. Romantic women like to be given sparkling gifts. Naturally, such a girl would not allow him to touch her until he had paid his proper respects. This was the key. Oh, he knew that one bracelet alone would not be enough. But he was certain he was on to something. He stuffed it in his shirt pocket.

"Found you a pretty lady, did you?" asked the old quartermaster.

"Ah, Gabriel. I didn't see you." He grinned proudly. "Aye, she is as lovely a prize as I've seen."

Gabriel hobbled toward his young captain, favoring his good leg, smiling with his tender blue eyes. "She is a strange one, though," he warned amicably.

Marques was startled. "What did you say?"

"I said she is a strange one," sighed the quartermaster, lowering himself cautiously into a wobbly chair.

"How remarkable," mused the captain, tugging on his short beard. "That is exactly what I call her, 'strange one.' But how did you know? You saw her only at breakfast, and did not even make her acquaintance."

"I'm an old man," admitted Gabriel. "I see things in an instant that a young man cannot see for weeks. When you have so little time left, you cannot afford to be slow-witted."

Marques smiled affectionately. "Gabriel, you're not so old as that. I've seen you aim a musket as well as any of my young recruits."

"A musket, yes. But my sword arm is weakening."

"There will always be a place for you on my ship," Marques assured him. "The men appointed you as quartermaster to advise me and keep an eye on me. I expect you to do just that for the rest of your days."

"Well, that's exactly what I'm doing," Gabriel countered with a spark. "I am advising you and keeping an eye on you. You've got yourself a strange girl."

Marques bent one knee and knelt to the floor, looking his sitting friend in the eye. "I confess that's what drew me to her. She wasn't afraid when we attacked her ship. She walked right up to me and stared, as though she were curious to see what a pirate looked like."

"Beware of women with clouds in their eyes," said Gabriel soberly. "They may love you, but they will never see you."

Marques didn't understand. "You have lost me, old friend."

"Have you bedded her yet?" asked the old man frankly.

"Nay, not yet. But I think I know my error. She wants me to feign courtship, to go through the motions of romance, and all of that nonsense. I think I can do it," he shrugged. "Why not?"

Gabriel shook his head. "Oh, Captain. What I would have done to have your handsomeness when I was your age."

Marques was embarrassed by the compliment, and looked away.

Gabriel sighed. "Captain, you want so little from a woman. Fun, flattery, pleasure. But don't you see that a woman like that is incapable of giving so little?"

Marques scowled. "What are you talking about?"

"I know women like that, Captain. You won't be able to win her with a few trinkets and carefully thrown compliments. That isn't what she wants."

Marques was intrigued, and leaned closer to his friend for further advice on capturing this challenging maiden. "Really?" he asked. "Well, then, tell me. What is it that she wants?"

"Your very blood."

When Marques returned to his cabin, he found Isabella talking playfully to a spotted dog. "No, no," she laughed. "That's not 'shake,' that's more like, 'stomp your foot.' You silly!" She laughed again, giving the dog a happy squeeze.

Marques was moved to grin himself. "Made a friend, have you?"

Isabella gasped, stepped away from the dog, and backed herself against a wall.

"Hello, Scruffy," he greeted, scratching the dog's neck.

Isabella fumed bitterly at him. "His name is not Scruffy."

"What's that?" Marques sauntered deeper into the room, closing the door behind him. He fiddled with his shirt, threatening to take it off.

"I say, his name is not Scruffy," replied Isabella indignantly. "That is a horrible name. He has feelings, you know. How would you like to be called Scruffy?"

Marques chuckled, his lips curving devilishly beneath his small beard.

"His name is Pedro," Isabella announced.

"Pedro?" he asked, "Really? And what makes you think that?"

"He told me," she replied, though she knew he would not understand.

She was right. Marques looked at her warily, as though she were the crazy relative everyone tries so hard to pacify. His smile was weak. "Well, just so long as he didn't tell you to jump overboard, I suppose it's all right."

Isabella glared angrily.

"Oh, don't look so distraught," he told her. "If you're going to be eccentric, the best place to do it is aboard a pirate ship."

Isabella watched him pull off his white shirt. She didn't mind now, because she was angry, and knew she would feel no attraction for him. Even though he had a magnificent chest. It was so bronzed, he clearly spent some time on deck without a shirt, so strong, he must enjoy lifting heavy equipment. And there was just the right amount of soft, dark hair. She could scarcely believe those arms. Never had she seen such inviting, such powerful arms. Her eyes traveled downward to where a line of hair led from his bellybutton to . . . She faced the wall with a jerk. "What are you going to do with me?" she asked, for the question had riddled her many times this afternoon.

"What do you mean?" he asked, deciding to leave his breeches on. They were not too dirty, though he needed a clean shirt for supper.

"I mean," she asked bravely, digging her fingers into her crossed arms, "are you going to kill me? Are you going to bring me somewhere? When will I be leaving the ship?"

Marques enjoyed the power her helpless wondering gave him. Her life depended on him. Her fate was in his hands. How precious, to be complete master over something as beautiful as Isabella. His pleasure in her plight made him pause before answering. "What do you wish I would do with you?" he asked.

Isabella did not know whether this was a trick, but it felt like one. So she answered, "I don't know," just to avoid falling in a trap.

"You don't know?" he asked. "Or you don't want to tell me? Because I assure you I am not so callous as to grant the opposite of your wish, only to be a bastard. You may turn around now," he added. "My shirt is replaced."

Bashfully, she turned and saw that where there had been a hard, massive chest, broad, naked shoulders, and a sturdy, bronzed pair of arms, there was now a clean silk shirt. She could not lie to herself. She found him more handsome than any man she had met before. It was horrible to think that such a fine, massive specimen of a man had turned to evil, and was now completely beyond the ability to love and be loved. He would have made someone a handsome husband. "I wish to go to Madeira," she said anxiously, "I wish for you to drop me off on one of the islands, and leave me."

"Is that where you're from?" he asked casually, straightening his collar.

"No, I am from Costa Verde."

"Then why Madeira?" he asked with a raised eyebrow.

"Because I . . . I've always wanted to see it."

Marques laughed in his pleasure. "So you were on an adventure, were you?" He moved toward her, every step making her cower closer to the wall. "You were on an adventure when I found you," he mused, ignoring her attempts at retreat. He let her back up until she was flat against the wall, and then he captured her. He rested one hand against the wall, directly beside her head, and used the other to caress her cheek. Her cheek was like that of a porcelain doll—so white, so flawless. He let his thumb venture over her cheekbone, and then her jaw. She would not lift her eyes to his, but he looked right at her. *What a strange woman,* he thought, for the hundredth time since they'd met. *A woman by herself on an adventure? And now so shy and timid?* "It appears your adventure turned out more exciting than you'd planned," he teased her darkly.

Isabella could not bring herself to speak. She was flushed by his touch, and longing to slip into her imagination.

"Why were you going to Madeira?" he demanded.

Isabella tried to shake his hand from her face, but could not. He would not be budged by her fragile protest. "I don't have any reason," she answered softly. "I just thought I was too old to stay at the convent."

"Convent?" he nearly laughed. "Are you joking? They put up with you at a convent?"

"What is that supposed to mean?" she snapped.

"Only that I wonder how they handled a girl who thinks dogs speak to her."

"Animals do speak," she insisted. "You only have to be perceptive enough to hear them."

"Fine," he relented, "animals speak. Now you say you're running away from a convent?"

"Not running. Just leaving."

"Very well." He clasped her wrists in his hands. "Then you're in no hurry." He leaned into her for a kiss. She was unreceptive, but he snuggled her lips anyway.

"I want to leave," she whispered, flushing.

"No you don't," he replied sternly, pulling her into a firm embrace. He bent her backward in a long, romantic kiss. He kept her from falling only with the strength of his arms. "You want to stay here," he challenged her, still bending her back. "You want an adventure; you want me to give you one, by force if necessary." He let her up, but pressed her against the wall. "Be honest with yourself," he whispered seductively. "You're curious. You're afraid; you don't want to be ruined, don't want to be hurt. But you forget something." He lifted her hand to his lips, and smiled devilishly. "It doesn't count if a pirate made you do it," he nearly laughed. "You won't be ruined, you'll be pitied. So as long as you're here, why don't you let me show you how we do things on the dark side of the earth? Let me show you how an outlaw takes a woman." He reached in his pocket and retrieved the sparkling ruby bracelet. "A lovely trinket for a stunning girl." He fastened it to her slim wrist, then kissed her hand. "That is yours forever," he assured her. "I will be gone, but you can always remember the evil pirate who kidnapped you, carried you to his bed, savagely violated every throbbing part of your bare body, while you ached and cried for mercy, and secretly yearned for more. And then you can settle into a calmer life, marry a bastard of dry land, and remember me only when you gaze on this ruby bracelet, which longs and fails to be as beautiful as its wearer.'' He bent down for another kiss.

But he was met by a hard slap across the face. It stunned him rather than hurt. "You ignorant, pretentious, self-absorbed idiot!" cried Isabella, face hot and red, fists clenched. "You think you know me? You think you know me just because I am a woman, and you think us all the same?" She looked him right in the eye, shaking her head in disbelief and exasperation. "I never said I was looking for an adventure—that was all your assumption. I am looking only for escape. Escape from people like you, who think that evil is glamorous, who think that hurting people is all in good fun! Do you want to know my secret fantasy?" she asked angrily. "My secret fantasy is for a brave and noble knight to come and rescue me from the likes of you! Someone who is moral and strong, someone who stands up for what's right, even when it makes others hate him. All of my life, I have longed for such a man, and never have I even met his like! Everyone I meet is just like you! Rude, selfish, mean, and cowardly!" She tore off his binding chain, and threw it at him. "And I will not wear your stolen goods! Give it back to its owner!"

Marques was angry. He could not remember the last time he'd been this angry. He grabbed the fragile lady and wrestled her easily to the cot. But then he stopped himself. He looked down at her frightened, squirming body, her distant eyes, and her wild yellow hair. He would not do it. He would not become the man she accused him of being. He would not hurt this brave, strange creature. Instead, he surprised her by drawing her into a sitting embrace. She wept into his shoulder now, scared by what had almost befallen her. Her pink face moistened his shirt as he stroked her satinlike tresses. He didn't say he was sorry. He didn't have to. The way she was holding on to him, trusting him with her sobs, showed that she knew he had decided not to harm her.

All he could think was that Gabriel had been right. Isabella was not like the other women he had bedded. It would not be easy to borrow her heart without breaking it. It would not be easy to touch her without some of her sticking to his hands. But this did not scare him away, as Gabriel had hoped. On the contrary, he had never felt so intrigued by a woman in all of his life. She was more than a challenge, she was a quest. The mission was to reach the very center of her heart, and once he got there, he had the strangest inkling of what he just might find. A heart not so very unlike his own. "Shall we go to supper?" he asked her.

Isabella shook her head against his shirt. "I can't eat that food. It has bugs in it."

He laughed softly. "That's true. I forgot how unappetizing that can be to newcomers. Why don't we at least get you some milk."

She sniffed. "You have milk?"

"But of course. What did you think all the goats on deck were for?"

She shrugged, separating herself from him, straightening her dress. Marques held out his hand, and helped her rise to her feet. "Are you all right?" he asked her solemnly.

She nodded.

He reached down and lifted the fallen bracelet. "Are you sure you don't want this?"

"Quite sure," she announced, regaining some of her stubbornness.

Marques muttered irritably, then dropped it in his pocket. "Don't see how a pirate is supposed to give you something that isn't stolen."

"Now you're beginning to understand why I shall never care for you," she said harshly.

Marques scowled as he flung open the door. He was more determined now than ever to prove her wrong about that. He would make her care for him if it was the last thing he ever did. For this was growing into more than an enticing game. It was becoming a battle for the love of an awfully strange woman.

Chapter Seven

Supper in the Great Cabin was even livelier than breakfast. The fare was the usual hard biscuits and questionable, dried meat, but the atmosphere was intoxicating. Lanterns were low, silver punch bowls were filled to the brim, faces were tired but cheerful, and all around, there was music and dance. One man played the fiddle beautifully while another sang quite badly.

Isabella, who did not ordinarily enjoy crowds, could not help smiling as the men leaped in the air, kicking, and often as not, fell to the floor. Some of them wore bandannas tied under their chins so they looked like women, while their partners swung them around brutally. Everyone laughed at this, including the female pirates, none of whom cared to join in the dance. There was clapping, which offered the dancers a rhythm for their steps, but most of the pirates were more interested in being comical than being adept. They did not listen to the rhythmic clapping, or the fiddle's melody. They just leaped and kicked and twirled until they fell.

Isabella saw Saada and Luisa sitting together again. She wanted to sit with them, for they had been so kind. But she had learned to see her own company as a burden on others, having been so unpopular at the convent, and feared the women would not welcome her for a second meal. She looked about for somewhere else to sit. The atmosphere was so rowdy, it frightened her. But at last, she spotted a kind-looking older gentleman sitting alone. "May I sit here?" she asked.

"Of course, of course," he replied cheerily, flashing her a look of welcome. "Sit anywhere you like, young lady."

She thanked him, and settled into the chair beside his. She found herself gazing at her own reflection. An enormous silver punch bowl was on the table before her, its coarsely carved flowering rim hiding its contents. "What is in there?" she asked the pale-eyed gentleman.

He rose from his seat and ladled some into a cup for her. "Here you go."

She hadn't meant for him to do that, but thanked him nonetheless. The liquid in her goblet was brownish red, and thick like egg nog. She wasn't sure she could drink it. But this abstinence from food and drink would simply have to end, she knew. Eventually, she would simply have to get used to the idea of eating something unappetizing, else she would starve before reaching dry land. She tilted the glass toward her nearly clenched lips. Most of its contents spilled on her upper lip, but a trickle landed in her mouth. She could see no napkin, so she used the back of her hand to clean her face. To her surprise, the taste wasn't all that bad. It was very spicy, and very sweet, not so different from the eggnog to which she had likened it. "What is this?" she asked her aging companion.

"Rfmfstn," he said with a full mouth.

"What?"

He worked hard to swallow, then said, "Rumfustian. Pirate beer."

"What's it made of?" She took another sip. It felt rather pleasant on her deprived taste buds.

"Mostly sugar and eggs."

"Where do you get the eggs?"

He pointed upward. "Chickens. Didn't you see them running about?"

She nodded while tipping back her cup, giving herself another mustache. "If it's just sugar and eggs," she asked, wiping her mouth, "then how did it get this color?" She found her glass empty, and leaned forward to refill it.

"Didn't say it was just sugar and eggs. Said mostly."

"Well, what else is there?" She giggled with delight as she sipped the top of her newly refilled cup. It tasted better with every sip.

"Well, there's uh, let's see, sherry, gin, ale, cinnamon, blood—"

She spit her drink onto the floor in a mighty blow.

"Bloodroot," he finished. "It's a plant."

She looked at the splash of liquid on the floor and turned red.

The old man broke into a chuckle. "No no," he laughed when she bent over, "don't try to wipe it up. That's what the galley boy's for. Believe me, there'll be worse spills than that before the night's through." He continued to laugh at the blushing Isabella, then said, "Did you really think we drink blood?"

She could not look at him. She watched herself fold and unfold her hands.

The old man's blue eyes twinkled. "You know, pirates aren't as bad as you think, young lady."

Isabella straightened her back in reply. She was tired of hearing pirates justify themselves. She would hold her silence, but she would not listen.

"We're pretty much like any other sailors," he explained. "We spend our days performing the hard work of sailing a ship. We spend our nights trying to forget our days. And when we pull into shore, we behave like a bunch of love-starved seamen. The only difference is we steal. But even about that, some men would argue. When a captain takes ninety percent of the earnings, and splits the rest among his hundreds of crew, that sounds like stealing to me. At least we never steal from each other.''

Marques arrived with a bucket of milk. ''Had to milk her myself,'' he announced. ''Galley boy didn't think anyone would want milk when there's Rumfustian aplenty. But I told him, from now on, put out a bucket each meal.''

''Thank you,'' said Isabella.

''Ah, I see you've met Gabriel, my guardian, the thorn in my side.''

''Yes,'' she said, though she realized she'd made the blunder of not asking his name.

''Gabriel here is the quartermaster,'' Marques explained. ''It is traditional for the men to elect one to keep an eye on their captain, and remind him of the crew's interests, so I don't get too big headed. Gabriel here is the only man who can fire me,'' he grinned, patting his friend on the back.

''And believe me, there've been times I've thought about it,'' teased the old man.

''Ah, nonsense. Uh oh.'' He wrinkled his brow. ''It looks like there's a fight at the gambling table. If you'll excuse me.'' He bowed to Isabella. ''Gabriel? Can I trust you with this lady?''

''If you're not too long,'' he teased.

''I won't be.''

When Marques had gone, Gabriel turned his grin toward Isabella. ''Men aren't allowed to argue while on board,'' he explained. ''That's why the captain has to break up their spat.''

''You mean they're not allowed to have even a little argument?'' she asked, disbelievingly.

''Not a single unkind word.'' He swallowed a chewy slab of salted beef. ''It's too dangerous,'' he explained. ''These are angry men, and good fighters. If they were to brawl on board, we couldn't run the ship. So we nip it in the bud. All disputes are written down, then settled by sword after we reach dry land. Whoever's still alive at the end of it gets back on ship, and vows not to squabble again until the next stop.''

"Well," she marveled. "At least it's . . . organized."

Gabriel gazed at her steadily. He didn't have to look long to know that everything he'd suspected of her was true. He had loved many women as a young man, had not sworn off them until the very last one met her doom. And she had been a woman of the stars, like this one. A woman who did not belong on earth, among mortals. Marques had to get away from this beautiful creature, for she was one of those who loved dangerously. He wished there were something he could say to stop this catastrophe while Marques's heart's juices were still untapped. "Marques is a fine captain," he began. "It isn't easy keeping a lot of malcontents in line for the duration of a long journey. It takes a strong man, and an intelligent one."

Isabella picked at a biscuit. The rumfustian had given her the courage to stomach it. "That's nice," she replied coldly, preparing herself to hear a speech about why she should cast aside her ideals and love him. Her back was rigid.

"But he isn't a tender man," Gabriel said, to her surprise. "He isn't right for a woman like you. He really cares only for his ship and his crew. Women are merely a hobby."

Isabella was startled. "Well, I had certainly guessed that, but I am surprised to hear you say so. You know that he brought me to this ship so he could ravish me, don't you?" The ale had made her frank. "He hasn't done it yet; he's toying with me. But it is only a matter of time."

"He isn't toying with you," objected Gabriel, knowing well that his friend was a man of honor. "He just wants to protect the honor of pirates."

"The *honor of pirates?*" she choked.

"Aye," he assured her. "Our captain is among those who believe that a pirate should always be a gentleman. Have you heard of Captain Roberts?"

"No."

"Well, ask Marques about him sometime. He is a gentleman pirate of the truest sort, and a hero to every pirate who thinks himself a man of honor. There are uglier, more savage pirates, of course. They hold Blackbeard as an idol, crazy brute. But we are all followers of Roberts here. Our captain, in particular, tries to uphold the standards of an outlaw gentleman on board. And that is why he does not harm you, child.'' Gabriel's eyes were caring and pleading. ''He doesn't want to be the brute the world would like him to be. If you refuse him for the rest of the voyage, I give you my word, the captain will let you go. He will be persistent, of that I am sure. But he will not ravish you, dear thing. Please . . .'' He looked at her strangely, as though he were in pain. ''Just hold your ground. He is a good man, but he is wed to his career. Refuse him, and you will be safely on your way. I promise you, the captain will not soil the name of all pirates, just for the sake of a night's pleasure.''

Isabella was taken aback. Was this man trying to protect her from his captain? No, it really didn't seem that way. It seemed almost as though he were trying to protect his captain from her! Yes, that was it. For some reason, he wanted her to stay away from the man who had abducted her. This was a very queer place. She had always imagined pirate ships would be dark, spooky, and fil'ʒd with haunting laughter. But she had never expected them to harbor the insane. She thanked Gabriel for his advice, then left the table. She was quite ready for a long night's sleep.

Strangely, she had trouble leaving the Great Cabin without first stopping to watch some of the dancers. They were so jovial, they made her smile despite herself. And the fiddler was superb. She stood for many long minutes, halfway between the music and the exit. In time, she found herself clapping her hands with the others. And then, she found herself going back for one last glass of pirate's beer. It was delicious, and helped her adore the atmosphere. Never had she seen such liveliness, having spent all her life in a convent. She couldn't believe that every evening held such a celebration. But why not? Why not celebrate every night of one's life? She smiled, a strange glow in her face that might actually have sprung from joy.

"Why won't you dance with me?" a heavyset pirate asked a woman.

She was dressed just as he was, and was, if anything, a bit heavier. " 'Cause I didn't join the ship to be flung about like some maiden," she chastised him.

"Then how about you?" he asked another.

"I'd sooner be thrown overboard," she laughed, downing a mug of rumfustian in one breath.

"Ah, women!" cried the pirate half-jokingly. "They're no good, any of them!"

Marques broke in with arms crossed. "You'll not insult your fellow crew," he warned. "Not aboard my ship." He was standing casually, leaning against the wall, enjoying the music and dance. But his face was uncompromising.

"Ahh!" cried the drunken pirate. "Why didn't I join Roberts' ship? He doesn't even allow women on board!"

"Doesn't allow gambling either," noted Marques. "So should I take your dice?"

This silenced the bumbling pirate, who bowed humbly in the wake of his captain's scolding. Marques, along with some others, laughed good-heartedly. It was not until then that his shimmering eyes caught sight of Isabella. She was standing so nervously, fingers near her mouth, yet she had not left. Her smoky eyes looked wondrously about her, amazed by everything they saw, and occasionally, her lips curled into a shy smile. The captain approached her with sturdy steps. "Do you dance, Isabella?" he asked, gently touching the small of her back.

Isabella cowered under his gaze, lowered her face, and said, "No, well, not except when I'm alone outdoors. Sometimes I dance by myself."

"Will you give it a try?" he asked, offering his hand.

"No," she blushed. "No, not with everyone looking."

He leaned down and whispered in her ear. "I'll tell you a secret. They're all drunk, and won't remember a thing come morning. They never do.'' He stood upright again, and smiled affectionately. ''Come,'' he winked. ''Just one song.''

Isabella did not want to be pulled into the crowd. She'd forgotten to tell him about her horrible stage fright, about how badly she longed for people not to notice her. And now it was too late. Everyone was cheering his captain on, and she was completely at his mercy. She had never been to a dance, never even been invited to one. She didn't know any steps, and didn't know how to be led. ''I ... I'm terrible at this,'' she told Marques feebly.

''Terrible at what?'' he asked. ''There is no right way. Just enjoy yourself.'' With that, he pulled her against him, causing all of the crew to shout and cheer. Isabella blushed at the feel of her breasts pressed against his hard chest. He looked her brazenly in the eye, his blue eyes like a ray, trying to penetrate her misty ones. Then he released her, sending her spinning, then just as quickly, brought her back to his chest. Isabella smiled. As long as she clung to him, she could tell, he would not allow her to embarrass herself. He lifted her by the waist, causing her to gasp, then spun her in the air with a twirl that felt like a gust of wind flowing through her bones. The audience cheered rowdily.

''Do that again,'' she grinned. ''Spin me again.''

Smiling brightly, he honored her request. This time, she arched her back and spread out her arms, imagining that they were sails, and she, a flying boat. He set her on her feet, and sent her twirling away from him. She started to forget that people were watching. She opened her arms and danced, just as she had always done around the convent. The audience saw that she had natural grace. With her striking white skin and her haunting eyes, she looked rather like a ghost to begin with. But dancing in those slow, circular, floating movements, she looked even more ethereal. When the captain captured her in his strong arms, she threw back her head, letting her loose, flaxen hair fall softly behind her. And when he moved, she let him pull her, let him guide her in sensual movements around the crowd. When the song was over, he bent her far backward, until her head nearly touched the floor. And she let him do this, even throwing a delicate arm to the side for dramatic effect. He straightened, taking her with him, and the couple faced an enthusiastic crowd. The men loved watching their captain dance, for it reminded them that they served under an elegant gentleman. And having no king, they needed such a role model.

Isabella had not heard the music stop playing. When she realized that the song was finished, she was disappointed, but when the captain asked her "Again?" she declined. She had enjoyed it too well. And somehow, she didn't think that was right—not on a pirate ship, not with the devil himself as her dance partner. She had heard much in her life about the seductiveness of evil. She wondered whether, perhaps, she was falling prey to just such a phenomenon. She wasn't sure. She wasn't sure that it was wrong to enjoy herself among these sinners. But just in case, she thought she'd best retire. "Then I will go with you," Marques announced. "Men! Bedtime is in one hour for all except the night crew. Lanterns out. Anyone who cannot sleep shall go on deck and be quiet while his fellow crew rest. Gabriel, please enforce the bedtime."

"Aye, sir."

Isabella couldn't believe it. "You give them a bedtime?" she nearly laughed.

"All pirate captains do."

"Why?"

"Because one or two night owls can prevent the whole crew from getting a good night's rest. It's my job to look out for the interests of the majority."

"I have to say," she admitted, "pirates are not exactly as I expected them to be."

"Is that so?" he asked, grinning, for sweeter words could not have reached his ears.

"I said 'not exactly,' " she reminded him. "They're mostly the way I imagined, just not exactly."

Marques scowled, but knew that he had won a partial victory. He planted her hand on his bent arm, and led her toward the cabin. "Did you finally eat?" he asked once they'd found sanctuary from the Great Cabin.

"Yes," she said, the loudness of her own voice stinging her ears. It had been quite boisterous in there, and she was left with an uncomfortable ringing.

"Good," he approved sternly, "for I'm afraid fresh food is something you will not see until landfall." He flung open his cabin door. "After you."

Isabella stepped into the darkness. It was strange, but their cabin already felt like her own room. When she saw Pedro still sleeping on her cot, she felt as though he were welcoming her home. "Oh Pedro!" she cried, lifting his heavy head to her shoulder. "Are you going to sleep in here?"

"No," came a loud voice. Isabella looked at Pedro inquisitively. Then she realized it was not he who had spoken. "He can come back in the morning," said Marques, grabbing the mutt by his scruff.

"No!" cried Isabella, hugging the poor creature with all of her might. "He is my friend!"

"Fine," said Marques. "And your friend may visit you again tomorrow. Come on," he whistled, making the dog move forward and out of Isabella's grasp. Marques shut the door firmly behind him.

"Why did you do that?" asked Isabella miserably.

"Don't want animals sleeping in my cabin," he explained, opening his collar.

"Then perhaps you should throw yourself out," she hissed.

"Ouch, that hurt," he smiled casually. "Now, if you'll excuse me, I'm going to remove my clothes."

Isabella faced the wall.

"You can watch if you'd like," he said provokingly, a mischievous grin on his face.

She did not think that deserved a reply.

When he'd changed into his knee-length sleeping shirt, he

told her she could turn around. "Now I'll look the other way while you dress," he offered. "Or if you're feeling generous," he added enticingly, "you might make the same offer I made you." He knew she would turn from him in disgust, but he enjoyed the flush he had drawn to her cheeks.

"Please look the other way," she said softly but firmly. She gathered her nightgown and corsets.

"You're not going to wear all of that to bed, are you?" he asked.

"All of what?"

"That." He pointed to her corsets.

Isabella shrugged. "Of course, I suppose. I always have."

"Don't," he urged her. "You'll be more comfortable without."

Isabella's eyes narrowed. "Is this one of your tricks? Are you trying to see me without my undergarments? Because if so, I assure you, you won't be able to tell the difference."

"Exactly," he said. "That's why you shouldn't wear them. I'm only wanting you to relax and be at ease. You're the only woman on the ship, you know, who wears all that fuss."

"I am?" Isabella was intrigued by this. She knew the pirate women wore no such things. "But what about Saada and Luisa?"

He shook his head. "No. They might've worn all that for the first few months, but they gave it up."

"But . . ." Isabella swallowed, fingering her corset nervously. "But without this, I would look . . . well, my waist . . ."

Marques rose to his feet. "If God had wanted your waist to be that small, He would've made it that way, eh?" He lifted the corset from her hands. He tossed it to the floor and wrapped his sturdy hands about her waist. "Seems to me your waist is already very small."

"I'm already wearing a corset," she informed him. "The one I'm wearing is even tighter than my night one."

"Take it off."

Isabella felt a flutter in her gut. "Wh—what?"

"Take it off."

She found herself stammering, looking up, spellbound by his beautiful, bronzed face. "I can't . . . my . . . my dress . . . it's . . ."

He went to work unbuttoning it for her. His fingers tickled her, made her giggle nervously and gently protest. But she was spellbound, and did little to prevent the dress from falling to her feet. Before she realized the full import of what she was allowing him to do, she found herself standing in her underclothes. To her, this was halfway to being naked under his masculine gaze. "Take it off," he said again.

Isabella was breathing heavily. She had never been so excited or so entranced in all of her life. She knew that if she removed the corset, not only her midriff, but her very breasts would be bare. The thought of doing it was thrilling. The thought of untying all of those laces and giving him a good look at her most tender body was intoxicating. But she could not do it. As light-headed as she was feeling, the candles so low, his heat so near, her mind racing through possibilities she had never considered except in her most forbidden fantasies, she could not strip for this pirate. So he offered her a scarf to hold over her breasts while he undid the corset himself. He did so with incredible expertise, as one who had spent half of his life unfastening such gear. Isabella clung shakily to the scarf as her corset was peeled from her moist skin and was thrown to the ground.

"See?" he asked soothingly, planting his hands on either side of her waist. "You have a lovely, delicate figure." He squeezed her bare flesh, tickling her bellybutton with a thumb. "I, myself, have always preferred a little cushion. After all, you are a woman, not a doll." He sneered at the crumpled corset with distaste.

Isabella wondered breathlessly what he would do next. He was touching her bare flesh, paralyzing her with his experienced gaze. She could hear a voice in the back of her mind, shouting "No! Stop!" but she did not move. She only looked up at her captain with the wondrous eyes of a girl who trusts because she must, and who might be willing to give her love in exchange for a little comfort and guidance. But Marques let her go with only a kiss. It was a firm kiss, not a seductive one. He would leave her wanting. He would leave her curious. He would leave her hoping she would find herself in this quandary again. "See, isn't that more comfortable?" he asked jovially. "Now go ahead, change. I'm very tired." He retreated to his cot, where he folded his arms behind his head and waited.

Isabella had nearly forgotten where she'd put her nightgown. She found it on the floor, and hurriedly replaced the scarf with it. She did not think. She did not allow her mind to return to the events of a moment ago. She merely pulled on her nightgown, leaving her corset tossed aside. Then she raced to her cot and slid beneath the covers. "All right," she announced, rolling over to face the wall, rather than him.

Marques blew out the candle. And it was only in the seclusion of darkness that he broke into a grin. What excellent progress he had made on this day! There was the little mishap with the bracelet, of course. But the evening had gone rather well. He was certain that within a matter of days, she would be his—heart and soul.

Chapter Eight

Marques fell into a most pleasant slumber. Always, when he slept in good cheer, his dreams brought him to his fondest memory. He had been a boy of about twelve. Having grown up on the breathtaking island of Madeira, his childhood left him with the permanent association between youth and the color purple. Purple had been everywhere. The sharp mountain peaks all around him had been a dark, bluish, slatelike color. The sunsets were a striking lavender. Purplish cliffs had plunged into an ocean accented with purple at nightfall. Even the black roads which wound up and down steep hills throughout the village center had taken on a purplish hue under the bright blue sky. His own hair, black as ink, he remembered as being nearly navy in color when the moon hit his looking glass in just the right way.

It was a very purple day indeed when he found himself playing ball with his friends that spring day. The rain had just left them, and the gray clouds were being struck by rainbows. Marques was the most athletic boy they all knew. He could outrun, outthrow, and outwrestle any boy at school. He loved running and falling over and over into the moist grass as the other boys tried to catch him. He felt alive only when he was moving, when he was competing, and perhaps, even showing off a bit. He was a handsome boy, the right size for his age, and developing a shadow over his upper lip much sooner than his classmates. His skin was always bronzed to a lovely color, and his eyes were quite striking in their electrifying blueness. But he didn't understand any of that yet. All he knew was that he liked playing rough, outdoor games, and that he especially loved winning them.

It was the only time he ever felt powerful, the only time he felt important, and the only time he forgot his troubles. He never confided in his classmates the truth about his suffering. But always, at the end of every game, he would look desperately at each of the other boys, and ask, ''Are you sure you can't play again?'' When they all insisted they must go home, he knew it was his time too. Sweaty, cheerful, and heart beating wildly from exercise, he loved the feeling of stopping, of letting a chilly breeze pass through his hot bones. And he loved the look of a darkening sky above on a beautiful Madeira evening. But he could not bear to go home. There was always some anger in his heart for the boys who insisted the game must end. For if they had been willing to play forever, he might never have returned to the place he dreaded most.

Most evenings, he would reluctantly bow his head and take his ball home with him, forcing his friends to swear by their grandparents' graves that they would return the next afternoon for another game. Then he would take the long way home. But on this night, when his friends had dispersed, he noticed something. It was a girl, fair as Isabella, with long, satiny hair that fell to her waist. Her eyes were long and blue, and she had already begun transforming into a woman. Marques had seen her before in church. He thought she was pretty, and he'd always wondered what her yellow hair would feel like if he touched it. It looked like it would feel slippery. But never in his life had it occurred to him that a girl might think about him, in the same way he thought about her. He wondered how long she'd been watching the game, and walked up to her. "What're you doing here?" he asked, not having any charms yet, to speak of.

She blushed, a reaction that Marques found strangely drawing. "I was just watching you play," she said nervously. "You did a really good job."

"Thanks," he said, tucking his ball under the arm.

He did not know that her friends had dared her to speak to him. He did not know how long she had spent biting her nails, working up the courage to approach him. But she did not want to return to her friends tomorrow in failure. He was the cutest boy in the whole village, and she thought that the next few moments would be critical. If he rejected her, she would replay this conversation a thousand times in her head tomorrow, and mourn. If everything went smoothly, if she at least managed not to make a fool of herself, then she would stay up all night with excitement. "I like watching you play. That is, all of you. I like to watch all of you boys playing."

Marques was puzzled. "Did you want to play with us?"

"You wouldn't mind if a girl played with you?"

He shrugged. "Why not?"

"That's very nice of you, Marques," she smiled. "Some boys wouldn't let a girl play. You're always very nice." She bit her lip furiously. Had she said too much? Had she been too obvious?

Marques, being a boy, and not knowing anything about courtship yet, did not realize that the girl was flirting with him. He was still trying to figure out why she had approached him. "Well, the game's over," he said.

"Yes," she observed. "Yes, it is."

Marques looked warily at the darkening sky above. He liked to be at least halfway home before the world turned pitch black. It was very hard to navigate the roads at night, especially since they were black themselves. "Well, bye." He started to leave.

"Wait!" she called. "Could you . . . could you maybe walk me home?"

"Why?" he asked. "Are you lost?"

"No," she replied anxiously. "It's just . . . it's just . . . well, it's so very dark out, and night noises scare me. But if I had a friend with me, it wouldn't be so bad." She was proud of herself for thinking of such a good excuse to walk with him. Yet she feared he could see right through her, see how she really felt, and maybe laugh at her.

Fortunately, he was a twelve-year-old boy, so there was absolutely no danger of his seeing through her. "Well, where do you live?" he asked.

"Just that way," she pointed.

Marques sighed. She was pointing in the wrong direction. Her house was nowhere near his, and it would be miserably dark before he made it back. Still, he thought she was pretty, and he wanted her to like him. It was a serious dilemma. To walk home and have a pretty girl be angry? Or keep her company and risk getting lost, maybe not finding his way home till morning? For the rest of his life he would be thankful he made the right decision. The couple had not traveled more than a quarter mile when the girl stopped and asked, "Marques? Have you ever kissed?"

It was on that night that he discovered something more pleasurable than playing ball. He discovered that a woman's soft lips could make him forget his troubles at home. Day after day, secret meeting after secret meeting, year after year, his studies brought him even richer joy. To meet a girl in the woods and kiss her was a pleasure. To meet her in a field and touch her was ecstasy. And eventually he learned that to meet her in an empty schoolhouse and go wild was the most maddening escape from life he could ever have wished to find.

Soon, he found a new girl every week, eager and willing for his tutelage. Some of them were shy at first, others were bold, but they all came to him because they had heard he was a very handsome and exciting boy. He learned to like both kinds: the girls who blushed every time he kissed them, and the ones who returned his kisses with fervor. In fact, it was the variety of personalities and responses that kept him so engaged. He really adored them all. And eventually, his friendly ball games with friends turned into passionate matches of jealousy, all of the other boys wanting to know how he got so many women to love him. "Beats me," he'd shrug casually, then tackle whoever was in his way. He continued to win the games, but was not so disappointed when they were over. For now, he almost always had something better to do.

The memory made him smile in his sleep.

Isabella, however, could find no rest on that night. She got up, wrapped her cloak over her nightgown, and sneaked from the room, careful not to let the door creak as she shut it. It was above deck, with the wild night wind whipping all around her that she found her sanctuary. Her nightgown blew up several times, exposing her porcelain legs, but there was no one to see, except for the fabulous white moon above. She was just about to cry out to the sky, confident that no one could hear her above the noisy wind, when suddenly she was startled by a noise behind her. "Isabella," said a soft, feminine voice.

Isabella turned to see Luisa, standing with arms crossed tightly and silky black hair blowing all around her. "Oh, hello," said Isabella, uncomfortable with the notion that she'd been watched.

"You might want to hold your cloak shut," the girl warned. "There's a lookout on the rigging." She pointed above.

When Isabella lifted her chin, she saw a telescope aimed directly at her legs. "Oh my!" she cried, frantically pinching her cloak together in the front.

Luisa laughed gently. "Don't worry," she said. "The men will never bother the captain's woman. Not openly, anyway."

A shadow cut across Isabella's face. "Don't call me that," she pleaded. "I am not his woman."

"Really?" Luisa looked surprised, even enough so to brush the hair from her eyes, letting her pox marks show.

"Yes, really," said Isabella mournfully. "I hope you won't take this the wrong way, Luisa. But I wish to be gone from here. I wish to be rescued."

Luisa pursed her lips. She seemed to be thinking. "That's odd. Because I'd do anything to have the captain look at *me*." She lowered her face self-consciously.

"Really?" asked Isabella, becoming nervous.

"Oh yes," said Luisa, standing nearly a head shorter than her companion. "Of course, I know that he never would . . . I mean, nobody would . . ." She seemed to have embarrassed herself, and now turned her face away. Speaking to the wind now, she said, "I just think you're awfully lucky. He's such a handsome, dashing, and really a fair, generous man."

Isabella didn't know what she should and should not confide in Luisa. The woman was good-hearted; anyone could see that. But she was also a pirate, and obviously didn't understand the evil of her ways. "Well, I think he is merely a swarthy gentleman of darkness," said Isabella. "His handsomeness is only to conceal his black heart."

Luisa burst into a chuckle. "Oh, Isabella," she laughed, visibly unable to contain herself. She started to speak several more times, but could only burst into another fit of hysterics. At last, with face red and eyes still smiling, she said, "You really are dramatic."

"It is the truth," she insisted.

Luisa shook her head, a trace of sorrow crossing her eyes.

Isabella was perceptive enough to see it. "Is something wrong?"

"Oh, no," said the dark-eyed girl. "It's just, well," she sighed heavily, "I guess as pretty as you are, you can afford to be picky. I guess you can have just about any man you want."

"That's not true," said Isabella.

Luisa thought her companion was being modest, so rather than ask her more, she stated simply, "You know, I used to be beautiful."

"You still are," said Isabella, though she knew she was telling a fib.

"No." Luisa smiled as she shook her head. "No, I know that I'm not anymore. You see, I had small pox." She looked at Isabella until she got a nod of understanding, then continued. "I suppose beautiful is an overstatement, but I was awfully pretty." She smiled at the memory. "All of the grownups used to say so. They used to say I'd be a heartbreaker." She laughed uncomfortably. "But then the small pox came, and . . . well, everyone thought I wouldn't make it, of course. But I did. I lived through it somehow." She smiled, but there were tears in her eyes. "And when the doctor summoned my mother to my bedside, and told her I was all right, do you know what she said?"

Isabella shook her head.

Luisa's tears became more visible. " 'My God, your face.' Not, 'Thank God you're alive,' or 'Oh, my baby. I love you so.' Just 'My God, your face.' That's it." Luisa winced, and the tears suddenly fell rapidly. "All she cared about was that I would never again be beautiful."

"That is awful!" cried Isabella, finding tears of her own.

Luisa stopped the oncoming embrace with a firm shake of her head. "Oh, no, that's not the worst of it," she assured her. "The worst is that I found out my mother was right." The stars shone on her glossy eyes for just a moment. "It is better to be dead than to live in this world as an ugly woman. My life was nothing but misery from that day forth. Boys wouldn't go near me, girls wouldn't be seen with me, and no one would hire me, for fear my face would scare off customers."

Isabella was nearly brought to her knees by sympathy. "Is that why you became a pirate?"

Luisa looked surprised. She completely broke free of her sad thoughts, and gazed inquisitively at her companion. "Is what why I became a pirate?"

"That . . ." said Isabella, "that you could not find work or a husband. Is that why you were forced to become a pirate?"

Luisa broke into a smile, and then a laugh. Her moist eyes gazed upon Isabella with disbelief, but also pity. "Oh no," she said, "no, no. That's not why I became a pirate. I became a pirate because it was the right thing to do."

"The *right* thing to do?" asked Isabella, aghast.

"Yes," said Luisa proudly. "It was Marques who told me. He said that a world that doesn't want me is a world that doesn't deserve me. Join him, and my talents will be put to good use. They will be put toward the cause of causing trouble for a world that is in desperate need of some troublemakers." She giggled at the memory.

Isabella could not hear this nonsense. It was easy to see how a girl with such a poor opinion of herself could be swept into the darkness, but it was a shame. "Marques is a smooth talker," she said bitterly.

Luisa shook her head. "You just don't understand." She rubbed her cold arms, which prickled with goosebumps. "Well, I think I shall go to my hammock now. It's getting awfully cold up here."

Isabella was sorry to see her go. She had enjoyed talking to someone—someone relatively normal. "Sleep well," she said.

"Thank you," Luisa replied shyly. "You too." She began to back away.

"And Luisa!" Isabella cried.

"Yes?"

"Thanks . . . thanks for talking to me. I . . . I hope I didn't say anything too terrible. I have a way of doing that. I guess that's why I've never had a . . . a friend."

Luisa smiled. "You have one now, if you like."

Isabella nodded. Then as Luisa turned away, she cried out one more time. "Luisa!"

"Yes?" asked the girl, a little more anxious this time.

Isabella swallowed. "I uh . . ." She chewed her lip. "I . . . I wanted to tell you something."

"What's that?"

Isabella took a step nearer. "I wanted to tell you that . . .

well, that . . ." She met the girl's eyes steadily. "That your life wouldn't have been as different as you think. I mean, without the . . . the . . ."

"Scars?" asked Luisa.

"Yes," Isabella sighed, "the scars. You see . . ." She smiled nervously, then gaining a nod of approval, continued. "Beauty brings you a lot of flattery. But . . . but it doesn't bring you love. Trust me. It doesn't bring you love."

"You've never been in love?" asked Luisa.

"I've never been loved. No one has ever loved me." She confessed this with a stoic face, and distant eyes. "It is the truth, Luisa. A man might give you a gaze for your beauty, or a kind word, or an obscene word, or maybe even his hand in marriage. But he will not give you his heart. That goes only to the woman who stirs his soul with something more."

Luisa nodded appreciatively. "Thank you. But it would be nice to receive a gaze once in a while."

"And I," said Isabella, "would give a thousand gazes for just one chance at true love."

"I'm sure you'll find it someday," Luisa promised her. "You're very nice."

"I'm strange," Isabella confessed, with lowered lashes, "and no one seems to like that."

Luisa smiled. "There's no such thing as strange on this ship," she said. "Good night."

Isabella smiled as her friend disappeared into the stairway. She didn't know whether it was the late hour or her vulnerable feelings that made her do it, but she started to giggle. It was true, she realized. Everyone on this ship was nearly as strange as she was.

Chapter Nine

When morning came, Isabella was still very tired. She had not gotten enough sleep, and dreaded the thought of rising. But she was not the sort who could bear to sleep long past sunrise, so she rose. Of course, Marques, leaning over her cot, whispering, "Wake up," did nothing to improve her mood.

"I'm coming," she whispered back, then turned to her side, trying to force her eyes to flutter open. It took several deep breaths and several moments of silently coaxing herself before she really lifted her lids for the day. But when she did, her blurry morning vision showed her something she had never seen before—a man undressing.

Marques was turned away from her, and did not know he was being watched. Drowsily, Isabella observed him, her mind too tired to resist the temptation. She saw him strip completely to his bare skin. She saw his naked shoulders, his strong, muscled back. She watched as he freed his dark hair from its ponytail. It fell in wild waves to his shoulders, tickling them, accenting their golden tone. Then she saw something she knew she must not. But she did not look away. She saw his buttocks, strong and round, muscular and lightly bronzed. And if she had been honest with herself, she would have known that she longed to reach out and see what it felt like. Would it feel spongy under her squeeze? Firm like thick leather? Or a combination of both?

She sensed he was about to turn, and quickly shut her eyes. She heard some rustling of clothes, then felt his breath on her cheek. "Isabella? Do you wish to sleep through breakfast?" he whispered. "If that is what you wish, just nod, and I'll leave you be."

Isabella let out a false yawn, accompanied by a dramatic flutter of the eyelids. "Oh, my," she exclaimed. "Is it morning already?"

"Yes."

She had never noticed before what a very nice voice he had. It was deep and well textured. "Well, I supposed I shall get up then."

She sprang to her feet with an energy that a freshly wakened soul could never have. Then she gathered up some clothes. She looked at her velvet dress. She was tired of standing out so brightly among the sailors. It was a beautiful and tasteful gown, but this was neither a beautiful nor a tasteful place to be. So somehow, the dress felt inappropriate. She wanted to look like everyone else today. She looked at her corset. Going without one at night was one thing, but dare she appear in public without one? Wouldn't everyone notice? Wasn't it obscene?

Marques could guess her thoughts, for his savvy about women had improved greatly since his earliest blunders as a twelve-year-old. He smiled thoughtfully, and approached her. "I forbid you to wear this," he said, tossing the corset to the floor. He thought she would be thankful to have the decision taken from her hands.

"Forbid me?" she asked. Her expression was not quite defiant, but rather worried. She was not sure what her status was aboard this vessel, but had hoped she was not a slave.

"Yes," he said gently.

She looked at her velvet dress. "What about this?"

"Do you want to wear it?" he asked.

"Well, I'm not sure," she explained. "It's a little hot for the weather, and ..."

"Then I forbid you to wear that too," he said, yanking it from her grip. He tossed it on his cot. "Just put an apron over your sleeping gown. That will be more comfortable."

Isabella looked at the fallen garments. "How can you forbid me?" she asked.

"I'm captain of this ship," he explained cheerfully, a smile crossing his mischievous lips. "I get to tell everyone what to do. That's what's so great about being captain."

"But you don't tell anyone else what to wear," she challenged cautiously.

"How do you know?" he asked. "Maybe I lay out their wardrobes every night before bedtime. Now go, put on your apron and let's eat." He gave her a friendly smack on the backside, causing Isabella to narrow her eyes at him. But he did not notice. He was cheerfully fixing the buttons on his cuff.

Isabella was glad, after all, to be wearing her nightgown and apron. And truth be told, she looked just as stunning in her new, simple garb as she had looked in that lush velvet dress. Her white bed gown flowed gracefully all around her, no longer stiffened by harsh framework. And the white, lacy apron blended in perfectly, making her look like an angel in layers and layers of flowing white. Many a pirate choked on his breakfast when the captain came whistling into the Great Cabin, this soft, lovely kitten on his arm. But she did not notice the pirates ogling her, for she walked with her eyes to the floor.

To Isabella's delight, there was milk waiting for her on the dining table, just as Marques had ordered. And to her even greater delight, both Luisa and Saada were eagerly waving her to their corner of the room. No one had ever done that before. Isabella's face lit up when she saw them. "Marques?" she asked. "May I sit with them?"

"Of course," he replied, "and I shall sit with the men." He

kissed her hand, then backed away, not turning to walk until he felt he'd paid his proper respects. Then he joined his groggy, but boisterous men at the table's far end.

Isabella approached her new companions with a grin she could not prevent. It was so exciting to be included. Not a single girl at the convent had ever waved Isabella to the seat beside her. Every time Isabella had approached a seat in the dining room, she had done so apologetically, knowing that no one had especially wanted her there. That old habit was haunting her still, as she lowered her gaze and asked, "You don't mind?" before taking her chair.

"Of course not," giggled Luisa. "Come, I've been telling Saada all about our talk last night."

Isabella reached for a biscuit. These, she was now willing to eat, after having braved one last night. The infested meat she would still not touch. Saada held understanding in her midnight eyes as she watched Isabella daintily pull apart and inspect each bite of her biscuit before eating it. She could remember how hard it was to get used to pirate food. "Isabella," she said, her voice rich and low, "Luisa told me you don't fancy our captain. Is that the truth?"

Isabella looked up timidly, worried that perhaps Saada was offended. But she saw that the woman was sending her an expression of something between humor and respect. " 'Tis no secret," replied Isabella frankly, "I am a captive here. Why should anyone think me anything other than eager to be free?"

Saada widened her eyes and pursed her lips into a comical expression, causing Luisa to break into laughter. "You should've met some of the other women," Luisa explained. "They're usually starry-eyed by the end of the very first day." She giggled some more, adding between breaths, "It's so ridiculous."

"What do you mean?" Isabella couldn't help asking, though she suspected she understood.

"Well, he just drops them off on the shore somewhere as soon as he gets tired of them," she said. "But they always come to the Great Cabin talking about how in love they are, and all the sweet things the captain did for them, trying to make us all jealous. It's ridiculous!''

"You're the first one," Saada announced proudly, "to say, 'Hey, I don't care *how* handsome he is, I have my own life, and I want to get back to it.' " The way she said it was so dramatic that Luisa and Isabella both laughed with her. "So tell me." Saada put a fist in her chin, and leaned forward. "You must have a husband, right? Or a lover you're being faithful to?''

Isabella shook her head. "No, there's no one," she said quietly.

Saada frowned in surprise, batting her eyelashes rapidly. "Well, good for you," she said in a high tone. "Good for you. You don't need a man." She nodded her approval.

"Actually," Isabella confessed nervously, "I ... I'm not alone by choice. I ..." she bowed her head. "I wish I had someone."

Saada could feel the sadness in those words, and responded instinctively by giving comfort. "Well, don't worry about that," she said lightly. "We'll take care of it. You know, New Providence is crowded with men. There is nothing but men from one end of town to the other. You just wait until we get there, Isabella. Luisa and I will find something nice for you.''

Luisa's grin showed that she was game. "It's true," she said softly. "Even I can find men in New Providence.''

Isabella wished Luisa would stop saying such things. It made her uncomfortable. "Well, I don't think I would want to meet men that way," she said, trying quickly to turn the subject from Luisa's scarred skin.

"Oh, don't worry," Saada assured her in a high voice. "They're not all pirates." She smiled warmly, letting Isabella know that she was not offended, but understood perfectly why Isabella had been wary of meeting the sort of men she and Luisa knew. "A lot of them are just regular land folks.''

"What exactly is New Providence?" asked Isabella.

"It's where we're heading," Saada explained, "Didn't the captain tell you?"

She shook her head.

"Oh, well, it's the island where we sell our goods after we've stolen them. The place is all set up for pirates. Pubs that serve pirate beer, women that uh ... serve pirates too," she laughed. "There's no sign of the law anywhere. We're completely welcome. In fact, around here, we call New Providence 'The Nest of Pyrates.' You'll love it."

"But there are nonpirates there too," Luisa was quick to add.

"Yes, that's right," said Saada. "We'll find you a dry land man. You'll see."

The galley boy came in to shoo everyone out. It was time to start the day. At least that was the case for everyone but Isabella, who had nothing to do. Marques fetched her, and offered his arm. "Did you eat well?" he asked.

Isabella's companions had already fled. "Yes," she said.

They walked a ways in silence before Marques noted, "You're being awfully quiet, even for you. Is something the matter?"

"No," she whispered. "I'm just thinking."

"About what?"

Isabella was startled. "About what?" She shrugged. "I don't know. It's never occurred to me to think *about* something before. I was just letting my thoughts run freely."

Marques smiled. "Don't see why a dreamy girl like you would ever want to return to their world," he muttered.

Isabella didn't catch all of it. "What?"

He paused and thought about repeating himself. But he decided against it. "I've many things to do," he announced. "Will you be able to entertain yourself?"

She nodded.

"Until supper then." He kissed her hand and backed away. Then he turned briskly on his heel.

Isabella watched him go with a certain sadness in her eye.

Everyone had told her that her instincts were exactly right. Even his dearest friends and faithful crew were eager to admit that he was a womanizer and a poor choice of suitors. Then why was it that every time she heard this, her heart sank? What had she felt when Luisa had told her about the other women? Was it jealousy? Was it relief that she had not been so gullible? Or was it fear that a piece of her was just as impressionable as those poor women had been. Fear that she was in danger of becoming one of those lovestruck, brokenhearted creatures. It was natural, she told herself. She was confined to his company, given no choice but to notice him. And he was handsome and charming, as so many evildoers were. It was not her fault that she was weakening. It was not her fault that she nearly hoped he would try to undress her again tonight. It was natural. It was the fate of a captured damsel to be tempted so. She only hoped that someone would come and save her before it was too late.

Chapter Ten

Isabella did not dance with Marques that night. Strangely, he did not invite her to. That he was trying to create suspense, that he was wanting her to become anxious for his company, did not occur to her, for she was not at all savvy about the ways of courtship. She ate her meal in silence, while Luisa and Saada chatted about their day. She enjoyed the music and the raucous dancing; but not as much as she had last night. For she was filled with confusion. Isabella had always believed in destiny, but hers was becoming foggier by the moment. Was she really meant to reach the island of Madeira? Could the fates have spoken any louder than to have her ship intercepted by pirates? Clearly, they did not want her to reach that island. So what did they want? There was nowhere in the world where her arrival would be expected. She had no clear vision of her future, except that she wanted to be swept off her feet by a handsome knight. And frankly, she thought, he was running a bit late.

As a babe in the convent, she had waited for him. In those days, she imagined him in the form of a relative, perhaps split in two. Perhaps he was a couple, an aunt and uncle, wealthy and loving, eager to rescue her from the harsh nuns, and the frighteningly cold convent life. Perhaps they would be wealthy, and offer her a room filled with toys. Or perhaps they would be poor, and she would have to help them raise their crops. But surely, they would take her to a place where she would be surrounded by friends, none of whom would believe how unpopular she'd been at the convent. They would take her to fairs, let her ride ponies, and read her a story every night before bed. She waited for them, knowing well that she must have a relative out there somewhere. She prayed in the way the nuns taught her to pray. And when that didn't work, she invented her own prayers. But they never came. Many a night, she cried herself to sleep, glaring angrily at the full moon outside her window, for it was either too stupid to hear her wish, or too callous to grant it.

As the years passed, and Isabella blossomed to maturity, her life changed. The convent girls still did not care for her, but she stopped trying to make them. She had grown very self-reliant, for whom did she have but herself? She was content to ignore the other girls, so long as they let her be. And though it hurt her when the nuns would force her to sit still while they sliced off her lovely hair, or chastised her for being so naughtily beautiful, she learned to stay calm. For secretly, she now expected him more than ever. He was no longer the aunt and uncle who would love her and buy her a pony. He was now a handsome gentleman, a lover, a shining knight, outraged by the way his lady had been mistreated. He would come for her, she knew. It might be in the middle of the night while she slept, or he might ride by as she danced through the woods. But he would come. She had no choice but to believe this, for it was her only hope.

He had not come in time to rescue her from the convent. No, she had been forced to do that herself. But here she was on a pirate ship, and where was he now? She had to believe he would come, she could not lose faith, for she believed in this knight just as surely as the nuns had believed in God. He was out there somewhere, he had to be. But she was, she admitted to herself, experiencing a crisis of doubt. If he did not come for her now, when she had been kidnapped, and worse yet, was gradually being bewitched by a villainous pirate captain, then when would he come? What was taking him so long? Had he not watched her from afar since her childhood? Had he not waited for her to mature so that he might make her his bride? Wasn't it time to steal her from the cruelty of the world, and whisk her off to his castle?

She looked about the Great Cabin with invisible tears in her eyes. What would life be like, she wondered, if there really were no knight out there? It was almost impossible to imagine. No knight, no rescue, just this. Ordinary life, all alone in the horrendously savage world. And no one watching or waiting to save her. She could not bear the thought. She had to resist it. Yet, she was growing more desperate by the day. And more drawn to the darkness, from which her knight was supposed to save her.

"Hello," said Marques.

Speaking of the devil.

"I'm sorry for having neglected you," he lied, bowing courteously. "Are you ready to retire?"

Isabella sighed miserably. "Yes, I suppose so."

Marques made the usual announcement about all crew returning to their hammocks, and extinguishing lanterns, then offered Isabella his arm. "My lady."

"I wish you would not feign courtship," she griped softly. "It doesn't suit you."

"Would you prefer I cursed and spat, as a pirate should?" he teased.

"Yes," she answered without hesitation.

He laughed jovially as he led her to his cabin, his blue eyes twinkling with delight. But as soon as his cabin door was closed, his face changed. He lit a short, red candle with a determination and intent that Isabella did not understand. Then he loosened his collar, and sat mysteriously on Isabella's cot. He leaned forward, his elbows resting on his knees and he looked at her soberly, hauntingly. The candlelight did strange things with the striking color of his eyes. There were moments when it seemed to make his pupils red instead of black. There were moments when Isabella could see a perfect reflection of flame on his golden face. He was deliriously handsome. His face could not have been carved more exquisitely, nor been bronzed to a more perfect color. His fashionable beard could not have been more flattering, nor could his hair be a shinier black. His energetic physique she dared not examine, though his strong shoulders were so clear in the dim light.

Isabella stood stiffly before him. She did not ask why he was staring at her so, for she could sense his reason. She touched her gown uncomfortably, feeling its whiteness, testing its ability to protect her from his gaze. Her long hair was waving wildly down her back. It looked as soft as it felt—even softer, for its pale gold sparkled whenever the candle flickered. She was expecting him to say something. She could feel what was happening between them, though she could not meet his eyes to be sure. The time had come for him to test her resolve, and she could feel tension like a thickening of the air all around her. She had known this night would come. And strangely, she was not afraid. She was resigned, and oddly . . . excited.

"Why don't you undress for me." His voice was soothing, but this had been a request, not a question.

Isabella was startled by his words. "Surely you don't expect me to cooperate?" she asked softly. "Surely you don't think I will make it so easy for you to ruin me."

"I said nothing about ruining you," he stated flatly. "I only want you to undress."

"Wh—what?" Her surprise was so great that she actually smiled. "You are joking."

His head shook firmly. "I just want to look at you. Go on." He nodded as though fully expecting her to comply.

Isabella laughed. "I will not."

"Please."

"No."

Marques continued to watch her as though he still believed she might lower her gown at any moment. His eyes were fixed on her, his hands clasped as he bit his lips in delicious anticipation.

At last, Isabella found herself asking, "Why should I?"

It was then that Marques knew he had her. He had piqued her curiosity, and that, in his experience, was something which would lead any man or woman to do anything. "Because I asked you to," he answered in a dark whisper, his handsome face catching rays of candlelight, "and because I can hear your heart beating."

"What?" Isabella was intrigued by the strange words he spoke. It was as though he were finally speaking in her own tongue, that watery language which comes so close to making sense, but barely falls short.

"I can feel your pulse," he said softly, deeply. "I can feel you growing warmer."

Isabella felt as though he were casting a spell upon her. She could now feel her own pulse, she could now hear her own heartbeat, and she suddenly felt very warm.

"I won't touch you," he promised her, "but wouldn't it be delicious to let me look?"

"You are pure evil," she gasped, her knees feeling weak.

"Would it be easier if I took it off for you?"

Isabella's head shook from side to side, but she knew she was being pulled in. The lights were so low, they were so alone, and he was so handsome in the flickering candlelight.

"How about if I made you an offer?" he smiled devilishly.

"Wh—what?"

"Take off your clothes for me, and I promise I will never ravish you."

"But . . . but I thought you already said you would never . . ."

"Yes, yes," he conceded, "but this time, I'll mean it."

Isabella was not thinking clearly enough to question this. The mind which would have told her to challenge his promise was giving way to a warmth between her legs, exciting her and urging her to go forth. Somehow, she managed to retreat into a far corner of her mind, a place where she could watch herself do something so delicious as undress before this fearsome pirate without feeling it was she who did it. She said, ''Then I must?''

To this, he replied, ''Oh yes, you certainly must,'' and managed not to laugh.

She closed her eyes and lifted a trembling hand to her sleeve. Slowly and quiveringly, she lowered her gown. She pulled it from her shoulders, offering him a good look at how her lemon hair looked against her snowy chest. Then she looked at him inquiringly, not sure she could venture to show him her breasts. He gave her a nod of encouragement. And with that, she lowered the gown to her belly. She turned her head away as though she could not see him, as though she were so caught up in the evil of her actions that she forgot she was being watched. But she knew that her breasts were peering at him, vulnerable and white, pink crested and rapidly hardening. She knew that if he wanted to grab them, he could. But he did not.

''The rest,'' he urged her patiently. ''Show me the rest.''

She let the gown fall to the floor. She tossed her head backward as though she were making love. He saw the tender curve of her hips, her long, shapely legs, and the pale wisps of silky hair that lay between. Isabella had never felt so raw, so sinful. She could never have brought herself to look at his piercing eyes now. ''Turn around,'' he ordered softly.'' She did so with speed. ''Slower,'' he commanded, an annoyed edge in his voice. ''Do it again, and do it more slowly.'' This time, she turned at a gentle pace, allowing him to observe the plumpest part of her otherwise slender body. By the time she faced him again, she was red in the face, though still weak in the knees. Marques saw that, and wisely ended the game.

''Thank you,'' he said, to Isabella's surprise. ''Thank you for letting me see you. You're breathtaking.''

Isabella did not reply. She did not even look at him.

He rose heavily to his feet, and though Isabella winced, afraid that he was going to break his promise, he was merely retrieving her nightgown. "Here," he said, lifting it from the floor. "Might as well put it on again."

She took it from his hand but did not hurry to put it on. She was still very far away.

His voice remained gentle. "If you want to sleep in my cot tonight, I'll hold you. Would that make you feel better?"

Isabella slid on her nightgown.

"Did you hear what I said?" he asked. "You're welcome to sleep with me. I'll be a gentleman about it."

The sound of her own wrathful voice surprised even Isabella. "You wouldn't know the meaning of the word 'gentleman.' "

He did not let that phase him, though she had touched one of his tender topics. He continued to stare at her, standing calmly within inches of her quivering body. "Be that as it may," he said soothingly, "I would be happy to offer you tenderness. Come."

"No, thank you," she replied coldly.

He found this deeply puzzling. Why wouldn't she want tenderness after she had just willingly exposed herself to him? It was most unusual, and Marques would know. He had never so much as kissed a woman who didn't want at least a tender squeeze in return. But then it occurred to him. Perhaps, she was not a maiden. Of course! Why had he assumed as much? She was raised in a convent, true. But convent walls were not impenetrable. And she was comely to the point of being an outrage to any man's senses. Obviously, she had been taken before, and probably without gentleness. Perhaps she was unaccustomed to afterward formalities in the bedroom.

Believing he had unraveled her mystery, Marques smiled. "I'm sorry," he said. "You undoubtedly mistrust my intentions. But I assure you," he swore, lifting her hand to his soft lips. "I would not betray you, and I would never, ever hold you still or silence your cries." He kissed her fingers, sealing that promise. "But I see that you are suspicious, and probably with good reason. Therefore, I bid you good night." He bowed gracefully and backed away, blowing out the candle before undressing and retiring to his cot.

Isabella returned to her own cot in complete darkness. She lay still for a long while, eyes wide open, focused on the watery porthole. She let the waves under her back soothe her. She couldn't think of any reason in the world to share Marques's cot. All of her life, she'd had only herself for company, and it no longer occurred to her that she should turn to another for comfort. "It's all right," she imagined her knight whispering from beside her pillow, "Everything will be all right. I shall come for you, and when I do, I shall forgive your foolish brush with temptation." But his voice seemed so faint within her mind. And Marques's breathing was loud. That was the problem with reality, she decided. It was so terribly loud.

Chapter Eleven

When Isabella opened her eyes, dawn was just beginning to break. The cabin was dark, and the shallow sea through the porthole was specked with orange. She didn't usually see this time of morning. She felt that no one on earth was awake yet. No one except her and Marques. For she saw him sitting at his desk, writing on parchment with a quill pen. He was already dressed, but his hair was loose. His back was to her, but he knew that she was watching him. And stranger still, she knew that he knew. She let him write for a few more moments, listening to the scratching sound of his scribbling disturb the silence. She felt at peace. Enough so to ask, "Why do you tie your hair up?" She thought it looked so beautiful, falling about his shoulders.

"Gets in the way," he replied in a voice soft enough for morning.

"What are you writing?" She set up on her elbows, and breathed in the stillness of the new day.

"A letter." He still did not look at her, but continued writing.

"Do you always wake up this early?"

"Yes."

She sighed pleasantly, closing her eyes, wondering whether she should return to slumber. But everything in her said no. Her eyes did not want to stay closed. They were pleased with the cool darkness all around them, and wanted to be allowed to soak it in. At last, Marques finished the last word in his letter, and thrust his quill into its ink pot.

"There," he announced, spinning around. Isabella was startled by how handsome he looked in the early light, his face so natural, his blue eyes so striking. "Would you like to take a walk on deck?" he asked kindly. "No one else is up yet."

Isabella was delighted. "Yes," she grinned, wanting so much to see this intoxicating dawn in full view.

"Pull on your cloak," he advised. "It's cool."

"All right." She sprung from her cot, and ran for her apron. She fumbled to tie it on rapidly, for fear the sun would rise before she saw it. But Marques stopped her racing hands with a gentle smile.

"We have plenty of time," he assured her. Then he reached around her and tied the apron himself. His hands were steady, and Isabella liked the way they felt against her as they worked. "There you go," he said, patting her side. "And here's your cloak."

"Thank you," said Isabella. He stared at her until she agreed to look into his bright eyes. When she did, she was rewarded with a smile.

"Let's go." He offered his arm.

Isabella took it, then crept out of the cabin with him, grinning and tiptoeing as though committing a crime and worrying she might be caught. She was determined not to awaken anyone on board and disturb the silence. It felt like her very own special morning. "Do you suppose," she whispered to Marques, "that there are spirit folk who live only at this time of day, then scurry away when the humans arise?"

"It's possible," he said, having no objection to fantasy. "That would seem to be an excellent life for a fairy."

They climbed the stairs to the upper deck, and immediately, Isabella was hit by a gust of bitter cold wind. But she loved it. It caught her hair, blowing it away from her startled face. Now, she felt truly alive, her mouth opening automatically to gasp in the cool air. She and Marques were alone up here. All she could see beyond the dark wood rails were ocean and sky. And both were magnificent. The ocean roared a song, welcoming the sun, and warning all that another difficult day on the planet earth was being called to session. The sky was still navy blue, save a breathtaking streak of lavender, and another one of pink. She had never seen so much sky in all of her life. The constant wind seemed to push the sky nearer and nearer to her disbelieving eyes. "If I died today," she called over nature's symphony, "I would be content. For this is the most beautiful morning I have ever seen."

"Then will you wake with me?" asked Marques. "Will you wake with me every morning to watch it? No one ever has before."

She nodded her promise. Her face was already moist from drops of seawater flying on to her cheeks. Her arms were tightly nestled under her dark cloak. And her eyes were almost invisible, as they blended in with the coming fog. "Have you always loved the sea?" she called.

"Always," said Marques, rocking against the railing, his sturdy body testing its strength.

"Are you sorry when the ship pulls into port?"

"Miserable!" he cried. "I hate the shore, and all who call it home."

"Why?"

"Because they are stagnant like the land, and as cruel as a desert."

"But the sea can be cruel," she called.

"Nay, it is never cruel! Cruelty has no reason but itself. The sea always has her reasons."

Isabella closed her eyes, and listened to the water. Which was louder, the sea or the wind? It was the wind which gave the sea its voice. So didn't that make the wind louder? "I would like to be buried at sea when I die," called Isabella.

"You think a lot about death," he observed. "It's the second time you've mentioned it."

"That's because I know that my savior will at least be there, even if he never comes for me here. I do not fear death."

"Didn't know you were such a devout Catholic," he said.

Isabella was puzzled. "Devout Catholic? What makes you say that?"

"All that savior stuff."

"Oh no," she laughed at the misunderstanding. "No, no. I'm not talking about Him. No, I'm talking about my other savior. The knight who is going to rescue me from your ship." She said this matter-of-factly, as though it were not a peculiar thing to say at all.

Something poked Marques's heart, and he found himself staring pitifully at the girl. He moved closer to her, the wind slapping his midnight hair into his lively face. "This knight," he began gently. "This knight is coming to rescue you?" She had mentioned this before, but he'd thought she was speaking figuratively. When she said she was waiting for a knight in shining armor, he'd just assumed she meant an upstanding, land-loving type of gentleman. He'd never dreamed she was being literal.

"Yes," she explained, surprised by the concerned expression he wore. "I'm sure I told you before. There is a knight out there somewhere, waiting for me, and someday I'm going to find him. I only have to keep searching for my destiny, following my heart, and I know he will come."

Marques did not laugh. His eyes showed signs of wanting to fill with tears when he asked, "How long have you been waiting?"

"Forever," she admitted, turning away from him. "But I don't want to hear you lecture me that he will never come. He will come, and I will not lose faith."

"When you say forever," he ventured, reaching for her hand,

"do you mean to tell me that you've been waiting for him since girlhood?"

Isabella nodded.

"Then my ship is not the first thing you've longed to escape."

Isabella blushed. That was why she was so quiet all the time. Whenever she started talking, really talking, people thought she was mad. "You must think me insane," she apologized.

"There's no such word on a pirate ship."

She appreciated his kind words, as well as the sincere look on his face. But she knew what he must think of her. "I know I imagine a lot," she explained. "Ghosts and werewolves and being queen of my own country . . ."

He broke into a smile. "Queen of your own country, eh?"

"But this is different!" she cried. "Those things . . . I don't know whether they really exist—ghosts and all of that. Sometimes I think they do, and sometimes I think maybe they don't. But this I am sure of! There is someone out there watching over me! I can feel him!"

Marques nodded. "Maybe there is."

This calmed Isabella considerably. "I'm . . . I'm sorry to have said so much. That should teach you to talk to me," she smiled weakly.

Marques returned her smile. Then he added, "I just wonder what would make a little girl so desperate for escape that she would befriend the spirit of death."

"That is none of your business!" Isabella hissed. "In fact," she remembered, tightening her cape, "I should not even be speaking to you. You are, after all, the enemy of my true love, being both a criminal and my abductor."

"I'm sorry I've woven my way into your story, and in such an unfavorable role." He couldn't help cracking a cynical smile. "So will you marry your knight when he comes?" he asked. He was merely curious how this all worked.

"But of course!" she cried. "He will steal me away."

"And that's why you're still unmarried? Because you've not yet met a knight?"

"Actually," she confessed, "no one has asked me. No one at all."

Marques shook his head. "I don't believe that. You're too fair."

Isabella narrowed her eyes, wisdom superimposed over dreaminess. "Well, believe it, Captain. There are few men brave enough to take what they imagine to be the first prize."

"I would," he replied confidently.

"Yes," she agreed, "you would. But what good does that do me? You're a pirate! Would you have me marry a pirate?"

Marques's face froze into a fixed, angry expression. "I'll ask you to stop insulting my people. Say what you will about me, but leave my profession out of it."

"Profession?" she scoffed.

The sun was now rising, and Marques was ready to go below. "I mean it, Isabella. You've not seen me angry, but you will if you don't stop criticizing my crew." With arms crossed, he leaned away from the ship's railing, and moved toward the stairway.

"But they are *pirates!*" she called after him. "It isn't that I don't like some of them, it's just that, well, they are *pirates!*"

He turned to her one last time. "In answer to your question, no. I would not have you marry a pirate. And you needn't worry that any of us shall ask," he scowled. "But I have treated you well, and my crew has accepted you. Can you say as much for those you would respect?"

Isabella watched him walk away, and truly, she felt guilty. She had never meant to hurt his feelings. And what if Saada and Luisa heard what she had said? Would it hurt their feelings too? But they were all pirates. They were all loathsome criminals. Surely, they shouldn't mind hearing it, for surely they knew it themselves. But she could see that she was in error. They obviously did mind hearing it, and they obviously couldn't see it themselves. She would have to make a choice. A choice between liking them individually and shunning their kind. It would not be an easy choice, for she did so like Luisa and

Saada. But Marques . . . how could she ever see him as anything but the seductive creature of darkness that he was? Would she even want to see him as something else? If he were something else, that would confuse everything. She would not be his helpless prisoner, and last night when she disrobed . . . she couldn't bear the thought. Of course, he was everything she presumed him to be and worse. It must be so.

Chapter Twelve

It had been so long since she'd seen another ship on the horizon, Isabella was startled. She had never quite considered the matter before, but now that she did, she realized that her situation was a dangerous one. Should Marques's ship be caught while she was aboard, she'd be at risk of hanging with the rest of the crew. Yet telling the truth about her capture would bring the lesser consequence of embarrassment. For what young woman wanted to confess that she'd been at the mercy of dozens of filthy pirates for days now? Her rescuers would assume what she herself could not believe wasn't so—that she'd been used in the most belittling and dishonoring fashion imaginable. Yet telling her rescuers otherwise could implicate her as a pirate. For who would believe that a young lady could be captured, then treated with courtesy aboard such a villainous vessel?

Marques had been summoned to deck at the first sign of another sail. He was now studying something through the telescope, and the crew breathlessly awaited his announcement. "Not pirate hunters," he said gravely. "It's corsairs."

This caused everyone to gasp, groan, or wince except for Isabella, who had no idea what corsairs were. She squeezed Pedro, rubbing his spotted fur as though comforting him, when it was she who needed reassurance. One of the crew spoke up. "Can we take care of them with cannon fire, Captain?"

Marques looked stern. Isabella had never seen him when he was truly at work, deeply engaged in his job. He looked like a different man. There was no humor in him, no lightheartedness. His jaw twitched agitatedly and his eyes were set to kill. "It appears we could outgun them, barely," he announced. "But we would suffer great damage, perhaps be sunk if they aim well."

There was a hush in reply to his grave analysis. The captain was still deep in thought.

"I believe," he said at last, "we would be better served by battling them man to man. That way, at least our ships would be spared."

The crew was silent. The enemy sails drew nearer. "I can smell them," said one young man eerily. "I can smell the bleeding slaves."

Marques turned to Gabriel. "Quartermaster," he said sternly, "I ask that you bring all women below deck except the fighters."

Gabriel knew his captain was worried. "Aye, sir," he replied kindly.

Isabella found herself being lifted by the elbow. "Wait!" she begged Gabriel. "Let me take Pedro! Let me take the dog!" This suddenly became the most important matter of the moment. For by focusing on Pedro's safety, she was able to have less concern for her own.

"Fine," snapped the old man, "take the dog. But hurry!"

She could not lift Pedro, for he was a fair-sized mutt. She was forced to call desperately to him as she made her gradual exit from the deck. All the while, Gabriel kept shouting at her to speed up while the other civilian women followed him eagerly. "What is going on?" Isabella begged of Gabriel as he grabbed Pedro by the scruff of the neck and hurled him into the cabin, and was just about to do something similar to Isabella. "What are corsairs?"

"Enemy pirates," he explained gruffly. "They come from the Near East, and make slaves out of Christians. Governments roll over because they're scared of them. It's easier to chase folks like us. But we won't be made slaves. And we won't have you sold for one either. So stay in the cabin. I'll lock the door. Hurry, you crazy lass! Hurry!" He shoved her in none too gently, then sealed her in as promised. Isabella was glad to be away from danger, but she was still scared. Snuggling Pedro, she buried her face in his salty coat. What was happening on deck? If these enemy pirates, these corsairs took over the ship, that little lock on the cabin door would offer no protection. Oh, whom should she root for? Pedro, sensing her distress, licked her as he would his own pup.

A cannonball was fired. "Men!" Marques called boldly, his proud presence and strong frame giving them all much-needed confidence. "That is the signal that they want us to surrender. We shall pretend to do so. When they board us, I want all fighters to rush in and save this vessel. Corsairs fight well. Their attackers are called janissaries, and will use intimidation as a tool in their favor. Their language is foul and threatening, their fighting techniques ungentlemanly. Their swords are better than ours, but their swordsmen are not." He paced before his lot of wild and free-spirited fighters, a proud glint in his eye. "You are capable of beating these men. And I shall be fighting at your side. Do not be intimidated, do not be hesitant. Your freedom is at stake. If these men win, we will lose not only this ship, but our lives. For I think we have all learned that life in chains is not worth living. One final note," he reminded them sternly. "If your captain is caught, it is everyone's duty to make certain that he is not made a slave. I would not tell each of you what course to choose should you find yourselves at auction. But it would be a dishonor to you all if your captain became a piece of merchandise. You are each and every one of you ordered to grab any opportunity to kill me, should I be placed in chains. Is that understood?''

"Aye sir!" came a chorus of male and female voices.

"Then fight!" he cried.

"Aye sir!"

"I can't hear you!" he cried.

"Fight!"

"Again!"

"Fight!"

"Now go hide!" he ordered, "José, raise the white flag!"

This was done with some hesitation, for no pirate enjoys even pretending to retreat. But the gesture was a success. For soon, Marques's vessel was being grappled by a strangely long and narrow ship. Its sails looked like they had once been part of a circus tent, for they were gaily striped with orange. Immediately, all fighters were glad they'd been warned about the janissaries, for their cries were loud and frightening. Wearing ballooned pants, matching turbans, and carrying shimmering curved swords, the janissaries leaped aboard the captured vessel, seeking its captain as their first prize.

Marques tossed his hands in the air, in a helpless gesture of surrender. But anyone looking at his eyes would have known that surrender was impossible for a man like him. As soon as his own fighters ran to the deck with cries of their own, he elbowed his captor hard in the ribs, and drew his sword. A gruesome battle began. The corsairs fought hard, for their captain might kill them if they did not. And the pirates fought hard, for their captain would lose respect for them if they did not. And this, to them, was worse than death. For they loved their Captain Marques, and lived every day of their lives to impress him.

The corsairs cursed all the while they fought. It was their tradition, for hurting the opponent's pride and confidence was half of the battle won. The pirates also yelled as they dove in for heavy blows, but they never cursed. Marques would have berated them for it. Slaves watched the battle from the skinny corsair ship. They were chained together naked, row after row of bright red bodies, so badly sunburned and so badly whipped. It was their job to row the ship in calm weather. And they could not stop even to eat. The crew shoved pieces of bread into their mouths from time to time, making sure that they wouldn't pass out. But they were never permitted to stop rowing until they reached Algiers, where they would be sold. They now scratched their faces and stretched their necks, enjoying this moment of stillness. They cheered on the pirates against their captors, though many thought the pirates would probably kill them. That was all right. Death would be a relief, so they continued to cheer.

Marques had never been as quick with a sword as he would have liked. He was a strong fighter, able to fell a victim with a single, fearsome blow. But in practice, he tended to focus on strength rather than agility. So he was sometimes a little slower than his opponent, which frustrated him. But today, he was having no trouble. The corsairs looked ridiculous to him in their bright orange costumes. They did not look like men at all, but clowns. And his dislike for cowardly, overly decorated men gave him the added edge he needed to fell one after the other. He was careful not to glance away, despite the temptation to see how his crew were faring. For one moment of lost attention could cost him a gash or a lost limb, or his life. He took heart in knowing that his crew were loyal and strong. They were undoubtedly doing well. And it always tickled him to recall that a third of them were women. He would have loved to see the look on a corsair's face after being struck to oblivion by a woman's sword. The temptation of seeing that alone made it difficult not to glance away.

As it turned out, though Marques was quite right to keep his eye on his own battle, there was one disaster which could have been avoided, if only he had looked away just once. For a handful of corsairs had slipped past the battling pirates and made their way below deck. There, tucked behind flimsily locked doors, lay unarmed, unsuspecting, and completely unprotected women. Isabella heard a pounding at her door.

Chapter Thirteen

Isabella clung to her dog. She believed the pirates had been defeated. She believed that she was about to be greeted by her new captors. She had never dreamed these corsairs might kill her. The thought had never come. But now, as she winced at every pounding of the door, she realized this just might be the end of her. She could sense the anger and determination on the other side of that door. She could hear the violence in that loud thumping. And even Pedro tried to get away from her, tried to scurry into the corner where he would feel safer. She closed her eyes, too fearful to witness her own demise. When she heard the door break down, and it landed with a thump on the floor, she jolted. But she did not rise to her feet, and she did not open her eyes.

It was just as well, for the startling colors of the corsair uniform would have shown her exactly what she hated most in the world: the unavoidable brightness of reality. With her eyes closed, she could gain some distance from her fate. But one look at the very real faces of three merciless corsairs within inches of her would have done her in. "This must be the captain's lady," said one, in a tongue she could not understand. He pulled her to her feet by tugging at one sore elbow. Isabella feared he would wrench her arm from its socket.

"Beautiful," said another in the same strange language. "Looks like a Swede."

"Stairs clear? Can we get her out of here?"

"No. We'll have to wait for the fighting to end."

"Then let's try her out. We've nothing else to do but wait for the path to clear."

Isabella could not understand his words, but she understood his intent. She turned her head to the side and did not struggle. Even when she felt one of the men press against her in a threateningly suggestive way, she did not open her eyes. She was like a rag doll in the corsair's arms. She talked to herself without making a sound, moved her lips like one in a trance. She felt one of the men grab the hem of her skirt, tearing its white cloth from her thigh. She was pressed against a wall now, laughter and strange talking all around her. She was maneuvered and shoved this way and that against the wall, as the men tried to ready her for the ravishment. She tried not to resist, as she did not want them to worsen the damage to her already bruised and scraped skin. She felt a hurtful hand upon her tender breast, and wincing from the pain, she began to sing softly to herself. It was a sad, whispery song that her mother had once sung to her. The men could not hear her over their own boisterous mayhem. And certainly, the men on deck could not hear her woeful song. Strangely, she did not think about crying out for help. For Isabella had learned to expect almost nothing from anyone. In her dreams, men came to save her from certain doom. But in reality, no one had ever saved her from anything.

Above deck, the pirates were victorious over their enemy. Sweaty and dripping with blood, they yelled at one another in voices so worn and wild that no one could understand the words.

But they all knew somehow that they were being congratulated. There was not one corsair still fighting. They had all either fallen or retreated, offering themselves for capture. It had been a close battle in the beginning, but once the scale began to tip, the pirates' advantage did nothing but grow. Every time a corsair fell, his companions saw it, and felt that much weaker and warier. And every time a corsair gave up, everyone who witnessed it was tempted, just for a moment, to do the same. Gradually, those still fighting were up against more than one pirate. When more were defeated, it became one against four, and then five, and then eight, until even the strongest corsair fighters could not go on.

"Let me guess!" called Marques to the galley slaves. "You want us to cut you free!"

The slaves, though exuberant over watching their captors fall, were nonetheless, barely strong enough to hold their heads up. As Marques approached the first line of them, all chained up to the oars, he had to cover his nose with a handkerchief. The smell of their dying bodies was wretched. "Javier!" he called. "Get me an axe! These chains are strong!"

One of the slaves, who must have been a strong youth a few weeks ago, but was now foggy eyed and trembling from hunger, was the only one who dared speak to Marques. "Are you going to kill us?" he asked.

Marques got on bended knee to talk to the boy. "No," he said reassuringly, looking him in the eye. "We'll let you rest a bit, and then we'll send you off with this ship. You can keep it. We have no need to carry a ship in tow, not this far from anyone that would buy it."

None of the slaves believed this fairy tale, but many of them wanted to. Only the young lad who had spoken believed Marques. For he was looking right into the man's shocking eyes, and knew he saw sincerity there. "But aren't you a pirate?" the boy asked faintly.

"Aye, that I am," nodded Marques. "And when you sail

off, well fed and well clothed, I want you to tell the world that you were saved by pirates. Got that?''

The boy didn't understand. "Why? Why are you letting us go?"

"Because we are like you—the battered slaves of the world. And we look after your kind. Those who would tell you we are evil are only trying to rob you of our protection. Protection against them. Got that? Now, return my favor and spread the word." He rose to his feet and left. "Hey, Gabriel! Is there any chance some of them slipped past us?"

"I don't think so, sir."

"No, wait, sir!" called a heavyset woman pirate, her forehead and sword both wet. "While I was battling, I thought I saw from the corner of my eye one or two of them head downstairs. I'm not sure of it, but I thought I saw something."

"Men, back me up!" called Marques, storming down the stairs with a hand on the hilt of his sword.

Isabella's breasts were now bare to every man in the room. Her head was limp, her breath coming forth in gasps. A few tears moistened her eyes, but did not fall from her closed lids. She kept them to herself, safely behind her own lashes. The shame and the terror of being stripped before gawking strangers had given way to a new, and more fearsome concern. Would they kill her? When it was over, when she had been humiliated past all redemption, and brutalized beyond repair, would they leave her be? Would they sell her into slavery? Or would they simply cut her throat? The last is what she feared most of all, for not one man among them showed any sign of remorse for what was being done to her. Not one of them showed any sign of having a conscience or a mother, or the capacity to sit up late at night with his thoughts. They were all laughing and cheering.

None of her attackers were worried about the battle upstairs. They all believed that their own men were winning, and clearing the way for an escape with this beautiful captive. They were all astonished when Marques, backed by seven of his men, broke through their crowd. "Enjoying yourself?" he asked the man whose hand was under Isabella's torn skirt. Marques's eyes were filled with murder, the tip of his sword prickling the man's throat.

Wisely, the corsair tossed up his hands in surrender, getting them just a little caught up in Isabella's gown on their way out. Marques's men grabbed the other two round the neck, holding knives against their ears. "What shall we do with them, Captain?"

Marques face was stoic and callous. "It's simple," he explained, his eyes and sword still fixed on the man before him. "Any part of them that touched her, we cut it off."

The corsairs gasped, their eyes widened in horror. Would the captain believe that they had not raped her yet? Just having their hands cut off was nightmarish enough, but what if he believed them to have touched her more intimately?

"Isabella," he asked sternly, his sword drawing a little blood from his captive's neck. "which of these men has lain a hand upon you?"

One of the corsair's cried out, "You're not going to believe a woman, are you? She'll lie!"

But Marques eyed him icily. "Would you like your tongue removed as well?"

The man bowed his head.

"Isabella," Marques repeated, "which of these men is guilty of touching you?"

She could barely hear him. No longer being held up by the corsair, she gradually collapsed into a crooked, sitting position. She still would not open her eyes, even though the ordeal was over. She did not want to see anyone's face. She did not want to see light. Even breathing hurt her chest. Just being alive was painful.

"Isabella?" Marques cast her a glance from the corner of his eye. When he saw her limpness, he ordered his men to grab the corsair he held hostage at sword point, and he raced to help her stand. "Isabella," he whispered hoarsely, wrapping his arms about her waist. "Can you stand?"

She used his shoulder as a prop, and let him gradually raise her to her feet. Once standing, she found she could not stay that way on her own. So she buried her head in Marques's warm chest, and held his waist. When he returned the embrace, she found she could not hold back her sobs. Her body shook with each sob, like a loud, rhythmic pulse. And soon, Marques's shirt was dripping with a new kind of saltwater. "Kill them!" he shouted, his voice vibrating against Isabella's ear. "Kill the bastards! Cut off their limbs, wait till dawn and then kill them!"

Isabella shook her head wildly against the brutality she was hearing. The thought of something so horrific befalling absolutely anyone was enough to make her find her voice at last. "No," she whispered. Realizing no one had heard, she tried again. "No. No. No." Finally, the last no was heard by Marques.

"What is it?" he asked gently, trying to lift her face, but finding she was determined to keep it near him.

"Don't," she whimpered, "Don't . . . don't hurt them."

"What?" he shouted, pushing her forcefully from his body, and holding her at arm's length. "Isabella, what do you mean?"

"Don't . . ." she stammered weakly. "Don't . . . don't."

The men looked at their captain questioningly.

"Follow my orders," he told them.

The men started to take the corsairs, but Isabella broke in once more. "No!" This time her voice was loud. "Don't!" she cried, opening her eyes. The light nearly toppled her. She waved a hand over her face to shade them. "Please," she begged Marques. "Please don't do anything so terrible to them. They didn't . . . they were going to, but . . ." She swallowed, and could not bring herself to explain.

"They didn't rape you?" Marques asked frankly.

"No!" she promised him, "No! They didn't!"

His eyes did not soften. "But it was not their consciences

which stopped them. What they did was more than enough to warrant death on my ship. Men, take them!''

Isabella fell to her knees. ''Don't!'' she begged, tugging at the leg of his breeches. ''Please! I beg of you. I'll do anything. But don't let them suffer so brutally on my account. I won't be able to live with the guilt.''

''*Guilt?*'' he cried harshly. ''What guilt? You've done nothing wrong!''

''But I will have, if I do not stop you from torturing them.'' She took a deep breath. ''Kill them if you must, Marques, for the honor of your ship. But don't do it for me.'' Her eyes were soft, like mist from the heavens. ''And do it quickly,'' she begged. ''Make them walk the plank or something, but don't cut off their limbs. Don't make them live that way until dawn, and then kill them. Just do it quickly, or don't do it at all. I beg you.'' She kissed his leg.

Marques was looking at his crewmen with puzzlement. They only shrugged, for they were wondering the same thing. ''Isabella?'' he asked.

''Yes?''

''How is making them walk along planks a punishment?''

''Oh, you know,'' she explained. ''They walk the plank, and then they get eaten by sharks.''

''Which plank?''

''The, uh, the one that sticks out over the water.''

''Why would we have a plank sticking out over the water?''

''Well, I don't know!'' she cried. ''It's just what I heard!''

The pirates all shook their heads at one another, and tried not to smile. It was amazing what stupid myths were spread about them on dry land. ''Oh well,'' Marques sighed, ''I cannot deny a lady who is on her knees to me.'' His men seemed to agree. ''Very well,'' he resigned. ''Take them to the brig, and we'll decide what to do with them later. Go!''

As the riffraff were hustled out of the room, Marques shouted, ''And get the carpenter! Tell him to fix my damned door!'' He kicked the fallen wood with agitation. Then, left in peace, he turned to Isabella. "Are you hurt?" He cradled the weeping woman in his arms. He rocked her back and forth, enabling her to stand with the strength of his own back. "Did they hurt you?" he repeated, kissing the soft hair on top of her head.

"No," she sniffed, but her sobs told him otherwise.

"They must've frightened you terribly," he whispered consolingly. "You poor child. If it's any consolation, I assure you they'd not have ended your life. There was never any danger of that."

"I don't care," she wept. "I don't care what they would have done with me after . . ."

"Well, it didn't happen," he interrupted firmly. "It didn't happen, so don't be afraid. It's all over now." He made every consoling gesture he could think of: stroking her hair, rubbing the small of her back, whispering hushes. But none of it had any effect on her sobbing. "I'll be here all night," he promised her. "I won't let anything happen to you. I'll not leave you alone again. Just stay here with me. Everything will be all right." When her weeping increased, he muttered, "You poor thing. They must've scared you to death. I'm sure I would've been scared, were I a maiden in such a state."

"It isn't that," she said so quietly, he couldn't hear.

"What?" he asked, separating himself slightly from her moist face, giving her the opportunity to speak with free lips.

"It isn't that," she repeated, surprising him by pulling away completely. She paced to the porthole, and watched the moving water with a fist in her mouth. "I'm not hurt," she assured him boldly. "And I know it's safe now. I'm not weeping about that." She spun around and looked at him face on. "It's just that no one has ever saved me before."

He shrugged, unable to resist the temptation to lighten her spirits. "Well, I'm sure they would have. Probably just never had the opportunity. I mean, how many men get to fight off a pack of corsairs for a lady?"

She did not laugh. "I mean it," she said, tears still running down her cheeks. "No one has ever saved me before."

He frowned, and took a couple of swaggering steps toward her. "Well, then I'm honored to be the first."

She did not appreciate his taking this opportunity to flirt. This was a very serious matter to her. "Marques, even when my parents died . . . no one . . . no one tried to help me." She swallowed some pain. "I've learned not to expect it."

"Well, some nuns took you in, didn't they?" he asked reasonably.

She shook her head, her eyes warning him not to contradict her. "They did what they thought was their duty. They felt they must raise me so I would not become so wicked as my parents. They didn't like me. They thought I was evil, spawned from the evil of a thousand generations."

He raised his eyebrows. "Your family sounds colorful."

"Don't mock me!" she cried. Having never heard her raise her voice before, Marques found himself instantly silenced. She was a passionate yeller. "The nuns had no love for me," she told him miserably. "They did it for God. A god who has never listened to my prayers, or never responded to them. I don't know which." She spat this last part with an anguish that was thinly disguised as bitterness. "You're right," she said softly. "The nuns are the only ones who ever tried to help me. But they did not manage to save me." She looked him pointedly in the eye. "But you did. You saved me."

"Well," he was tempted to flush, "I try to be helpful."

Isabella shook her head scoldingly at him. "Oh, stop being such an ass," she begged him. "Don't you understand?" She moved toward him, and surprised him by taking his strong hand in both of hers. He let her raise the hand to her cheek, where she moved it across her face lovingly, and then kissed it in a show of respect. "I am indebted to you," she swore.

Marques was beginning to like the sound of this. "When you say indebted . . ." he began.

But she stopped him by placing his hand at her breast. "You have fought for me, and you have won," she announced boldly.

"When you say I have won, do you mean . . ."

She pushed his fingertips past the torn edge of her gown, until they rested securely on the very crest of her bare breast. "I am yours," she said humbly, though she felt pride in announcing something so very romantic. "I am yours to do with as you please."

Marques couldn't help grinning at this most surprising triumph. But only for a moment. Then he pulled her roughly against his chest.

Chapter Fourteen

There may have been a quiet voice in Marques's mind which questioned all of this. Was it right to take Isabella, merely because he had accidentally become a hero in the fuzzy fairy tale of her life? Did she really understand what she was agreeing to and why? Did her madness come and go? Would she regret this in an hour? Or was hers a permanent state of delusion.

Fortunately for Marques, he could not hear the soft voice which longed to nag him. The louder voice of conquest played glorious trumpets in his head, pushing away every other song. Isabella was a prize beyond all imagining. In this late afternoon below deck, lanterns made pictures across her face. She looked even less human than usual, with one cheek in shadow, and the other glowing brightly. Her silky hair tossed over one shoulder, her thin hands clasped nervously, her beautiful face wearing stripes of shadow. She looked like a spirit of the fog, come to offer Marques a night of pleasure unlike any he had known before. Surely, she was not human, but a creature of mist. Her eyes so distant, her face so flawless, surely she would take him to heaven on this night, that ethereal world from which she had sprung.

Her flesh seemed to melt against him in their embrace. Her back was not rigid, but completely flexible. Every part of her seemed to be capable of molding and shaping itself to fit him perfectly. "You are beautiful," he whispered close to her ear. His lips moved against her neck, his hot breath bubbling her skin.

"Do not flatter me," she pleaded. "Beauty means nothing to me. It has no heart, no fire, no motion. It is but a cold statue of a fact."

"Then shall I tell you you're elegant?" he whispered, moving his kiss to her porcelain shoulder. "Shall I tell you you're kind? Shall I tell you that your visions inspire me to be heroic?"

"Tell me only the truth," she begged. "Tell me only what you believe, and spare me your seduction. I am here because of your actions, not your words."

Marques had spent a lifetime researching the art of saying the right thing to a woman. To stop uttering words of romance took a great deal of willpower on his part. But he stopped himself, bent down, lifted her in his arms, and carried her to the cot. Isabella let herself be carried, and even wrapped her arms about his neck and looked at him endearingly. It was a glorious feeling to be carried by the man who had saved her. Even if he was Marques. He lowered her gently to his cot, had her lie down comfortably, then knelt. He took her hand in one of his, squeezing reassurances. His brilliant blue eyes looked boldly into hers. And his free hand began to explore.

Isabella felt her skirt inching up beneath his powerful hand. "What do you like?" he asked.

Isabella could not speak of such things. Her head turned away from him, her voice came out as only a heavy breath.

"It's all right," he assured her, leaning into her lips. Before he kissed them, he added, "You can tell your lover anything. Anything you like, anything you want to do. You must speak up, so I can pleasure you. Nothing you say leaves this room."

He kissed her quivering lips, then crawled beside her onto the cot. He pulled her into his arms, and drove into her mouth with a strong, ungentle kiss. "Tell me," he urged her.

Isabella was shaking her head. "I . . . I don't know. I . . . I've never . . ."

"You're a maiden?" he asked skeptically.

She nodded.

"You don't have to say that to me," he assured her, lifting one of her white hands to his mouth. He sucked on a finger, eyeing her steadily, then pulled it out, adding, "I've no special preference for maidens. I would not view you as soiled goods."

"But it's true!" she insisted, rather indignantly.

Marques sensed she was about to sit up, and could not allow that. So he softened his voice, and pretended to agree with her. "Very well," he consented. "You are a maiden. Then at least tell me this." He rolled on top of her, capturing her wrists in his hands, and her eyes with his own. "What have you always *wanted* to do? Granted, you have never done it."

Isabella was dumbfounded. "I . . . I . . . I've never thought of it before." She struggled from his grip, not to get away, but just to have the freedom to do so. He would not release her.

"Tell me," he smiled. "Tell me how you hoped this would be."

And then, Isabella did what she always did to ruin his seductive games. She spoke of romance. Her pupils got big, and a glow crossed her forehead. "I had always hoped," she confessed, "that it would be so beautiful that I could not hear the clamor which surrounded it, that the transition from earth to sky would be so fluid that I would not feel the pains of takeoff, or the crunch of landing."

Something about that made sense to Marques, and he kissed her again, this time with a strange beating in his heart. For a moment, he almost thought he saw golden specks in the air between their lips. My God, he was becoming as dreamy as she was. He let go of her wrists, and pulled her into an intimate embrace, letting her feel his manhood against her hips. He rolled her to one side and then the other, holding her tightly, never letting her come close to falling from the bed. He thought he could hear her heart beat. He knew it was impossible, but he really thought he heard it. He rolled to his back, lifted her above him, then lowered her lips to his. He was not noticing her porcelain face anymore or her perfect cheekbones. He was watching only the specks of light which he swore were forming between them.

"How is it done?" she asked, feeling more comfortable with him than ever before. "Show me how to do it right."

He could feel her nervousness as if it were his own. He could sense her uncertainty, and suddenly knew, to his great surprise, that she was truly a maiden. He had been so sure she was not! But then, he had been using his old tricks to look into her. And now he was seeing her on her own terms. Now he knew the truth. "I assure you," he smiled kindly. "There's no danger of your doing anything wrong. I'm really the only one who can be a failure."

She laughed with him, just from the joy of sharing a joke, though she didn't quite understand it. He rolled her smiling presence onto her back, and proceeded to spread her hair over the pillow. He couldn't resist that. It was so yellow and soft. "Don't be afraid," he whispered, not intending to sound like a vampire about to bite, but sounding that way to Isabella nonetheless.

He lifted her skirt all the way to her waist, and Isabella clutched him. Her bareness frightened and shamed her, but only in the most delicious way. She felt the cloth of his breeches rub against her tickling, private skin. "Wrap your legs around me," he said darkly, his eyes sparkling the way they always did at this moment, the moment before his feast. She obeyed him, if for no other reason than to bury her nudity, and hide it from his view. To her delightful surprise, she found herself wanting to rub against him, now that she was snuggled there. Marques shot her a savvy smile. "Not so fast, you little vixen," he teased. He unbuttoned his breeches as quickly as he could without seeming anxious or unsettled.

Isabella threw her head back when Marques tore the cloth between her breasts, freeing them to be humbled and excited by his gaze. She seemed to be trying to escape him, Marques observed. She seemed to be reaching upward with her arms, lifting her chin and searching for something beyond their two bodies. But he had no time to ponder the meaning of this. It was sexy, the way she reached and arched, her eyes closed. Her lips pressed together into a rosy kiss for no one. Isabella felt him taste her breasts with his tongue; then she felt the cloth between her legs become bare skin. She was no longer arching against his dry breeches, but against his own rough skin. It was warm and golden. And feeling it between her legs felt sinful. She wrapped her legs tighter around him. But he pushed her away.

"No," he said, with some urgency, "I need to pull away for a second so I can go in."

"Go in?" she asked, flinging her eyes wide open.

Marques smiled. "Yes." He kissed her tenderly on the lips, then asked, "Don't you know how it's done?"

"I thought we were already doing it!"

Marques chuckled, but stopped as quickly as he could. "No," he said, brushing away a piece of hair which had fallen over her face. His smile was still bright. "But do you feel what I'm doing now?" He gradually, cautiously entered into her virgin flesh.

Isabella's gasp and vivacious nod told him that she felt it well.

"Good," he said, warming her forehead with his breath. "Am I going too fast?"

"No," she said quietly, squinting her eyes hard, concentrating on the sensation of being intruded upon in this strange manner. It felt strangely noble, strangely selfless.

Marques continued his slow journey into her. Soon, he found that it was absolutely true. She was a maiden. He had taken only a few maidens before, and always hated this part of it. He had not become a lover only to bring pain to his conquests. He always liked to believe that he was giving as much as he was getting. That is why he always made certain to cater to a woman's fantasies. But this moment was always a tough one. "This will hurt," he warned her. "But I shall reward you for your pains, I promise."

Isabella could hear the years of rehearsal behind that line, and the smooth way he finished it with a kiss. But she did not care, for she was far too intrigued by these new sensations she was having, by her strange glimpse at a new spectrum of emotions, living alongside all the ones she had known about, yet always remaining invisible before. These emotions, these yearnings, these tickles of excitement wove themselves into every aspect of the world around her, she was sure. Yet she had never seen them wrapping around people or moving destiny, because she had never experienced them herself. It was fascinating.

Marques broke blood with a thrust he'd hoped would be more gentle. Isabella arched, her face cringing. But she received his kisses with nibbles of her own. She was not wounded, only further intrigued. Intrigued by a pleasure that could spring from pain. "Does it hurt you too?" she asked.

"It hurts me to see you hurt," he replied slyly, kissing her bottom lip, bringing it into his teeth.

When he released her mouth, Isabella admonished him. "You speak as though I hear, but do not think."

Marques had never met such a challenging woman. None of his practice, none of his expertise helped him at all against her strangeness. "I believe that you think," he replied warmly, "but I believe this is not the time to think." He plunged deeply into her, feeling heat all around his member. He could feel her heart beat at his very tip. It was impossible. Could a woman's heart beat so heavily that he could feel it throbbing around his stiffened manhood? He felt her body heat stream into him, warming him, making him dizzy.

Isabella had never known a man could reach so far into her body without wounding her. She felt as though he had found a secret entrance into her belly, into her bones. She felt that he was folded inside her, and that she was keeping him safe and warm. She opened her eyes and saw how very handsome he was, his bronzed face moistening in his pleasure, his ink black hair falling from its ponytail, his shoulders bearing such impressive spheres of muscle. She touched his elegant face, thinking, "How could a pirate be so fair?"

He slowed his movements, thinking she was trying to tell him something by her touch. "Shall I be more gentle?" he asked, kissing the hand that fondled his face.

"No," she replied dreamily. "I just want this to last forever."

He smiled triumphantly, then continued his thrusts, fearing that "forever" was a feat even he could not perform. But he was glad she was enjoying herself. And he tingled her ear with his tongue, encouraging her to enjoy it more. Her heat, her energy was growing stronger in his bones. He could not believe that a woman could be so contagious, so powerful, her presence so infectious that she seemed to be entering him though she was the one being entered. Marques felt a strange weakness, as though a foreign power had invaded him and taken over his senses. He thrust madly into her, becoming greedy in the absorption of her heat. Her waters mingled with his, as deep within her body, he danced.

Isabella felt completely ravished, completely opened up and revealed. She loved the feeling, and urged her lover to press deeper, gripping his powerful shoulders, pulling him tighter to her breast. She started to feel as though she were weightless, as though Marques were holding her down from an otherwise certain flight to the ceiling. Every time his member reached the peak of its thrust, she felt a tender, explosive part of her had been touched and teased. She tried to make him touch that place in her, over and over again by lifting her hips up against him, forcing the thrusts to go deeper. They were both near madness by now. Marques was thrusting as deep and fast as he could, but Isabella was wanting him to work harder. "I love you!" she screamed, when in fact, she meant, "I love this."

"I love you too," he said, out of habit. For what ladies' man would be fool enough to deprive his lover of such easily spoken words?

And yet, when Marques burst open in his excitement, splashing Isabella with a tidal wave of his thrill, then collapsed against her in a panting, weakened, vulnerable state, they both had the strangest thought simultaneously. Perhaps they had actually meant it? They looked at each other, startled. Their eyes shone frightenedly in the dark. No, they decided at the same time, relaxing in each other's arms. That was not what they had meant. They did not love one another. For clearly, Marques was a lover, not a "loved one." And clearly, Isabella was . . . well, she preferred men who weren't real. They were so much more charming and benevolent.

"Thank you for saving my life," she said to Marques, stroking a strand of black hair from his eyes. "And thank you for . . . for that," she grinned shyly. "I liked it."

"Well, you can thank me," he said suavely, taking her hand to his lips, "but not just yet. Give me a moment to recover, then I'll give you good reason to thank me."

She laughed. "What do you mean?"

"Just a moment," he promised, turning onto his back, closing his eyes and taking several more deep breaths. He could not remember a bout of lovemaking that was as exhausting or as thrilling as the one he'd just had. Of course, he couldn't remember very many bouts of lovemaking at all, for they tended to blend in with one another in his memory. But this one would always stand out in his mind. A few more deep breaths, and he was ready. "All right," he grinned, sitting up on the edge of the cot. "Come here."

"What?" She propped herself on her elbows.

"Come here," he repeated, lifting her into his lap.

"What?" she laughed, but did not resist being brought to him.

"No gown," he ordered seductively, pulling at it. "Go on, take it off."

For some reason, she felt ashamed to do so. He was completely bare skinned. If she removed her gown as well, sitting on his lap would feel positively shameful. The thought did arouse her a bit. "I can't," she replied nervously.

"Do I have to tear it off?" he smiled, "I don't mind. I'm going to have to find you a new one as it is."

"Yes, tear it off," she instructed. "That will be less embarrassing for me."

She laughed as he did this. In fact, they both gave a smile. "But you have to let me get it from under you," he said, urging her bottom off the torn shreds. She let him clear away what little was left of the gown, then sat her bare flesh upon his thigh. "That's better," he said with a kiss. "Now come, rest your head here." He lay it gently upon his shoulder. Isabella snuggled her cheek against his neck. "That's a good girl," he teased her with a kiss on the top of her head. "Now just relax."

He held her securely on his knee with one arm, while his free hand touched her tenderest spot. Isabella jerked away. "It's all right," he whispered, urging her head to rest again. "Just close your eyes." She did so and, this time, did not react when he touched her. At first, she was too worried to enjoy it. She feared he would pinch her too hard in the wrong place and it would hurt. But of course, this one thing she did not have to worry about with Marques. He knew what he was doing. Gradually, she came to trust his fingers. They were rough and callused from hard work, but he knew their strength, and exactly how much pressure to apply where. He knew when to use a circular motion, then how to sense that the lady was ready for a stronger, back and forth movement.

Isabella started to squeeze his strong arms with all her might. She started to whimper into his ear. Nothing had happened yet, but she could feel it. She knew something spectacular was about to happen to her. "Give me a pretty cry," Marques urged her. "I know you can." He squeezed her in anticipation of the event. "I'll bet you have a beautiful voice when it's free. Cry pretty for me."

Isabella broke into a fit of tremors and a whispery cry for more. Her mouth flung open wide and wrapped around Marques's hard shoulder, sucking it, tasting its salt. "No," he said, shaking her off, "Cry out loud." Without the buffer of his shoulder, she was forced to yell out with a clear voice. Marques grinned mightily, for this was his favorite sound in the world. More beautiful even than the cold ocean waves first thing before dawn. "Thank you," he said once she had crumpled against him, unconsciously begging him for the use of his strength.

"No, thank *you,*" she replied, letting him lift her up, then settle her onto the cot.

He wrapped his arms about her and squeezed. "Are you all right then?" he asked, rocking her. "Was your first time all right?"

"Marques," she breathed with moist face and closed eyes, "I shall never forget this so long as I live."

That brought a deep smile to Marques's lips and eyes. It was what he hoped all of his lovers felt—that he had provided them with an unforgettable night. And in this case, he could say the same in turn. She had been magnificent. She *was* magnificent. He had never met any woman like her, and he could not have been more pleased to make her strange acquaintance.

Isabella breathed heavily as Marques planted amorous kisses along her wrist and arm. "So," she sighed dreamily, "now that I am yours, what sort of a wedding shall we have?"

Marques dropped her arm.

Chapter Fifteen

"You're . . . you're joking, right?" he asked her with a weak smile.

Isabella's eyes flung wide at the sound of his strange words. "What? Joking? But of course not."

"But . . . but . . . when did we ever mention marriage?"

"I remember it quite clearly," she informed him. "You saved my life. I told you I would be yours now. And you accepted my offer by bringing me to your bed."

Marques reflected on those events with a tremble in his strong heart. "No, no . . ." he objected. "No, you told me a long time ago, you see, that you would never marry a pirate."

"It would not have been my first choice," she admitted with a sigh. "But one cannot fight destiny. I do not love you, it is true. You are objectionable, false, thoroughly unromantic, violent, immoral—"

"All right, enough. Get on with it."

"But," she finished, "you are obviously not the dark-hearted demon I suspected you were. You rescued me like the truest of knights. And so, it is a matter of honor that I wed you now."

"You really don't have to do that," he assured her. "You can send me a thank-you note, and we'll call it even."

Isabella laughed. "What do you mean? Why, you don't think I'd be willingly bedded by a man who would not make an honest woman of me, do you?"

Marques ground his teeth. It was time to tell her the truth. "Isabella," he began cautiously, "I am a pirate."

"Yes, I know."

"And a pirate," he went on, "is a pirate forever. I will never settle on dry land."

"What's wrong with dry land?"

"It is filled with people I don't like," he explained flatly. "It's divided up into all of those despicable countries and governments."

"Which country don't you like?"

"All of them. I hate all of them. So you see," he said, taking her hand with care, "I can never return to that world."

Isabella lowered her eyes. "I see," she replied thoughtfully. "And I cannot say I don't wish you'd told me sooner, for I do."

"I apologize for the misunderstanding."

"But I can accept this," she stated boldly. Marques felt relief in every one of his muscles. "You're right, it was insensitive of me to expect you to change."

"Not insensitive," he chimed in smoothly. "It was perfectly understandable."

"No, no, it was insensitive," she insisted. "I should have realized right away that I cannot force a pirate to live on dry land. It was thoughtless, and I am sorry. So it is decided."

"Thank you," he breathed, covering her hand with kisses.

"We shall live on board this ship after we're married. I'll get used to it. I promise." She bounced gaily to her feet.

Marques watched helplessly as she pranced about the room, looking for something to wear for supper. There was a weary smile in his eyes, for he was not unable to see the humor in this predicament he had brought upon himself. "Isabella, I . . .

I assure you, that any man would be the luckiest on earth to have you for a wife.''

"Why, thank you," she smiled over her shoulder.

"But I fear I am unworthy," he ventured.

Isabella remained stubbornly dense. She could not see the truth when her imagination was so firmly superimposed upon its images. A knight always desired the hand of his rescued damsel. It could be no other way. "You're worthy enough," she assured him, "after what you did. Oh, what do you suppose it will be like, being a married couple aboard a ship like this?''

"I shall lock you in the cabin and beat you often," said Marques, standing up. He found the velvet dress she was searching for, and handed it to her with a toss.

"Oh really?" she laughed, catching the gown. "Now, seriously, Marques. This is important. A girl dreams of her wedding all her life! I only want to know what it will be like . . . after the honeymoon.''

Marques looked her right in the eye. "There will be no wedding, there will be no honeymoon, and there will be no 'after the honeymoon.' I'm sorry, Isabella. I cannot marry you.''

Isabella thought this must be a joke. She twisted his words into every creative coil in her mind, to see if she could change their meaning. But no matter what she tried, the words remained callous. He was not smiling. "What?" she asked, looking right at him. There was a terrible silence. Isabella's heart began to fall.

"I'm sorry," he repeated. "I care for you deeply. But I shall always be a bachelor.''

He waited intently for her reply. He wanted a sign, any sign that she had heard him, that she understood. That she was not suffering. But he got none. Isabella seemed to be frozen. Her eyes had left him, her face had paled, and he could not tell whether she still breathed.

"Isabella," he pleaded, taking her hand. She jerked it from him. "I'm sorry," he repeated. "But listen. It isn't as though I'm abandoning you. You may stay on board this ship as long as you like. Why, I've always need for another pirate. And while you're clearly not a fighter, I'm sure you've talents. What do you say to that, eh?'' He was feeling rather generous, for he had never made such an offer to one of his lovers before. ''It's equal share in all profits, a reasonable work schedule, great parties. And you don't have to sleep with the rest of the crew for a while. We can remain lovers. I would really like that.''

Isabella's eyes grew positively demonic. Their soft grayness darkened into ominous, stormy clouds. ''You have taken my innocence!'' she shouted. Marques could not believe what a startling shout she possessed. ''And now you would leave me *ruined?* Have me sign my life to you and your ship when you will give me nothing of your own life?'' She struck out at the air, finding nothing to receive her rage. She clasped her own hair, and pulled until it hurt. ''How can you do this?'' she demanded, tears coming to her eyes, and not from the pain of her scalp.

Marques was moved. He wanted to console her, and yet, he could not relent. He reached for her, but of course, she tore herself away. He found his own eyes moistening. He had never meant to do this, never meant to hurt a creature so strange and so vulnerable. He felt as though he had captured an exotic bird, clipped its wings, then announced he did not want a pet. He did not believe that bedding women was soiling them. But he could see that she did. And he could see that returning her to the uncivilized world of land was now unthinkable. She would be chastised; she would feel an outsider. Even more so than she had before. ''Oh Isabella,'' he pleaded, ''you have not been ruined. For it would take more power than that of a mortal man to ruin something so exquisite as you.''

''Stop it!'' she cried, covering her ears. ''Stop talking to me as though I were lovestruck rather than deceived!''

''But I—''

''Stop it!'' she repeated. Then she tossed her chin into the air. "You have no conscience. You care for no one but yourself. And you obviously hate women."

He nearly laughed at that. "I assure you, nothing could be further from the truth."

"Bedding women is not loving them!" she fumed, "Only loving them is loving them."

Marques bowed his head. He would accept her scorn. He knew that he deserved it well.

Isabella began to consider her fate. She worked thoughtfully at fastening her gown, no longer loving its rich color, or bathing in its lush velvet. Her heart was too weak to enjoy beauty right now. "Just tell me why," she whispered, still working on her gown.

Marques looked at her with surprise. "Why what?"

She did not look at him. "Why can you never commit to one woman?"

"Oh that." He stroked his short beard for a moment, thinking.

Isabella broke into his thoughts. "Is it because you have practiced so long to be a seducer? Would all of that hard work go to waste should you finally settle with one woman?"

He smiled at her thought, but shook his head. "No, that's not it," he said softly.

"Are you sure?" she asked skeptically, " 'Tis an old story. A man learns to enjoy a game so well that he is disappointed to win."

Game. She had mentioned games. The thought of them always brought him back to those purple mountains in Madeira. How he had loved outwrestling the other boys! And how true it was that winning only made him want to play again. Not unlike chasing women, he supposed. Yet, he knew that was not what this was about. He shook his head again.

"Then what?" she demanded. "Just give me that much. Give me a reason I can carry with me. A reason that does not make me feel gullible or unwanted."

Marques longed to tell her. But he had never let a lover

come to know him that well before. "I just . . ." He stopped, shaking his head at himself. He couldn't tell her.

"Then you won't give me even that much?" she asked. "Well, fine." She was finished dressing, and now looked for her hairbrush in the dimness of flickering candles. "Then I see that you are exactly what I always suspected you to be. A despicable, ruthless pirate." She faced him proudly, stroking her hair with a brush as though preparing for the journey out of his life "You have done well to try to convince me that you and your kind are noble, and you nearly had me persuaded. But now I see you again for what you are. Evil. Nothing but evil. And I wish nothing more to do with you."

Her words stung him where it hurt most, but he resisted the urge to retaliate. He said only, "You are wounded, but you will see that I am right, that I would make no kind of a husband. And I hope you will decide that my ship is the best place for you." He didn't want her to go.

Isabella barely heard him. "Just drop me off the next time you reach shore," she said stonily. "Anywhere will do. I don't . . . I don't have anyone anywhere who is . . . expecting me." Sadness struck her face, but only for a moment. "Just bring me somewhere nice."

"Our next stop is New Providence," said Marques. "It isn't a place for a lady to live. It's only a place to drink."

"I'll manage."

"But you hate dry land as much as I do," he reminded her. "You don't belong there."

"I don't belong *here!*"

"But none of us belong. That's what's so perfect about it." He reached for her hand, but it was yanked away. Undaunted, he asked, "Don't you see that there is strength in numbers? One strange woman cannot survive out there, but a ship full of us can rule the waters."

"Why do you want me to stay?" she demanded. "So I can be ravished again by the likes of you? Get away from me!"

"The ravished part is optional," he pleaded. "You may sleep with the crew."

"You are despicable," she spat. "I hate you!"

"Oh, come now. I'm offering you something much better than marriage! To join a pirate ship!"

"Oh yes, Marques," she drawled. "That is every woman's dream."

He looked puzzled. "Isn't it? Wait! Where are you going? Isabella, please!" He caught her by the elbow.

"Unhand me!" she demanded. He tossed both hands in the air as though in surrender. Again, she made to leave.

"Wait!" he cried. "Don't go. For God's sake, there's nothing out there but ocean. Where are you going?"

"To supper," she announced. "And I'll thank you not to speak to me while I'm there." She slammed the door behind her.

Marques was left in the cold wake of a slammed door. "Oh good," he said to the empty cabin, "then you'll think about it?" He dropped his head in his open palm. What had he done?

Chapter Sixteen

"You look sad," said Luisa.

Isabella did not want to be sad. She wanted to be angry and indignant. Surely, her justified outrage should have blocked the way to sadness. Yet she found herself to be a little bit limp. The Great Cabin was so boisterous this evening. The fighters were drinking heavily and dancing gaily, but she could not feel their exuberance. "I am a little out of sorts," she confessed, "but I won't let it ruin anyone's fun."

Luisa smiled affectionately, and took Isabella's hand. This startled her, for she was hardly ever treated to such tenderness by another woman. She looked surprisedly at Luisa, who only gave a warm look of assurance in return. "Do you want to talk about it?"

Isabella glanced warily at Saada, who pretended to be paying no attention, but could surely overhear. "Well . . . I . . . I don't know."

"Is it Marques?" Luisa guessed, for what else could it be? Isabella flushed at her own transparency. "Yes."

Luisa's dark eyes smiled. "Oh well. I suppose you've fallen in love with him then, have you?"

"Oh no!" cried Isabella.

"Still not?"

"Of course not!"

Saada could no longer pretend she wasn't eavesdropping. She joined the conversation in both voice and posture. "She really knows what she wants," she chuckled. "That's what I like about you, Isabella. If you don't like him, then you don't like him, and that's that. Wish there were more like you. Maybe some of those men wouldn't get so full of themselves."

Isabella felt compelled to protest. "This has nothing to do with liking him," she explained. "He may be charming, but he is an evil, treacherous man, and I will never love him."

"What do you mean?" asked Luisa, a little dreaminess showing in her slumped shoulders and twinkling eyes. "I think he's devastating. He's so handsome."

"Noticing a thing like that doesn't make you in love," said Isabella.

"But he's also so brave, and such a good captain."

"Then you admire him," shrugged Isabella. "That isn't love."

"But he's also so kind," argued Luisa. "He's such a gentleman, and always so courteous."

"Then you enjoy his company, but don't you see? None of that is love. Attraction, admiration, the want of friendship. Those are all fine things, but they are not love. Love is a gust of wind; love is a swelling of the heart. It can never occur within someone whose soul is too dark to breed it."

This time, it was Saada who protested. "That is very European of you," she said, tilting back the last of her pirate's beer. "Where I come from, love is something that is built intentionally between two people who admire each other. We don't wait for a gust of wind. We create the wind through our own actions."

Isabella studied Saada's full cheekbones, clothed in rich,

moist skin. "Where are you from?" She had seen enough Africans to know from which continent Saada had sprung, but she could not tell the country.

Saada set down her goblet with a bang. "I realize I brought that question upon myself, but my answer is still the same." She shot Isabella a gentle, but warning look. "I do not discuss my past. I am a pirate, and that's all you need to know about me."

"I'm sorry," said Isabella.

"Don't apologize." Saada looked at her empty goblet. "I'm going to get me some more rumfustian. Do you want some?"

"No, thank you."

As Saada hurried off, Luisa took Isabella's elbow. "Come, don't be sad," she said. "Let us dance."

"You and I?" laughed Isabella.

"Why not? The men all dance together. Come!" She whisked her grinning, fair-haired companion to the floor. Some of the men took notice of their arrival, and gathered round so they could watch the two ladies twirl about. Others paid them no heed as they continued to leap and shout to the rapid fiddling.

Luisa put her hands out in front of her and clapped. Then she spun around twice, finishing with a clap over her head. Now, Isabella took her friend's arm, and they walked in a circle, heads held high. They separated, twisted, and clapped, then joined arms again. Within a few more refrains, they were both kicking up their feet, spinning uncontrollably, and laughing as they tried to stay upright. Some men cheered as they drank. Others accidentally bumped into them as they danced. The room seemed to be spinning. There was music in the fiddle, music in the crew's laughter, and music in the lanterns gleaming all around them. Isabella didn't ever want to stop dancing. She didn't ever want to go to bed, and she didn't ever want the bowl of punch to run dry.

Only once, as the songs played on and on, and the ladies continued to spin and clap, was Isabella reminded of all the sorrows which had befallen her on this day. She attempted a very difficult turn, and failed miserably. Laughing, and grasping at her skirts, she nearly fell to the floor. But Marques caught her. She hadn't realized he was standing there. She found herself wrapped in somebody's arms. She looked up, saw his handsome face, allowed him to help her to her feet, then glared at him to let him know that saving her from a fall would never again be enough to earn her trust. For the one moment in which he held her, her body recalled the joy she had felt in his arms only hours ago. She nearly betrayed herself by enjoying the feel of his strong hands assisting her to her feet. But stubbornly, she returned to her dance partner, grabbed her arm, and urged her into another spiraling twirl. By the end of it, they were both laughing again.

Some of the pirates started passing out. This was, Isabella learned, quite normal after a victory celebration such as this. She herself, was not ready to retire just yet. She crept up to those who were slumbering at the table, snatched their mugs, and finished their drinks for them. She had rather grown to like the thick, sweet and spicy drinks of the outlaws. It pained her when the fiddler announced he was quite finished for the day, and began to pack up. She worried that at any moment Marques would call the whole evening to a close, and her joy would come to a screeching halt. Luisa grabbed her with an adventurous smile and said, "Come! Saada and I are going on deck!

"Ladies!" Marques called, as he saw them launch into their scurry. When they stopped and faced him, he bowed. "May I ask where you are headed? I am about to impose curfew."

Isabella's heart sank. But Luisa curtsied and cheerfully announced, "We're only going on deck. We'll be very quiet." She turned to Isabella. "It's all right. We're allowed on deck after curfew. Just nowhere else."

"Very well," said Marques, fixing his gaze on Isabella, "but be certain Isabella doesn't stay up too late, or she'll wake me upon her return."

Isabella could not believe her ears. Surely, he did not think she would return to his cabin! "You needn't worry," she assured him, "for tonight, I plan to sleep with the crew."

"I'm so sorry," he replied blandly, "but I'm afraid that isn't an option. We've a shortage of hammocks in the crew's cabin."

Isabella met his mocking eyes with fury. "You told me I could sleep with the crew," she recalled in a deep whisper.

He could not let Isabella go. "I said you may sleep with the crew once you become a member of it," he informed her with a dark smile. "You have not agreed to join, so as our guest, you will enjoy whatever hospitality is offered. In this case, it is my cabin."

Isabella leaned into him and hissed too softly for her companions to hear, "I shall sleep in your cabin as though I were a corpse. I shall sleep as though you were oceans away."

"I invite you to try," he grinned.

Isabella was about to say something seething in reply, but Saada interrupted their spat. "Captain, did you invite Isabella to join our crew?" She looked excitedly at her friend.

"The invitation is there," shrugged Marques.

Luisa squeezed Isabella's hand. "Oh!" she cried. "You might join the ship and stay? That's wonderful!"

Isabella tried to protest, but was interrupted.

"You ladies had best hurry and go on deck," said Marques. "I'm about to round these men up for bed. And remember, Luisa . . . don't keep Isabella up too late." He winked mockingly at the fair-haired woman, enjoying the look of rage he received in turn.

"Oh, this is so exciting!" cried Luisa, pulling Isabella to the stairs. "I can't believe he's letting you become a pirate! What an honor!" Isabella rolled her eyes as the three women raced to the deck, where the night was lost in fog.

When they stepped outside, Isabella felt as though she were walking into a cloud. The moisture of the night hit her like a cool cloth upon her forehead, and she tried to gasp in a breath of the thick air. "How beautiful!" she exclaimed, looking up at the starless sky. She could not see to the far end of the ship, for there was no moonlight, no lanterns, and mist everywhere. She needed Luisa's hand to guide her to a railing. And Luisa needed Saada's hand to do the same.

"Good thing Saada's a navigator," Luisa joked, causing Saada to chuckle back.

When at last, the women made it to a railing, Luisa hoisted herself up, and balanced on its narrow rim. Isabella was impressed by her bravery. It would be a horrible thing to fall in. But Saada appeared to be equally brave, for she, too, made herself comfortable on the ship's tenuous rail. "Sometimes," Luisa told her still-standing companion, "on nights like this, Saada and I play hide and seek on deck. You can't see anything in this fog, so it can take a long time to find someone!"

"Especially if they get stuck behind a gaff," said Saada with a humorously goading look.

Luisa burst into laughter. "Oh, that's right! One time, we were playing, and I was hiding between a sail and its gaff. And Saada spent nearly an hour trying to find me. And then . . ." Her laughter forced her to pause. "And then I couldn't get out, and she had to go pull the night navigator from his shift to help pull me." The three of them laughed as Saada distributed something from a lovely gold canister, about the size of a pill box. "Snuff?" asked Luisa.

Isabella was stunned. "No, thank you," she replied impulsively.

Luisa shrugged, taking some in her mouth. "The captain doesn't let us smoke, because of all the flammable things on board. So we just use the snuff."

Isabella watched as Saada put some in her mouth as well. "The nuns said ladies never use tobacco," she objected, though there was no scolding in her tone, just curiosity.

"We aren't ladies," grinned Luisa, chewing. "We're pirates."

Isabella couldn't help smiling back. This ship was like a bizarre little island, though it was always moving.

"So when are you going to sign on to the ship?" asked Saada.

"I'm not going to," replied Isabella miserably.

"But you must!" pleaded Luisa. "We want you to!"

"I can't," she said. "I am looking for something. I'm not sure what it is, but I know it isn't here."

"A destiny?" suggested Luisa.

"Perhaps," Isabella shrugged. "It may be that I don't have one, that there's nothing for me out there. But I must keep looking, mustn't I? I cannot give up while there's even the smallest chance that there is a fate out there which waits for me."

Luisa worked hard to repress a giggle at the flamboyant way in which Isabella spoke. "Well," she replied diplomatically, "maybe this ship is your destiny. Maybe this is your kingdom. Maybe this is what you were meant to find."

"Not with Marques on board. My fate could never be with someone so unchivalrous. I can't stand to be near him."

"Why not?"

"Because," moaned Isabella, "he took my innocence."

Luisa's mouth dropped open. "The captain forced himself on you? I can't believe it."

"No," groaned Isabella, becoming more mortified with each sentence she was forced to utter. "He didn't force himself. I came to him willingly. That's what makes it so awful. But it was only because he had saved me from those horrible corsairs, and I got so caught up in the romance of it." She shook her head defeatedly, thoroughly disgusted with herself. "I just thought it would be so romantic to be swept away to the bed of a hero, to let him ravish me, to give myself to him in my moment of salvation."

Saada and Luisa looked at one another, and then spat out in uncontrollable laughter. They tried to silence themselves, but could not. They were delighted that Isabella had not fallen madly in love with their captain as so many dim-witted women before her. She had just fallen in love with her own drama. Crazy people were so much more fun than stupid ones. "Well, it all ended well," Luisa assured her with that tender look that always made Isabella feel so unconditionally accepted.

"Yes," chimed in Saada. "At least you had some loving. And it isn't as though you'd want to bring him to the altar. Our captain wouldn't make much of a husband, but I'll bet he's a fine lover." She said the last of this with a positively comical expression of deviousness.

Luisa squeezed Saada's hand. "That's so true. I sure wouldn't have minded being rescued by him."

"It's the part after that I'd be looking forward to," said Saada, pretending to fan herself. "I'll bet he looks like a fine piece of man without that shirt on."

Luisa gasped, then broke into a giggle, covering her blushing face with trembling hands.

Isabella did not laugh. "It's easy for the two of you to joke," she scowled, crossing her arms, "You're not the ones who have humiliated yourselves."

Luisa cocked her head. "Oh, Isabella, don't be so sad. You wouldn't really want the captain to marry you, trust me. He's not the type who could be faithful. Better to know that up front, and move on than to find yourself bound to him."

"That's right," said Saada. "I love my captain, but when it comes to women, he's no good."

Luisa agreed. "Really, Isabella, he's no good."

"She's no good," said Gabriel, who had been invited into the captain's cabin. "You did the right thing, sir. Better to toss her back before she tries to tie you down."

"But she's so intriguing!" Marques cried, pacing the length of his room. "In one moment, she's like a lost little puppy whom I just want to snuggle, and the next moment she bites me. She seeks protection from the sunshine, and then she runs out in the rain! I can't figure her out, and I can't stop trying. It's as though I've stumbled into her storybook, and I can't leave until I see how it turns out."

"Storybook, exactly," said Gabriel. "That's why you must push her away. You could never meet her expectations. Not when you haven't even read the script she has imposed on you."

"But I feel such a fool!" cried Marques, banging his desk, causing a crinkle in his map, which he quickly tried to smooth out. "A lovely woman like that. Imagine! A woman willing to forgo a civilized life, and spend her life on the sea, all because a pirate saved her. What a rare, unworldly creature. When will I ever find a woman that strange again? When will I ever find a woman who hates the world as much as I do?"

"Doesn't matter," said Gabriel. "You're not a marrying man."

"I hope not," muttered Marques.

Gabriel's face grew stern. "What do you mean, you hope not? I thought you hated matrimony."

"Not for other men, Gabriel. Just for myself."

Gabriel had wanted desperately to steer the conversation away from marriage. He did not like Marques's obsession with this strange woman. He knew the dangers of loving a woman like Isabella. He knew her kind, and he did not want to see a young man make the same mistake he once had. Yet he felt that his captain needed to talk, and would not deprive him of the opportunity to do so. "Marques," he said in rare form, addressing his captain by first name, "I know what you're going through."

Marques scowled. "You do not. You have no idea what I live with."

"Yes I do, Marques. I know about . . . about your fears."

Marques shot him a look that was something between angry and pleading. "How can you know? How can you understand if you've never met him? You have no idea what it was like."

Gabriel's heart softened with sympathy for his young captain. "I know that your father was an unkind man, Marques."

"Unkind?" he shouted. *"Unkind? Is that what you call it? The man beat me every day of my life!"*

"I know that was hard, Captain, but I don't see—"

"That's right! You don't see." He paced passionately to the far side of the room, arms crossed defensively. "What am I supposed to do, Gabriel? Become somebody's father?" He did not look at his quartermaster, but waited for a reply. When he got none, he continued with clenched teeth. "I couldn't go home, Gabriel. That's how bad it was. I couldn't go home. I stayed out late with my friends every day, because I feared him." He paused, closing his eyes as he recalled, "I would've killed him, if I'd had the chance. I'm not lying about that. The bastard beat me, and he beat my sister, and he beat my mother. And I couldn't stop him. I was half his size until it was too late to matter."

"But you've done so well for yourself since then! Despite all, you made something of yourself."

Marques had to laugh at that. "Gabriel, do you know how I became a pirate?"

With a puzzled expression, the quartermaster shook his head. "No, as a matter of fact. I suppose I've never asked you." This seemed strange to him in retrospect.

"One day," said Marques, "my mother gave me some coins and told me to leave, told me I was old enough to work and get away from that god-awful house. I wouldn't go. I couldn't leave her and my sister alone with him. I may not have been big enough to fight him yet, but at least when I was there, there was some chance he'd choose to beat me instead of them. So I didn't leave home until the day he died. On that very day, I skipped his funeral and went off to earn some money, to bring it back to my mother and sister. Got a slave job at the docks. Had to carry boxes of cargo from merchant ships, and I was good at it. But if I didn't work fast enough, they took a whip to me. Sometimes they did it in advance, just as a warning. Half the time, when I'd finished after a twelve-hour day, they didn't give me my pay. They took out 'expenses.' Expenses they'd made up. So that's when I realized that men are all the same—men of dry land, anyway.

"Well, I came to watch a pirate ship come into port one day. Everyone attacked, and ordered me to do the same. But I thought, 'Who am I fighting for? You? Him? You all treat me like dirt. I'm rooting for the pirates.' The pirate captain saw me there, a sturdy young boy who had been rooting for him to win. And well, you know the rest. He let me join his crew, then put me in line to succeed him in command. My mother eats well now. Even had her house fixed up. Of course, I'm not completely up front about what I do, but ... well anyway. We're all better off without that man. The entire world's better off without him."

"I'm sorry," said Gabriel. "But still, if you really wanted to marry, you could."

"Gabriel, there are only two things keeping me from becoming my father. The fact that I'm a pirate is one. The second is that I am not wed, and have no children. As long as that is true, there is no danger of my becoming just like him. Otherwise, what's stopping me?"

"Your heart?"

"My heart is strong because it is free!" Marques cried. "The wind keeps it clear of rot. But how do I know it would remain sturdy if it stayed still?"

"Marques Santana," scolded Gabriel. "Every man on this ship has sworn his life to you because he believes in the sturdiness of your heart. We all trust in you absolutely, that you will not become a man like your father. Do you call all of us mistaken?"

Marques swallowed his uncertainty.

"Do you expect me to believe you would beat a woman?" asked Gabriel.

Marques slowly shook his head. "I couldn't do that," he snapped. "You know I couldn't."

"And if you had a son? Do you expect me to believe you would beat him?"

Marques evaded the question. "I ... I would be a poor father. I cannot teach a boy to survive in a world I cannot tolerate."

"But would you beat him?"

"Of course not."

"Then why do you worry so?" pleaded the old man. "Why don't you trust yourself?"

Marques tugged thoughtfully at his beard. "I don't know," he nearly whispered. "I just feel I have to be cautious, feel that if I'm not careful, I'll accidentally slip into his shoes."

"Don't you see," Gabriel countered, "that there is no magic step that will make you turn into your father. No single movement that will make you transform. It's in everyday life that you gradually build and define yourself. It's taken a long time to become who you are, and it would take a very long slide of negligence to undo it."

Marques flashed his eyes at the quartermaster. "Then you think I should marry Isabella?"

"Oh, heavens no!" cried Gabriel. "The woman's a lunatic!"

"But that's what I like about her," explained Marques as the men headed out of the cabin. "You'd have to be crazy to marry a pirate, anyway."

"Not *that* crazy! Can't you just settle for a *little* crazy?"

"The question is, Gabriel, will a *little* crazy settle for *me?*"

"Well, just because you shouldn't be afraid to marry doesn't mean that you must! Wouldn't you rather just have lots of different women?"

"Yes, but I think I'd better have one bound to me before I get old and ugly. You know. Just *before* I get old and ugly. That way, I can enjoy womanizing right up to the very end, but at the last minute, just before I fall into old age, I can reach out and pull someone down with me."

"Good thinking."

Marques laughed. "Thank you for lending me your ear, old man."

Gabriel's smile was genuine. "Anytime, friend." He started to make his exit, but the captain stopped him.

"Oh, Gabriel?"

"Yes?"

He reached for the ruby bracelet, the one he had tried to give Isabella. "If I uh . . . if I bought a bracelet with money I've stolen, would you say I had stolen the bracelet?"

Gabriel scratched his cheek. "Hmmm. The bracelet is paid for, so I suppose not."

"I see," said Marques thoughtfully. "What if rather than money, I made a fair exchange of one piece for another, with a bracelet I had stolen. Would I be stealing the new bracelet?"

"Hmmm. No, I suppose not. Not if the seller were willing to take a bracelet instead of money."

"And if the seller had stolen the bracelet? Would I, as a buyer, be stealing it as well, just because it had been stolen once before?"

"I . . . guess . . . not."

Marques dangled the ruby bracelet before his friend's eyes. "Have you got one in your sea trunk of about the same value?"

"Well, not a bracelet. But I've a silver necklace in there I don't need."

"Would you kindly trade?"

"Certainly."

"Thank you, old friend," he grinned devilishly. "You have just enabled me to give my lady an honest gift."

Gabriel grumbled his way out the door. "For a man who's afraid of marriage, you certainly do spend a lot of time trying to trick pretty women into loving you."

"I'm just wanting to make amends for breaking her heart," Marques insisted.

Gabriel grunted. "Sounds like trouble to me. But good night."

"Sleep well, old friend. And bring me that necklace!" he shouted down the hallway.

Chapter Seventeen

Isabella crept into the cabin late that night. Her head felt lightened by the sounds of the ocean and the company of nice friends. But as soon as she tiptoed into the cabin, she felt the stinging feeling that Marques had won this battle. Indeed, there had not been a spare hammock in the crew space. Isabella suspected Marques had seen to it. Now, she was being forced to creep into his bedroom like a concubine, and it made her furious. She thought Marques was asleep at first, and was glad of it. But when she stubbed her toe in the dark, it made a noise which summoned him to his feet. "No need to rise," she said, glimpsing his beautiful form, now poised upright on the cot. "I'll make it to my cot just fine."

"Here, let me light a candle for you."

"That isn't necess—" She was too late. He was already setting one ablaze, giving her an even clearer look at his powerful physique, exaggerated by the shadows of the night. "Why do you use candles instead of lanterns in your cabin?" she asked, tossing herself on her cot.

He did not tell her it was for romantic ambiance. "I just

prefer candlelight,'' he lied. Now he could see her in all of her wind-blown glory. Her hair was tangled and waving across her pillow. Her face was fresh and moist with saltwater. ''Did you enjoy the party?'' he asked, unable to keep himself from grinning. She looked so fresh, so tempting.

''Yes,'' she told him. ''Except for the fact that you were there.''

''Still angry?'' he grinned.

''I am not angry,'' she retorted, ''for how can I be angry at someone who is incapable of decency? Rather, I should pity him.''

''Oh good, I'm glad you're not angry.'' He returned to his cot, conscious of not making any swift moves to seduce her. He knew he had taken several steps backward in the game of winning her, and would have to gradually make them up. ''So you have been enjoying the company of Saada and Luisa?'' he asked, trying to change the subject. ''They are fine crew.''

Isabella, though she had not planned to engage in any small talk, was now reminded of something she had been dying to ask. She tossed it around in her mind and decided there would be no harm in venturing. ''Can you tell me what made Saada become a pirate?''

Marques scratched his face, trying to recall. He had so many crew to keep track of. ''Well,'' he said thoughtfully, ''I believe she was on a slave ship, headed for the Americas, and—''

''*What?*'' Isabella was aghast. ''What did you say?''

Marques shrugged. ''The slave trade is big, and growing. I'm not sure how she got picked up, but we had pulled them over to rob them of other loot. Naturally, we handed the ship over to the slaves on board after executing the captain. I was looking through the gold and such, distributing it among my crew, when I noticed Saada. She was an educated woman, able to speak fluent Portuguese as well as Spanish and English. I hadn't thought to invite any of the slaves to join my ship because I'd assumed they couldn't understand me, and I don't know any of the African tongues. But when I heard her begging for her life, as they often so mistakenly do when we rescue them, and heard she could speak in tongues I understood, I decided to offer her the life of a pirate. It was a good decision, for she is an excellent navigator, and a brilliant mathematician.''

Isabella's mouth was hanging open. ''No wonder she won't talk about it,'' she reflected to herself. ''How awful!''

Marques shrugged. ''Has the world given you any reason to think it's too kind to do such a thing?''

Isabella's eyes froze on him. She almost told him something, something she had never spoken of to anyone. But she caught herself, and just shook her head.

Marques continued. ''And Luisa,'' he tried to recall, ''was working at a bar I was patronizing one afternoon. Her employer was a bastard, calling her an 'ugly tramp' and telling her she was scaring away customers with that face of hers. I couldn't stand to watch it, so I scribbled down the name of my inn and handed it to her. Told her to come talk to me if she wanted a better life.''

Isabella recalled what Luisa had once told her. ''Marques told me that a world which does not want me is a world that does not deserve me.'' Isabella could see that both Saada and Luisa had done the right thing for themselves by joining the ship. And yet . . . they had turned to a life of wickedness, had they not? It was all so confusing.

''But what I find most interesting of all,'' said Marques, feeling that this light conversation had eased some tension between them, ''is how I came across a young lady traveling alone to an island where she had never been.'' He rose to his full height and stepped nearer to her.

Isabella leaped from her cot and backed herself against a wall. ''Do not touch me.''

''Don't worry,'' he said, but did not cease his strides toward her. Isabella trembled when she felt his warm hands upon her neck. Then she felt something cool wrap about her throat. ''A peace offering?'' he suggested.

Isabella looked down at the thick, silver band he had fastened to her. It was beautiful. "I told you I won't wear stolen goods," she snapped, though she was struck by the beauty of the piece. She had never seen silver so clear and shimmering.

" 'Tis not stolen," he said, kissing the hollow of her neck. "Ask no more. Just know that I paid for it fair and square."

"With stolen money?"

"Earned money," he corrected her. "Money I worked hard to get."

"By stealing it?"

"You ask too many questions. I should think a romantic ought to know better than to ask so many questions. It only makes life less fuzzy and soft."

"Are you seducing me again, Marques?" she asked, though for some reason she could not bring herself to stop his lips from touching her throat. She could feel his hot breath against her hair, and his strong hands stroking her shoulders.

"Would that be so terrible?" he whispered against her tender ear.

"Yes," she replied, beginning to melt against him.

"Why?" he asked, gradually lowering his hands to her breasts.

"Because you will not marry me, and I have learned I wouldn't want you to anyway."

"Excellent," he replied. "Then we are in agreement. Now there are no obstacles." He cupped her breasts and massaged them through her gown, kneading them, encouraging them to grow warm and sensitive in his palms.

"I will not be your lover," she informed him, though her will was weakening and her head growing light.

He felt the tips of her breast grow hard, inviting him to venture further. "Why not?" he whispered. "What is so important about matrimony? If we are both enjoying ourselves, then what harm is it?"

Isabella felt so betrayed by her body's longing, that her face, if Marques could have seen it, wore an expression of sheer turmoil. She wanted to do it again. She wanted to lie on that cot with him, and experience all of those strange sensations again. But her words were firm. "If I cannot trust you with my heart, then I must not trust you with my body. And you have betrayed my heart."

"How have I betrayed it?" he asked. "I have been tender."

"You plan to abandon me when I have served my purpose," she explained. "That is not kind, and it is an insult, and my true love would never do it. So you must not be him."

"I'm sure I'm not," he admitted, lowering his hands to her slim, soft waist. "But why not have some fun with me while you wait for him? Hmm?" He brought her earlobe into his mouth, and tickled it with his firm, hot tongue.

Isabella's body was melting. But she was strong. Her strength came from a lifetime of relying on herself for companionship. She could always trust herself, but no one else. "I do not trust you," she said. "You will break my heart. I cannot love as you do. I cannot love halfway. When I succumb to a man, it will be with my body, heart, and immortal soul. You aren't faithful enough to handle that. You have no faith in true love."

His hands slipped into the cup between her legs. Pressing firmly, nearly lifting her from her feet, he whispered, "Be my lover, Isabella. I will treasure you. I will be gentle and firm. I cannot promise you forever, but I can love you now. And in any way you please. I can be rough, tender, gentlemanly, or savage." He started moving his fingers in circles, stimulating her tenderest spot beneath the cloth of her dress. "Any way you like it, that's how it will be."

Isabella pushed him away. "Do you want to know how I like it?" she asked his stunned face. "I like it in a wedding chamber, with a man who has sworn himself to me. I like it with a man who is noble and good and sure of spirit! That's how I like it." She spun around and began undressing for the night. Her face was not angry, but determined. "I shall keep the necklace," she announced. "I shall keep it as a token to remind me always of what a fool I nearly was, how easily I was seduced by treachery. And every time I look at it, I will remember that I must never fall prey again to the likes of a villain like you.''

Marques swallowed, a feeling of shame coming over him.

''But it is not a token of love,'' she continued, still undressing, ''for you have none for me. You may watch me remove my gown,'' she added coldly, ''as I imagine I have no secrets from you now. But I will not play 'lovers' with you. Drop me off when we reach New Providence, and do not come for me again. You think I cannot make my way in the world alone. But I assure you, I shall do better on my own than I could ever do with an untrustworthy man. There is a destiny which awaits me, and it is not with the likes of you.''

Marques had been scorned by brokenhearted women before, but never quite so skillfully. He genuinely felt like a bastard. He couldn't believe it. She had shamed him beyond imagining. He could think of no way to defend himself. He felt the stupidest, most childish, most immature man alive right now. All he could do was nod, and mutter, ''Well, you can't blame me for trying.''

Isabella turned to him icily. ''Yes, I can. And I do.''

Chapter Eighteen

After that, days passed like a heavy weight falling. There were no more obstacles, no more dramas interrupting the course of a long workday, a jovial supper, and a silent night. Isabella did nothing all day but play with Pedro, read books on Marques's shelf, and wait for the sight of shore. Marques did nothing but work. At dinner, they did not eat together. Isabella talked with her new friends, and felt for the first time in her life that she was part of a circle of women which would not be the same without her. Marques watched over his crew during meals, and occasionally, joined the gambling table. At night, Isabella played above deck with Saada and Luisa until as late an hour as she could manage. Then, she would creep into the cabin, hoping Marques was already asleep. He usually pretended to be.

Though she hated herself for it, she often fantasized about letting him touch her again. Sometimes at night, she lay in her cot and knew that he was also awake. She knew that if she wanted to, she could rise from her bed, go to him, lower her gown, and fall into his arms. It was tempting. It was enticing just knowing that she could do it. She had so enjoyed their one night together, and wished they could do it again, just one more time. But she was too proud, too wise about her own heart. She stayed put, and let him suffer in the knowledge that if he had not spoiled everything by being the cad he was, then he could be having her right here and now.

Marques felt ashamed in her presence now, though he wouldn't let her know it. He knew what she thought of him, knew that she thought him a man with a child's heart. And he wanted desperately to explain it all to her, to set her straight, if for no sake other than his own pride. If she had known his father. If she only knew what he was saving her from. It was not childish of him to refuse marriage, he was sure. It was the most mature thing he could do, the most responsible thing he could do. He knew what he might become if he settled into marriage, and he could not subject any woman to that. It was for her own sake that he refused her. But how could he make her understand? And why, he wondered night after night, why did he care so much what she thought?

Wasn't she a woman like any other? An unusually pretty one, of course. But still, couldn't he replace her at the next dock? He would have liked to be her lover for a while more, but if he could not have her, why couldn't he just settle for another? He tried to fix his mind on New Providence, and all of the women who would await him there. Women who loved pirates, women who wanted to be taken for a ride on powerful boats. But he imagined Isabella's yellow hair fading into the distance as she walked away from the dock. Her face would be so ethereal, her beautiful body so vulnerable to the stares of unconscionable men. Her head would be dreaming up princes and knights. His teeth were grinding. My God, he didn't want her to wander off. He didn't want to leave her in the hands of the dry land men, the men he hated so, and whom he knew would hurt anything weak enough to allow it. He couldn't trust the world with Isabella. She thought she could make it on her own, but she was too sensitive, too unaware. He could not watch her fade away into the distance, alone and lost. He cared. He really cared. And yet . . . it was impossible. He could not give her what she needed. He could not be her knight. He would have to leave her to the world, and let her learn the hard way that there were no knights. And that pained him, for he wished she might always believe.

"The Nest of Pyrates!"

Everyone could see land now. The sturdy old ship had to weave its way between hordes of others just like it, each bearing an ominous flag of black and red. Isabella shuttered. She had gotten so used to her ship now, and all the crew on board. But seeing unfamiliar pirate ships all herded together like a fleet, and hearing the shouts and songs of pirates she had never met, was positively frightening. She stayed close to Luisa. "Isn't it exciting?" beamed the dark-eyed girl. "We're finally going to get a holiday! Oh, just wait until you see how much fun it is! Then you'll change your mind about leaving. I'm sure of it."

Isabella could see that no one else shared her timid feelings. Some fighters hung over the railing, shouting playful insults at pirates aboard neighboring ships. Isabella could see past the traffic that they were heading toward a sandy island, brightened by lush green palm trees. Crumbling wooden houses lined the coast. "Those are the taverns," explained Luisa excitedly. "They might not look like much, but they're so much fun! You know what pirates believe? We believe that when we die, instead of going to Heaven, we just get to stay right here in New Providence. Isn't that funny? I mean, I'm sure we don't really believe it, but isn't it a nice thought?"

Isabella wasn't so sure. She hoped that her Heaven would be a lot quieter than this. And much, much more solitary. Her old shyness was returning to her, and she did not want to meet anyone new. She didn't want any of those frightening strangers to notice her, or gawk at her, or yell something crude. The pirates' songs were rowdy and ominous. She felt surrounded by them. She was panicking, wishing they were deep in the ocean's empty vastness once again.

Suddenly, she felt a hand upon her back, and it was not Luisa's. It was a strong hand, a firm hand. She looked up with a start. "Isabella," Marques said, squeezing her waist with affection, "I wonder if you would be willing to stay with the crew for a few days before running off. I'll spring for your accommodations, and you can look around, decide whether this is really where you'd like me to leave you."

Isabella was so relieved, she could have wept. All of her yearning to leave the ship just to escape Marques seemed so petty right now. Compared to an island of rowdy, unfamiliar pirates, Marques's ship was heaven. "Yes," she said haughtily. "I appreciate your offer, Captain, and I accept. But I assure you, I have every intention of finding a job here and settling. I shall not reboard this ship."

"Good," he nodded, smacking her backside in that way she despised, then strolling off to tend to the anchor. She felt much calmer now that she knew she would have a place to stay for her first few days. She even felt calm enough to take interest in the snowy white seagulls that flew overhead. She would imagine that she was one of them, flying in to shore, barely touching ground, then fleeing at the first sign of trouble. Yes, she could do this. She could face this land of pirates, just as the seagulls did.

"What do you mean there's no room for us at dock?" Marques shouted to one of the dock workers.

The boy shouted something in turn, but no one could hear him.

"I can't hear you!" Marques cried. "Look! Just make room for us!"

He listened hard this time, and seemed to catch the boy's words.

"I'm not sailing all the way around to the other side of the island!" Marques shouted. "My crew is weary!"

The boy shouted something again.

"What?" Marques called. He still couldn't hear, so he muttered, "Never mind," and picked up a musket. He aimed it steadily at the dock boy, who started waving his arms and screaming. This time, everyone heard.

"I'll make room! I'll make room!"

"Poor lad," Marques chuckled, to his crew's delight, "Not easy being a dock boy at a pirate port." He tossed the musket to the floor. "Wasn't loaded," he assured Gabriel. "Just wanted to remind him who his customers are."

Gabriel shook his head. "Imagine working at a place like this, and telling your customers to get in line and be patient! What is he thinking?"

"I don't know," laughed Marques. "He's young." He whipped around and faced his crew. "All right then! Six days shore leave!"

Everyone cheered.

"Anyone not on board exactly six days from this hour will be left behind. If you have any loot you'd like to trade for gold, give it to your quartermaster, and he'll take care of it. Eat well, drink well, love well. But remember that you represent your ship and your captain. So I require you to behave as gentlemen, even if others do not. Here are my rules. Never throw the first punch. Make sure your opponents are approximately your own size. If not, refuse to fight them, even if it means appearing cowardly. Never use a weapon on an unarmed person. Do not strike a woman, even if you happen to be one. A lady pirate against a local damsel is not a fair fight. Do not cheat at the gambling tables. Do not rob fellow pirates. Always tip generously. And don't short-change a prostitute. Pay her what she's owed. *Got that?*"

"Yay!" they all called.

"All right." Marques motioned for a plank to be lowered to shore. "Shore leave begins now!"

There was a huge rush of restless pirates, storming past their captain. Luisa grabbed Isabella's hand and pulled her to the dock, nearly twisting her arm by mistake. Marques was the only one who remained calm, for he had to be the last one to leave the ship. He stood cross-armed by the exit, silently counting his crew as they scrambled by.

"Where are we going?" cried Isabella, banging against heavyset pirates as Luisa pulled her in tow.

"First to the inn!" she cried. "Wait till you see it!"

As soon as her feet touched sand, Isabella was hit by a warm breeze. She had to admit it was pleasant. Palm trees swayed above her head, bright sunshine warmed her hair, and soft sand was filling her shoes. The farther she and Luisa walked, the less dense was the crowd. She began to feel as though she could actually breathe. But suddenly, her knees gave way, and she fell to the ground. This frightened her, and she looked up at Luisa pleadingly. But the excited girl only laughed. "Oh dear!" she giggled. "You haven't got your land legs yet. Come, get up. The only way to find them is to keep walking." She urged Isabella to her feet, then helped her along by the waist, lending what little support her small body could give.

Somehow, the two of them hobbled their way to a broken-down inn, its porch half rotted, its gray paint peeling terribly. "Here we go," beamed Luisa, assisting her friend up the untrustworthy steps. "Two from Captain Marques Martinez Santana's ship," she told the innkeeper.

Isabella looked around her. The inn was right on the beach, and was filled with the sound of crashing waves and the tweaking of seagulls. The windows were tall with some panes broken. The wooden floor was filthy. And the innkeeper was so old, he could barely see his account book. "Captain Marques Martinez Santana?" he repeated, squinting painfully, trying to read his own writing. "Shall I charge it to his account then? He's always been good about paying."

"Yes, please," said Luisa.

"Can I have your names?"

"Luisa and Isabella."

"All right then," said the innkeeper, scribbling, "When he

comes by, I'll tell him that two beautiful young ladies charged a room to him.''

Luisa giggled and flushed. "Thank you." She took Isabella's hand, and pulled her up the creaky stairway. "See?" she squealed. "Even I'm considered pretty in a town like this. Just so long as you're female—that's all they care about."

"How touching."

The women's room had a lovely view of the water. There was a door that opened onto a huge balcony. And when Isabella stood on it, she felt as though she were back on a sailing ship. The winds were so strong, and the waves were so loud. Inside, the room was filled with sunshine and light. And while the floors were dirty, and the oil lanterns cracked, the ugly beds were spectacularly soft and comfortable. The first thing she did was dive onto one, and sink into its softness. "Oh, I think I shall just stay here," she moaned. "This bed is so nice."

"You shall not!" cried Luisa, "You shall nap no longer than an hour or so, and then you shall come with me to the Parrot's Cage. It's one of the best pubs," she promised, "though Saada always prefers the Peg Leg. Secretly, I think she only likes it because she met a dashing gentleman there once, and she always keeps the ridiculous hope that he'll return. I mean, what are the chances that they would arrive here at the same time again? She doesn't even remember his name, and can't ask for him! So we'll go to the Parrot's Cage unless Saada forces us otherwise. She's staying at a different inn right now, you see. She always stays at this place farther inland, because she likes it best, and that's why we never stay together. I simply must have an ocean view! But we'll meet her later when—" Luisa's chattering stopped abruptly. In fact, it stopped so abruptly, that Isabella lifted her head from her soft, plush pillow.

"What is it?" she asked.

Luisa was looking out the window, squinting hard, worry all over her face.

"What is it?" Isabella repeated anxiously.

Luisa frowned. "Hmmm. Corsairs. Wonder what they're doing here."

"Corsairs?" Isabella nearly leaped from the bed.

"Yes," said Luisa. "I can see their turbans quite plainly. This is odd. This is very odd."

"What are they doing?" Isabella demanded.

"They seem to be just walking around like everyone else," said Luisa suspiciously, "But it's very unusual. This island belongs to the pirates. I mean, the corsairs have never been banned, but they don't usually venture all the way from the Mediterranean to the Caribbean. It's a very long trip. They usually frolic in Morocco."

Isabella was more wary of this place than ever before. "Will they bother us?" she asked. "Should we tell Marques? Should we return to the ship?"

"Return to the ship?" Luisa laughed, moving her eyes from the window, "Of course not! We just got here! Oh, I'm sure it's nothing," she assured her friend. "I'm sure there's a good explanation. We'll just ask someone when we get a chance."

Isabella's mind wandered back to that frightening afternoon. The corsairs pinning her to the wall, stripping her of her dress and her dignity, preparing to strip her of much more. She remembered their savage shouts. "I don't like this," she told Luisa. "I don't like corsairs."

"Oh, don't be silly," said Luisa. "I'm sure they're harmless."

Isabella tilted her head. "Luisa?"

"Yes?"

"Have you ever heard the expression 'famous last words'?"

Chapter Nineteen

Marques was in need of rest, just as surely as his crew. It was not easy being captain. When the crew were feasting, he was monitoring their feast. When the crew were drinking, he was keeping track of their drunkenness. When the crew were gambling, he was making sure the winnings were given fairly. When the crew were going about their workday, waiting for orders, he was on guard for any sign of danger. Sometimes he felt like a parent, a guardian who could never rest, never let down his guard, never stop worrying about his charges, and whose pay was nothing but respect. Of course, respect was a fine thing to have. He loved being captain, for he was a born leader. When his own captain had died, there'd been no question of who would take his place. Marques was a sharp and self-confident soul, a man who was able to keep tabs on his own frolic. He loved to lead, and loved to be followed. But there was a certain relief for him whenever the ship pulled into port. His children were on their own for now, and what happened to them was not his problem. He could indulge himself.

He wasted no time in doing this. Within an hour of securing

the ship's anchor, he was checked into his favorite inn across town, unpacked, dressed in his finest red velvet, and lounging at the Peg Leg. His black hair was slicked cleanly into a gentleman's pigtail. His breeches and long coat were smashingly red. His belt and buckled shoes were strikingly black. And all over him, golden jewels and buttons glittered. This was the standard outfit for an off-shore pirate captain. His elaborate plumage was what separated him from all the crewmen gallivanting about. The only thing Marques left home tonight was his feathered hat. He did own one, but was so accustomed to a head free of wigs and other coverings, that he could hardly stand to wear it. The velvet and jewels would be enough to reveal his status on the island. Of course, he did not fail to carry weaponry. Six pistols, three knives, and a sword were strapped to him by sashes. This made him more lightly armed than most, for after all, each pistol could be fired only once. Still, he felt reasonably prepared for trouble.

"Marques!" An enormously breasted beauty barely gave Marques time to find a seat. She threw her arms around him, and screeched. Bending her knees so her feet were off the ground, she encouraged him to lift her. This, he did, and added an affectionate kiss on the cheek as a bonus. "How are you?" she asked in English.

Marques spoke English reasonably well, though with a heavy accent. "I am well, Margaret. And you are lovely as always." He lowered her gently, then brought her hand to his lips.

"I love the way you say my name," she grinned. "Mahrd-go-rdet." Her hair was chestnut, as were her long, sensual eye lashes. Her cheekbones were strong and exotic. But it was her lips that always melted Marques. She had a wide mouth, and her lips were so full and plump.

Marques twinkled his eyes at the lady. He didn't like being told he had an accent, because it made him feel he should study his English harder. A pirate must be educated, he told himself. Roberts had no accent in any language. But he supposed that if the lady liked the way he said her name, then there was no real harm in this case. He welcomed her onto his lap as he signaled for a drink. Crewmen shouted when they wanted a rumfustian. But a pirate captain gave only the most delicate indication with a twitch of the hand. "You are very bold," he teased Margaret, "taking to my lap so quickly." He wrapped one arm around her beautiful, robust hips, and used the other to drink. "How do you know I've not married since last we met? Hmm?"

"Didn't figure it mattered," she laughed. She had a wonderful smile, and an intelligent glint in her eye. But she was not dreamy like Isabella. She did not believe in knights. Marques wondered whether she ever had. Had she ever been a little girl, looking out a window and wondering whether a knight would come for her? When had she learned the truth? When had she learned that there was no such thing as true romance, but only romantic postures?

"Well, as it just so happens," he jested, "you're in luck, for I have managed to go another year without being wed."

"No!" she cried sarcastically. "I can't believe it! You? Still a bachelor? And I thought you were just itching to tie the knot. Buy me a drink?"

He made another gesture at the bartender. "And what about yourself, Margaret? Am I to believe that such a seductive creature as you has not been swept to the altar?"

"Hard to believe, I know," she said coldly, "but most men seem to pay in cash rather than diamonds."

Marques took a long time swallowing his gulp of pirate's beer. What a crude comment she had made. Why did it bother him? To imply that a wedding ring was payment for sex did not strike him as funny right now. It struck him as revolting. Isabella would never have said such a thing. She could never believe such a thing. She would resist such a crass notion at every turn. Wedding rings were tokens. Symbols of a promise. A promise that a gentleman would never break his lady's heart. How he wished more people saw the world through Isabella's eyes. He tried hard not to stiffen under the weight of Margaret's body on his knee.

"How long will you be in town?" she asked.

"Six days," he answered, trying out another swig of his drink. He tipped the bartender for bringing a glass of wine to Margaret.

"Six days?" she asked excitedly, taking her wineglass in both hands. "Great! That'll give us plenty of time, huh?" She rubbed her nose against his ear.

Six days with a woman who wanted only his money seemed like a long time all of a sudden. Six days with a jaded entrepreneur who had no secrets to tell him, no fantasies to confess to him, no magic to show him. Margaret didn't know anything that he didn't know. She knew all about the world, and so did he. But Isabella knew about something else, something invisible, something sacred. "Now, don't be greedy," he teased. "Surely, you plan to share me."

"If that's what you want," she shrugged. "Shall I bring a friend?"

He glanced at her scoldingly. "That is not what I meant, young lady. I am a one-lady-at-a-time sort of gentleman."

"Ah!" she cried, placing a sarcastic hand over her heart. "What values!" She laughed, her eyes lighting up with intelligence.

Marques smiled with her. "Well," he said with a sigh. It was a sigh of defeat. "Shall we throw some dice and see whether we can't buy you some perfume with our winnings?"

"I'd rather have a fur," she grinned.

"In that case," he smiled, pressing a kiss to her forehead, "we'd best do very well at the table. Come, be my good luck charm." He nudged her to her feet, and tossed some coins at the bartender. She took his arm, and they walked to the rowdy gambling room.

Marques saw immediately another young lady whose acquaintance he always made a point of renewing. She was a redhead. He had always been taken by red hair. She had a round, white face and clear, blue eyes. Her figure was plump and delectable. It was time to practice his French. "Hello," he said, in the best accent he could manage.

She recognized him immediately, and burst into a grin. "Marques!" She planted a kiss on each of his cheeks. Isabella would have been furious if she'd been the woman on his arm, watching him receive a kiss from another woman. But Margaret didn't care. She was looking the other way, still enjoying her wine.

"You haven't aged a day, Veronique." He bowed courteously.

"Ah, your French is improving!" she praised him. "I would hardly know you don't speak it!"

This pleased him tremendously. "Margaret and I are going to try our luck with the dice," he informed her. "Would you be so kind as to join us?"

She looked warily over her shoulder, then motioned for him to lean in. He did so with an attentive ear. "I am with another man tonight," she whispered. "But I think he is leaving tomorrow. May I join you then?"

"But of course," he replied, lifting her hand to his lips.

She blushed at that, for even after all of these years of selling herself, she still had some girlish tenderness for Marques. He sensed that, and he loved that about her. When he took Margaret to the bedroom, he could make her moan, but it was only because he did certain things to her body. She couldn't help it. But Veronique would sometimes moan from anticipation or giddiness or even a little fear. And that was so much more exciting. "If I can get away from him, I will," she promised.

"Don't get in trouble for me," he said sternly. "If you've been paid, then do what you must."

"All right," she said, then bounced away.

Marques watched her go with some regret. She walked right into the waiting arm of another man, then snuggled her head into his chest. This was his notion of a sensitive woman? How pathetic, he thought. He had always considered Veronique to be one of the more genuine, one of the softer, more vulnerable women he regularly bedded. And just look at her. She could throw herself at a stranger without even trembling. He couldn't picture Isabella in the arms of a stranger. She would scream, weep, and brutally scold him for his lack of honor. Oh, would he ever meet anyone else like her? Was this his fate? Hardened women without dreams? He gave Margaret's bottom a firm squeeze. She did not object or squirm away from him as Isabella would have, but grinned attentively. "Yes?" she asked. "Do you want something?"

The answer was all too clear to him now. He did want something. But there was nothing in this room which would appease him.

Chapter Twenty

Luisa, Saada, and Isabella arrived at the Parrot Cage just before nightfall. Luisa had changed her dress six times before deciding on a black gown to match her straight hair. Saada looked ravishing in red silk. Its vibrant color brought out the striking darkness of her skin, and its square, low-cut neck amplified her already impressive bust. Isabella was the only one who had tried to dress modestly. The nuns had taught her never to reveal her beauty in public, and now was the first time she rather agreed with them. The last thing she wanted on an island full of rowdy pirates was to draw attention. Saada had lent her a pale turquoise dress, which fit loosely but, at least, was the right length. She wore all of her petticoats, framework, and corseting beneath it. And she tied her hair into a very modest knot on top of her head, covering it with a tiny white puff of a hat.

"Take off your cape," Luisa urged her. "Relax, let's have fun." She was feasting her eyes on all of the gentlemen around her, both handsome and otherwise.

"I'd prefer to keep it on for a while," said Isabella, covering her ears from all of the noise.

Saada found them a table, and arranged the chairs. "This spot should give you a good view," she chided Luisa. She shook her head at Isabella. "Isn't she just awful when she cuts loose?"

Isabella smiled shyly, and took a seat. She was relieved to be sitting. It was so much less conspicuous than standing.

"Oh, look at that handsome pirate over there," squealed Luisa, covering her flushing face with both hands. "Isn't he beautiful?"

Saada waved a black lace fan coolly before her face. "He sure is."

"Oh, he's too handsome for me," Luisa told herself aloud. "He'll never look at me. I should set my sights lower."

Isabella wasn't sure how she could set her sights any lower than upon a drunken pirate. But she had learned from listening to all their prattling that Luisa and Saada both thought pirates were the most desirable men alive.

"Oooo, I see one for me," said Saada, fixing her gaze on a tall gentleman in a plumed hat.

"Oh stop that," Luisa scolded her. "That's a captain. You can't have a captain."

"And why not?" asked Saada, putting a hand on her hip.

"Because every woman in town will be trying to get a captain. Too much competition. Oh look!" she cried, trying not to point. "A blond pirate! Oh, he must be Dutch, do you think? I just love blonds."

"But do you speak Dutch?" asked Isabella, trying nervously to join in the conversation.

Saada laughed. "I don't think speaking is what she had in mind."

Luisa batted her eyelashes playfully.

The next voice Isabella heard was that of a strange man. She jumped, because he had crept up behind her. "Ladies," he said, bowing gracefully despite his rugged attire. He was wear-

ing baggy clothes and a red scarf around his head. A very nice
sword glittered at his side from a sash. "Duyuspeekenglish?"
he asked, causing all of the women to shake their heads confusedly. "Do you speak Portuguese?"

They all nodded.

"My ship has just pulled in from England," he told them
as well as he could. "May I buy you pretty ladies some drinks?"

Luisa became suddenly shy. She bowed her head and
wouldn't look at him. Isabella knew what she was doing. She
was trying to cover her scars with her hair. Saada was fanning
herself with cool, easy motions, a cold and confident look upon
her face. "How long are you in port?" she asked, motioning
for him to sit.

"Ten days," he told her, then shouted to the bartender.
"Bombo for the ladies!" He jingled some coins in the air. "Is
bombo all right?" he asked them.

"Yes, it's fine," replied Saada, who was the only lady brave
enough to speak at the moment.

The stocky man noticed Isabella. She'd known he would. It
had only been a matter of time before he saw her hiding those
golden locks and that elegant face of hers. "My name's John,"
he told her. "John Rivers. And who might you be?"

Isabella looked to her friends for help. She did not want to
talk to him.

"That's Isabella," said Saada, "and she's sensible enough
not to speak to outlaws she doesn't know." She finished this
with a bright smile, lifting the rejected man into good cheer.

"Ah, that is wise," he agreed. "And you?" he asked Saada.

"I'm not sure I should tell you my name," she teased with
a very straight face. "How do I know you're not a pirate hunter
in disguise? Maybe you're trying to trap us into revealing our
identities to the authorities."

"Good point," he laughed. "Does that go for your friend
too?" He motioned toward Luisa.

"No," said Saada, taking this opportunity to promote her
friend. "Luisa here isn't afraid of pirate hunters. In fact, we're

pretty sure she is one. So the more you tell her about yourself, the better.''

John chuckled again, just as the bombo was brought to the table. Isabella looked at the thick, white beverage with some interest. Her silver mug was quite elegant, and when she brought the liquid to her lips, she found it sweet and pleasing. She worked up the courage to look around her. This place was not so different from the Great Cabin, only it was bigger. Pirates were shouting and drinking. There was a huddle of gamblers in one corner. It really was just the dry land version of the very same life they all boasted at sea.

''Do you ladies have comfortable lodging?'' John asked, giving each of the three women a glance.

''Let me guess,'' said Saada saucily, ''you can provide us with even more comfortable lodging. Is that it?'' She grinned intelligently.

''Oh no,'' he drawled, ''I would never suggest such a thing. Of course, if you were looking for a place to stay, it wouldn't be right of me to turn you away, now would it?''

''Mmmm,'' said Saada with her mouth full of bombo. ''You're a real gentleman.''

Luisa finally managed to squeak out a question. ''Are you on Captain Johnson's ship?'' It was a dumb question, she knew. But Johnson was the only British pirate captain she'd met.

''No,'' he said, ''can't say as I've heard of him. My captain is Jackson.''

''Oh,'' she smiled, trying to be courageous enough to maintain eye contact.

''And what about you ladies?'' he asked, looking right at Isabella. ''What brings you to a place like this? You don't look like fighters.''

''I told you she doesn't speak to strangers,'' Saada reminded him. ''It's a good thing you're cute, because you're not very bright.''

He laughed along with her, but added, ''Well, won't she at least take off her cloak?''

"Maybe she's cold," said Saada. "And what business is it of yours?"

"Just thought I'd like to see that pretty face a little better." He winked at Isabella.

Isabella could not take any more of this. She did not like being put on display for rowdy men to examine, evaluate, then harass. She did not like watching Luisa work up her courage just to gain the attention of someone not nearly worthy of her. And she did not like this John fellow. "Excuse me," she said, rising awkwardly to her feet. "Excuse me." She tried her best to nod politely to everyone present without quite looking at them, then made her way to the door.

The cool night air hit her hard when she first stepped outside. But it was not a chilling wind, it was a soft, fishy-smelling breeze that tickled her neck. She looked up and saw palm trees waving overhead. This was much better. She felt much freer in the open air, much more comfortable. There were gangs of pirates shouting to one another, crowding the sidewalk, and walking with swaggers. But they did not take much notice of her, for her black cape blended into the night sky. She leaned against the Parrot Cage's wooden wall, taking several deep breaths of lovely, tropical air. This is what it would feel like, she realized, to blend in. This is how other people felt. No one stared at them, no one suspected them of being mad. Everyone just went about his business, as usual.

"Are you all right?"

Isabella was startled. But it was only Luisa. "Oh yes," she sighed in relief. "Yes. I'm sorry. Did I pull you away from your . . . your friend? I didn't mean to."

"No," smiled Luisa. "He wasn't really my type anyway. To tell you the truth, I think he was more interested in having either you or Saada. And Saada didn't want him, and you . . . well, you left."

Isabella could see that Saada was exiting the pub as well now. "I'm sorry," Isabella said to Luisa. "I guess I'm not very good company."

Saada smiled pleasantly when she saw her companions "There you are. Say, why did you run off like that?"

"I'm sorry," Isabella apologized again. "I just wanted som fresh air. I didn't mean to pull you away from John."

"Pull me away?" she laughed. "I just wish you'd brough us with you. He wasn't worth the time of day. Come on, let' go to the Peg Leg."

"Ohhhh," griped Luisa. "You only want to go there becaus you think that man will be there again." She turned to Isabell and explained. "A long time ago, she met a handsome gentle man, bedded him only once, and now she thinks she's goin to find him again."

"I did not bed him," Saada corrected her coldly.

Something in her eyes told Isabella that it was true, Saad still thought of him.

"Oh, you did too, and you know it!" cried Luisa, takin each of her friends' hands, and leading the way to the Peg Leg

"I did not," Saada insisted. "We don't all give ourselve away to every set of blue eyes, you know."

"Does that mean me?" griped Luisa. "It had better not!"

Saada laughed. "Oh, come now. How many times have w come to New Providence? And how many times have you lef without getting bedded at least once? Never!"

"That doesn't mean I'm cheap," said Luisa. "I just happe to be in a hurry. We don't come here often, you know, and w don't stay long."

"Well, I prefer to get to know a man before I bed him," said Saada.

"Yes, but at one meeting every year or so, you could b ancient before you get to know someone."

"If he knows what's good for him, he'll wait," she sai mischievously. "Even at a hundred years old, I'll be the bes thing that ever happened to him."

Luisa burst into laughter. "Oh, I wish I had your self-confi dence!"

The Peg Leg was a little classier than the Parrot's Cage. I

had red carpets, and low lighting. The gambling was in a separate room from the drinking. "Now you two stay here," instructed Luisa. "I'm going to approach those men while I've still got my courage. Don't come over, for goodness' sake! Or else they'll want you instead."

Isabella and Saada agreed, and both wore looks of amusement as Luisa hopped toward a group of drunken pirates. "May I sit here?" she asked sweetly, bouncing her skirts.

"Far be it from me to turn away a lady," said one.

"You sit anywhere you like, doll," said another.

She smiled brightly and sprung into her seat. "So what were you men talking about?" she asked.

"About how much we were wishing a pretty young lady would join us," said one.

Isabella smiled. Luisa would be just fine now. She looked at Saada, but found her friend to be gazing intensely about her. Clearly, she was looking for that mysterious love of hers. Isabella was dying to see what this man looked like. What sort of a man could steal the heart of such a headstrong woman as Saada? It appeared she would not find out tonight, for there was no sign of him. Saada tried not to show her disappointment. "Shall we gamble?" she asked.

"All right. But I don't have any gold."

"I've got plenty," said her friend, leading her toward the gambling room.

Isabella was excited by the dimly lit back room. It was elegant, despite the grubbiness of the patrons. There was a real chandelier overhead, and a red carpet underfoot. Golden lanterns shimmered upon the gaming table, making the piles of forfeit gold sparkle, and the fateful dice glow with promise. "Let's watch a couple rounds before we start betting," suggested Saada.

"That seems a good idea." Isabella tried to watch the game attentively, holding her cape tightly about her shoulders. But she was instantly distracted by the faces of the gamblers. They looked so anxious, so worried, almost as though they were having no fun at all. Some of them looked downright angry. How sad it would be, she thought, to lose a pile of gold to one toss of the dice. She let her eyes wander about the room, examining each man and woman. The women were interesting too. They hung on their men's arms, cheering them on and pretending to care about the outcome. Only a few of them played.

Isabella remembered with some startle that there were prostitutes on this island. She wondered whether some of the women in this very room were. But they all looked so normal! Wouldn't a prostitute stand out? Wouldn't she carry a sign or have a depraved look in her eye? They all just looked like ordinary women. She studied each gown and each face with interest. Her eyes wandered to the tables, set away from the gamblers. And that was when she saw him.

He had a shapely brunette on his lap. He was squeezing her, kissing her, whispering in her ear. He smiled devilishly, and brought a cup to her lips. He seemed to be urging her to drink from it. When she did, he cleaned her plush lips with his tongue. She looked at him adoringly. He looked at her with fire in his eyes. Isabella could not move. She could not breathe. She just kept staring at him, swallowing, and breathing hard. At last, a warm tear fell from one of her eyes. She didn't know that it would hurt this much. She didn't know that she still cared. She couldn't believe that she had been so quickly replaced, and had truly meant nothing to him. He kept laughing and joking, as though he knew Isabella was watching, as though he was trying to torment her. Undoubtedly, he was delivering all of the same romantic lines to this woman that he had once tossed at Isabella. His hand squeezed that woman's breast, openly, publicly, tenderly. And Isabella fled.

"Wait!" called Saada, but she was not heard. She looked around confusedly, trying to see what had caused her strange friend to run. When she caught sight of Marques and his whore, she scowled. Both hands on her hips, she shook her head and muttered, "Oh, you've really done it this time, you good for

nothing . . . Isabella!'' she cried again. She ran outside, but it
was too late. The girl had disappeared into the crowd of pirates.
There'd be no finding her now.

Isabella ran through the night until she could run no more.
She wanted to reach the ocean, wanted to throw herself into
its violent waves and wake from this terrible dream. But she
seemed to be going the wrong way. She turned around and
slowed her pace, trying to smooth out her breathing. The streets
were winding, and her head was spinning. She wasn't sure
where she was anymore. How could she have done it? How
could she have lain with such a man? How quickly she had
been replaced! He had never loved her, never cared for her.
He had been tricking her all along. It was humiliating. How
she wished she hadn't told anyone of it! And now here she
was wandering around in . . . where was she? She seemed to
have wandered away from the crowds a bit. The sidewalk
was growing gloomy. Where were those ocean sounds coming
from? Perhaps if she followed them, she'd make it to the inn.

Oh, why did it hurt so much? Why did it make her feel so
small to see him doting on another woman? Was it just the
humiliation? Or was it something else. Did she secretly wish
to be in that woman's place? Did she wish that had been her
own breast he squeezed? Was there a piece of her that had
hoped he would change his mind and marry her? Had tonight
dashed all hopes of that? And where on earth was she going?
Nothing looked familiar anymore. Ah, she caught sight of a
sail ahead. She would head for the boat, then use the sandy
beach to guide her home to the inn. Strange sail, she thought,
getting nearer. Funny colors. Something familiar about it. All
those orange stripes. Just as her foot hit the sand, a moist cloth
covered her mouth, and she knew no more.

Chapter Twenty-one

She woke up once, saw nothing but a lantern swinging overhead. Then she returned to her painful slumber. She woke up again, felt the ocean moving beneath her back. Then she let it gradually lull her back to sleep. Once more she awoke. She felt she had been drugged. Something was not right within her mind. Everything was so cloudy. Wood was splintering under her hand. She was pierced by a prickly shard of wood, but she did not remove it. She saw a drop of her own blood, thought about picking at the splinter, but was too weak. The lantern overhead was still swinging. She smelled rotting fish. Oh, it was awful. That smell. She was going to be sick. At least, she thought she was going to be. But instead, she fell asleep once more.

"Hungry?"

Isabella sat bolt upright. She was not sure how long she'd slumbered. She couldn't seem to open her eyes all the way. She squinted against the light. She felt her splinter again, and this time, yanked it out. "Ouch," she hissed, sucking on the wounded hand.

"Hungry?" the voice repeated.

She looked up and screamed. She screamed so loud that the sound itself brought her to her feet. She raced to the wall, clung to it, dug at it, but did not turn her back on her abductor. He was wearing an orange turban.

"No need to scream," he said in fairly competent Portuguese. "I'm only bringing your breakfast."

Breakfast? Was it morning? There were no portholes in the cabin. Everything seemed so dark and gloomy. The swinging lantern did so little to shed light on this filthy little room. Her abductor wore baggy balloon-style pants, pointed boots, and a heavily embroidered shirt. His beard was short and triangular. She could only pant at the sight of him. The memory of the other corsairs she had met . . . the memory of what they had done to her . . . she could not bring herself to speak.

"I'm the only one on board who speaks Portuguese," he told her, "so if you have any questions, direct them to me." He scratched his turban. "So, uh, do you have any?"

She was wide-eyed and silent.

"All right, well, enjoy your breakfast." He started to leave.

But at the thought of being left alone again, Isabella was shaken into sensibility. She must know what would happen to her. She must know where she was going. She mustn't let him leave without telling her what would be her fate. "Wait!" she cried, her voice coming out with a scratch against her throat.

He turned around easily. "Yes?"

"What . . . where are we going?"

"I thought you might want to know that," he laughed. "But you didn't ask, so . . . well, I just figured you were happier in your ignorance." Isabella didn't return his smile, so he cleared his throat and tried to look serious. "We're going to Tunis. It's a lovely city-state on the north coast of Africa. Really beautiful. The wine is superb, the people are friendly as can be, and you'll go wild for the local cuisine. Can't wait to get there myself."

"But what . . . what . . ."

"You'll be a slave," he informed her lightly. "That part of it rather stinks, I agree. At least, it stinks for you. Doesn't really bother me personally."

"But why . . . why . . ." Her throat was terribly dry.

"Because you were there," he shrugged. "We didn't mean any trouble by coming to New Providence. Just heard it was a great place for shore leave, decided to try it out. But as we were getting ready to set sail, there you were. We thought about leaving you be, but then we remembered that we *are* corsairs, after all. So we grabbed you."

"Then you came to New Providence for . . . for—"

"The whores. Yes, that's all. Boy, what an unlucky break for you. Really unfortunate. You might want to look into getting a new guardian angel."

"You . . . you believe . . ."

"Believe in guardian angels? No, of course not. I'm a Muslim. I was just making fun of your religion, but I guess it was to no avail. Speaking of Islam . . ." He looked over each shoulder to make sure he was alone. "You might want to consider having a vision of Allah as quickly as possible. This is between you and me, but a tip to the wise. We only enslave Christians." He winked.

"But . . . but . . ."

"But is it a good religion? Pretty good. You have to face Mecca once a day, which gets to be tiresome. But the holidays are splendid! You'll love them."

"But . . . but . . ."

"But how do you convert? Well, that's the tough part. See, the captain has to really believe that you've had a change of heart. Seems a lot of our prisoners have sudden visions of Mohammed once they discover their fate. It makes the captain get a little skeptical. So what you must do is win his trust and seem to be gradually converting. That's the way I'd go. If I were in your position, which . . . praise Allah I'm not."

Isabella was trying to catch her breath, trying to regain her senses. "But, sir . . ." she began.

"How do you win the captain's trust?" He shrugged. "Easy. You're pretty good looking . . . for a Christian. So if you set your mind to it, I'll bet you could make friends with the captain. And don't forget to call him 'rais.' That's our word for captain. When you meet him, be really nice and call him rais."

"I . . . I . . . there must be another way," she said pensively. "I can't . . . I can't just . . ."

"Throw yourself at him? Sure you can. I would." He chuckled, "I mean, if I were in your shoes, there's *nothing* I wouldn't do."

"Don't go!" she cried. She couldn't believe she was beckoning to a corsair, but he was her only contact, her only hope. He was human. A human corsair. It seemed impossible, and yet it was so.

"I have to go," he apologized. "I have other chores to do. But if you get bored, you can always just start crying out at the top of your lungs. That's sure to get you some company fast. Just kidding," he added with a chuckle, "Whatever you do, don't do that." He made a casual exit.

Isabella was left in the horrendous silence of this cabin. No sound, so little light. Only a nauseating movement of water below. And a horrible stench. For perhaps the first time in her life, she did not think, or even imagine. Her mind was paralyzed, and her body frozen in a strange kneeling posture.

Chapter Twenty-two

"What do you mean she ran off?"

Luisa was humble before her captain. She didn't feel responsible exactly, but she hated to be the bearer of bad news. Particularly to a man she admired so deeply, and whose warmth she so craved. "I didn't see it myself," she explained. "I heard Saada shouting her name, and when I looked up, she was already gone."

"Why didn't you go after her?" Marques growled.

"I thought she was just returning to the inn," she answered defensively. "I didn't see any reason to follow her. And I was . . . well, occupied. I didn't return until this morning. And it's then that I learned she had never returned. The innkeeper said she'd not been in all night." She bowed her head in regret.

"And you've no idea what set her off?" he demanded.

"Actually, Saada told me what it was," she admitted meekly.

"What was it?"

Luisa did not want to say. She winced at having to relay the message. "She . . . she saw you, Captain. With . . . with another woman."

Marques's face froze into an unreadable expression. When his jaw twitched at last, he asked, "Where is Saada? I want to hear this from her."

"She is ill this morning," Luisa explained. "Had too much to drink. I fear she hasn't done anything all day but grunt and beg to be left alone. I ran to her just as soon as I found Isabella missing, and it took a great deal to get her to tell me as much as I've told you."

Marques lowered his eyes. "What did she tell you? Exactly."

Luisa felt cautious, but proceeded as best she could. Her hands wrung together as she spoke. "She said that the two of them went to the gaming room—we were at the Peg Leg. And that Isabella saw you . . . well, the way you always are on shore leave," she blushed. "And then . . . well, she just ran off."

"Angrily?" he demanded.

"Mmmm, no, I think she was more . . . hurt."

That's what he'd been afraid of. He crossed his arms pensively. He paced to the window. Looking out, he saw crowds of people. All of them the same; none of them remotely reminding him of Isabella. Of course, he knew she had no right to be angry. They had agreed to separate, agreed that she should go her own way, and he go his. But what difference did it make whether she had the right? The point was, he had wounded her, and he knew it. For it was not the infidelity which troubled her, but the casual ease with which he had caressed another woman. She had watched him engage in loveless pleasure of the flesh, and felt that's all he was capable of, felt he had not valued their passionate night together one bit. Marques was surprised that he could guess her mind so well, but he was sure of it. He was certain that this was what had made her run off. And he wished he could punish himself for his idiocy. For the sake of one night's amusement, he had forever lost the only woman to whom he had ever lent more than a passing thought.

And goodness only knew what was happening to her now, he worried. Was she alone on this rowdy island, trying to find work? Or had she paid some sailors to grant her passage? He couldn't bear to think of it. Had he, in his carelessness, driven her to danger? Or worse? Could he have driven her to lose faith in love? How he never wanted her to lose faith! How he never wanted her to change, never wanted her to become just like everyone else. "I'll send some men to search for her," he announced with resolve. "Let's hope she's still on the island."

Luisa could sense his doubt about that. She left with her head hung down, for not only had she been forced to break terrible news to her captain, but she knew that she may have just lost a very dear friend.

"Gabriel, I can't live with this," Marques cried out. They were walking at an anxious pace, glancing this way and that, but heading nowhere in particular. "I thought I could let her go. I wanted her, but I could let her go. I was wrong. It's been only a few hours, and I miss her so badly it aches. My God! I don't even know that she's still alive!"

"I'm sure she's fine," the old man assured him.

"You know what?" Marques spat frantically. "It doesn't even matter. Even if she's safe, I'm still not happy. I want her back. I don't want to set sail without her. I don't care whether she's gone and married a millionaire and become the happiest woman on earth. I want her back."

"Why?" asked Gabriel nervously.

"I don't know!" he cried, loudly enough to be heard by the whole town, if it hadn't been for all of the other noise. "I just want her. I just miss her, and I want her back."

"You want to marry her?" asked Gabriel, working hard to keep up with his captain's frantic strides.

"I don't know. I don't know," he muttered desperately. "I haven't thought it all through. I just . . . I just know that I'm never going to find anyone like her again, and it hurts."

"But Marques," Gabriel pleaded, "she's no good for you."

"You know? I'm sick of you saying that." He tossed his arms into the air. "What do you have against her anyway?"

Gabriel stopped walking, but it took Marques a long time to notice. When he finally did, he stopped and faced the quartermaster. "Captain, let me speak to you a moment. Calmly," urged Gabriel.

"Oh blast it all!" he cried. "I can't be calm!"

"Just for a moment," Gabriel pleaded. "Just lend me your ear for half a minute."

"All right," groaned Marques. "What is it?"

Gabriel moved nearer. "Marques," he said, his blue eyes weary with age, "I once had a lady very much like your Isabella."

Marques nearly screamed. "Is that all you're going to tell me? A miserable tale of lost love? Come on. We're in a hurry."

"Hear me out," insisted Gabriel.

"All right, fine. You knew a lady like Isabella, and she broke your heart."

"No," said Gabriel sternly. "She didn't break my heart. She took her own life."

Marques was startled. "Really?"

"Yes," said the old man. "You see, she loved me. Don't ask me why anyone would love a crazy, filthy pirate like me. But in my younger days, I always managed to draw a few women to my side. Perhaps I was not as handsome as yourself, but there were always ladies who preferred outlaws, who craved the freedom that only a lawless sod would grant them."

Marques found himself intrigued.

"I loved many of them," Gabriel recalled. "But this one was different. She was not only attracted to my lust, but sought my heart. And that is what killed her."

"You've lost me."

"She was a dreamer. She thought there was such a thing as happily ever after. She thought she could find it, even with a pirate. I broke her heart, Marques. Not because I wanted to, but because no matter how I tried, I was still a mere mortal. And I could never be good enough for her."

Marques gave this some thought. "Well, perhaps you could

have talked to her, explained to her that all men have both some good and some bad in them.''

Gabriel was shaking his head before Marques's sentence was even finished. ''She could not hear me, Captain. I was not from her world.''

Marques felt a bit flustered. ''Well ... well, what finally drove her over the edge?''

''Caught me in the arms of another woman,'' he admitted. ''But if it hadn't been that, it would have been something else. I could not please such a woman. No man could.''

Marques grinned his relief. ''Oh! So you cheated on her, eh? Well, that explains it then. You don't have to be a gallant knight just to refrain from infidelity, old friend. You blew it, and you know it. Don't tell me she was impossible to please. She just wanted you to be faithful. Three quarters of the women in the world want that.''

''I could not have pleased her,'' Gabriel insisted angrily. ''No matter what I did.''

''You don't know that!'' Marques cried indignantly. ''You didn't try!''

''I did,'' said Gabriel. ''I gave her everything!''

''Hmm,'' said Marques with some amusement. ''Caught you in bed with another, and killed herself. Rather flattering, actually.'' He stopped walking and thought about Isabella. ''Oh no. You don't suppose she ... No she doesn't like me that well.''

''Let her go!'' Gabriel warned.

Marques turned to him without apology or understanding. ''Gabriel, old friend. Listen to me.'' He put his hands on the older man's shoulders. ''I know that Isabella isn't perfect. I know that she doesn't understand how the real world works, and that she doesn't see people as they are, but as she imagines them to be. I know that,'' he assured Gabriel with a nod. ''But there are problems with me too, old friend. You may not have realized this,'' he smiled twistedly, ''but I am a thief and a killer. I live on a boat, and I refuse to get married. Do you really think I should be fussy? Do you really think I should turn away a wonderful woman just because *she's* got problems?" His grin broadened. "Now come, Gabriel. I heed your warning, and I appreciate the thought. I shall be careful of Isabella's insanity, I promise. But what you don't realize is that I am more adventurous than you are, old friend."

"How is that?" asked Gabriel reluctantly.

Marques sprung into his next step. "I've always wanted to try knighthood. Didn't realize it until now, but I think it should be fun. What do you think?" he asked, drawing his sword. "Shall I have it sharpened and polished?"

Gabriel returned his friend's smile for the first time. "Marques, you are a character."

"Call me Sir Marques from now on," he teased.

The old man relented with a sigh. "Very well, then. It's your life. Now where do we find this damsel in distress?"

"Not sure," answered Marques pensively. "Let's check the docks."

Chapter Twenty-three

The *rais* turned out to be a charming man. If you happen to be charmed by sweaty ogres who treat their camels better than they treat their wives. But Isabella was repulsed by him, and found herself clinging to the cabin wall in a frantic retreat when he intruded upon her solitude. He was a tall man, a massive man with vacant dark eyes that never quite met her own. If she had met him on a crowded street, she would have known that he was a captain, would have known that he was accustomed to being obeyed. He showed no signs of having the perceptiveness or the interest in others that comes from a lifetime of having to please. He had never learned how to gain someone else's affection or approval, for it had never been necessary. Isabella could see that he'd been born into a high station.

"He wants you to turn around," said the translator, whom Isabella was learning to like. Not because he was such a nice person, but because he was human, and he could speak to her, and he was her only contact with her destiny.

Isabella shuttered at being asked to turn around. She looked to see whether the *rais* carried a whip, but saw that his massive hands were bare. Questioningly, she looked again to her translator. "You know," he said, twirling a finger in the air. "Spin around so he can look at you."

She sighed her relief. He was not going to harm her, only examine her. She turned around slowly, her arms outstretched, feeling like a horse for sale. Not once did the *rais* look her in the eye. His gaze moved from stoically fixed above her head to scrutinizingly set upon her slim figure. She heard his voice, low and stern, but could not understand his words. "He wants you to come closer," said the translator. Isabella did so, though with a trembling in her knees and hands. She could not lift her chin. She was too ashamed. "Now he wants you to jump up and down and scream nonsensically."

Isabella looked curiously at the turbaned young man.

"Just kidding," he grinned. "I just thought it'd be funny if you really did it."

She wanted to laugh, but could not. Her stomach was churning. Her shaking was getting worse.

The *rais* spoke again, and his translator said, "He says you're very lovely."

"Thank you," she muttered with a hint of sarcasm.

The *rais* reached for her hair. She pulled away.

"Let him do it," the young man warned. "I saw him strike a woman once just for refusing him a kiss."

Isabella was shaken by that announcement, and stilled herself. With wide, petrified eyes she allowed him to finger her hair as though testing the fineness of silk. "He says you have a lovely face," said the translator. "Says you're a little too skinny and he wants me to feed you more. But he says your face is perfect."

"Should I be flattered?" she asked softly, with a trembling voice and clenched fists.

"Sure, why not?" he shrugged. "If you're going to be a slave, you might as well be a valuable one, right? I mean, imagine getting sold for a pair of socks or something. How embarrassing that would be!"

Again, Isabella wanted to laugh, but couldn't. "Does he speak any Portuguese at all?" she asked quietly.

"No. He thinks he's way too important to open a book and learn something. Though I'd not say so in a tongue he understood."

The *rais* barked something that made Isabella jolt. She was standing so close to him, that she could feel the vibration of his booming voice against the front of her body. Petrified, she looked to the translator, but he was busily chatting with the *rais*. Within moments, the *rais* had turned on his heel and left the cabin, leaving Isabella and her companion trembling in an awkward silence. "What . . . what was that?" she dared to ask. "What did he say?"

The young man scratched his head. "Ummm, you're not going to like this."

"*What?*" she demanded breathlessly.

"Well, he uh . . . he wants me to draw you a bath."

Isabella felt her dirty hair. "Well, that doesn't sound so bad."

"And then he wants me to bring you to his cabin."

"*What?*"

"It'll be all right," he said anxiously. "This is the opportunity you needed to win his trust."

"But I don't want his trust!" she cried, crossing her arms and turning away. "I don't want anything to do with him!"

"Don't be afraid," begged the young man, who had a weakness for soon-to-be-ravished ladies. "I'm sure it'll be all right. He knows what he's doing. He's got sixteen wives after all. Believe me, he knows all about women!"

Isabella glared at him.

"Well . . . well," he stammered, "I'm sure he won't harm you. He would never do anything like that, I mean he . . ." He scratched his beard pensively. "Actually, he does have a sadistic streak. Last week, he had me flogged just for missing a spot when I was sweeping. Can you believe that? He had me flogged for that! As though anyone would care that the deck wasn't

clean. What an overblown, self-righteous, coldhearted piece of
. . . But hey!'' he added quickly. ''He's handsome.''

Isabella dropped her forehead against the cold wall. She
could not take this. It was all too much.

''Oh, try not to be so upset,'' urged the young corsair, ''I'm
sure everything will turn out all right for you in the end. Don't
you think? Who knows? Maybe uh . . . maybe someone will
rescue you.''

Isabella began to weep. Arms crossed defensively, she wrinkled up her face and began wetting the wall with her tears.

''Is it something I said?''

Isabella shook her head, nearly splintering her forehead in
the process. ''No,'' she wept, ''It's just that . . . that I suddenly
don't believe anymore.''

''Believe what?''

''That he'll come,'' she wept. ''That my knight will rescue
me.''

The translator wasn't certain what to make of that.

''I have waited,'' she sniffed, clutching her gut. ''I have
waited, and waited, and waited. He didn't come for me at the
convent, nor on the pirate ship, and where is he now?'' She
was no longer speaking to the young man, but only to herself.
''I have had faith, and what has it brought me? Nothing at all.
He would have come by now if he could. No knight would let
his lady suffer this long. So I can only reason that he is unable.
Unable because . . .'' She wracked out a tremendous sob.
''Because he does not exist,'' she wept through clenched teeth.

''I see . . .'' said the wide-eyed, partially disturbed corsair.

Isabella took several deep breaths, experiencing how it felt
to be alive, to be still living and breathing, yet knowing that
there was not a soul out there to keep watch over her. No
mythical, benevolent knight to look after her safety, and rescue
her from danger. To be alone. She kept breathing steadily, and
found that she was all right. Disbelief was not as painful as
believing, and feeling that she'd been abandoned. ''It'll be all
right, though,'' she sniffed weakly.

"That's the spirit," said the boy, not knowing that it was better to keep his mouth shut and let the lady ramble.

"It'll be all right because Marques will come," she announced boldly, lifting her forehead from the wall. "I know this, not from faith but from experience. He is courageous and loyal, and not at all unclever. He will discover what has become of me, and he will come."

The corsair wondered whether this Marques fellow was real or not. He offered her a weak grin. "Sure he will, sure he will."

She thrust her chin into the air and turned to her translator boldly. "He will rescue me not as a knight, but as . . . as a friend." She squinted distantly, thoughtfully into the eyes of the only person who could hear her realization. "And perhaps that is good enough. Perhaps a courageous, loyal friend is worth more than a thousand knights."

Chapter Twenty-four

"Hey, you!" Marques and Gabriel jogged toward a dock boy, their weapons jangling all the way. "Boy!" Marques called over the strong wind. "Come here!"

The boy looked as though nothing could have sounded less tempting. For what fool would want to run toward a couple of angry pirates, shouting and weighed down by weapons? He simply glimpsed them from the corner of his eye, then went on tying his knot.

"Come here!" cried Marques, coming closer still, until the boy could no longer ignore him. "I have need of information."

"I don't know anything," said the sandy-haired lad with caution."

"Can you tell me which boats have set sail in the past twelve hours?"

"Docks have been quiet," the boy reported, relieved that this was all the captain wanted. "Three ships have just arrived, and only one has departed."

"Did the ship carry any civilian passengers? The one that departed?" Marques demanded.

"Doubt it," said the boy. "Didn't see it leave myself. My shift just started. But the boy before me said only one ship had left during the night—and it was a corsairs.' "

Marques and Gabriel looked at one another. Then Marques's gaze recaptured the boy. "What were corsairs doing here?"

"Don't know," he shrugged, trying to seem casual under the frightful glare of a pirate captain. "The dock boy didn't want to let them anchor, but there was no law against it, so he had to. As far as I know, all they did was drink and gamble like everyone else."

"And when they left, they took no passenger?"

The boy frowned. "Don't know, Captain. I doubt it, but nobody saw them leave till they'd already set sail. Can't imagine a bunch of corsairs taking a civilian passenger."

"Me either," said Marques, looking squarely at his quarter-master. "I don't like this."

"Neither do I," said Gabriel.

Marques tossed the boy a coin.

"Thanks!" he cried, his face lighting up at the sight of gold glowing in his very own palm.

Marques did not reply. "If the men haven't found her on the island," he told Gabriel, "I'm going after that corsair ship. Tell the crew that I'll not deprive them of the shore leave they were promised. Anyone who wants to stay, can stay. But those who come with me can share in the loot we take from the corsairs."

"Aye, sir," said Gabriel, turning on his heel.

"And Gabriel?"

He turned to see his captain's bright blue eyes, so full of hope and adventurousness. "Thank you for not trying to dissuade me. Thanks for . . . for letting me play the hero."

Gabriel smiled warmly. "It suits you, Captain."

"Do you think so?" he grinned. "I guess I'd like to believe that. Yes. I think I'd really like to believe that."

Chapter Twenty-five

Isabella tried to imagine that the bath water was melting her skin, melting her body, and freeing her soul of its worldly entrapments. She stretched out in the tin tub, resting her feet on its top, letting her hair float around her like a halo. She lifted her hands. They were pruned, as though they really were melting. She dropped them into the water once more, spreading her fingers, letting thick, warm water collect between them. She held her breath, and let her face fall under, baptizing herself, wondering how it would feel to drown. When she could hold her breath no more, she came up with a gasp, welcoming in the stale air of the prisoners' cabin.

"Sure you don't need any help?" asked the translator, whose name turned out to be Samir. He had reluctantly agreed to face the other way while she bathed, but resented not being allowed to indulge in this one little potential perk of his otherwise tedious job.

"I don't need any help, Samir." Her eyes were closed, and she was trying to forget what the future had in store for her. If she looked an hour ahead, she would see herself in the bed of that horrible *rais*. If she looked a month ahead, she would see herself wearing shackles, and being put up for auction. If she looked a year ahead, she would see herself scrubbing floors or planting crops for some horrible, cruel stranger. So she preferred to bask in the moment.

"Are you ready?" he asked.

Isabella sighed heavily. "I shall never be ready," she replied. "But if my time has come, then I will dress."

Samir fidgeted with a lacy gown. "The *rais* ordered me to have you wear this," he announced uncomfortably.

Isabella opened her eyes, and felt surrounded by the color white. "How strange," she said, squinting at the satin, "that he should have me wear the color of purity, when his intentions are so violently impure."

Samir shrugged. "Makes perfect sense to me. It's like ravishing an angel. He'll probably want you to act really demure too."

Isabella sat upright. "What did you say?"

"Oh, you know," he explained. "It's just one of those things with us men. We like something to be holy before we defile it. Just one of those quirks."

Isabella, for possibly the first time in her life, was forming a plan. "Samir?"

"Hmm?"

"Are Muslim women very docile and obedient?"

He laughed. "That is indeed a fantasy, and believe me, we work hard to keep the dream alive. But in reality—"

"And the *rais?*" she interrupted. "Is he used to women who are timid and chaste?"

"Well, sure, I guess. I mean, every woman he beds is either married to him or is about to be sold by him. I imagine they're all pretty, er, uncomfortable."

Isabella grinned. It was so exciting. For the first time in her life, she was not going to escape this by drifting into her imagination. She was going to escape it by using her wits. "And if I were bold with him?" she asked. "Do you imagine that would repel him?"

"If you challenged him, he'd have you flogged," Samir warned.

"But what if I didn't challenge him?" she asked. "What if I were nice . . . overly nice? Do you think that might turn him away?"

Samir shook his head. "I don't know. I don't know what he'd think. But if you'd like to try it on me first, we could see how it plays out. You know, give it sort of a test run."

She shot him a look of annoyance. "Stop that, Samir. I'm quite serious. I think I just might be able to rescue myself."

Marques paced before his crew, arms clasped militaristically behind his back. "Men! I want to thank you all for joining me."

"And women!" cried Luisa.

Marques gave a low bow. "And women. I apologize for my carelessness." He rose again. "I thank you all for taking time away from your shore leave to come on what is really a personal mission of mine. As some of you may have noticed, there was a lady on board our last voyage named Isabella, to whom I have taken quite a fondness. I have reason to believe she has been captured by corsairs, and I aim to bring her back. As she is not a member of our crew, I require none of you to assist me. However, I am glad that so many of you seem to agree that it is our duty as outlaws to rescue innocents from the world we reject. We know that corsairs are more like men of land than like ourselves. We know that they will harm anyone who is not strong enough to stop them. And we, as the only free people on earth, must do what we can to rescue a lady from their merciless grasps."

There was some clumsy applause, but mostly muttering and cries of "Yay!"

"Now, I know we cannot devote ourselves to rescues and chivalry," he admitted soberly. "We are pirates, after all, and must make a living. So I tell you this. When we overtake the corsair ship, which we will, then you may all divide the treasure amongst yourselves, leaving me completely devoid of a share. I want only one thing, the woman. Agreed?"

There were a couple of rough cheers.

"All right then. To work!"

The crew dispersed, heading cheerfully to their tasks. In truth, though they all enjoyed the frolic of shore leave, none of them felt at home on dry land. Their swinging hammocks were their only true beds. The Great Cabin was their favorite restaurant. Their legs cramped when there was no motion under their feet. And they could not breathe unless the salty air was whipping into their noses and mouths at a ship's speed. They were all glad to be home. Not one man or woman felt deprived at having to return for an early sail. They could hardly wait for the fiddling and dancing that night.

Gabriel leaned warily against the ship's rail. "Don't mean to dampen our rescue plans," he said to the captain, "but has it occurred to you there may be a problem?"

"Impossible," said Marques. "Our ship is faster than any skinny corsair vessel."

"Not that," said Gabriel. "I mean the other problem. Isabella."

"Huh?"

"Captain, we don't know for certain that she was kidnapped. Suppose she simply bought passage. Suppose she isn't eager to return to your embrace. After all, wasn't she running away from you? Isn't that how we got into this mess? You did take her virginity, then refuse to marry her, if you recall."

"She'll give me another chance," he replied confidently.

"How can you be so sure? Even if she were kidnapped, she might say, 'Thanks for rescuing me, now please drop me off at the next port.' She made it clear she doesn't want to be your mistress.''

"It'll be all right.''

"Why do you say that?''

"Because,'' Marques shrugged, "I'm going to rescue her. I'm going to be her knight. She'll have to love me then—it's in her plan. And Isabella always follows her plan.''

"Did you know I have always wanted to make mad passionate love to a corsair?'' Isabella told the *rais*. He could not understand her words, but he disliked her demeanor. She had yanked her sleeves from her shoulders, allowing her dress top to hang from her breasts. She had torn her skirts and petticoats to expose a shapely, bare leg. "How embarrassing,'' she observed, pretending to have just noticed. She licked her finger, and ran it up her own leg, then placed the finger on his tense lips. She was doing a good job of acting, and she knew it. Her imagination was lending her the power to pretend. To imagine that she was someone else. To see through the eyes, to think through the mind of a woman who was wanton, who was afraid of nothing, who would willingly bed a stranger. It was not so different from imagining a faraway land. She was imagining a faraway person.

The *rais* shook off her finger, then pulled her into his strong arms. She touched his cheek with a seductive grin. This angered him. He grabbed the offending hand by the wrist, and flung her mercilessly to the floor. It hurt. Isabella's arm felt bruised by the fall. She wanted to weep, but she knew that weeping would be the end of her. That is what he wanted. He wanted her to be frightened, wanted her to beg for mercy and cower from his touch. She must not give in. Her scheme would only work if she plunged into it head first, without hesitating or backing down. She remained on the floor, and struck a seductive pose. She forced herself to smile at her dumbfounded captor. "Is this your idea of seduction?'' she asked him calmly.

Growling, he lifted her, and carried her to his cot. She pretended it was not frightening to be held by someone she did not trust. Instead of panicking, she wrapped her arms about his neck and let herself be tossed to the bed. He fell on her. He did not kiss her, but groped at her body, trying to intimidate her with the roughness of his hands upon her tender skin. She laughed as though he were nothing but a joke, and planted kisses on his neck. He kept shrugging her away, trying to stop her affectionate reply to his violence. But she was stubborn. She would not cower from him, and she would not plead for her innocence. It was infuriating.

At last, he placed a hand upon her breastbone, pinning her to her back while he struggled to lower his breeches with only one hand. This was it. Isabella knew that she had only one last chance to repel his advances. She had to believe she would still get out of this unharmed. She had to believe in herself. The *rais* freed himself from his breeches, and moved toward her with the first traces of a smile on his face. He believed he had won. He believed that no woman could be strong in the face of his brutality. But just when he was on the verge of success, she spoke amorously in his ear, urging him toward her with a squeeze. "You're driving me wild," she said in a tone that even he could understand. He cursed. It was the last straw. Even while on the threshold of his most brutal intimidation, this European vixen would not be humble before him. He had lost his interest. And suddenly, Isabella was lying alone. Her skirt lifted, her breasts nearly bared, she was no longer being breathed upon. Her legs and arms were free.

The *rais* flung open his cabin door. He shouted into the hallway, summoning a frantic Samir. The two exchanged words for a few brief minutes, and then Isabella found herself being hauled from the room by the elbow. She did not look back as Samir pulled her into the hallway, and the cabin door slammed shut behind them. But when they were out of ear's reach, she asked him, "What happened? What did the *rais* say?"

Samir smiled. "He said you are completely out of your mind."

Isabella covered her grinning mouth with both hands. In relief and joy, she burst into laughter. "Oh Samir! For the first time in my life, I am actually happy to hear that!"

He nearly shared in her laughter, but then, there was a loud boom.

"What was that?" asked Isabella.

"Sounded like cannon fire," he replied. "Come. We must get to safety before you are harmed, or worse ... before I am asked to help fight." He led her through many winding passageways. Frantic janissaries hurried past them, straightening their belts and clutching their swords. "Fighting men," mused Samir. "What a bunch of lunatics. Can you imagine hearing gunfire and thinking, 'Oh boy, I'd better run toward it!' Me, I'm happier just to be the one who mops up their blood after the battle's over."

He realized it would take too long to reach the prisoners' cabin. They were in everyone's way who was trying to get on deck. And soon, there could be enemies on board. He decided they'd best duck into his own cabin. "This should be safe enough," he said, latching the door behind them. "If the enemy makes it this far, we'll know our own men are defeated. So then we can do what any sensible gentleman does." He raised his eyebrows. "Switch sides. Swear our allegiance to the newcomers."

There was a porthole in this room, and Isabella was immediately drawn to it. She looked wistfully at a school of fish floating by in turbulent sheathes of aqua. She loved the ocean. She loved fish. And she loved the feeling of having finally freed her own self from danger. Of course, she knew what the commotion was upstairs. Of course, she knew that Marques had come for her. She'd known he would. She had finally put her faith in something worthy of it. And perhaps it was time she put her heart there as well. "Oh, please win this fight, Marques," she whispered to the porthole. "If you were mythical, I'd have no doubt of your victory. But alas, you are mortal. And you could perish. And if you did, you would do so without ever knowing how much I have grown. And how much I have grown to accept you. Just as you are.''

Chapter Twenty-six

Isabella could not bear to lend her thoughts to the battle upstairs. She did not want to consider the details of what was happening right above her head. She did not want to picture the blood, or wonder whose sword was drawing it. She did not want to guess whose yells were of victory, and whose were of mortal terror. She could not control it, she kept telling herself. Whatever was happening up there, it was completely out of her hands. This was not an easy thing to accept, not when her destiny was being carved beyond her line of sight. But to wonder, to guess, was to torment herself. And so, she kept her arms crossed tightly and forced herself to watch only the fish through the porthole. Beautiful fish, who did not know what it meant to be beautiful.

Even when she heard footsteps nearing the cabin door, Isabella did not turn. She would not wait anxiously by the door, frantic to learn whether it was her salvation or her doom which approached. She would wait patiently, disinterestedly, as one who knew that her soul would survive whatever fate did to her body and her life. She watched the fish. The fish didn't know that they were mortal, but what good would it do them to know? They could not save themselves. Even when the cabin door flew wide, she did not turn. She thought about her heartbeat, forced it to remain slow. She would show destiny that she had not clung to its verdict. That she had greater concerns than its trivial, heartless decisions.

She heard Samir try to scream, but his voice was muffled. He sounded as though he could not breathe. Isabella turned. Slowly, patiently, like an empress approached by a lowly messenger. Her eyes closed and filled with painful tears. "Marques," she whispered loudly.

His blue eyes were flashing with brightness and victory. One arm was bleeding, and hanging uselessly at his side. But the other was wrapped tightly about Samir's throat. The muscles in his forearm cut into the poor young man's neck, stifling him, turning him purple. "Isabella!" he called, though his eyes were fixed on his victim. "Are you hurt?"

She was so happy to see him, it ached. It made her knees tremble and her breathing ragged. But her moist face was nearly expressionless as she said, "I'm fine, Marques. Now let him go."

Marques curled his lips, exposing a set of painfully clenched teeth. "Not until he's suffered for what he's done." He forced his injured arm to move, to hold a knife to his captive's throat, while the good arm held still his prey.

Isabella became more firm, more present. "Stop that," she snapped. "He has done nothing. Let him go."

"Nothing, eh?" asked Marques, grimacing at his wiggling prey. "Is this not his cabin? Is that not his bed?" He shook the choking young man with a flex of his arm muscle. "Do you think it's funny? Dragging a young woman to your bed? Did you think there would be no consequence?"

Isabella grabbed Marques's trembling wrist, trying to force him to drop the knife which threatened Samir's throat. "He didn't harm me!" she cried. "Will you listen?"

"Ouch!" he grimaced, as she tried to twist his wounded

arm. "Are you mad, woman?" He was strong enough to keep the knife in his grip, and his grip near the corsair's throat, but he was suffering from her fingers digging into his wound. "You'll not stop me from killing this time, Isabella! I've seen you tormented by filth once too often."

"But he was helping me!" she cried, tugging at him. "He's not like the others! He's young! He brought me here for safety. Let him go! Marques!"

Marques drew a look of puzzlement. "He was helping you?"

"Yes!" she cried. "Honestly! Will you listen?"

He didn't want to, but he turned the boy loose. Samir touched his own throat with both hands, feeling the veins, stroking the muscles.

"I'm so sorry, Samir!" Isabella approached the blue-faced boy who was staggering aimlessly away from her.

"No," he rasped. "No, no need to apologize. All a misunderstanding. Could happen to anyone." His eyes were bulging, and his lips were pale, but somehow, he managed to regain his senses well enough to strike a picturesque pose upon bended knee. "Hail to the victors," he said, head bent low.

Marques looked questioningly at Isabella, who only shrugged with a smile.

Samir raised a sharp eyebrow. "You are the victors, aren't you? You beat the captain's men?"

Marques nodded.

"Then hail to the victors," he repeated. "I am forever at your service."

Marques looked again to Isabella. "Where did you find this boy?"

She shrugged cheerfully.

"I pray that you will have mercy upon my worthless soul," he continued, turban nearly touching the wooden floor. "But even more than that, I pray that you will allow me to serve you and to swab the decks of your mighty ship."

To Marques's quizzical look, Isabella shrugged. "I guess he needs a job," she explained.

Marques was not interested. "I don't like corsairs." He tried to turn his attention to Isabella, but the young man interrupted.

"Oh, but I wouldn't be one anymore!" he cried. "I would be a member of your crew. If you want, I could even change my religion."

Marques raised an eyebrow. "Religion?"

"Yes, I can convert to anything you please. For example, I love Buddha! Is that what you are? I'd make a wonderful Buddhist."

"I'm not a Buddhist," drawled Marques, shaking his head.

"Hail Isis?"

"They'll still burn you in Spain for saying that."

"Uh . . . Mary?"

"You're getting closer."

"Then Hail Mary! May she bestow mercy upon us all!"

Marques rolled his eyes. "Look, if you want a job, we'll talk later. For now, you'll have to go join the other prisoners. Go!" He pointed toward the cabin door.

"You won't regret sparing my life!" he cried, making a clumsy exit. "And what a lovely lady you have. Her beauty is . . . well, it's something I would never notice, of course, because she belongs to you. Right?"

"Go!"

When he was sure the coast was clear of that imbecile, Marques drew Isabella into his arms. Though she was a little stiff and hesitant at first, he held her close, and pressed her head into his shoulder. He rubbed her back, and secured her under his chin until she had relaxed, and gotten used once again to being in a man's arms. "Are you all right?" he whispered, the joy of holding her again bringing him nearly to tears. "Did they hurt you? Any of them?"

Isabella breathed him into her. She could not believe he was here, could not believe he was real and solid. She breathed heavily against his warmth, trying to suck in his very essence. His chest was so sturdy, so hard, and so very real. She wanted to knock on it, to pound it, to reassure herself that it would never give way. But she settled for fumbling nervously with his shirt, trying to sense the tough skin beneath it. "They tried to," she whispered into his shoulder. "But I'm all right. I outwitted them."

"Look," he began, squeezing her tightly, trying to mold her to fit him perfectly. Trying to make her fit so well that she could not be unhooked. "Whatever they did to you, it doesn't matter. That is, it matters. But only because I shall avenge your suffering. I would not think less of you for having been their victim. Do you understand me?" He lifted her chin with a sturdy finger.

Isabella shook her head and tried to speak, but heavy emotion slowed her, and she could make no sound before Marques continued.

"I shall see that your wounds are tended," he said, his eyes moist with caring, "and in no way shall it affect how I feel . . . no matter what they did. It will not change that I . . ." He swallowed, for he had said it many times. But he had never before meant it. "That I love you," he said bravely. To her quizzical expression, he replied, "Yes, 'tis so. I would not have come for you otherwise. You may think me a knight now, but I am not. I would not have come for a woman I did not care for." It was an embarrassing confession, and one he'd not planned to make. But he could not lie to her anymore. He loved her. And even if it cost him the price of her legs spread before him tonight, he would tell her the truth. He was no knight.

To his surprise, Isabella broke into a wonderful smile. "Oh Marques," she said, her gray eyes sparkling from tears and good humor. "You have such a good heart, but such terrible ears. You never listen," she laughed. "I told you I'm not hurt. I've not been ravished. And I do not think you are a knight."

"You don't?" he asked, with both surprise and, strangely, a little disappointment.

"Heavens no," she breathed. "Marques, I have not been ravished, but I have been frightened out of my wits. Frightened out of my dreams." She took a deep breath and looked him straight in the eye. "You are naught but a man, Marques Santana. Nor is any other man more than that. My knight is gone from the prison of my imagination. But I shall gladly take flesh and blood in his stead."

Marques didn't quite know what all of this meant. Were his problems with Isabella over now? Had she come to realize what he feared she never would? Or was she merely traumatized? "Does this mean that you will return with me?" he asked.

"What choice do I have?" she laughed. "Shall I swim home?"

"That's not what I mean," he said, returning her smile. "I mean, will you stay on board? Will you . . . will you give me another chance?"

"Of course I will," she said quietly.

"Oh Isabella," he sighed, wrapping her back up in his arms, squeezing her and rocking her from side to side. "I'm so sorry I made you run off. Those other women . . . they were just . . . it was nothing, I—"

"I understand," she said, pulling free from his embrace.

His eyebrow lifted. "You do?"

"Yes," she whispered, placing a finger over his lips. "I had rejected you, and women are your vice. People always turn to their vices in times of trouble. I understand."

She really had done some soul-searching, it seemed. And it appeared to be to his benefit. He shook his head. No. He had sailed a long way and fought a tough battle to be here. He had not come just to earn her forgiveness. He had come for her heart. "Isabella," he said, holding her firmly by both shoulders. "About marriage. I . . . I know that what went wrong between us was about that. I know that you don't feel comfortable as my lover. I know that you want that bond that is sealed by the men of dry land. And I resist that, I'll admit. But I . . . well, you see. I . . . when you were gone . . . I just . . ." He ran a hand through his haggard hair. "I just think that I should do whatever it takes . . . I don't think I'll meet someone else who . . . oh blast it all, Isabella! You remind me of things like . . . oh, I don't know . . . like stars and clouds and sunsets and cold winds, and . . . all those things that most men forget. All those things that I, too, will forget if ever I find myself wed to a hardened, jaded old woman. As long as you are with me," he said, his face growing suddenly calm. "I know that I shall never grow bitter. I shall never . . . never become so involved with reality that I forget to die and go to heaven. So I . . . if it's what you really want. If you . . . then . . ."

Isabella had let him suffer this long, only because she wanted to hear the flattery. Now she put him out of his misery by lifting a finger to his lips. "No," she said with a smile. "No."

"No what?"

"No, I won't marry you," she informed him tenderly. "Not only because that is the clumsiest proposal I have ever witnessed," she laughed, "but more importantly, because you don't really want to."

"I don't?"

"No," she smiled, shaking her head. "You don't. And I shall not accept a proposal from your frantic tongue and fearful heart. When you're ready, then propose to me with a joyous heart, and a tongue that is guided by it."

Marques bowed his head in shame. "I suppose I was rather tongue tied."

"It's all right," she said, standing on her toes, planting a kiss on his firm lips. She opened her eyes and looked at him squarely. They both breathed heavily, stared at one another's eyes, and then broke simultaneously into an infectious smile. "For now, I will be your lover," she said.

Marques couldn't believe his luck. *Stop that,* he thought. *Stop calling it your luck. That's what you call it when you win the heart of an overly fussy, and overly sought-after beauty. When you win the heart of a woman who loves so selectively, so deeply, so vulnerably as Isabella, you call it an honor.* He couldn't believe how he was being honored. He grappled her into a forceful, steady kiss, trying to melt her with his hot breath, trying to topple her with his forceful pull, and yet rescue her with his powerful arms. When he felt her heart quicken beneath her breast and her trusting arms cling to him for safety, he felt he had just won a victory more virile than any he had won with his sword. Could it be that a man was truly nothing without a woman at his side? Could it be that devoting his heart to a single woman would make him more a man than bedding thousands every had?

Chapter Twenty-seven

The ship was loud with festivity that night. The Great Cabin was wild with very fast fiddling and very bad singing. The corsairs had some fresh meat on board, so now, the pirates enjoyed it on their behalf. The meal was not elegantly prepared, but quite tasty. The rumfustian flowed plentifully from goblets. The silver bowls splashed red wine all over the Great Table. Men tripped over chairs as they danced, then laughed at themselves and went on prancing. Golden lanterns swayed to the rhythm of waves beneath the ship. And though the pirates wore their usual, comfortable garb, some of the nonfighting ladies wore bright and lovely gowns to celebrate Isabella's return.

Isabella felt as if she had come home. Marques had bought her a soft gown from New Providence. It was a comfortable gown, a pirate's gown, but it looked beautiful. Made of sturdy dark gray to match her eyes and to hide stains, it was trimmed with silver lace at the elbow-length sleeves, and at the low-cut neck. Her breasts were pressed together and lifted, exaggerating and revealing her beautiful, though modest cleavage. But the dress was warm enough to fend off chilly winds, and it was rather loose in the waist, enabling her to take deep breaths. She wore the gown now, feeling it was the most beautiful she had ever possessed, though it was practical. And around her head, she wore a red scarf, marking her for the first time as a pirate. Everyone thought she looked adorable with a kerchief tied around her forehead, and her long, pale hair flowing freely beneath it. She pranced into the Great Hall, delighted, but embarrassed by all the attention she was getting.

"Oh Isabella!" cried Luisa, throwing her arms about the slender woman. "I was so worried about you!"

"Is all of this for me?" Isabella asked meekly.

"Well, sort of," she hedged. "Actually, I think they just like throwing parties. But I'm sure they're glad you're back!"

Isabella smiled with some relief that all this was not really just for her. "Well, tell me," she asked. "How was the rest of your stay in New Providence?"

"Ugh! What a story that is!" Luisa cried, "But come, let's go sit with Saada first. If we don't hurry, all the beef will be gone. And it's fresh!" She yanked Isabella by the arm.

Marques had dressed up for the occasion, out of respect for Isabella. He wore his finest black velvet, and plenty of golden buttons and pins. His black hair was tied neatly into a ponytail. He stood stoically near the door, watching over his crew as always, making sure their festivities did not get out of hand. He swigged from a goblet of wine, and made a point of laughing at a joke periodically, so that no one would think he was grim. But he was a little bothered by his arm. He'd taken a fairly serious whack to the left bicep during battle today. And though the ship's doctor had wrapped it and told him it would be fine, Marques knew the danger. There was no treatment for wounds that did not heal by themselves. All he could do was keep it wrapped, and hope that it mended without assistance. Because if it got worse rather than better, there would be only one way to save his life. Amputation.

The thought made him queasy. Marques considered himself to be a brave man, but the thought of having his arm sawn off, without any way to ease the pain, the thought of having a hook strapped to a stump of his bicep—it scared him. But he kept smiling, kept drinking, and continued to keep a watchful eye over his crew. He would not let them see his worry. He would let them think that the wound was not as deep as it was. Only he and the doctor need know the truth. But the more he thought about his arm, the more he sickened himself with images of amputation, the more the arm pained him. After a while, he thought it would be best to disappear and go on deck, lest his men notice he was out of sorts.

"Saada's true love wasn't on the island, so she didn't enjoy herself at all!" Luisa announced.

"That's not true," said Saada coolly. "I just didn't see anyone interesting, and didn't care to throw myself at the first ugly pirate I saw."

"Oh, was that aimed at me?" asked Luisa with a grin. "For your information, he was not ugly at all! He was tall and lean and knew how to use his hands!"

Isabella was horrified to hear such crude speech. Perhaps she wasn't yet a pirate, after all.

"Oh, don't be embarrassed," said Luisa, pinching her arm. "You should hear Saada and me when we really get going."

When their laughter died down, both women looked at Isabella. They cleared their throats and drank silently for a moment, wondering how to approach the obviously intrusive and delicate subject they so desperately wanted to broach.

"So," said Saada at last, being the bolder of the two, "you must have had a very trying experience."

Isabella paid close attention to the slab of chewy beef in her hand. "Yes," she nodded, without looking up.

Saada and Luisa exchanged looks. "Are you all right?" asked Luisa timidly.

Isabella nodded, her mouth full of food, her eyes turned away.

The women were disappointed. They were, of course, genuinely concerned for their friend. They wanted to know what had happened because they wanted to share in her grief and console her. But perhaps even stronger was the urge to hear the juicy details of how she had been captured by corsairs and repeatedly ravished. There was nothing quite so thrilling as tragedy, so long as it was happening to someone else. "Have you seen the doctor?" Luisa asked, thinking that might just be the way to learn exactly what had happened.

"No," said Isabella quietly. "I told Marques there was no need."

"Oh." Luisa bowed her head. "Well, that's very good. Then they didn't . . . wound you or anything?"

Saada kicked her under the table.

Isabella finished her last bite of supper, then rose to her feet. "I'm . . . I'm fine. Really I am. But I, uh . . . I hope you'll excuse me if I go get some rest a little early tonight."

"Of course," said Luisa with wide, guilty eyes. "You should get rest."

"Thank you. I'm sorry," nodded Isabella, "I'm sorry. It's wonderful to be back. Good night."

"Good night," they said simultaneously.

When Isabella was out of sight, Saada kicked Luisa again. "Now look what you did!"

"I know," apologized Luisa. "I was being nosy. I feel terrible."

"And even worse, you didn't get any gossip."

Luisa looked at Saada with horror, and then burst into a dark giggle. "We are so awful," she laughed guiltily.

"Of course we are. We're pirates," grinned Saada.

"Oh yes. Pirates are hunted at all corners of the seven seas because of our horrible gossiping."

"That's right," laughed Saada. "That, and our terrible fashion sense."

They both laughed and refilled their goblets.

* * *

Isabella had thought she would find Marques in their cabin. This was the real reason she had returned. She wasn't enjoying being asked so many personal questions. She felt ashamed and embarrassed by her capture. She wanted to get away from the interrogation, and she wanted to do something she would enjoy instead. Kissing Marques had come to mind. But when she found the cabin empty, she was disappointed and decidedly unsleepy. She knew that Marques was not in the Great Cabin, so she wrapped herself in a cape and tried the deck. The air smelled clean and brisk. The wind was wild. The stars were magnificent. And Marques looked so handsome leaning against the rail in his black velvet, she could have eaten him alive.

"Is the party over?" he asked, seeing her float toward him like a spirit carried by the wind. Her yellow hair blew behind her, her pink cheeks were specked with saltwater, and her cloak blended into the night.

"Not yet," she said. "I just thought I'd come visit you."

"Well, I'm glad you did," he replied, inviting her to share the railing.

"I have missed you," she confessed, watching the black waves make war with the ship's sturdy starboard.

"Obviously, I missed you too," he replied, lifting one half of his mouth into a smile.

"Oh, how is your arm?" she asked, noting how his sleeve swelled over the bandaging.

"It's fine," he said, self-consciously grabbing it. "It'll be fine."

"Good," she replied. "Because I'd hoped you were not too wounded to kiss me." She flushed at her own daring.

Marques took on the look of a tiger. "Never," he said suavely. "Never too wounded to do that." He pulled her against him with his good arm. Isabella felt him against her, so hard and strong, and knew she had started something she could not stop. But she liked it. She liked it so well that she slipped into that tunnel of her mind which lay somewhere between her reason and her fantasies. Marques assaulted her with a gentle kiss, leaving her room to stop this now. When he released her lips, he looked at her questioningly, inviting her to turn away. And at first, that seemed to be her plan.

"I have missed your ship, Captain," she smiled, finding it somehow amusing to call him "Captain" in the midst of their passionate friendship.

Marques grinned, enjoying the sound of the word as it came from her lips. "I am glad."

"I have grown accustomed to your ways, I think. I am no longer wearing my corsets."

"Good." He nodded his approval. "Those things are barbaric."

Isabella's stomach tickled and taunted her as she prepared to say her next line. "In fact," she worked up her courage to say. She did not finish. His hand was still on the small of her back, pressing her gently against him, making her knees weak. "In fact," she giggled, turning bright red, "I, uh . . . I'm not . . ."

"You're not what?" he assisted. His face was blank, as he had no idea what she was going to say.

Isabella placed a trembling hand on his velvet coat. "I'm not wearing anything under my dress."

Marques' eyebrows shot up. "Madam," he said, moving so close to her that he was breathing on her forehead. "If I didn't know better, I would think you were seducing me."

Isabella gave in to the call of the wild ocean. "What could you possibly know that is better than that?" she asked.

Marques was so aroused he forgot all about his arm. With a firm finger, he lifted the skirts of her gown, not allowing her to pull away from him in shyness. His finger trickled up the bare flesh of her leg, then squeezed between her tight thighs. "My God," he observed, pinning her against him in a squeeze. "You really aren't wearing anything, are you?"

She shook her head.

He moved his finger into the folds of her thighs, and then into the folds beyond. She was moist. So moist that he knew she was waiting for him. He knew that she had really missed him. He violated her with a gentle glide until his hand could reach no further. "Shall we go to the cabin?" he whispered in her ear.

"No," she whispered passionately. "No, I want to stay right here. Right on the open deck with the wind in my hair and the oily sky above."

"We could be seen," he warned. "Not likely, but possible."

Isabella was perspiring now, she was so eager. "Let them see," she rasped out. "I want to make love outdoors, like birds, like dolphins. Like the gods themselves did before we came along and disturbed their peace."

Marques did not have to be held at gunpoint. He looked around him for a comfortable place to lay her down.

"Right here," she interrupted him, turning his cheek with a finger. "Right here on the rail." She backed herself up until she was nearly sitting on it.

"But you could fall off," he said.

"Keep me from falling off," she begged, reaching for his face. "Hold me up. Don't let me fall to my death."

Marques lifted her—with two strong arms—and placed her gently on the railing. He had to hold her steadily, or else truly, she would fall in. Especially the way she was leaning backward, letting her hair fall overboard, tempting the winds to topple her. He lowered his breeches, and noticed with a sly grin that Isabella was pulling down the top of her dress. "And I thought you were shy," he teased.

"Only when I'm thinking," she replied intensely. "Don't let me think, Marques. Take me."

Her knees were opened wide for him. All he needed to do was lift the skirt. When he did, and he saw her golden silk, he could not hold back. He had to taste her before taking her.

"No!" she cried, when she felt the softness of his tongue. "Don't tease me. Just take me."

"Don't give your captain orders," he teased slyly. Then he returned to his moist, tender feast. She struggled a little, and that scared him, for he did not want her to fall. But he held her firmly, and licked her with what were indeed teasing laps. He tickled her with his tongue, then paused, enjoying her torment. Then he did it again, until he felt that the game had turned truly cruel. He dove in with hard, circular, steady pressure. He loved the way she squealed. He loved the colors of his supper— all gold and pink. And he loved how tender and sensitive she was to every one of his tongue's flicks. He pulled away and looked once more. How lovely it would be to call this woman his. Was that why some men chose marriage?

He thrust his hips forward, readjusting his hold on her, making certain she was safe. "I'll do it slowly," he promised, not having forgotten that she'd been bedded only once. "Don't worry. I'll be very gentle."

"Don't be," she pleaded, her face wet from the ocean's splashing and from her own excited hunger. "Do it as it was meant to be done. Be rough. Show me how it feels to be you. I want to know. I want to know how you really feel. Don't hold anything back."

Again, Marques did not need to be threatened with a cutlass. He was only too eager to cater to the lady's deliciously indecent request. With a heavy thrust, he cut into her like a barbarian. Isabella yelled. She loved it. She had always wanted to understand what the nuns had tried to protect her from. And now she really knew. Marques kept pushing, and pushing, showing her no mercy and no gentleness. His teeth were clenched, and his body was a vessel of destruction. Isabella was being bounced brutally, a huge, wondrous smile upon her face. Her breasts were jiggling, raw and naked in the cold air. Her hair was dipping low, near the crashing waves. Every time she opened her eyes, she saw magic. The magic of night and starshine. And never did the thrusting slow down.

Marques had rarely gotten the opportunity to express his darker half in the bedroom. He had so perfected the art of seducing women and pleasuring them that he had nearly forgotten how to be savage. This was a joy. Somewhere in the back of his mind, he hoped that he was not hurting Isabella. But consciously, he simply watched her pink-tipped breasts wrinkle under the cold. He watched her shake, and felt his power to make her do so. He listened to the ocean—the ocean he loved more than life itself. And he felt just as evil and as rich as those black waters. Isabella was so fair, so delicate. And he was brutalizing her with his lust. It was glorious, and thrilling, and empowering. He burst faster than he ever had before. He forced his seeds into her, making her take them, making her swallow them into her womb. And then he took a deep breath.

"Are you all right, angel?" He pulled out of her with a gradual, careful slide.

She was red faced and panting. "No," she gasped.

He furrowed his eyebrows. "I was too brutal with you?" he asked worriedly.

"No," she whispered. "I just . . . I'm just not . . . finished."

"Oh, that!" he grinned, lifting her from the railing and placing her on her feet. "Well, I think we can take care of that." He squeezed her tightly, putting both hands on her naked bottom. She was limp against him, desperate for help, desperate to be freed of her lustful discomfort. He did not tease her. He slid his fingers into her from behind. He left one free so that he could stroke the front of her swollen flesh while the rest of his hand plunged into her. He rubbed her in this way, thankful for a lifetime of practice. This was, after all, not an easy feat. She breathed against him, absently digging her teeth into his black vest while her fingers clenched and unclenched against his biceps.

Marques stroked the front of her, while dipping over and over into her center. She became wild, feeling the sea breeze against her naked backside, and Marques's hand violating her in every conceivable way. She gasped and bit and then, at last, broke into a wild yell. A yell that lasted so long, it sounded like that of a wild dog. It sounded like a werewolf's cry. Marques held her and rocked her against him. "What a beautiful cry,'' he whispered. ''What a beautiful woman, what a beautiful ecstasy.''

Isabella whimpered against him, still shaking, yet feeling so comforted by his embrace. She wanted to stay there all night. She wanted to stay there forever. Marques kissed her hair, and rubbed her back. It seemed as though they were the only two people on earth, out there under the flickering stars.

''Hi, you two! How're you doing?''

Marques and Isabella jumped. It was Saada and Luisa. They were just coming up the stairs. They looked down to make sure they were mostly dressed. They were, thank goodness. Marques made a quick move to neaten up his breeches. ''Hello,'' Isabella greeted, terror in her eyes.

''Pretty up here, isn't it?'' asked Luisa, jumping up to sit on the rail.

''The party was getting dull,'' explained Saada, ''so we thought we'd see what the two of you were up to.''

''Nothing, as you can see,'' said Marques, grabbing Isabella by the hand. ''But I think it's time for us to retire.'' He led her forcefully toward the stairs.

''Good night!'' Saada and Luisa called in unison. They both waved like the most proper of ladies, then Saada handed Luisa some snuff from a canister. With the most complacent of smiles upon their lips, they watched Isabella and Marques disappear. Then at the same moment, they burst into laughter.

''We are so evil,'' said Saada. ''Why is it so much fun to embarrass people who are making love?''

''I don't know,'' laughed Luisa hysterically. ''But boy, we'd better rob another ship soon. Because you and I get so evil when we're bored.'' They laughed again. ''I'm glad I'm a pirate and I don't have to behave.''

''Yes, that's another thing pirates are famous for,'' Saada teased. ''We're out on these dangerous waters, gossiping, and embarrassing happy couples everywhere.''

They burst into another fit of laughter.

* * *

Isabella spent the night in Marques's arms. It was the first time she had ever shared a bed with a man—and slept. To her, it was another new, intriguing experience. She marveled that the arm he'd wrapped around her did not fall asleep. "I don't know why," he answered peacefully, "it just doesn't." She was surprised when he urged her to lay her head upon his bare chest. She could hear his heartbeat. Her fingers could not refrain from combing his coarse, dark chest hair. She wondered whether he minded her exploration of his chest and his belly. It was not an erotic search for her, but one based solely on curiosity. She wanted to know what a man felt like. "No, I don't mind," he assured her, "though if you start testing for muscle, I'll be forced to flex. Vanity, you know."

One candle still flickered in the darkness. Isabella had not wanted to blow it out. She wanted to keep her eyes wide open, to see as well as feel the presence of her man. Her man. Could she call him that yet? She supposed not. Without marriage, there were no promises. But she would settle for what they had, for she had never been so happy and excited in all her life. "Why do couples sleep together after they make love?" she asked, circling his belly button with a gentle finger. "What does sleep have to do with making love?"

Marques scratched his short beard. "Well," he mused aloud, "I suppose for the most part they simply collapse there. I mean, once you're in bed making love, why not just stay put?" He gave the matter another moment's thought. "But I suspect there is another reason. I suspect that most people like to know that their lovers are still with them, even after the heat of the moment has passed."

Isabella could not help asking the first question that came to her mind. "But you don't like women to stay, do you?" she asked. "When you bed a woman, you leave her to her freedom."

"I suppose that was true before I met you," he admitted

uncomfortably. "But still, I believe that even back then, whenever I would take a woman, I imagined for one moment that I was claiming her as mine forever. Just as," he added, "I imagine they pretended I would stay." He was suddenly muted by guilt. The thought had never occurred to him before. Not like this. Had he been a cruel bastard to all of those women he bedded? He suddenly thought of a thousand trusting brown eyes, and a thousand gentle blue ones. What had he done?

Isabella broke him away from his thoughts. "Do you believe in destined mates?" she asked, tickling his waist with her fingertips.

"What?" he asked disinterestedly. "You mean, people who were made just for one another?"

"Yes," she said dreamily, watching the candlelight dance on his rough skin.

"I doubt it," he said, "but I don't know. I've never understood much about magic or God or anything. Couldn't stay awake in church as a boy."

Isabella smiled and rolled to her stomach. She looked him right in his beautiful bright blue eyes. "I believe we were made for each other," she whispered, touching his long, dark hair.

"I know so little about you," he said, looking into her mysterious, misty eyes. "Tell me. Tell me something. Anything about you." He reached up and clasped her forehead in his palm. "Give me a glimpse at this woman who has stolen my heart."

"What do you want to know?" she asked.

"I don't know, uh . . . you were raised in a convent. Why don't you tell me how your parents died?"

"Murdered," she said distantly, deceptively emotionlessly. She felt she could tell him anything, felt that they were alone on this ship, the closest of playmates, the most bonded of bosom friends.

"Murdered?" he asked with a startle. "How awful!" He reached to comfort her, but she would not receive his gesture.

"It's too late to console me," she said, though there was no resentment in her voice. "It happened so long ago that medicine will only reach a scar. It's too late to heal the wound."

Marques swallowed. "Did they catch them? Did they catch the murderers?"

"They *are* the murderers," she told him. She ran her thumb along his eyebrow.

"What do you mean?"

"My parents were publicly executed. It was all good and legal."

Marques squinted in his confusion. "Why?"

She tried to smile. She rubbed her nose against his. "Do you want to guess?"

He shook his head, unable to think of a single guess.

"The Inquisition."

"Ohhhh," said Marques with a sigh. "Are they still doing that? I thought they'd lost some of their zeal."

"Some of it," she replied, "but not all of it."

He tried to ask something, but his voice caught in his throat. "Did you . . . did . . ."

"Did I see it?" she asked. "Yes." Her eyes were so foggy that he could scarcely see her pupils. "I was required to watch. They said it was good for me to see what became of heretics. Then the nuns took me in to make doubly certain I would grow up understanding Godliness. Kind of them, wasn't it?" she asked. There was so much pain in her that none of it reached her face.

"You poor thing," Marques whispered, touching her delicate cheek with his knuckles. "No wonder you . . ."

"No wonder I'm strange?" she asked. "Yes, the nuns noticed that too. That's why they were harder on me than on the other girls. They feared I had too much of my parents in me—feared if they didn't beat me, I would become as eccentric as they were."

Marques felt an ache for her that he did not know how to express. He didn't know what to do. He knew what she'd said was right, that it was too late to cure a badly healed wound.

She had already adjusted, already gone a little mad. He could not rescue her from the past. Blast it all. Why did he have to be a human? Why couldn't he have been a knight after all?

"What do you call them?" she asked wistfully. "Men of dry land?"

He nodded with an awkward swallow.

"Why do you call them that?"

It took him a moment to collect himself, to get over his pain at hearing her tale. But when he could, he croaked out, "Because they live on dry land, I suppose. And because . . . because they belong there. Because their hearts are not rich enough for the ocean. All they know of the ocean is its danger, never its beauty. All they know of passion is wrath." He paused to scratch his arm. "Isabella?"

She flashed him a bright smile. "Yes?"

"I do believe in destined mates," he announced.

She was startled. "You do?"

"Yes."

"Why the change?"

He lifted his left arm. Slowly, but without caution, he unwrapped its bandaging. Isabella gasped when she saw the horrible dried blood which encrusted his skin. "Look," he said.

"It looks terrible!" she cried.

He shook his head. "No. It's healing."

"It is?"

"Yes." He scratched it heavily. "It itches."

"So?"

"So that means it's healing." He tossed his bandage to the floor, and lifted Isabella over him. "And it only started itching when you told me your story, when you let me see who you are." He lowered her for an amorous kiss. "Thank you."

Chapter Twenty-eight

Isabella learned that the ship was heading for Madeira. The corsair vessel, which had been turned over to the galley slaves after being plundered of its loot, had carried some marvelous treasure. The crew wanted to sell their shares for more gold, and Madeira was an excellent place to do this. In addition, Marques and the other crew who'd been born there wanted to visit their families. Isabella didn't know whether to be delighted or petrified. It would be fun to meet Marques's family—the very idea of his having one was somewhat amusing. And yet what would they think of her? She was not his bride, not yet a sworn member of his crew. How would she be introduced? And how would she be received?

"You'll be my fiancée," Marques announced once she'd voiced her concern. "I'll not have you shamed before my mother."

"That is very kind of you," said Isabella with relief. "I was . . . worried."

He gave her a quick kiss on the cheek. "Did you think I

would introduce you as my lover? You know how men of dry land feel about women who are bedded out of wedlock.''

''Yes, I know,'' she said, ''but I feared you'd not want to lie.''

''Not want to lie?'' he chuckled. ''Are you joking? I'm a pirate. And speaking of lies . . . my mother doesn't know that, so keep it hush.''

Isabella's mouth fell open. She could not quite make the sound of laughter. She was too stunned. ''Marques!''

''Yes?'' he asked nonchalantly.

''Your . . . your . . . your mother.'' She began to tremble with laughter. ''Your mother doesn't know you're a pirate?''

He wrinkled his brow. ''But of course not.''

''Then . . . then what does she think?''

''Merchant,'' he shrugged. ''She thinks I'm captain of my own merchant ship, which is not quite a lie. We do carry goods overseas, and we do sell them. . . .''

''Marques! I can't believe you!'' she gasped, a huge, disbelieving grin on her face.

''You think that's bad?'' he asked. ''Wait until you meet my sister.''

''Why?''

''My mother thinks she's a successful businesswoman—owning and running her own family establishment.''

''And in truth?''

''The only 'family' members who frequent her brothel are discontented husbands.''

Isabella laughed outloud. ''I cannot believe this! How do you both keep this from your mother?''

''Wait until you meet her, and you'll understand. A sweet, endearing woman. But not the brightest one you've ever met.''

Isabella put both fists on her hips. ''Marques! How can you speak that way of your own mother?''

He put his arm around her, and urged her toward the cabin door. It was nearly breakfast time. They'd been up since dawn, watching the sunrise pierce the morning mist. Isabella had been true to her word, and had awakened with him each morning all week to sneak above deck before the rest of the crew, and watch this spectacular event. They were always furiously hungry by the breakfast hour, for they'd been up so long already without fare. "Actually," he said, escorting her toward the Great Cabin, "I thank her for not being very bright. If she'd been brilliant, she never would have wed my father, and then I'd not have been born."

"Marques!" she scolded him. "Now you insult them both?"

"No, no. I love my mother," he grumbled.

"And your father?"

"Glad he's dead." Marques walked briskly ahead, leaving a gaping Isabella in his wake.

Isabella did not ask again about Marques's father. She kept herself occupied during the day by milking goats, helping to clean up after meals, and playing with Pedro. In the evenings, if Marques was not too exhausted, they made wild love. If he was completely spent, they just snuggled in bed, letting their body heat mingle under the light of a flickering candle, which was not extinguished until neither of them could keep their eyes open a moment longer. They hated to sleep in each other's company. They wanted to savor every moment they had, wanted to be awake, and able to enjoy it. Even if they were too exhausted to speak. Pirates and drifting, penniless damsels never knowing what lied ahead. They had no illusions about their mortality. They kept grasping and pinching each other in their sleep.

But one morning, the crew awakened to the glorious sight of purple mountains rising from the ocean. Isabella could not believe it. After all these months, she would be returning to the start of her journey. Madeira. The convent girls had said it was magnificent, but she had never dreamed it would be like this. The island was really nothing more than a mountain which had grown too tall to stay underwater. The shore was nothing short of sharp cliffs plunging into the sea. There was no sand, but only pebbles and rocks, reminders of times when the cliffs had lost their balance. Isabella could see tropical plants everywhere that the rocks would let them grow. Banana trees, rows of sugarcane, and of course, how could an island call itself Portuguese without grapevines? Port was practically the national beverage.

"This is Funchal," Gabriel whispered in her ear. "It's the capital."

As the ship docked, she noticed that theirs was not the only vessel bearing a pirate flag.

"This island is plagued by pirates," Gabriel explained to her. "Isn't that endearing? To be called a plague?"

She smiled, but her eyes were fixed straight ahead. If she could have imagined paradise, this might have been it.

She felt quite useless as the men emptied the hold of treasure. She stood awkwardly on the pebbled shore, watching them sweat. But fortunately, the mountains kept distracting her. She could not believe how high they rose above her. And were the tops truly purple? Was the air around her truly purple? The town was paved with narrow, black roads, moving up and down steep hills. The hills between storefronts were so treacherous that the elderly rode in wheeled ox carts. A walk through town looked exhausting. But at least, it would be a beautiful stroll, for the black pebbled streets were lined with red roses. And the whitewashed storefronts looked welcoming.

"I'll take you shopping later in the week," Marques promised.

Isabella was startled, for she had not heard his approach.

"Didn't mean to scare you," he said, noting the hand which had flung to her breast.

Isabella sighed her relief. "This is the most beautiful place I have ever seen."

"Glad you like it," he said cheerfully. "And now for the best part. Ready to meet my family?"

Something about the way he said that made her very wary. And his mischievous grin didn't help either.

Chapter Twenty-nine

"Marques! Can it be? You're home!"

A short, pale-eyed woman with a gray bun full of hair wrapped her arms around her sturdy son's waist.

"And you've brought a lovely lady with you!" she exclaimed. She wrapped both arms around a very unsuspecting Isabella. So much for awkward introductions. It seemed Isabella was already part of the family, though she hadn't yet said a word.

"Oh, don't you look handsome," she said to her son. "Are you eating enough?"

"Yes, Mother."

"Are you remembering to stay warm at night? You know, it's awfully cold out there on the sea."

"Yes, Mother."

She looked lovingly at Isabella. "And by the way, who is this?"

Marques took Isabella's hand. "This is my fiancée."

"Oh!" cried the woman, clasping her cheeks. "How marvelous! You're finally getting married! But what happened to . . . what's her name? I thought you were going to marry her."

"She ran off," he replied hurriedly.

"I'll bet," said a deep female voice from the corner of the room.

Marques and Isabella both looked up to see a tall, handsome woman with long, chestnut hair, flashing blue eyes, and two fists on her hips.

"Oh, that's right!" cried the elder Mrs. Santana. "I almost forgot to tell you. Your sister is already here."

Marques smiled at the robust young woman as one reunited with an old friend, a friend with whom he had shared many secrets. "Maria," he said warmly, moving toward the girl in a fluid motion. He lifted her into his arms and spun her around. "Heavier every time I see you," he teased, dropping her with feigned exhaustion.

"And every time I see *you,*" she countered, "you seem to have a new true love. Who is this? Does she know your name yet?"

He scowled, showing her that he actually cared about this one. Maria instantly shut up.

"Well, come in," said their mother. "Come sit down, all of you. I'll bring you some port."

The house was modest, but charming. Buried in a grove of trees, a good hour's walk from town, it was small and white with a red tiled roof, and grapevines climbing all the way up its walls. The inside was sparsely furnished, but decorated with lovely, homemade lace. Even the couch was trimmed with Mrs. Santana's special pink crocheting. "It's so good to see you all," said the kind old woman. Catalina Santana had once had bright blue eyes like her children's, but with age, they had paled to cornflower. She was petite, but broad shouldered and well fed. There was a distance in her face, a lack of awareness. But that only made her appear kinder.

Her daughter, Maria, had a very different look about her. Tall and strong, she had thick, powerful chestnut hair. Her blue eyes were so big and round, that she seemed always to be startled. But her lips were narrow, tight, and savvy. "I'm just glad I made it here in one piece," she said, sipping liquor from her teacup. "What, with all of the pirates in this town." She met Marques's eyes with a sly grin. He shook his head scoldingly, but with a smile that said, "I'll get you for that."

"Yes," he said, stretching his arms out along the sofa, nearly touching Isabella's shoulder. "Well, I suppose it's the local culture that draws them," he said. "So many brothels and dens of sin."

"Oh yes!" exclaimed Catalina. "I hear it's just awful nowadays. You know, when I was young, we didn't have any brothels. Life was so simple in those days."

Her three guests all blinked rapidly at her, trying to think of some way to reply. Then simultaneously, they all broke into fidgeting. "Anyhow."

"Well, what I want to hear about," began Maria with delicious mischief in her eyes, "is the wedding. How exciting that you're engaged, Marques!"

He looked at her comically and coldly. "Why, thank you, dear sister. How is business going?"

"Quite well," she replied. "Oh my! I've just had the most wonderful idea! Mother? What do you say we go to town and have Isabella's wedding gown made while she's here?"

Isabella started to protest.

"Oh, no!" cried Maria. "I absolutely insist. Don't you, Mother?"

"Ah yes," said the elderly woman with a light in her eyes. "I remember when I was being fitted for my wedding gown. What a joy it was."

Marques was shaking his head at Maria. "I hate you," he mouthed, though there was a big grin on his face.

Maria kissed the air at him.

"Are you going to wear white?" Catalina asked Isabella, a warm smile upon her face.

Everyone froze. They couldn't believe what the sweet old woman had just asked.

"Well, she could also wear off-white or silver," the woman explained. "It's a lady's choice, you know."

Everyone relaxed.

Isabella did not know what to say. She looked helplessly at Marques.

"Well, what did your other fiancées choose, dear brother?" Maria asked snidely.

He scowled in her direction. "I don't know, my beloved angel of a sister. What do you suppose you'll choose? Oh, that's right. You're not yet engaged. I nearly forgot. Why is that?"

Maria grimaced.

"Yes," asked Catalina. "Why haven't you yet chosen a husband? Such a successful woman you are—running your own uh . . . place." She finished her sentence with a look of puzzlement, for she just realized she didn't know what sort of a "place" Maria ran. But the thought fled as quickly as it had come. "So why can't you use those same wiles to land you a husband?"

Isabella winced. Wiles. Wiles to land a husband. The thought repulsed her. It was so terribly unromantic. And yet, here she was, with no wiles at all, and surely enough—no husband. For a moment, she felt cheated, taken advantage of. She looked steadily at Marques's profile. He had nearly proposed to her on the corsair vessel. But she had not accepted his stuttering request. Because she did not want to gain a husband who did not love her passionately, and who did not ache to carry her to the altar. That was why she would never develop wiles. For who wanted a husband who had been tricked? Perhaps she was not missing out, any more than all of those women in the world who had reluctant men at their sides.

"I just haven't found the right one," Maria sang to her mother. She worked hard to think of a good change of topic.

"What?" asked Marques, still not satisfied he had repaid

her for those jokes at Isabella's expense. "You haven't met one single man in all of the days since you've left home? But I could have sworn I've seen you with men."

She scowled. "Enough," she mouthed. When he only grinned at her, she retorted by changing the subject. "Speaking of my successes, Mother. I fear mine are quite insignificant compared to those of your son. Tell us, Marques. How is the uh . . . merchant business going?"

"It makes a man hungry," he replied, quite finished with their game. "Mother, may we assist you in the kitchen?"

"Well," she said slowly, "if Maria and Isabella would help me carry in the heavy platters, that would be nice. I can't lift things as well as I used to."

"I can do that," volunteered Marques, rising to his feet.

"No, no, that's ladies' work," his mother objected.

Marques, who had been living and fighting alongside women for some time now, did not heed such senseless social conventions. "A lady's job is to do whatever she's best at," he said. "Same as a man's." He gave a kind smile to his aging mother. "And I happen to be very good at carrying things. Come, show me what needs to be brought in."

When he'd gotten his mother alone in the kitchen, Marques bent down and planted a kiss upon the old woman's forehead. "Mother," he said in a low voice that could not be heard from the parlor. "Please take this." He slipped her a pouch full of gold.

"Oh," she croaked excitedly. "You don't need to bring money every time you come home, Marques. Your father left me with a little stashed away."

"Take it," he repeated. "You don't have enough. I can see that the roof has not been repaired in twenty years, and you've not bought a single trinket for the parlor."

"Well, I don't like to be wasteful," she confessed.

"Just take it." He turned from her so there would be no further argument.

"I'm so proud of you," she said, wrapping both arms around

his waist. Marques struggled not to drop the platter of baked fish he had just lifted. "You have grown so tall, and so wealthy," she said, burying her face in his back.

"Well, a man must learn to take care of himself," he said distantly. "No one else will do it for him."

"I must have done something right when I raised you," she squealed delightedly, letting him out of her embrace with several affectionate pats.

Marques closed his eyes for a moment. "Well. . . ." He thought about all the years she had knitted quietly while his father beat him. "You . . . you tried your very best, and suffered much on my behalf. Come, shall we eat?"

"Of course," she answered warmly. "Oh Maria! Will you bring us a bottle of port from the wine cellar?"

"Yes, Mother!" she called back. "Shall I bring one for the rest of you, too?"

Catalina was not a gourmet chef, but she knew how to cook in bulk. There was enough baked fish, fried banana, and spicy sweet potato pie for ten people. Isabella had never been inclined to eat heavily, as she found her appetite usually quite eased by a small amount of food. More than one helping gave her a stomachache. But she was so relieved to be eating something other than pirate food, she found herself heaping fried banana onto her plate, just for the joy of tasting them. She hoped she would not make herself sick. "Isabella," Maria began after shoving a spoonful of sweet potatoes into her mouth. "Do tell me. Where are you from?"

Isabella chewed carefully, and did not reply until she had swallowed in full. "Costa Verde," she replied, lifting a napkin to her lips.

"Ahh, I've been there once," said Maria. "Nice place. So what did you do there? Were you a farmer's daughter?"

Isabella shook her head. "No," she said uncomfortably. "I lived in a convent."

Maria laughed outloud. "A nun? You were a nun?"

Marques laughed right back at her. "Try again, Maria. You can do it."

She was silent for a moment, pursing her thin lips. "Oh!" she cried at last. "You mean that you were *raised* in a convent."

Isabella nodded, her mouth full of fish.

"Then I imagine my brother had much to teach you," she smiled devilishly.

Marques scowled warningly.

Seeing that he was not smiling, even a little, Maria backed off. "So how did you two meet?" she asked diplomatically.

Isabella looked frantically at Marques. "I . . . I . . ."

"She was a passenger aboard my ship," Marques explained on her behalf. "She was trying to reach Madeira, and since I was coming here myself, I thought I would bring her."

Maria touched her heart. "Oh, Marques. What a gentleman you are. I suppose you agreed to it even before you saw her, eh?"

He scowled with amusement in his eyes. "But of course. I never notice women's beauty when I'm on the job."

Maria laughed heartily. "Good one." Marques joined in her amusement this time.

Catalina did not really understand what her children were talking about, but she loved to watch them bicker, for she simply loved to see them in motion. It was as though they were putting on a play for her, and she got to watch her very own children be natural, and be themselves. She always looked forward to their visits. Living alone was a hard thing for a woman who had once had a husband and two small children. "I'm afraid I don't have enough spare rooms," she apologized to her guests. "Isabella, do you mind sharing a bedroom with Maria?"

Isabella didn't want to. She liked Maria, because she could see that Marques liked her, but she felt that Maria was laughing at her. And she didn't want to sleep beside someone who thought she was a joke. But what could she say? *No thank you,*

I'd rather sleep with your son? Probably not a good idea. So she nodded hesitantly and murmured, "That will be fine."

"Don't worry," Maria nudged her, "I don't sleep much. You'll probably be unconscious before I even change into my nightgown."

Isabella smiled. She was glad that Maria didn't mind sharing a room. She was glad Maria didn't really have anything against her. Maybe she could live with being a joke for a few weeks.

Everyone helped clean the dishes, including Marques, despite his mother's protests. The guests thanked their hardworking hostess for an excellent meal, and then, the elderly woman announced her need to retire. "I have prepared all of your beds," she said, "and placed flowers in the vases. If you need anything, please wake me up."

Everyone smiled, for who would be crass enough to do such a thing? "Good night," Marques said to his mother, kissing her cheek with affection.

"Sleep well, Mother," said Maria, offering a strong hug.

"Uh . . . yes. Sleep . . . sleep well," said Isabella awkwardly, offering a little flick of a wave. She felt so out of place.

"Can't wait to have a new daughter-in-law," said Catalina assuringly. "But what ever did happen to that other one?" she asked Marques one more time.

"Disappeared," he repeated. "Just vanished. Good night, Mother."

"Good night." She crept into her bedroom, and closed the door as gently as a mouse.

Everyone sighed. They looked at each other, the three young people finally on their own and at ease. It was time to break out another bottle of port, and *really* talk. "Mind if I light a cigar?" Maria asked.

"Please do," said Marques.

"Want one?"

"No, thank you. But please offer one to Isabella." He disappeared into the wine cellar.

Maria stuck a thin cigar out in Isabella's direction. She shook her head, appalled. She did not know that ladies ever smoked cigars. Luisa and Saada has used snuff, of course. But somehow, she'd grown to see that as less shocking. Maria shrugged and lit up.

"Here we are," said Marques, planting glasses and a bottle of violet port before the ladies. "Ahhh." He collapsed on the sofa, and stretched out.

"Are you glad to be home?" asked Maria.

He shook his head. "Not really. But it's good to see Mother."

"Same here," she said, blowing out a smoke ring.

"Maria, I've wanted to talk to you," he began, leaning forward with concern. "I want to know why you're still working at that brothel. I thought I'd given you enough money to quit."

Maria laughed. "Marques, there is no such thing as 'enough money.' "

He smiled but remained persistent. "I don't like my sister having to keep such a job. I accept it as your choice, but I want to be sure you're not doing it out of necessity."

"Well, I'm not doing it for pleasure," she laughed. "There's nothing fun about catering to a bunch of sweaty old men."

"Then quit," he demanded.

"Marques, I can't." Her huge blue eyes were more honest than Isabella had yet seen them. "I have a lot of habits. I need the money."

"What habits?" he asked nervously.

She shrugged and looked away.

Marques swallowed. He rested his elbows on his knees and rubbed his rough hands together. Finally, with a gruff sigh, he asked, "Opium?"

She nodded.

He sighed.

Isabella blinked.

Marques bowed his head. "Maria, I know you're not a saint. Neither of us is. But wouldn't it be worth dropping the habit if it meant you could quit that job?"

"Nothing would be worth dropping the habit," she informed him. "It's my only pleasure, the only thing I look forward to."

He lifted his head and met her eyes once more. "What if I raised your allowance? Would that help?"

"Wouldn't be enough," she answered, eyes fixed on the wall. "Not unless you're raking in a lot more gold than I know about."

Marques breathed heavily, thinking, worrying.

At last, Maria changed the subject. "What about you, brother? Is all well? Are you happy?"

His eyes twinkled at Isabella. "Yes, I am."

Maria caught that look. "So this is real?" she asked, waving a finger between the two of them. "You two are really . . ."

"Not engaged," he said. "You know how I feel about marriage."

"About the same way I do, I imagine," she snickered, flicking her cigar ashes.

Marques shared her smile. "Yes, probably about the same way. But Isabella and I do plan to spend our lives together."

"Plans are cheap," Maria said flatly. "No promises means no promises. Remember that." She nudged Isabella. "Keep nagging him for that ring."

Isabella stunned them both by speaking. Her voice was quiet, and her demeanor shy. But her words were clear enough. "I don't want a promise or a ring," she said plainly. "I only want Marques."

Maria mouthed the words "Oh my!" to her brother. Nobody knew whether it was a compliment or an insult.

"Well, let us not stay up too late," suggested Marques, standing up. "Mother will be up early, and it would be nice of us to join her for breakfast."

"I agree," said Maria. All three of them stretched. "Our room is this way." She nudged Isabella. "Marques gets to pine away for you tonight. It's going to be a big, lonely bed, big brother."

"Thank you, I remember," he said. He carried Isabella's

trunk up a flight of stairs and into the ladies' bedroom. It was a lovely room with pink roses painted on the walls. There were two small beds and a tiny window overlooking a grassy field. Isabella could smell flowers, and didn't know whether the scent rose from the vases or from the distant fields whose smell was carried in the breeze. "Do you have everything you need?" he asked her tenderly. He wrapped his arm about her waist and squeezed, as though to tell her she had done well, as though to assure her it would get no worse than this.

"Yes," she nodded.

"I'm sorry for the separate bedrooms," he whispered.

"And I'm sorry I'm not the first woman you've brought here," she whispered back impulsively.

Marques was shocked. He pulled away from her and looked her steadily in the eye.

"I'm sorry," she said softly, shaking her head. "I'm sorry I said that. It's just ... it's just that I knew there were others, but ..." She looked him straight on. "I didn't know you'd brought any of them home to meet your mother."

"I had to," he explained. "I couldn't just drop a lady off at a strange inn. No matter how short a time I'd known her or how little I cared, I—"

"It's all right," said Isabella, head bent. She reached for his hand and gave it a gentle squeeze. "It's all right. I was just a little surprised. I know I have no right, it's just ... I just hope I mean more to you than they did."

"How can you even ask that?" he demanded sternly. "Isabella, I didn't even know any of them. You know how I was. I made it a point not to know them."

"I know," she hedged awkwardly.

He lifted her chin with his finger, forcing her to look into his striking eyes. "You are the only woman I have ever longed to know. You are the only woman who has ever made me yearn for something more than pleasure. I love you, Isabella. Don't let Maria bother you—we're just so close that she forgets to be polite."

"I know," she said, somewhat soothed by his words. "I know. I guess I just feel vulnerable tonight because . . . well, because you have a family here. You have other people besides me. And I have no one. I just want to be sure I won't be tossed away."

"Never," he said firmly, sealing his declaration with a kiss. "Besides," he whispered near her ear. "How can one toss away a piece of wind? You are my destined mate. Remember?" He smiled down at her.

"Thank you," she whispered. "I needed to be reassured."

"Good night," he said, pressing his lips upon her forehead. "If you have trouble sleeping, come find me, for I don't plan to sleep much tonight."

Isabella wrinkled her forehead. "Why is that?"

"Just can't sleep in this house," he said. "But I'll go to my bedroom and try. Good night."

She watched him walk away, then turned to the room about her. It was a cozy, feminine room. She wished she could have it all to herself. She bounced up and down a couple of times, arms crossed, the excitement of being in a new place chilling her. She peeked out of the tiny window and felt a wonderful, grassy-smelling breeze upon her face. She threw out her arms and spun. She loved the nighttime, she loved the stars outside. She loved the scent of roses all around her, and she couldn't wait to try out her new bed.

"Hi."

Isabella got a horrible pain in her chest. Panting, she clutched it. Her heart was pounding. There were few things worse than believing she was alone and then finding, to her embarrassment, that she was not.

Maria strolled casually into the room, tossing her own small trunk on the floor with ease. She bounced onto one of the beds, claiming it as her own. Isabella was glad to see it was the one farthest from the window. Maria undid a couple of braids, letting all of her brown hair fall to her waist. It was thick and coarse-looking, and absolutely beautiful. She reached in her trunk for a hairbrush, and went to work. Brushing out those beautiful masses would be no easy task. "Comfortable enough?" she asked. She had, indeed, observed Isabella spinning around senselessly, but she decided to do the nice thing, and not mention it.

"Yes," murmured Isabella. "It's a nice room." Her eyes were downcast.

"Sorry for teasing you earlier," said Maria, now that they were quite alone. "Sometimes I get casual around family. Hope I didn't hurt your feelings."

Of course, she had hurt Isabella's feelings. But Isabella knew that people never expected anyone to be so fragile, so she accepted the girl's apology. "I'm not hurt," she lied.

"Well, aren't you going to brush your hair?"

Isabella swallowed hard, and turned toward her trunk. She supposed she really should. She dug through her clothes and found her old hairbrush, then started toward her bed. But Maria snatched it from her.

"No, see?" said Maria. "This brush is no good." She wrapped it against her hand. "The bristles are too soft. You can brush the outside of your hair, and then the inside, but the middle stays tangled. Here, look at mine."

Isabella felt her brush.

"See, now that's a real brush. You could groom a horse with this thing," she laughed. "Here, come sit down. I'll brush your hair for you."

No one had ever brushed Isabella's hair before, except herself. She sat down tenderly upon Maria's bed, facing the wrong direction.

"The other way," said Maria, twirling her finger. "You have to face that way so I can brush the back."

Isabella turned around, and began to feel tender, gentle brush strokes through her hair. It felt wonderful. It felt strange. There was something bonding about trusting her hair to someone.

"What beautiful hair," said Maria. "How did you get it this color? Did you use chamomile or lemon?" She fingered it carefully, then drew her own conclusion. "Nope. This is the real thing. You're very lucky. Were your parents both blond?"

"Yes," whispered Isabella. She liked the way it felt when Maria touched the wispy hairs at her temple, gently drawing them into the rest of her mane.

"You must be Celtic Portuguese then, right? Or German Portuguese?"

"Celtic," said Isabella.

"Hmmm. Marques and I ... that is, our family is mostly Spaniard and Moorish. That's why we're so dark. So how did you and Marques *really* meet, eh?"

Isabella's eyes were closed. She was breathing to rhythm of the brush. "He kidnapped me."

"Really? Marques? Well, that's a story to tell the grandchildren, eh?" She laughed, but found she was laughing alone. "You don't like to talk much, do you," she stated.

Isabella blushed.

"That's all right," said Maria. "I like quiet people. Some of my favorite people in the world are quiet. In fact, all of my favorite people are quiet, because I can't stand to listen to anyone chatter except for myself." She laughed. "I think we're done here."

Isabella was disappointed. Her scalp was still feeling itchy, and still wanted to be brushed some more. But she rose from the bed and said, "Thank you."

"You're welcome." Maria stood up. She was a tall, impressive woman, the kind of woman nobody pushes around. Isabella admired people like Maria. She envied them. "Well," said Maria, "I guess I'll go entertain myself somehow. I'll try not to wake you up when I come in."

Isabella was startled. "You mean you're not coming to bed?"

"Not yet. I told you I stay up late."

"Why is that?"

Maria shrugged on her way to the door. "Just can't sleep in this house, I guess."

Isabella squinted curiously. "That's exactly what Marques said."

"Really? Hmm. Well, I guess you can kill a man, but you can't get rid of his spirit, eh? Well, good night."

"Good night."

Maria departed, clicking the door shut behind her.

Isabella blew out the lantern and hopped into her soft, bouncy bed before she could scare herself with thoughts of spirits living in the house. She wished Maria had not mentioned such a thing. She closed her eyes and enjoyed the sound of crickets chirping in the darkness. She loved the breeze which brought her such sweet smells. She loved the softness of her mattress, and the color of pink all around her. But she missed the ocean's roar. Dry land now felt so motionless, so hard. She wondered whether she could ever get used to it again.

Her last thought before she fell into slumber was one she had not wanted to hear. It was a thought which could only surface when her mind was relaxed, and her consciousness slipping away, for she would never have willingly brought it forth. It was, *Marques, will you ever marry me?*

Chapter Thirty

Saada and Luisa were sharing a room in town. They wished Isabella could have joined them, but knew that she had somewhere better to stay. The little inn was nothing but the upstairs of a bar. It was right at the top of one of the town's steep, black-paved hills, so no matter where they went, the trek home was tedious. The room was quiet and pretty during the day, offering a nice high view of the town, and the mountains. But at night, the bar was full, and the noise was unbearable. "Sometime I think I should sleep with Marques," griped Saada, yanking open a stubborn window. "Just so I could have a nice place to stay in Madeira."

"Sometimes I think I should sleep with Marques," giggled Luisa, "just so I could sleep with Marques."

They both laughed.

"Hello!"

"Oh no," they both groaned. It was Samir, who had been following them around ever since the ship had anchored. He was no longer a prisoner, but a deck swabber, just as he had been on the corsair ship. And a good one at that, Marques had observed. But he had recently taken up the annoying habit of following around Saada and Luisa, and it drove them crazy.

"Would you believe it?" he asked, "I managed to get a room right next to yours. Now we can spend the whole shore leave together!"

Saada fluttered her thick, dark lashes. "Samir," she suggested, "wouldn't you rather spend time with the men? Surely you don't want to be dragged around town by a couple of ladies. All we'll do is shop," she lied.

"Spend time with the men?" he cried, "Why would I do that? Why would anyone want to spend time with men?"

"Because you *are* one," Saada suggested.

"But that is precisely the point," he explained. "When I see a woman, I see a potential bed mate. When I see a man, all I see is competition. No thank you! I'll just stay with you ladies."

"But we are *not* going to be your bedmates," Saada explained coolly, a saucy fist upon her hip.

"Oh, I know," he said, "I know. Don't worry. But you see, even women who won't bed me are still more appealing than men, because at least I can imagine it. With men, I have to put so much effort into trying *not* to imagine it, lest I get ill."

Saada shook her head, but she was now smiling. She liked a man with spunk, even if he was ridiculous.

"Besides," continued Samir, "I need your help. Both of you."

They raised their eyebrows attentively.

"You see," he explained, "I would like to find a wife here in Portugal. I've always wanted to marry, but my social status is so low in Arabia, that I've not had much opportunity. I mean, when some men are taking sixteen wives, what does that leave for the rest of us? Makes no sense at all. But here, where men only get one, there are enough to go around! So I believe even I might get lucky. But I need your help."

"We don't know anyone to introduce you to," Saada said apologetically.

"That's all right, I'll introduce myself. But what I need you to do is teach me how to be attractive to heathens."

"Heathens?" Luisa and Saada asked at the same time.

"Yes," he shrugged. "How do I make myself desirable in the eyes of women who are on their way to Hell?"

Saada and Luisa looked around and behind themselves. "Who are you talking about?"

"You know," he shrugged. "People like you—Hindus or Christians or whatever you are. How do I appeal to you?"

"Well, you can start," said Saada, "by not calling us heathens."

"Hold on, let me write this down."

"Secondly," chimed in Luisa, "we are Christians. Not Hindus, not Buddhists, not Confucianists. Some of us are a little touchy about those distinctions."

"Interesting, interesting," he said, scribbling.

"Actually, I worship Mella," Saada informed her friend, "but I'm not from here."

"Fascinating," said Samir. "So you really see yourselves as different from all those other non-Muslim groups, eh? I'll be careful. All right now, what about the turban? Yes? No?"

"I guess it depends what you've got under there," said Saada. "Come, let's have a look."

He took off his turban to reveal long, silky black hair.

"Oooo, yes," said Saada with pursed lips. "Forget that turban."

"I agree," said Luisa.

"And the clothes?" asked Samir, standing up.

"Hmmm." Both women tapped their chins, studying him and reflecting seriously upon the matter.

"The pointy shoes have got to go," decided Saada.

"You don't like them?"

"Not even a little. How about you, Luisa?"

"Got to go," the smaller girl agreed.

"And the breeches?"

"Too baggy," said Saada. "We've got to see your legs.

What woman wants to marry a man without knowing first what his legs look like?"

"Not to mention his behind," added Luisa with a giggle.

Saada pointed at her like a scolding mother. "I wasn't going to say that. You said it, not me."

"I know, let's take him shopping," suggested Luisa.

Saada laughed. "Well, I was only trying to scare him away when I told him that women like to shop all day. But I guess that's not a bad idea."

"You would do that for me?" asked Samir.

"Absolutely," said Saada. "Come on, we've got to get you ready and eligible quickly if you're going to get a bride before the next sailing."

"Yes, let's go!" cried Luisa.

The three of them linked arms, with Samir in the center. He felt quite proud of himself, having a woman on each arm as they skipped down the steps, through the bar, and out onto the peaceful sidewalk. "Boy, this place is not at all like New Providence," said Luisa sadly. "It seems almost barren. Beautiful, but barren." She looked up at the mountains, letting the wind send fragrant roses her way. "I sure miss sailing. I just hate being stuck on dry land. Stuck is exactly how it feels too. It's as though your feet grow heavier and there's no place to wander."

"You must be crazy!" cried Samir. "I hate the sea! Being on a ship is just like being in a floating closet, trapped beside smelly men, and getting sick every few hours."

"Then why did you become a sailor?" Luisa asked indignantly.

He shrugged. "It beat becoming a eunuch. I may not get to protect hoards of beautiful wives, but at least I can still *appreciate* hoards of beautiful wives, if you know what I mean."

Luisa looked at Saada, but found her friend to be staring emptily into the distance. She was not listening. She'd not heard a word they'd said. Something was wrong. "Saada? What is it?"

A slow, sophisticated smile came over her plush, dark lips. "He's here," she said, her voice like wind.

"Who's here?" asked Luisa her hands on her hips.

Saada was silent.

"Oh no," groaned Luisa, "not this again. That man you met in New Providence all that time ago? You're still looking for him? Oh, come on, Saada! He's not going to be in Portugal. He wasn't even Portuguese! What are the odds?"

Saada blinked at the mountains, as though they had spoken to her, and she understood. "He's here," she said with a nod. "I can feel it."

Luisa grabbed both her companions roughly by the elbows. "Come on," she said to Samir, "let's go shopping. I apologize. It seems my friend is losing her mind."

Chapter Thirty-one

Isabella awoke from her slumber feeling refreshed and surrounded by the scents of grass and orchids. She rolled to her left, and then to her right, taking in the luxurious feel of a real bed under her back. The ship's cots were so much harder. When she opened her eyes, she saw perfect sunshine streaming through her window—not too bright, but just light enough to welcome her to the day. With a sigh, she pushed herself out of bed. Stretching her arms overhead, she looked at the place where Maria should have lain. The blankets were a mess, so she must have been there sometime in the night, but she was gone. Isabella opened her trunk. The only dresses she had now were her wine velvet and her gray cotton. The wine dress was too warm for the fall weather, and the gray one was too casual for shore leave. She couldn't wear her sleeping gown as she sometimes did on the ship. She didn't know what to do.

She twisted her hair as best she could while she pondered the matter. She had always been so terrible at fixing her own hair. She knew that no matter how hard she tried, it would be messy, and she wished she could just leave it down. But on dry land, it was proper to wear it up, so she tried. The gray dress, she decided.

Maria knocked and opened the door at the same time. "Are you goint to eat?"

"Oh, uh . . . yes," stammered Isabella. "I'm . . . I'm sorry I'm late."

"Don't worry about it," said Maria. "We started without you, but we saved some."

Isabella finished dressing and hurried downstairs. How mortifying to be a guest in a strange house, and not awake until everyone else had eaten! She rushed down the stairs, her girdle pinching her, the framing under her skirt swaying and bumping into things. But when she arrived at the breakfast table, she found that everyone was talking and laughing and slouching jovially. No one cared that she'd overslept. "Let me get you some bread," Catalina offered, her pale eyes sparkling as she rose to her feet.

"Did you sleep well?" asked Marques, standing and offering her a chair.

"Yes," she said quietly. "Yes, very well. I'm sorry I'm late."

"Late for what?" asked Maria. "We're not going anywhere."

Isabella smiled her gratitude.

"We're going into town today," Marques announced.

"We are?" asked his sister.

"No," he replied, "Isabella and I are."

"Oh, just forget your sister the minute you find a lover," griped Maria. "Don't worry about me. I'll be fine here with Mother. Why, I'll . . . let's see . . . sweep? Scrub floors? Help with the cooking?"

"I'm not holding you here," he said. "If you want to go out, then do so. But Isabella and I have a special mission today," he said with a twinkle in his eye. "We're going shopping."

Isabella frowned. "Shopping? For what?"

"Gowns," he told her, "and jewels and perfume, and anything else your heart desires. You have only two dresses, and that isn't fitting for the lady of a pirate captain. If pirates are to be recognized as civilized gentlemen, then our ladies must want for nothing. Today, we go into town, and I hold my pouches of gold wide open."

"Oh, I couldn't," said Isabella, and she meant it.

Catalina swept into the room at that moment with some fresh, hot bread. All mention of pirates and their ladies had to stop. "What's the matter, dear?" she asked, having caught the very end of the discussion. "What can't you do?"

"Marques wants to take her shopping," said Maria, helping herself to a slice of the new loaf of bread. "But it seems Isabella isn't used to being spoiled."

"Oh my," said Catalina, filling up a plate of breakfast foods for her guest. "You really must let him buy you things, dear. After all, he's going to be your husband."

Isabella looked worriedly at Marques.

"Yes, well," he said, rising anxiously to his feet. "Look at the time. Come, Isabella. We must get to the shops before they all close in ... uh ... nine hours or so. Good day, Mother. Sister." He bowed courteously to each.

"Goodbye, big brother," Maria called brightly.

He scowled, but not without love in his eyes. He took Isabella by the hand, and hurried her away.

Marques and Isabella nearly ran from the house, sighing exhaustedly when they reached the outdoors. Then they looked at each other, and started laughing. Marques reached for her hand, and Isabella squeezed his in return. "See, now, don't you wish you had a family?" he asked sarcastically.

"I still do," she confessed, "but I see there were a few ... complexities I was spared by not having one."

He gave her a playful wink. "Come. I'll race you to the top of that hill."

"But I'll be hot and out of breath by the time we reach town!" she protested.

"No, there'll be plenty of time to cool off afterward. We're more than two miles away. Come."

"You don't mean it? I'm terrible at games."

"I'll bet you've never even played chase."

"Not willingly, but I was forced a couple of times to join in the girls' games, and . . . and whatever team I was on, lost!"

"Come on," he laughed. "I'll give you a count to five handicap."

"No."

"One! Better hurry."

"Marques, I—"

"Two!"

"I can't run. I—"

"Three! You've almost lost your handicap."

Isabella bolted. She ran as hard as she could, as though for that one moment, nothing mattered but reaching the top of the hill. She was laughing and gasping before she was halfway there, but she thought that perhaps for the first time in her life, she understood why people liked to run. As it turned out, if Isabella had any atheletic talent, it was the ability to flee with great speed. She moved as though she weighed nothing at all, and could probably have outrun anyone her own size. Still, Marques had the advantage of height, and decided to start his count to five over again. Then still, he steadied his pace to keep his margin of victory to a minimum. "I've got you," he said at last, just before she reached the top. He tackled her affectionately, knocking her to the grass, but making sure she fell on his own arm.

"It's not fair," she gasped, clutching her ribs. "You weren't wearing a corset!"

"That's true," he admitted, rolling her onto her back. "But still, you lost and must pay the consequences." He pinned her arms to her side. She panted heavily, her breasts heaving up and down. "Now, what did we say the prize would be?"

"We didn't!" she cried breathlessly, a delighted grin on her face. "We didn't say!"

"No, no. I'm quite sure we did," he teased, "What was it? Ah yes." He dipped down for a kiss. His lips tasted hers, softly and warningly, like a prelude to something dangerous. "I remember now. The victor gets to kiss the loser anywhere he chooses."

"Is that right?" she laughed. "Well, then, here you go. Here's my hand." She thrust it into the air.

"Hmm, a lovely hand," he agreed, tickling it with a couple light kisses. "However, I think to choose something else."

"My cheek?" she asked, turning her head to the side.

"Hardly." He smiled devilishly, then reached for the hem of her skirt.

"Marques!" she cried, appalled but still grinning. "Stop that! What are you doing?"

He smiled mysteriously, then reached under her gown and tore open her bloomers, leaving a completely bare passageway to her womanhood. Isabella shuddered, but he soothed her with a kiss on the brow. "Now, now. Don't be a sore loser."

Her face flushed bright red. "I can't believe you're going to do this," she said as a final protest.

He knelt beside her bent knees. "Open them," he whispered, stroking her fair hand.

"I will not!" she cried, smiling and blushing.

"Come now," he ordered lightheartedly.

Isabella bit her lip and spread her knees wide.

"Good girl," he teased, then lowered his lips to the pinkest part of her.

"Quickly!" she cried. "Get it over with! I'm so embarrassed!"

"Mmmm." He sat propped on one elbow, his eyes mellow, his smile taunting. "A man likes to take his time, Isabella." He fingered her provocatively, making swirls and zigzags along her tenderest skin.

"Stop that!" she begged.

He leaned over and kissed her. He kissed her right between her bare, open legs. He snuggled his lips into her nest, and rubbed her, then departed with a couple of affectionate pecks. "There," he said, "now, that's how a pirate kisses a woman."

She reached for him, and pulled his face to hers. She kissed him passionately, urging him to do more. But he pushed her away with a devilish smile. "Now, now," he said. "You know, we are in public. What sort of a man do you think I am? Control yourself."

"Marques!" she yelled.

But he was already rising to his feet, offering her his hand. "Come," he said, "we've got to get to town. Remember? We're in a hurry."

"Marques!" she screamed. "You lie back down here right now!"

"I'll tell you what," he said, scratching his beard. "See that hill up there? If you can beat me to the top of that one, I'll let you have your way with me. If not, well . . . then I guess I get to keep my virtue."

She was already running.

"Only three-second handicap this time!" he called out. "Oh well," he shrugged, "better make it fifty seconds. One! Two!"

By the time they arrived in town, Isabella and Marques were both exhausted. And suspiciously sloppily dressed. Shirts were not tucked in properly, corsets were poorly refastened, sleeves hung off shoulders, and breeches were tugged up crookedly. But nobody in town seemed to guess that they had been up to mischief. They were so properly linked at the arm, and chatting so charmingly with one another as they walked, that it seemed they could have been nothing other than the most respectable of couples.

"Here we are," said Marques, opening a jingling door wide for his lady. Isabella stepped into the tiny dress shop, which was all filled with light, and quaintly situated between a jewelry shop and a garden of flowers. Isabella had black pebbles caught in her shoes.

"Hello," greeted a beautiful woman at the sound of her jingling door bells. She had hair so thick that it would not stay up in a bun, but had to be braided and tossed over her shoulder. Her face was delicate and narrow, built of tiny bones like those in her wrists. "May I help you?"

Marques bowed. "Yes, please. I need some gowns made for my lady."

The woman looked at Isabella. "All right," she said, chewing on her lip. She had an intelligent spark in her eye, a competence for evaluation. She was studying Isabella's beauty and flaws, making sound guesses about what would flatter her and what would not. In less than a second, she had completed her visual research. She had taken note of Isabella's perfectly small waist, and the narrow hips that needed to be padded. She had noticed the fashionable milky skin, and also the foggy gray eyes that would disappear if not brought out. She saw the lovely, lemon color of the hair, but also its wispiness and lack of strength. She took note of the beautiful shape of the breasts, and the neck that was not quite long enough. Every woman was a puzzle, and there was nothing this dressmaker enjoyed more than playing with the pieces, trying to create beauty through the simple art of rearranging the given parts. "How many dresses do you need?" she asked.

"Twelve," said Marques.

Isabella gasped. "Marques, no. What am I going to do with twelve dresses? I can't even wear them on the ship. . . ." She stopped talking. She felt she should not have mentioned the ship. For what sailor carried women with him, unless he was a pirate?

But the dressmaker smiled. "You're a pirate then, eh?" She got out her account book. "That's all right. In my experience, pirates are the best tippers."

Marques appreciated her understanding. "I'll pay you up front if you prefer," he had the humility to say. Some people did not trust pirates, and while he didn't like it, he knew that in some cases, there was reason for their worry.

"No, that's all right," she said, chewing on the end of her feathered pen. "You look like a Roberts pirate. Is that right?"

"Absolutely," he bowed.

"Roberts pirates are always very respectable," she flattered him by saying. "You can pay afterward like everyone else. I really don't mind. I just need twenty percent up front."

"As you wish."

She scribbled something in her account book. "All right then," she said, straightening up. "Let's get to work." There was nothing she enjoyed more than working with a new customer. This was not much of a job in some ways, but she put her whole heart and soul into it. "What fabric do you prefer?"

"Some silk, some cotton," said Marques, holding Isabella around the waist.

"And what style do you prefer? Sack gown? Formal?"

"Some of each."

She scribbled something in her book. "Now, what about colors?"

"I'm not sure," said Marques, turning to look at his lady, "I hadn't thought about that."

The dressmaker chewed on her lip, studying, thinking. "I think a nice red might look good."

"Red?" asked Marques. "Isn't that a bit bold for her fair complexion?"

"Not if we choose just the right shade," said the woman, turning Isabella's blushing cheek in her slender hand. "Scarlet would be too bright, I agree. But a softer rose petal might be just the thing. Here, let me show you." She sifted through some panels of cloth on her shelf, and found one in just the right shade. "Here, see?" She held a smoky rose swatch to Isabella's cheek. "The subtle pink in it really brings out her flush. And the redness is striking against her yellow hair. Don't you agree?"

Marques was impressed. "Yes, you're right," he said. "That's brilliant. Say, have you ever thought of working on a pirate ship? I could really use a personal tailor, and someone to redesign our flag and emblems.''

''I'll get back to you,'' she laughed, clearly uninterested. ''Now, what about the second gown? Light green, do you think?''

''That wouldn't match her eyes,'' he hedged. ''Shouldn't only green-eyed women wear green?''

''Ah, amateurs!'' she teased. ''No, that's not how it works.'' She fished through her shelves for another swatch. ''You see, matching colors compete with the eyes. It's contrasting colors which emphasize them. And let's not forget the hair. Gray against yellow hair is perfectly drab. But spring green on the other hand . . .'' She held up the swatch of lime-colored silk. ''See? Pale green and yellow are smashing together.''

Marques shook his head. ''I admire a woman who is brilliant at her art.''

''Why, thank you,'' she grinned. ''You'd be surprised how little respect people have for dressmakers. Just because we're women, people think the job doesn't require any skill.''

''I admire anyone who is excellent at what she does,'' said Marques. ''I'll entrust the dressmaking to you. My input appears to be useless.''

''Really?'' she asked, clearly flattered by his trust. ''You just want me to make them however I see fit?''

''Yes.''

She reached under her dress for a sketch book. ''Great. Now, just hold still,'' she said to Isabella. ''I just want to make a little drawing of you so I can remember what we need to do.'' In two minutes, she had drawn an absolutely uncanny representation of Isabella. ''There we go. Now let me get some measurements.'' She wrapped a rope about Isabella's waist, gawking at the slimness. ''Boy, you're thin.'' She scribbled down a number, then measured the bust. ''All right,'' she said, a little less impressed by this measurement. ''And hips?'' Isabella flushed as the woman fastened her rope snugly about her. ''Hmmm . . . all right.'' She measured her legs, once again impressed by what she read. "You're a tall woman. Good thing he's tall too," she smiled, glancing gingerly at Marques. "You make a nice couple."

Isabella was too embarrassed to thank her for the compliment. "All right, we're done here," she announced, scribbling down the length of her long torso. "Check back every couple of weeks to see whether I'm ready," she told Marques. "It all depends how busy the shop gets, and how often I get inspired."

Marques bowed low. "Thank you, madam."

"Thank you!" she called back.

Marques escorted his lady from the shop. Isabella felt as though she were walking on air. She had never felt so flattered and spoiled in all of her life. "The jewel shop is right next door," Marques said with a kiss upon her hand. "I promise this will be more fun than being measured was."

"I thought it was fun," Isabella confessed shyly.

Marques glanced her way, and thought she looked like someone coming away from her own birthday party. Obviously, she had never been taken shopping before. Obviously, she had never had her looks fussed over before. He was delighted he could make her feel so precious. He held her before the jeweler's window, clutching her waist with both hands, peering over her head at the window display. "See anything you like?" he asked.

Isabella liked it all. Sapphires, emeralds, rubies, gold and silver, onyx, mother of pearl, topaz, diamonds. Even the jade made her ache. "No, I . . . I don't really need anything," she said bashfully, for she could never tell him how much she yearned for something beautiful and sparkling.

"Still worried about using a pirate's money?" he asked.

"No. You're my beau now, and I'll treasure your gifts."

"Then choose," he urged her. "What catches your eye?"

She was staring at a silver brooch, perfect for holding a cape in place. It was big and oval, and in its center was a white cameo. The Virgin Mary from a profile, looked lovely and gentle and forgiving. Circled all about her were diamond chips.

It was too expensive, she told herself. It must be. She could not ask for one of the most expensive pieces in the store. She had to lower her sights. She had to choose something smaller, something made for a lady on a budget. She moved her eyes away from that twinkling cameo brooch, and tried to find something more modest. But Marques had already seen her stare.

"You like that one?" he asked, pointing.

Isabella swallowed. "No," she said, though it hurt. "I . . . it's . . . it's too big. How about that?" She pointed to a small, golden ring with an elephant carved in its green jade stone. "I like elephants," she said.

"You like cameos better," he observed. "Come, let's see whether we can afford it."

He led her by the hand into the cluttered jeweler's shop. A man with a looking glass greeted them gruffly. He did not like pirates. "What is it?" he asked.

"The cameo in the window," said Marques. "The brooch."

"What about it?" asked the man.

Marques didn't like his rudeness, and gazed at him with contempt. But he would try to buy that brooch for Isabella, even if it had to be from a pirate hater. "Tell me the price," he said. "Whisper it so the lady won't hear." He leaned forward as the man mumbled something at him. Marques stood straight, stroking his short beard. Isabella could tell the price had been high. Marques started unfastening some of his own golden trophies from his waistcoat. Solid gold buttons, pins stolen from the Far East—he laid these before the wide-eyed jeweler. "This should be more than enough."

The jeweler held his looking glass to the pieces, unable to believe what beautiful possessions filthy pirates could own. It was nearly impossible to get hold of some of these buttons that were made in China, Siam, and India. He hated to do business with a pirate, but he could not turn away this wealth of jewelry. "Looks fair," he said mildly.

"Then get me that brooch."

Isabella tugged at Marques's sleeve. "Marques, no. I know how you value your treasures. Don't part with them."

"Oh, I've got plenty more where those came from," he assured her, "and I'll 'acquire' more before the year's out. Now, don't argue." He gave her a friendly pinch.

The jeweler brought out the piece, and Isabella's eyes fixed on its sparkle. Was it really to be hers? "How shall I wrap it?" he asked.

"No need," said Marques, holding it up to the light to make sure it was as valuable as he'd thought. It seemed to be well made. He pinned it at Isabella's breast. "There you are," he said, sealing the gift with a kiss.

Isabella thought she might cry, but would not do it in front of the jeweler.

"Good day," said the jeweler grudgingly.

Marques bowed stiffly, then departed. "Are you happy?" he asked Isabella, bending down to meet her soft eyes.

"Oh Marques," she nearly wept, touching the giant piece of silver. "I've never had anything like this. I . . ."

He was even happier than she was. His smile showed it. "Come," he said, taking her hand, "let us get some perfume. What do you like? Jasmine? Rose? Lilly of the Valley?" He led her down a steep hill, toward a little diner and perfumery. "We'll get something to eat afterward," he suggested.

Isabella was grinning, though her head was bent. So much fuss, so much attention she was receiving today. She wondered whether she could ever look anyone in the eye again. "I've never smelled any of those perfumes," she confessed. "We weren't allowed to wear any at the convent. But I like the sound of the last one you said."

"What was that? Lilly of the Valley?"

"Yes, it has a nice name."

He grinned. "I bet you'll like it. It has a very clean scent."

"Marques," she said, planting her heels so he could drag her no farther.

He turned around. "Yes, what is it?"

She frowned. "I hope you don't think I'm materialistic, just because I'm letting you buy me all these nice things. I hope you don't think I'm taking advantage."

Marques shook his head, his blue eyes sparkling. He refrained from saying what he really thought. *I've had whores who made me buy them more.* Instead, he said, "Isabella, if I had only one shard of gold, and I had to choose between eating or using it to put a smile on your face, I would spend it on you."

"Oh Marques!" she cried, flinging her arms around him. "That is the most romantic thing anyone has ever said to me!"

He returned her hug with fierce affection. "Well, it's about time," he said. "It's about time someone appreciated you. I know I always will."

Isabella gave him a look, and it was not a kind one. Marques apologetically lowered his gaze. He knew what she was thinking. He knew he should not have said "always." He knew that he had reminded her of what he was not giving. He knew that a few trinkets, no matter how expensive and thoughtful, could never replace a happy ending to Isabella's life story. But he wasn't ready, and didn't know that he would ever be. He took her hand, careful not to meet her disappointed gaze. "Come," he said. "There is still more to the afternoon. Let us enjoy it." Isabella cast him a very odd look then. It was a very serious look, one which said she would follow him for now, but one which also let him know that his time was running out. She accepted his hand with tenderness, and led him toward the sunset.

Chapter Thirty-two

By the time Samir arrived at the inn's pub, he looked quite the smashing marital candidate. Saada and Luisa had done a good job on him. His long, shiny black hair was tied neatly in a bow, then tossed over one shoulder. His thickly lashed brown eyes stood out much better without the turban, which had concealed his brows. He was not a tall man, but he was nicely sleek, and that could now be easily seen, thanks to his new slim-cut breeches. They were olive and gold, had a matching vest, and a lovely coat that flapped behind him. His new black shoes were shiny, as was the square, silver buckle which adorned them. He felt quite certain he was ready to go on the hunt.

"Now, first thing's first," instructed Luisa. "Choose someone to be your first victim . . . err . . . target."

They all looked around the room for eligible-looking women. "I like her," Samir said, pointing.

"Don't point," Saada snapped at him. "It's very rude. Now let me have a look." She casually peered over her shoulder and saw a slender pixie of a woman trying to enjoy her soup.

She had lovely chestnut hair and eyes, and an awfully nice bonnet resting beside her. "She looks a little wealthy," she said worriedly. "Not dirty rich, but a little too classy. See her bonnet?" she pointed out to Luisa.

"Ah, yes. It's a nice one."

"But all right," sighed Saada, "you've got to start somewhere, so why don't you go up to her and start a conversation. You remember everything we told you?"

"Don't call her a heathen. . . ."

"Not on the first date anyway."

"Don't tell her I'm a pirate. And make good eye contact."

"That's right," said Saada. "Now give it your best shot."

As he strolled away, both women buried their heads in their hands. They couldn't stand to watch. They just knew he was going to do something wrong.

"Hello, sweet lady," he began. "May I join you?"

She pursed her lips and gazed upon him with suspicion. But then she nodded indifferently, and returned to her soup.

"There is something I would like to ask you," he began.

She looked up with only her eyes.

"Would you be my wife? Would you scrub floors for me, cook all my meals, work in the field, give birth to my children, raise them while I sail around the world, agree with all of my opinions no matter how uninformed they are, obey my orders, look at no other man, try your hardest to pleasure me in the bedroom on the nights when I come home, and someday, welcome my second and third wives to the household? Please? What do you say?"

Slap!

Saada and Luisa came rushing to rescue him. "What happened?" Luisa gasped, as they struggled to keep him on his feet.

"I don't know," he said. "I guess it was what you thought— she's too wealthy for me."

"Well, what did you say?" demanded Saada.

"I just asked her to marry me, and . . ."

"Oh, well, you can't do that!" she cried. "Women need time to become attracted to you before you bring that up. You should just ask her to go for a stroll with you. You do that a few times, and *then* you break the bad news about wanting her hand in marriage."

Luisa nodded her agreement.

"Well, all right," he said, straightening out his waistcoat. "But I tell you, in Arabia, a woman would be burned at the stake for striking a man like that!"

"In Arabia," Saada reminded him with a fist upon one hip, "you would be a eunuch. So stop your whining and let's try again."

"Very well," he said, "but let's hope the next one is not so arrogant. There is nothing worse than a haughty woman."

"Fine," said Saada. "So who will be your next victim?"

"Target!" Luisa corrected her friend with a firm elbow.

"You say it your way, I'll say it mine. Now, who will it be, Samir?"

"How about her?" he asked, twitching his head spasmodically.

"What are you doing?" asked Saada with a squint.

"You told me not to point," he reminded her, still jiggling his head.

Saada rolled her eyes, then both women inspected the next target. She was a fair-haired lady with green eyes and rosy cheeks. She was very young, and looked even more so, all dressed in white. "She's very pretty," said Saada worriedly. "A skillful man could have her, no matter what he looked like. But you—well, all you've got is your looks. She might be out of your league."

"How can a woman be out of a man's league?" he asked indignantly. "Men are always above women."

"Welcome to the eighteenth century, Samir. She's too good for you. Pick another."

"No," he insisted. "I want her."

"Fine," snapped Saada, tossing up her hands. "It's your humiliation."

Quite determinedly now, Samir spun around on his heel and marched toward the blond beauty. An enormous pirate with anchors branded into his rocky arms strolled past Samir without seeing him, then took a seat beside the lady. She welcomed him with a bright grin. "Nobody's been looking at you?" he asked in a deep voice. "Because if they have, just tell me, and I'll kill them."

Samir returned to Saada. "Not my type," he announced.

Saada was not listening. She had that dazed look on her face again. Her chin was turned toward the window, her eyes fixed on the mountains. "Saada?" Luisa asked worriedly. "Saada?" She reached for her friend's elbow. But Saada shook her off.

"No. Leave me be," she said in a beautiful, possessed voice.

Samir and Luisa watched her leave the bar as though she were being summoned by some ancient god. "What is it?" asked Samir.

"Probably that man again," said Luisa dreamily.

"It's scary," he said, crossing his arms and shaking. "You've said there's no way that man could be here, and yet, it's as though she's possessed by some madness. She really believes. It's frightening."

"Do you know what's even scarier?" Luisa asked.

"What's that?"

"I see him. He's right there."

Chapter Thirty-three

Saada thought he looked like a panther. Sleek and dark, he moved with stealth and grace along the black paved roads of Funchal. He wore a gray wig, tied with a black bow. He wore the most dignified of outfits, with slim emerald breeches and a matching coat, laced in silver. His coat flapped behind him in the strong mountain wind. Saada followed him for blocks. She did not cry out to him, but waited for him to feel her presence. When at last, at the very edge of town, he cocked his head in puzzlement and turned, his breath was completely halted. "Saada," he said into the wind.

"I waited for you," she told him, lips pursed challengingly, eyes coldly fixed on him. She did not let him see the shaking in her knees or hear the pounding of her heart.

"I meant to return," he said, his voice low and powerful.

"Then why didn't you?" she demanded. "Do you take me for a fool?"

He shook his head. He had round cheekbones, skin like chocolate, and eyes like the richest mahogany. "I was captured," he told her, sending a prayer out to the mountains that she might believe his wild story. "I was going to return to you, I swear it. I have never stopped thinking about you, never stopped dreaming of you."

"Don't feed me lines," she said. "If you dreamed about me so much, where the hell were you?"

He couldn't help grinning. She was as beautiful as he'd remembered. Her figure was so plush, the sides of her like waves of the ocean. Her lips were so full and velvety. Her skin was between polished oak and the deepest gold.

"What are you smiling at, you fool?" she demanded. "I asked you a question!"

"I'm sorry," he said, though his smile did not dim. "It's just that I know you might turn and leave me now. And I want to enjoy this moment, seeing you in front of that purple mountain, the wind blowing on your face. Just let me have this moment."

Saada rolled her eyes. "Yes, and you can have a lot *more* moments too, if you'll just explain yourself!"

"I was captured," he begged her to believe. "When we met in New Providence, I swore we would meet there again. I promised you I would come back, and make you my bride." He bent his head in shame. "That night was the longest one of my life, and it was the first night that ever seemed real. When I look back, all my memories are of a man halfway dreaming, always thinking, and never experiencing the life around him. But that night was different. That night had color and texture. I can still feel the first ray of blue sky we saw that morning. I remember how it looked like gray light across your face. How your hair was coming loose from its braids, and resting on my pillow like strands of wool. I remember your smile, and how it looked in the sunrise, with all the shades of pink and purple behind you. I remember the sound of the ocean that day, and the shape of your body in that green dress. I remember how you shared things with me, things you had never told anyone else. And how I listened, thinking, 'We've got to stay in this hotel room. We've got to lock the door, and never let anyone in, never let anyone drag us from here and thrust us back into the world of drudgery.' I remember asking you to be my wife, and I remember knowing without any doubt that you would say yes. Because I could see into your heart that night, and I knew your deepest mind." He paused, unable to believe that she was really here again, just as magnificent as ever.

"That's right," she said, "I remember all that too. But it still seems like you're forgetting a part."

"Which part?"

"The part where you ran off and never came back for me, you bastard!"

Omari threw out his hands in self-defense. "No, no. I can explain. Saada, really! I can explain. You see . . ."

She put a fist on her hip. Her eyes were hard, but her ears were secretly wide open.

"My ship was at port in the British Colonies of North America. We were just unloading our cargo, and preparing to sell it for some awfully nice prices, when suddenly, I was grabbed by my coat and asked where I thought I was going. Saada, they thought I was an escaped slave! I tried to straighten them out. But it turned out that shouting, 'No, no. I'm just a pirate!' was the wrong way to defend myself. I never promised you'd be marrying a brilliant man—just a handsome one."

Saada smiled. Her heart was beginning to warm.

"So they dragged me off," he explained. "They branded me, put chains on me, beat me, and made me work in a field."

"And you call that a reason to keep me waiting?" she asked, her eyes beginning to fill with tears.

"I knew you'd never accept my excuse," he joked, sharing in her smile, "so I vowed that I must break free. I wouldn't work for them at first. I became a pirate to avoid a life of slavery, as did, I suppose, all of the other pirates in their own way. And I wasn't about to give up my freedom now. It was awful, Saada. They hardly fed us, they barely gave us shelter, we were all bug bitten and stinking and rotting of illnesses nobody would bother to cure. There were children there, and women . . .'' He stopped himself. This was no tale to be telling a lady. She had not seen this horror with her own eyes, and it was better she remained innocent. He must not frighten her with tales of suffering beyond what she could imagine.

"In any case," he continued more cautiously, "I would rather have died than stayed there. But I decided not to do away with myself. And for only one reason—you.'' He melted her with a honey-warm gaze. ''Whenever times were the worst, when the babies wouldn't stop crying, when the mosquitoes wouldn't stop biting, when my muscles wouldn't stop aching ... I remembered your face in the early morning light, and it was as though you were there again, smiling before a purple sky. I knew that you probably hated me now. I knew I'd been gone too long, and you must have thought I abandoned you. And I knew that if I died right then and there, that I would never get to straighten things out with you. And that's what kept me going. And that's what gave me the strength to escape. And that's why I've been traveling these seas in search of you ever since. Oh, Saada, tell me you've not wed another!'' The thought made his face crumple into a wince.

Saada would have wept if she hadn't had so much pride. But as it was, she looked at him poutily and said, "Well, I'd like to torment you a little longer by telling you it's none of your business. But I guess you did a good job finding me. No, Omari. I haven't married anyone else.''

Before she'd finished speaking, he had her wrapped in a glorious embrace. Both of their mouths were open, sucking in the mountain breeze. Both of their hearts were pounding, and neither of them wanted to be the first to let go. So neither of them did. Not for minutes, and maybe not for hours. When at last, they broke apart, they casually joined hands, as friends who had never once been away from each other, and peacefully walked into the sunset.

Chapter Thirty-four

Marques would not take Isabella home until he had first taken her somewhere else. He wanted her to see the field where he used to play ball. When at last, around sunset, they reached a clearing in the woods, he spread out his arms. "Here it is," he said, not believing how powerful were the memories that it brought back. The grass rose all the way to his shins, and he could see the purple mountains from here. A small, white wreckage of a shack was all that remained of his old church. "I spent most of my youth in this field," he told Isabella. "I came out as soon as I was done with my chores at home, and did not leave until darkness forced me out."

"Were you a very good athlete?" she asked, looking about her at what seemed to be a pleasant, but ordinary field.

"I was the best," he boasted with a wry grin. "I was the fastest and the strongest."

"And the most humble?" she asked endearingly.

"No, not that," he confessed. "Come, let's see what's left of the old church." He took her hand, and led her through the grass. He felt as though he were fourteen again. He wondered what had become of all his old friends. Of course, none of them had really been friends. They were merely competitors on the field. But they had known each other's strengths and weaknesses to a tee. And Marques was sure he would recognize any one of those boys in a split second if he saw him today.

"Oh dear," said Isabella, sniffing the musty air. "It appears your church caught fire."

"Hmmm," he agreed, rubbing his beard. "It does. I wonder when that happened." He helped her step over a crumbled entranceway, then led her to what was once a pew. The inside of the old shack was blackened now, and smelled badly of ash. Marques could hardly recognize it. It hardly brought back any memories—it was too disfigured. Of course, most of his days in there had been spent just trying to keep his eyes open. He'd always hated sermons almost as much as he'd hated waking up for them. But still, he had thought this place would bring back some spark of memory—even if it were a sleepy one. But nothing.

Until he saw where the back room used to be. The wall between the chapel and the office was now crumbled. He remembered that room much more vividly than he remembered this one, and for a very shameful reason. He had brought more than one young lady back there on days when the priest was away. He could remember a few of those girls. There'd been one with big eyes and brown ringlets. And then, that beautiful blond. He wondered where they all were now. Probably married. And him? He looked at the smoke-eyed beauty at his side. He'd found a woman more beautiful than any of them. He'd found a lover more intriguing than any other on earth. He'd found someone who'd opened his mind to the possibility that there was magic all around him, someone who would not let him grow old. And yet, he was too much of a fool to wed her. He wrapped his arm about her, and closed his eyes as she relaxed into his chest. There was nothing so wondrous as having a lady snuggle against one's aching chest.

"Isabella?" he asked.

"Yes?" She was staring at the church ruins all around her, wondering what memories they were triggering in Marques.

"When I told you in town today that"—he swallowed—"that I would always love you, that I would always appreciate you . . ."

"Yes?"

"I meant it."

"That's nice," she sighed into his coat.

"So we might as well get married, right?" he asked stiffly. The words had come out more easily than he'd thought they would. It was a spontaneous decision, perhaps a reckless one. But he feared losing her, feared being left alone, and thought he should ask quickly, while the mood still grabbed him.

Isabella became rigid.

"I mean, if we're going to stay together forever, which I want desperately, then . . . then we should just take the plunge, right?" He seemed to be talking more to himself than to her.

"Take the plunge?" she asked indignantly, sitting upright. "Take the plunge? As in, dive into frigid water? As in, get it over with? Do you dread it so much, Marques? Is marrying me so traumatic that you must get it over with in one daring swoop?"

"No, no," he objected, trying to ease her back into his arms. But she would not budge. Her back was straight, her hips were inches away from his, and her eyes were fuming. "It isn't that at all," he pleaded.

"Then what is it?" she cried. "Tell me why! Tell me why you make me feel as though by accepting your ungracious proposal, I would be robbing you of your very life!"

"It isn't that way," he explained, reaching for her, longing desperately to feel her warmth at his side once more. "I just—"

"Tell me," she demanded, now on her feet. "You have wounded me, Marques. You make me feel as though I am not worthy to be anyone's bride. You make me feel that anyone who married me would see it as a chore. Now all I ask is that you explain to me why."

"Isabella—"

"Don't!" she warned. "Don't try to soothe my feelings. Don't tell me that any man who married me would be the luckiest man alive. Just tell me why you don't want to be him. That's all I want to know."

Marques knew he would have to explain. He knew there was no way to put this off. But he felt he sounded ridiculous as he muttered, "Oh, it's just ... it's not you ... I just don't want ... you know ... to be like my father."

"How would marrying me turn you into your father?" she demanded.

"Well, it wouldn't," he stammered, "not by itself. But you know, it's all baby steps. First you get married, then you start farming, then you have a son and daughter, and ... I'm sure it happens gradually, but—"

"This is ridiculous," said Isabella indignantly. "You are not your father and I am not your mother. I can't believe your father, dead though he be, still has such a hold on you that you would deprive yourself of life just to spite him."

"Isabella, I ... you don't understand."

"What don't I understand?" she demanded. "Tell me. Make me understand."

"My father ... he ... he was a bastard. I lived in mortal terror of him. To become him would be worse than death. Don't you understand that?"

"I understand you're hurting," she said, her eyes the color of tears. "And I understand that you've spent your life rebelling against that man. But I cannot be part of this. I thought I could—I thought we didn't need marriage because it was not important, but now I see that marriage is very important to you after all. Your failure to wed me is not an oversight, but an insult. And so I must inform you that I will no longer be your mistress. Nor will I marry someone who fears the altar, and fears me. Because I may be shy about accepting fancy jewels and gowns," she said, unfastening her cameo and handing it to him, "but I will settle for nothing less than the most devoted and grateful of husbands. Marques, I grew much when I was taken by those corsairs. I grew to accept you as a man, and not a villain. But now I am the only one of us who has grown. I had feared it, but I wasn't sure of it until now." He would not take the cameo, and so she set it on the remains of a pew. "If you'll excuse me," she said, so distantly that he could no longer read her emotions. "I'm going to pack my trunk. I'm sorry it has to end this way. If you need me, I'll be at the inn with Saada and Luisa." She turned around without any doubt or hesitation and stormed out of the chapel, turning only one last time as she reached the door. "And Marques? Don't even think that I won't be able to survive on my own. I may not be the worldiest of women, but I am a survivor. I've always been." And she left. It was simply time for her to go. The wind was calling her again, just as it had on that fateful day at the convent.

Marques watched her float away, then he swung out with his fist, striking hard at a piece of ragged wood. Then he cursed. And then, despite all he'd ever believed about himself, he leaned into a muscular arm and let out a sob. He knew she would not return. He had gotten to know her that well. He knew that once she was gone, she was gone forever, and he would never see her again.

Chapter Thirty-five

"I'm so glad you're going to share this room with me," said Luisa. "Saada has disappeared with her knight in shining armor, and now I'm all by myself."

Isabella liked the little room. It was not as pretty as the one at Marques's house, but she liked the view of the town from the window. And sharing a room with Luisa would be so much more relaxing than sharing one with Maria had been.

"So did you and Marques have a big fight?" asked Luisa, opening Isabella's trunk for her and putting things away.

"Not a big one," said Isabella cautiously. "But ... it's over." She turned from the window to the room, and rushed to stop Luisa from doing her unpacking. "Stop that, Luisa. I'll do that."

"Oh, I'm sorry," said Luisa, dropping her arms to her sides. "I just have this instinct to take care of you. Marques always said ... well, never mind."

Isabella grew pale. "Marques always said what?"

"It's nothing," said Luisa, moving away from the trunk so Isabella could unpack by herself.

"What did he say?" she demanded.

"Well." Luisa thought hard about the best way to put this. It really hadn't been an insult, after all. "He just said that, well, that you're more romantic than practical," she smiled. "I guess that's why I have this instinct to look after you."

Isabella's face got hot. "Marques thinks I can't take care of myself?"

"Oh no!" cried Luisa. "No, he never said that!"

"But he meant it, didn't he?"

"Uh . . . I . . . he never said that."

Isabella bowed her face into her fist. It was not his fault. She had no right to be angry. Of course, he thought her perfectly incompetent! What had she ever done to make him think otherwise? The truth was, she had never taken care of herself in her life. She had always resented her captivity, first at the convent and then on the pirate ship. But never had she succeeded in proving she could live without it. Yes, it had been time to leave. It had been time to show Marques that she did not need him, or anyone else. And more importantly, it was time to show herself. "Do you have plans for the rest of the day?" she asked Luisa.

"Nothing important," she replied. "I just promised Samir I'd walk around with him some."

Isabella took a deep, cleansing breath. "All right, then." With courage, she looked Luisa in the eye. "Shall we part until bedtime then? I have some errands to run."

"Certainly," beamed Luisa, "but promise me you'll play with me tomorrow, all right? I've missed having you around."

"All right."

"I'll bring some cake and tea back to the room with me tonight," vowed Luisa, "and we can stay up and talk."

"That would be nice." Isabella thought it really did sound pleasant. A female roommate. Two independent women sharing the stories of their day. This would be delightful. Who needed a husband? There was a knock at the door.

"Ugh," groaned Luisa, though Isabella could tell she was

not really upset. "That's Samir. You'll have to get used to his dropping by every time he feels like it. When Saada was here, he just wouldn't leave us alone. I'm coming, Samir!" She opened the door.

"Isabella!" he cried, looking not at all the man she had once known. His turban was gone, and in its place was a head of silky black hair dropping well past his shoulders. His beige outfit was stylish and trim. "So glad to see you again," he said. "You know I have come to realize that I owe my good fortune all to you. If it hadn't been for protecting you, I never would have been singled out to join Marques's pirates. And it has been such a blessing after working on the corsair ship. You people spend more time dancing and drinking than you spend working. There are beautiful women everywhere. It's a joy."

"I'm glad you like it," said Isabella.

"I didn't say I like it," he corrected her. "I said that after working on the corsair ship, it is a blessing. I'm still hoping to get a superficial wound and make it on the pirate welfare roll so I can stop working."

She was glad he hadn't changed too much.

"Well, let's go, Samir," said Luisa, tying a bonnet's ribbon under her chin. "I promised you a walk, so let's take one. Goodbye, Isabella," she said, kissing her on the cheek. "I'm sure your evening will be nicer than mine." But her grin and her squint showed that on some level, she would enjoy this little excursion, even if it were only because she hoped to acquire some funny stories about Samir's gracelessness.

Isabella watched them go with joy, and then with an ache in her heart. She missed Marques already. She'd been gone two hours, and she already wanted to talk to him, wanted to curl up in his arms while she worked up the courage to do what she was about to do. But she had to stop thinking that way. She did not need his comfort or his encouragement. She did not need him at all. With forced confidence, and a straight back, she did her best to fix her hair. Then she tossed back her shoulders and bounced down the stairs. She was on her way to becoming an independent woman—self-confident, capable, unafraid. She would build her own life, beginning tonight. She would make all of her own arrangements. The resolve felt good. She was in control, she was joyful, and she was tingling with hopes of a bright new future. Nothing would stop her. Absolutely nothing. Except . . . perhaps . . . a world full of strangers.

Oh God, she thought when she stumbled into the downstairs pub. There were people everywhere. Crowds of them. She felt suffocated, she felt stared at. She wanted to run back upstairs and hide. Glasses were clanking together, men were laughing loudly—at her? No, probably not. But she really shouldn't be there alone, should she? Now, at least one of them was definitely staring at her. She caught him right in the act. She should just sneak away while she still could, right? It just wasn't safe. All these people . . . many of them criminals, no doubt. They were talking so loudly. The smoke, the liquor, the voices . . . they were making her dizzy. Why, if she stepped from this ledge, she would be forced to rub up against strangers, to squeeze by them just to cross the room. She would have to be touched. By real people. Strangers were so unpredictable. How did she know that one wouldn't draw a pistol and shoot her right here and now? She could see many weapons hanging from silken sashes.

She closed her eyes and thought about her breath. Breathe, she told herself, clutching to the banister. Just breathe. "Can I help you?" This came from a gruff old man in an apron. He was carrying a tray of drinks.

"No," she said frantically. "No."

He started to walk away, but Isabella punched herself on the leg. She felt stupid. She turned as though to walk back up the stairs, but she just couldn't bring herself to do it. If she went up there and returned to that little bedroom, with nothing to do all night and nothing to do again tomorrow, she would be forced to suffer with the knowledge of her own cowardice. If she didn't pull herself out of her shell right now, then when would she? "Stop!" she cried.

The aproned man turned and looked at her as though she were mad. "What is it?" he asked.

"I . . . I'm looking for a job," she blurted out. "I—"

"Good," he said. "Follow me. We can use your help right now." He turned and walked away. Stunned, Isabella paused only a moment, and then raced to follow him before he was lost in the crowd.

"I . . . I could do dishes," she stammered, "or I could"— she swallowed—"I could help cook, or—"

"You'll be a waitress," he informed her. "That's where I need help." He led her into a hot kitchen, which was filled with smoke and burned-out employees.

"Hey, watch where you're going!" one yelled at him as the owner tried to get past.

"Watch your mouth," he retorted. "Or you can find yourself another job."

"Oh, and who will replace me?" the heavy man sneered. "A pirate? Come on, you know you have too many customers, and not enough help."

The gruff owner did not reply, but only found an apron for Isabella. "Put this on," he told her, tossing it at her breast.

Isabella looked at it warily. A waitress? This wasn't what she'd wanted. A job, yes. A nice quiet job where she could scrub dishes and daydream. But to wait on customers? What if they were mean to her? "Umm, sir, I—"

"Smiling is optional," he shouted at her over the kitchen's clamor. "You don't have to be pretty about it, or even polite. Just get their orders, and get them right. If anyone hassles you, spit in his food. Or his face, for all I care. Now, go."

Isabella frantically tied the apron around her waist. "What . . . what do I do again?"

"Just get out there and ask people what they want to eat! You can ignore the ones at the bar. They're just drinking. But go see to the tables."

Isabella was so shaken by his tone of voice that she found herself obediently scurrying out, completely forgetting that she'd meant to turn down the job. She literally stumbled into a massive pirate, who caught her in two strong arms just before she fell to the floor. "Are you all right, sweetie?" he asked jovially.

"Yes," she replied. "I'm sorry. I'm very sorry." Then she pulled out of his clutches, and scurried toward the tables. There was another waitress, a small young lady with jet black hair and a badly soiled gown.

"You the new waitress?" she called over the deafening noise of customers.

Isabella nodded, her mouth hanging open.

"I've already helped this half of the room!" she called. "You help that half!"

Isabella nodded. But when she turned about to see how angry her half of the room was, she wasn't at all certain she should have. These men had not been fed in a while. "Umm, umm . . . may I help you?" she asked a nice-looking couple sitting at the nearest table.

"Hey, what about us?" called a rowdy bunch who had pushed three tables together so they could arm wrestle. "We've been waiting longer than they have!"

Isabella apologized to the couple. "I'm sorry. I'll . . . I'll be right back." And she pushed her way toward the table of arm wrestlers. "May I help you?"

"Wait a minute!" called a plume-hatted pirate captain from a corner table. "They've not been here as long as I have!"

Isabella apologized again. "I'm sorry, men. I guess I'll have to go wait on him first."

"Not so fast," said one, tugging at her skirt. "You take our orders first. We're hungry."

"But the captain—"

"You want me to tear this skirt right off you?" he threatened. "Right in front of everyone?"

Isabella looked over each of her shoulders to see whether she might find help. But her boss was nowhere to be found. In fact, she could barely see anything through the standing crowds of men. "I'll . . . I'll take your order," she promised. "What would you like?"

"How about a piece of you?" he asked, and his eyes told her he wasn't joking.

"I said I want service!" called the pirate captain, rising to his feet in the corner of the room.

"Just a moment, sir!" she called.

"No, *now!*" he demanded. "Or I'll have you fired!"

"But . . ." She looked around her frantically.

"So what do you say?" asked the evil-eyed arm wrestler. "Come up to my room?"

The nice couple stood up and left the establishment, griping about poor service and how they must speak to the owner.

"I'm in a hurry," she begged. "Just tell me what you want to eat, so I can help the pirate captain."

"What about me?" asked another arm wrestler. "Don't you want to hear my order? Say, you're beautiful," he added, catching a glimpse at her angelic face. "Do you want to play cards for clothes later on?" A lot of the men laughed at that.

"Come on, I'm serious," pleaded the one who was not laughing, but still clutching her skirt. "I can make you feel good."

"Get over here!" demanded the captain, his eyes fuming.

"Actually," cried someone from another table, "we've been waiting awhile too. Do you mind?"

Isabella looked helplessly toward the voice, but her pleading face gained no sympathy. "Are you coming?" he repeated.

"I'm losing patience!" yelled the pirate captain.

"I'll have the baked trout," said an arm wrestler.

"And the key to your room," laughed another, causing the others to join in his cruel delight.

"Hey, I'm trying to talk to you here," said her assailant.

Isabella burst into tears. She pulled free from the man who tried to hold her, causing her skirt to rip, though luckily, not all the way off. The arm wrestler was left with a long strip of cloth in his fist, while Isabella ran to the kitchen, pink-faced and sobbing, her gray dress ruined beyond repair. Some of the men laughed as she ran. "I can't do this," she told her boss, untying her apron and thrusting it in his hands. "The customers are animals, and they. . . ." She was crying so hard, that she couldn't finish her sentence. "I just can't."

Her boss showed no sympathy. In fact, he looked disgusted. "What?" he sneered with a disbelieving squint. "You can't what? You can't just ask a bunch of people what they want to eat? Put this apron back on and get out there! I don't have time for this."

Isabella was shaking her head. "But—"

"What's the matter with you?" he asked. "I've lost waitresses before, but never in the first ten minutes. Now go!" He slapped the apron into her hand, and stormed away.

Isabella felt miserable. She was ashamed of herself, knowing that anyone else could survive this job longer than ten minutes. She felt perfectly incompetent, and perfectly helpless. Yet she could not go back out there. The men would tease her even more violently than they had before. They had all seen her burst into tears. The angry ones would be even angrier, and the drunken ones would be one drink closer to sloshed. Not only did she not want to face them now, but she was already scheming about how she might avoid them on her way downstairs in the morning, in case a few came in for breakfast. But it was that thought which changed her mind. The thought of tomorrow. The thought of waking up in the morning after this terrible failure and not having the courage to try for another job. She would have to return to Marques, begging him to take care of her, to rescue her . . . on whatever terms he saw fit. No!

She tied the apron back on. If she was going to lose her job tonight, she would go down with dignity. She would rely on the only strength she had—her imagination. She would pretend to be brave, she would pretend to be someone who could not be pushed about, she would pretend to be like Marques. A leader. And most importantly, and with the most difficulty, she would pretend not to be afraid. She marched back out into the dining room. Anyone who got in her way, she gave him a light push and a quick "excuse me." She walked right up to the most patient-looking person she could find. "Hello," she smiled. "May I take your order?"

"Yes, thank you," said the tender woman, dining alone. "I would like some prawns in butter, if you don't mind."

"Certainly."

"Hey!" the pirate captain called. "Where the hell did you go? Get over here! Now!"

But Isabella was prepared. She put both fists on her hips and cast her eyes angrily in his direction. So vivid was her imagination that she nearly believed she was a new person, a stronger person, a person with the same mind as her own, but a different heart. "You may be captain on board your ship," she yelled out, "but here, ladies are served first. You're next!" Then she removed her eyes from him, and thanked her other customer. "I'll bring it out just as soon as I can. Do you already have a drink?"

"No," said the woman, "but I think I would like a glass of port."

"Certainly."

"Hey, we're next!" cried someone at the arm-wrestling table. "Don't serve a filthy pirate before you serve honest sailors!"

"Filthy pirate?" sneered the captain.

"That's right," he said. "Filthy, stinking robbers with no respect for the law."

"Whose law?" called the captain, reaching for his pistol. "We didn't agree to your laws, so why should we obey them? And if you had to obey *our* laws, you wouldn't have such a filthy mouth!"

"Settle your disputes outside!" Isabella broke in. "You!" she called, pointing to the captain. "You're next! And you!" she called, pointing to the arm wrestlers. "You're being penalized because that one tore my dress!" she said, jerking her thumb at the evil-eyed sailor. "So you fellows are last!" Oddly, this caused some of them to chuckle, rather than scream, for they all knew they'd misbehaved.

"All right, what do you want?" she asked the pirate captain.

"It's about time," he grumbled.

"And the more you complain, the longer it'll take," she countered, "so hurry up."

"I'll have the squid."

"Anything else?"

"A little faster service next time."

"Only if you show a little more patience," she retorted, spinning on her heel and approaching the next customer.

When she finally reached the table of rowdy arm-wrestlers, she announced, "If anyone touches me or asks for the key to my room, I spit in all of your food, got it?" She waved her finger at each of them, making sure they'd all heard. "I mean it. One more rude remark from any of you, and I'm not bluffing."

They were quite understanding, and gave their orders without a snicker or a jeer. When halfway through, someone called from another table, "Hey, waitress! Get over here, I don't have all day!" she spun around and glared.

"Too bad! Wait your turn!"

"This is ridiculous," he sneered, having just come into the diner and not yet realizing what he was up against. "I'm not going to tolerate this kind of service."

"Good!" she snapped. "Then get out, and empty up a table for someone more patient!" She smiled. She was starting to get the hang of this. It was even sort of . . . fun.

As the evening played out, Isabella earned more and more respect. Men stopped harassing her, stopped shouting at her for service, and even began to thank her humbly when she brought their meals and drinks. What a world men live in, she thought. They respect you only when you're mean, and walk all over you when you're not. There can be nothing admirable about success in a world like that. And yet, she was enjoying this achievement. She was enjoying being an intimidator instead of a victim. She did not feel like a better person for it, but she certainly felt more capable. She had wanted to prove that she could survive on her own if she had to, even in this world of predators. And now she knew, without a doubt, that she could.

"Did a good job," her boss praised her gruffly at the end of the night. "Tell you what. If you stay on, you can have that room upstairs for free, eat all your meals here, and I'll throw in a little spending money—not much, mind you."

"I'm not promising to stay forever," Isabella warned, "but I'll give it another try tomorrow night."

"Good enough," he said. "Oh, and by the way. My name's Paulo."

Isabella laughed. It seemed funny that until now, they had not been introduced. But the diner had been too busy for them to take time out for such formalities. "I'm Isabella," she said.

"Nice name. See you tomorrow." And Isabella knew that this would be the extent of their acquaintance, for however long she worked there.

She sprang upstairs, exhausted, but feeling so proud of herself that she didn't think she could fall asleep yet. She opened the bedroom door cautiously, in case Luisa was in bed. But Luisa was wide awake, wearing her white sleeping gown and arranging little cakes on a tray. "Oh, Isabella!" she cried delightedly. "Where were you? I thought you'd be home before now. I was starting to worry."

"You don't need to worry about me," Isabella informed her proudly. "I was simply at work." She said this with a grin and a bounce.

"At work?" asked Luisa, "What do you mean?"

"I have a job, working downstairs at the diner—well, the bar. But some people eat there. I am a waitress."

Instead of being thrilled, Luisa just looked confused. "Why?"

"Because I am going to support myself," Isabella announced crossly. "I am going to be independent, and never again sit around idly, waiting for a man to rescue me from the world. I shall face it myself from now on.''

Luisa looked hurt. Her face lost all color. ''Isabella? Does this mean . . . does this mean you're not going to set sail with us again? You're not going to be a pirate?''

Isabella had forgotten that Luisa was still hoping for this. She felt rather guilty all of the sudden, and changed her expression to one of compassion. ''Oh Luisa!'' She wrapped her arms around her friend's small frame. ''Of course, I want to stay with you, and Saada, and everyone . . . but I just can't!''

''But why not?'' asked Luisa into her shoulder. She was afraid that Saada was about to vanish from her life, and now it seemed Isabella might too.

''Because,'' cried Isabella, pulling away, ''I have not sworn to the ship. I am not a real pirate. The only thing which kept me there was Marques. Don't you see?''

''He's what keeps all of us there,'' Luisa objected. ''We stay because we love our captain, and because we love our way of life. Don't you love those things too?''

''Yes,'' said Isabella, ''but I'm afraid I've loved your captain a bit *too* much. And now, I mustn't stay on the ship.''

''But why not?'' Luisa demanded frantically. ''Why can't you? I'm sure he wouldn't object. I know he wouldn't!''

''Because I mustn't take anything from him now,'' explained Isabella sadly. ''Not even a job.''

Luisa felt defeated, but she had too kind a spirit to let her disappointment spoil their friendship. ''Well,'' she said, ''perhaps you'll change your mind later. Come, let's have some tea before it gets cold.''

Isabella was anxious to do this. Nothing sounded better after the night she'd just had than to slip into her comfortable sleeping gown, brush out her hair, and enjoy some hot tea. Once she'd gotten all ready, she and Luisa sat together on the windowsill, looking down at the quiet, moonlit city. They sipped tea, nibbled on spice cakes, and basked in the peace of being the only two people still awake in the whole beautiful mountain town. A cold breeze blew in, but they would not shut the window. They just tightened their wraps and kept looking out. "Did you have fun with Samir?" Isabella asked at last.

"Oh yes," Luisa smiled girlishly. "He's so funny. All he talks about is finding a wife, but he makes such a fool of himself whenever he tries to meet women! You should see him." She giggled.

Isabella's smile was distant.

In the silence, Luisa got up the courage to ask the most obvious of questions. "Are you thinking about Marques?"

Isabella nodded regretfully.

"I don't blame you," said Luisa. "He's so handsome! If I ever had a beau like that, I'm sure I'd pine away for him too, after he, you know . . . ended it."

Isabella was shocked. "After he ended it? What makes you think it was he who ended it?"

"Well, I don't know," Luisa shrugged. "I just assumed. Well, I mean, he never stays with anyone for very long."

Isabella shook her head. "No, no. I ended it," she said, pointing at her own breast. "I'm the one who said goodbye."

"What?" Luisa gasped. "Are you crazy? Why would you do that? He's perfect!"

"Nobody's perfect, Luisa."

"Close enough! He's handsome, smart, the head of his own pirate ship. Isabella! Why did you go and do a thing like that?"

Isabella gazed out at the moonlight. "Oh, Luisa," she sighed. "It was hard, I'll admit. But . . ." She leaned her head against the wall, and halfway closed her eyes. "I may not believe in knights in shining armor anymore, but I still believe in love. I would not be myself if I became wholly realistic. I will always believe in love."

Luisa was puzzled. "He didn't love you?" she asked.

"Not enough, Luisa," Isabella replied, shaking her head back and forth against the wall. "Not in the way that I need."

Chapter Thirty-six

The ocean water was growing cold for winter. Marques knelt on the rocky shore, one knee facing the sky, the other crammed between two round stones. Seagulls were making a squealing ruckus, but not as much as the wind. Marques's hair was flying wildly from its ponytail, slapping his cheeks, tickling his eyelids, threatening to fill his mouth at every breath. He missed his ship. Every time he made landfall, it was this way. The first few days were peaceful, and the rest were trying. He was not made for land, to grow and blossom like a tree. He was made for the ocean, to move, and feel, then move some more, like the stupidest of fish, and the wisest of dolphins. He cupped a rock in his fist and studied it. It was round, blunted by the water's poisonous salt. The ocean was at war with the land. She killed that which did not love her.

"Do you know why I wish to be buried at sea?" he asked Gabriel.

Gabriel was startled. He'd been standing behind the captain for some time now, watching his stoic face as it confronted the ocean's madness. But he had not announced himself. How did the captain know he was here?

"I want to be buried at sea," continued Marques, "so that my body will fertilize nothing. So that I donate nothing to the continuance of wretched dry land." He turned his head and smiled. "Didn't think I knew you were there, did you?"

"No sir." Gabriel was somber. He looked like someone attending a funeral—his eyes reverent, his face blanched from grief, his head bowed respectfully.

Marques studied him hard. It took him only a moment to guess what had happened, what was on the old man's mind. Then he returned his thoughts to the ocean. "We're not like other men, are we, Gabriel?"

"No sir."

"We cannot love with our feet planted firmly on the earth, but only with the wind in our faces."

Gabriel closed his eyes. "Captain . . ."

Marques cut his eyes to the side. "Yes, Gabriel?" he asked solemnly.

"I fear I . . . I must tell you."

Marques waited patiently, but no further words emerged from the quartermaster's lips. The two men waited in painful silence. "She's gone, you know," said Marques.

"Who is?" asked Gabriel, "You mean . . . the, uhh, woman, the, uh . . . Isabella?"

"Aye."

Gabriel took a step backward. "Oh, I see"—he bowed—"then this is not a good time."

"It's a perfect time," Marques corrected him. "I like my bad news all at once, the same way I like my good news. That way the two don't dampen each other's mood."

Gabriel didn't think this was a good idea. "No, sir. I . . . I really think it's best I approach you later. It's not—"

"It's all right," Marques interrupted him, closing his eyes, trying to hide and curl up within himself for just a moment before braving his fate. "It's all right," he repeated with a sigh. "I think I already know what it is."

"You do?" asked Gabriel doubtfully.

Marques met the quartermaster's eyes. "It's over, isn't it?" he asked with a swallow.

Gabriel nodded.

Marques bowed his head as one who had just become a widower. He rubbed his face hard.

Gabriel stepped forward. "I just wanted you to know," he explained. "I just wanted you to hear it from me before—"

Marques raised a halting hand. "It's all right, Gabriel. I understand."

Gabriel thought about running off, but decided to settle himself on the rocks instead. His captain probably needed the company, even though he wouldn't want to talk.

"It was only a matter of time, wasn't it?" Marques asked distantly.

"Aye, sir. It was."

"Men like you and me . . . we're. . . ."

"Soon to be extinct, sir."

"Aye," breathed Marques, "soon to be extinct."

Chapter Thirty-seven

"Oh, Luisa! You must come downstairs for supper tonight! You must see me at work." Isabella made two fists and pretended to be jabbing with them. "You won't even recognize me down there. I'm tough, I'm bossy, I don't take anything from anyone! Oh, tell me you'll come!"

Luisa laughed delightedly. "Of course I will. And I'll bring Samir too," she added casually.

Isabella was not fooled by her lightness. "You've been seeing an awful lot of him," she observed with a knowing squint.

"Well, how can I avoid it?" asked Luisa. "He follows me everywhere I go."

"And you've never suspected that's because he likes you?"

"What do you mean 'likes'?" asked Luisa defensively. "I'm sure he likes me just fine. But not any more than he'd like anyone who let him tag along."

Isabella's intuition was telling her differently. "I don't know, Luisa," she said slyly. "It may be that you go off and get married, leaving me here alone, the last spinster in Madeira."

Luisa let out a forced laugh. "Oh please! I'm not getting married. Just look at me." She pointed to her pockmarked cheeks. "Who would marry me? And besides, I'm already sworn to Marques and the ship. I'm already married in a way."

Isabella thought it best to let the subject drop before she accidentally persuaded Luisa never to see Samir again, just to prove a point. Still, she couldn't help adding, "I didn't know it was possible to be married 'in a way.' I thought it was rather yes or no."

Luisa scowled, though she had the sort of face which looked sweet even when it was puckered in annoyance. "Well, then, I am *very* married to my ship. And besides, if anyone's going to wed, I'm sure it will be you. With your beauty and all."

Isabella hated this topic. She didn't like discussing Luisa's scars or her own facial perfection. It made her feel as though they'd been in a race, and she herself had won. When in truth, Isabella would never have chosen to compete against anyone for anything. "There's a big difference," she said, "between being beautiful and being loved. Nobody falls in love with a face."

"No," Luisa agreed sadly, "but at least they give you a chance. At least they see you and want to meet you. And that's the first step toward falling in love."

"And the last step in most cases," laughed Isabella darkly. "They meet me, find out how strange I am, and decide to try someone else. I don't know whether I'll ever find a husband, Luisa."

"I'm sure you will," Luisa promised. She did not feel too sorry for herself to look upon her friend with compassion. "I know you'll find someone wonderful, Isabella." She squeezed her slim hand. "You'll find someone who wants somebody a little different. I know you will."

Isabella's smile suddenly filled with tears. "I thought I already had." She leaned into Luisa's loving shoulder and sobbed tears she hadn't known were there. "I miss him, Luisa!

I miss him! I really thought he was the one. I really thought he loved me.''

Luisa squeezed Isabella with all of her might. "He did," she promised. "I know he did. And he still does too. I know it."

"But he didn't love me passionately. He didn't love me with a vengeance."

"How do you know?"

Isabella lifted her chin and sniffed. "Because he hasn't suffered for me, and he isn't willing to."

It was a harrowing night at the bar. Orders were shouted so rapidly that Isabella struggled to remember what she'd heard. Twice she brought the wrong meal to the wrong customer and was scolded for it. "Hey!" her fellow waitress Emilia cried out, coming to her rescue. "Tell the brute he's lucky you brought him any dinner at all!" Isabella smiled her thanks, and moved on. There were hoards of anxious customers, and she knew that the longer she kept them waiting, the drunker they'd be when she arrived at their tables. At least, she did not fear them anymore. If last night she had learned to bellow, then tonight her lesson was about disinterest. She learned not to care whether the customers liked her or not as she moved from one table to the next, doing her best. But that was a hard lesson for a sensitive woman to learn.

Luisa was dutifully impressed by her friend's management of this ornery bar. Luisa had never feared the gay lawlessness of pirate life, but in a bar like this one, where pirates clashed with ordinary sailors, tension was high and fights were always on the brink of explosion. She would not have wanted to work here. She was glad to see that Isabella was able to handle herself, but more importantly, she was glad to see the confidence that being able to handle herself brought. Yes, Luisa had always seen it. Her strange, beautiful friend, like everyone else, had been given the same number of curses as gifts. And while Luisa envied Isabella for her loveliness, she knew well that Isabella had a secret shame about herself, a lack of confidence that kept her from showing the world her beauty. It was this shield, this fear that Luisa saw melting as Isabella strutted around the room giving orders. Luisa's heart swelled, for she loved to see a kind person triumph in this hostile world.

"Do you like your supper?" Luisa asked Samir.

Samir had learned to enjoy the way Luisa's face scrunched up when she smiled, and the frequency with which this occurred. "Yes, it's fine," he said, "but I wish they would stop filling my cup with port. Alcohol is expressly forbidden in the Koran. You'd think they would at least ask before pouring."

"They *don't* think," Luisa explained. "Around here, we think no one in his right mind would be without spirits."

Samir grunted.

"Anyway, I thought you never liked being a Muslim that much," she teased, taking a hearty swig of her own drink.

"It's as good as any other religion," he said, "and after I've put all this work into being a good Muslim, I'm not switching horses now. I think I still may have a good shot at getting into heaven."

"I'm sure you have an excellent shot," Luisa encouraged him.

Samir met her black eyes with his own. He found her to be a most interesting foreigner. "You know, there is something that really bothers me," he said flatly.

"Oh? What is that?"

He leaned into her, digging his elbows into the table as though about to reveal a very private secret. "I can't seem to find a Christian woman to marry," he said softly, as though in confession. "I don't mind marrying a Christian, and there seem to be plenty of them. But why won't they marry me? What is it that I don't understand about them?"

Luisa was touched by his sobriety. Normally, she made light of his ridiculous attempts to win a bride. He seemed so blatantly clueless, and so obstinately stuck in the middle ages when it came to love. But right now, he looked vulnerable, like a man who was pained by rejection. Luisa's heart softened. "Well, perhaps," she suggested, "perhaps you aren't saying the right things."

"Like what?" he asked. "I tell them I want to court them or I want to marry them. What is wrong with that?"

"But do you tell them they are beautiful?" she asked.

He shrugged. "No. Should I?"

"Of course," she laughed. "A woman doesn't want you unless she thinks you're in love with her, or that you might come to be."

He squinted suspiciously. "Is this some sort of a heathen thing? In Arabia, all they want is to be taken care of."

Luisa laughed outright. "How would you know what they want in Arabia, Samir? You never speak to the women there. How do you know that they don't wish for love?"

"But what is important about love?" he asked. "Will love feed a woman or clothe her children? Of course not. It is a man's sense of obligation that should matter to her."

"Well, I'm sure that matters too," said Luisa, "and I'm sure that a lot of women will be happy to learn of your strong sense of obligation as a family man. That's a very attractive thing, Samir. But a woman needs more. She needs to feel that you love her."

"Well, after ten or twenty years of living together, I'm sure I'll love her."

"No, Samir. That's the kind of love you have for a mother or a sister. That's like comfort in seeing a familiar face. That, too, is important. But that's not the only kind of love a woman wants you to have for her."

"Well, what other kind is there?" he asked.

"Oh, I don't know how to explain it," she said, wistfully spinning the port around in her glass. "Romantic love is . . . it's when you see something magical in someone else . . . something that she can't even see herself. It's when you get butterflies every time you're around someone." Luisa moved her eyes dreamily about the room, in an uncharacteristically fanciful expression. "Oh, the butterflies wear off in time, of course. But you always remember them. And even fifty years later, if you look at her, and you really try, you can remember what it is that she taught you, what magic she reminded you of, that was so important that you couldn't risk letting her out of your sight again, lest you lose the jewel she has accidentally placed in your palm. Now, that's love."

"Ahhhh," he said, stroking his beard, "I think I understand now. You mean a woman wants to know that you look forward to seeing her every day."

"That's right," she smiled.

"And that her eyes remind you of the mysteries of the night sky."

"Uh-huh."

"And that when you're with her, you feel like an important person, like somebody's really listening."

"Sure, why not?"

"And that you wonder whether her scent is as soft as her looks. But you don't want to lean over and see, for you fear she would be startled like a shy deer."

"You're getting the hang of it."

Samir's eyes grew hooded in the midst of his overpowering emotion. "That you love even her imperfections," he continued in a whisper, "because they keep her modest. And without them, you fear you'd never have a chance with her."

"Uh-huh. Something like that, I guess."

"But is it enough?" he asked with a startle. "Is that kind of love enough to make a marriage? Just because you long for a woman, after all, doesn't mean she'll be good at cleaning the house," he said pensively.

"That's another thing I've been meaning to talk to you about," she ventured, leaning into him a bit. "You have a way of . . . well, I don't mean to offend you, but . . . you have a way of speaking to women as though you're looking for a workhorse. We don't like that."

He looked surprised. "Really?"

"No, really," she assured him. "We really don't."

"Hmmm. But surely a woman knows that she must earn her keep."

"No, Samir. Surely, in fact, she does not want to be told that."

"But unless a man is very wealthy, his wives cannot simply frolic."

"Wife, Samir. One wife. That's all you're allowed here."

"Sorry."

"Well, look at it this way," she explained. "All right, let's say that your wife must work, for practical reasons. You need someone to help you with your crops or what-not. Fine. But a woman wants to be told that you'll be building a life *together*. The way you put it, it's as though she'll be your employee. As though she's working *for* you, instead of *with* you. Do you understand the difference?"

"Hmmm." He fondled his shiny black beard. "And this difference is important to a woman?"

"Yes, very important."

"I see," he said. "But—"

"Hey!" A burly sailor nearly knocked over their table as he passed them. "That's an ugly woman you got there. Shame on you, beating your wife till she looks like that." He and his friends laughed uproariously as they settled themselves into a table nearby.

Luisa's eyes and heart sank. She was used to this, of course. But she wished desperately that the cruel men had not taken the table beside hers. She wished they would disappear into the crowd. She could not sit there now. She would have to excuse herself, leave a perfectly good meal behind, and flee to her bedroom. How she wished they had not insulted her in front of Samir! It was humiliating, and there was something else . . . She wasn't sure what. Perhaps she had hoped Samir did not know she was ugly. Why she should think this, she didn't know. Just because he was from a foreign country? Is that why she'd thought maybe he was unaware? It didn't matter now. She'd been publicly shamed, and she had to leave. But Samir's voice halted her impending flight.

"Yes, lucky you," he said casually. "I am dining with a nice young lady, and you're dining with six smelly men. Boy, do I feel like bad."

The sailors were quiet, for they never expected their rudeness to be challenged, not when they so outnumbered the couple. "Well, I'd rather eat by myself than with an ugly tramp. What did you do? Pay one gold piece for her at the docks? Well, if you did, you got cheated!" The sailor who'd made this come-back was congratulated by laughter and pats on the back.

Samir didn't wait even a moment to reply. "Yes, I can see you're a great judge of beauty. What's that scent you're wearing? Eau de dead fish?"

One man rose to his feet. He was about a foot taller than Samir, and a hundred pounds heavier. "Hey, what are you?" he bellowed. "Some kind of an Arab or something? You don't look like you're from here."

"Thank you for your interest," said Samir as though on the verge of falling asleep, "but unlike you, I prefer the company of women. So I'm not interested in getting better acquainted, as handsome as you may be."

The man knocked over the couple's dining table, sending goblets and plates smashing to the ground. Samir, who had seemed so complacent, was now on the sailor's back, jamming his fingers in his eyes before anyone had time to take a breath. Samir screeched and howled, using sound as a vehicle of terror, just as the janissaries always did. He kicked out behind him, planting his heels in the groins of oncoming assailants. His hands nearly gouged out his victim's eyes. "Stop it!" the man cried, spinning blindly. "Get off of me!" When Samir did not let go, and the pain only worsened, he panicked. Fearing the loss of his eyesight, he cried, "Please! Let go! Please!" And when Samir leaped down, the sailor was bawling like a baby.

"I'm going to have to ask you to leave," said Paulo, the

inn's owner. "I saw you sailors start the fight. Now, you get out of here before I have my men throw you out."

The sailors eagerly departed, none of them bold enough to look around them at the jeering faces. Luisa threw her arms about her victorious Samir. "I can't believe it!" she cried. "You really beat them! Those men were huge!"

"Yes, but very, very dumb," he told her. "And besides, I had to." He brushed his fingers triumphantly along his waistcoat. "They were insulting you."

Luisa's face lit up. "You did it for me? Just for me?"

"But of course," he shrugged. "You're the only person who's befriended me since I came to this heathen land. It's natural that I should defend you."

"Oh Samir," she said, head shaking, tears in her eyes. She threw her arms around him again, and this time, gave him a big friendly kiss on the lips.

"Hmm," he said when she'd finished. "I think I just learned something else that Christian women like."

"What's that?"

"Blood letting. I'll have to remember that. You like your men romantic and violent."

"Make a note of it," she teased, diving into him for another kiss.

Isabella came bouncing out of the kitchen, her apron tossed aside and her hair free from its bun. "All right, Luisa! My shift is over, I . . ." She saw the two of them locked by the arms and lips. "Oh great," she moaned, turning away. "Now I'm the only one who's not in love."

Luisa broke free of Samir's kiss so she could smile at him. The two of them locked eyes and grinned. When Isabella caught her eye from the corner, she said, "Oh, Isabella! I'm sorry, I didn't see you. Here, let me get ready. I'll go back to the room with you."

"No, no," Isabella protested, tossing up her hands. "You stay here. Have a good time. Someone should. I'll see you in the morning."

She ascended the stairs with lead feet and a heavy head. The dreariness of work had a way of repelling her from thoughts of love, and she could not stand thinking about Luisa and Samir. All she wanted to do was sleep. The last thing she wanted right now, she thought, opening the bedroom door, was to be reminded of something as disappointing, treacherous, and downright depressing as love. She swung open the door. She could hardly wait to slip into her bed gown, and into her cozy sheets. Her mind would be too filled with smoke and breaking dishes and men shouting orders from across the room to dream about anything even remotely related to love. Yes, first she would make herself a nice cup of tea, and then . . .

"Marques!"

Chapter Thirty-eight

She had never seen him look so stern or so callous. There was no humor in his gaze tonight, no laughter in his eyes or lightness in his step. He looked fierce. "Where have you been?" he demanded. "I've been waiting for hours."

"What are you doing in my room?" she countered. "How did you get in here? And why?"

"Answer my question first," he ordered. His bulky arms were crossed, and something in his gaze was frightening her.

"I . . . I was working," she muttered, uncomfortable with his accusing gaze. "I have a job now, working downstairs at the pub."

His expression was incredulous. "Why?"

"Why not?" she asked.

"Did you think I wouldn't take care of you?" he demanded. "Just because you left me? Did you think I would leave you penniless and unprotected?" He tossed her a pouch filled with gold. "I came to bring you this, and one of your gowns is ready too." He pointed toward a package tied in a pink bow. "I don't appreciate your underestimating me. Is it because I'm a pirate? Is that why you thought you couldn't depend on me to take care of my own?''

Isabella knew better than to confess to something that would so deeply offend him. "No, Marques, no. I . . . I know you're a gentleman.''

This seemed to appease him somewhat, as his posture relaxed. His eyes, however, remained deadly.

"I just thought I should fend for myself for a while," she continued. "I just thought—''

"Well, you were wrong," he snapped. "You should have known I would look after you." He moved to the window, and stood in the faint moonlight as one who was either defeated or tired of fighting. Isabella could not tell which. He leaned against the windowsill, one arm overhead and looked out blankly, as though he could see nothing.

"Marques, what is it?" she implored him. "What is the matter? I know this could not all be because I have taken a job." Her heart ached at seeing him so pained and rigid.

Marques took a deep sigh. He hadn't planned to tell her anything, but now, it seemed the only thing to do. She was the only person in the world to whom he longed to confide. He could not resist sharing this with her, though a piece of him nagged him for not concealing his pain. Isabella was different from other people. She would listen, and she would care. "Roberts is dead," he announced icily.

Isabella gasped. "That pirate you admire so much? The one who—''

"Hunted down and murdered," he reported. "His men tossed him overboard so that his body would not be defiled by lawmen.''

"Oh, I'm so sorry," she told him with a heavy breath. "I know how much you admired him.''

"It's not just that," he continued, spinning around to show her the bitterness in his bright eyes. "The antipiracy laws have passed. They're rounding us up, executing us, covering our bodies with tar so we won't rot, then hanging us in cages to teach children a lesson.''

Isabella's jaw fell open. "But . . . but what do you mean? I . . . well, it's always been against the law, hasn't it?''

"Yes," he said sharply, "but not like this. Killing us used to be one of their projects. Now it's their *only* project. They're expending all of their resources to do it. Every country which has ever been troubled by pirates has banded together. They're letting people starve while they pour money into having us hunted down. They're printing false reports about revolting acts committed by pirates against civilians. They're stirring up hostility, and getting their people to support any action it takes to have us all eliminated.''

"But . . . but Marques, you've been hunted before.''

"It's over!" he shouted, making her jump. "It's over! We can't compete against entire navies! We can't defend ourselves against countries who will stop at nothing to kill us! They're even executing those who accept our money on dry land.''

"What?" she gasped. "That doesn't make sense.''

"Terror," he explained. "They want to spread terror, then turn around and blame us for it.''

"But Luisa . . .''

"Nobody knows yet," he told her dryly. "Word hasn't reached this island yet. It'll be safe here for a few months more.''

Isabella's heart was racing. "Then you must leave!" she cried. "You must leave this island before we're found!''

"If we set sail, we'll be killed," he broke in. "All ships are being pulled over and inspected. It's safer here for the time being.''

"Then what . . . what will you do? Where—''

"I don't know!" he yelled, and it was not until then that Isabella realized he had never raised his voice at her before. It was startling. "Do you think I know what to do?" he asked accusingly. "Do you think I have some magic plan to save us all from death? Well, I don't!" He grabbed her by the elbows and shook her roughly. "I don't know what to do, Isabella! Everything I've worked for, everything I am! It's gone! Damn it! I'm a robber like everyone else in this world, but I am not a murderer! I have never killed a civilian, and I never will! They want to hunt me down, put my body in a cage, and spit on my memory! And you ask me, 'What shall I do?'! Why don't you tell me?"

"Marques, stop it," she breathed, closing her eyes against his hatred. "You're scaring me."

He released her and turned away. He faced the wall, took some deep breaths, and tried to control himself. He must not frighten a lady. No matter what happened to him, no matter whether he had a future or not, he must not stoop to frightening a woman.

"Marques," she pleaded, approaching his turned back, "please don't be angry—not with me."

He shook his head. "I'm not. It's just . . ." He grimaced hard, successfully preventing tears. "Roberts was such a fine gentleman. So civilized." He paused for an eerie moment as a horse clopped by outside. "I have known so few civilized men."

Isabella wrapped her arms around his waist, and sank her head into his back. "I know, Marques. I know." She felt his hard stomach, and the muscles that rippled under his silk shirt. She hated him for not loving her as he should, but he was still a friend, and he was in so much pain, it was tangible. Right and wrong had grown so fuzzy in her mind. It was all so confusing when the good guys kept acting like bad guys, and even the bad guys had their moments of beauty. But Marques was here and he was real, and that was something she could believe in. She lifted her hands to his pounding chest. He was so warm, so hard and strong. She rubbed him a bit through his soft shirt.

"What are you doing?" he scowled, whipping around and grabbing hold of her wrist.

Isabella was speechless. She hadn't been thinking about it. She'd just done what seemed natural.

"Are you trying to arouse me?" he asked bitterly, releasing her wrist with a toss. "What the hell are you trying to do to me?"

Isabella just shook her head, but no words emerged from her lips. She could not think of an excuse, and she could not stop looking at his menacing eyes.

"Don't play games with a man who has lost everything," he warned, taking a few sauntering steps toward her.

Isabella backed away, but met his eyes with strength.

"If the stories they're printing about me were true," he said roughly, "I'd thrash you right now, just for the hell of it. I'd have thrashed you a long time ago."

She closed her eyes against his fury. "Marques—"

"Don't 'Marques' me," he warned, letting her back herself against a wall. He did not go so far as to trap her, but stood near enough that she could not move without touching him. "You abandoned me for not marrying you, even though I proposed marriage!" he laughed. For a moment, this made absolutely no sense to him, though an hour ago, he'd understood. "Then you didn't tell me where you were going. I hunted you down, found out you'd taken a job as a *barmaid*." He emphasized the word, as though her new occupation were an embarrassment to him. "I asked you why, and you made it sound as though you needed the money, as though I'd not have the decency to take care of a woman I loved. Then I pour my heart out to you, and you try to *arouse* me? Are you insane?" He let out a little snort. "Oh yes, that's right. You are insane. I forgot."

"You take that back, Marques," she gathered her courage to warn. "I mean it. You take it back."

"All right," he gave in easily, planting a hand on the wall beside her trembling face. "I take it back." He narrowed his eyes at her and stared, as though he were trying to kill her with his gaze. "Now why don't you tell me what the hell you think you're doing?"

She turned her face away.

"Don't do that," he said angrily. "Don't avoid me." He manually turned her cheek until she faced him. "Look me in the eye," he said, squeezing her cheeks together, "and tell me what you want. Do you want this?" he asked bitterly, using his free hand to fondle the hem of her skirt.

She slapped his hand away.

"No?" he asked cruelly. "Then what is it, Isabella? Are you just trying to torment me? Am I not suffering enough for you today?"

Isabella was getting angry. "Let go of me," she said, trying to wiggle from his clasp.

He did so without hesitation. "You haven't answered my question," he reminded her hotly. "You haven't told me what you want. So what is it?"

She didn't like his tone. She didn't like the way he was handling her, or the way he was making her feel like a selfish child. "Just calm down," she commanded. "Don't you have anything better to do than harass me?"

"No, I really don't," he said abruptly. "I have nothing to do. I'm unemployed. Men are looking to have my head cut off, and my lover has run off. So no, Isabella. I've got nothing better to do, and nowhere better to be. So what do you want?"

"I hate you," she spat, though she didn't mean it. She just didn't like this side of him.

"Oh really? Do you hate me?" he asked sharply. "That's nice. I'm pretty used to that, after all. How does it feel to be one of the crowd, Isabella?"

"You are so full of yourself, Marques!"

His blood was beating into his veins so rapidly that he felt drunk. "Hey, somebody has to like me. Now, how about it, Isabella? What do you want from me? Do you want me to drop dead? Do you want to turn me into the authorities?"

"Oh, you would like that," she whispered through clenched

teeth. "That would really wrap up your life nicely—to be betrayed by your lover and sent to your death. Well, I won't facilitate your drama!"

"Then what do you want from me?" he scowled. "Do you want a little blood out of my veins? Do you want me to crawl to you?"

Isabella screamed. "Yes! That's exactly what I want!"

"I'm sure you do! Gabriel was right about you, you know. Nothing's good enough for you!"

"Maybe *you're* just not good enough for me!"

"*What?*"

"You heard me! Maybe you don't have what it takes to be my lover!"

"You listen here! I love you as no other could!"

"You don't love me with a vengeance!"

"Love you with a vengeance? What is that? One of your vague, romantic notions which I can never fulfill?"

"Call it what you like!"

"I love you like a madman! I love you with a blood that boils and a spirit that aches!"

"Then prove it!"

"How?"

"Make love to me, you idiot!"

Chapter Thirty-nine

It was Isabella's first time making love out of rage. She was driven wild by this new realm of arousing possibility. Marques was rough with her, touching her where he pleased, and not stopping to see that she was at ease. She, in turn, was aggressive by her own right. She dug her fingers into his loins, trying to arouse him, and trying to subjugate him. He cast a look of annoyance, and tried to pry away her angry fingers, but found that every time he moved a hand, it was replaced with a vengeance. And so he gave up, and went on trying to ravish her before she got the chance to ravish him.

"How does it feel?" she panted.

He looked up from the porcelain white breast he was about to devour. "Why do you care what I feel?"

"It makes it more exciting," she said, rotating her hips in anticipation, "if I know what you're thinking."

"I'm thinking nothing," he told her, then dove in for a hard suck against her sensitive, pale pink nipple. Knowing that this caused her a twinge of pain excited him. He believed he could make her feel whatever it pleased him to make her feel—pain, passion, fear, arousal. It was his choice, and he loved it.

Isabella knew that her own power was as great as his, and that with every touch and glide of her finger, she could make him even stiffer with need. "Thinking nothing," Isabella sighed, her eyes closed mysteriously. "Interesting." She tried also to think of nothing.

He put a hand on each of her knees and separated them with mighty force. When he had her spread wide, he grinned victoriously, believing he had won a battle. But she believed that she had won, for now, he needed her more than ever.

"Do it with passion," she begged him distantly. "Make it rough so I can really feel your troubled heart. I want to feel everything about you."

This took Marques aback somewhat. He paused, and looked at her in surprise. "I swear, you are the wildest woman I have ever met," he couldn't help saying. "Are you sure you were raised in a convent?"

Her foggy eyes looked up at him as though she were far away. And he knew why she was so wild. It was because she was free—her spirit roamed the unexplored waters, and no one had ever been able to drag her back to earth. Marques suddenly had second thoughts about taking her roughly. His anger was melting. He loved this woman. He loved her as instinctively as he loved freedom, as he loved the ocean. It was as though she'd been made for him. And as angry and confused and hungry as he was, he did not want to defile her with his hatred. He wanted to empower her with his love.

"Isabella," he whispered in her ear, "I want to move into you gently. I want to give you warmth."

"No," she pleaded, closing her eyes, shaking her head as though in a trance. "I still feel the bite of my own rage. I want to explore rough waters. I want to feel wrath surging through our joined bodies."

"No, Isabella. I can't. I have no rage against you. I'm not even angry anymore."

"Try to be," she begged.

"I can't. I love you."

She opened her eyes wide and glared at him, as only the neediest of women can do. "How about if I tell you that Captain Roberts is nothing but a common criminal," she suggested, "that you and your pirates are nothing but overgrown children rebelling against your families, and that I'm secretly in love with your quartermaster."

Marques squinted for a moment's ponderance. "Hmmm. All right," he relented, "that pretty much did it." He spread her wide, preparing her for a merciless penetration. He pushed her arms out until they flung open like wings. He massaged her tender breasts until they hardened, and asked to be rubbed more fiercely. At last, he spread her thighs boldly apart, stretching her muscles, challenging her limberness. And once he had her in this most submissive of postures, he pressed into her—more gently than she had requested. But he would not be more callous, for he knew that her insults had only been in jest.

Isabella gasped from the precious pain. Her mouth wide, she sucked in air as though she were breathing fiery rage. "Ahhh." She let out a sound that sounded like a wounded woman's last breath. "Harder, Marques." As he broke into her again and again, she wore a strange, open-mouthed grin. She felt she was being attacked—attacked by a werewolf. And with every bite into her flesh, she grew stronger rather than weaker.

"Tell me you love me," he ordered, his eyes slicing into her. "Tell me you're in love with a lawless, stinking bastard of a pirate."

"Why?" she breathed dreamily. "Why do you want me to love what you are—and not just love you."

"Because I want to win," he told her sharply, emphasizing his words with a distinctly insensitive thrust. "I want the loveliest woman in Portugal to choose a pirate over dry men."

"I am not a prize," she countered softly. "I will not be your token of victory."

"Say it!" he cried, startling her with his loud voice, and by stopping his movements. He propped himself over her, both arms straining to hold all his weight. He looked down at her as one who had a captive. She could feel him still hot and hard inside her. She felt completely open to him, completely unable to refuse his demand.

"All right," she said quietly, uncertainly. "Marques, I love a pirate. Not all pirates—just you. And if that means something to you, then I'm glad. But it means nothing to me."

Completely unsatisfied, he was nonetheless unable to argue that she had given in to his bidding. Angrily, he returned to the task of ravishing her. He kissed her amorously upon the lips and caressed her breasts with a hot breath. Isabella responded like an animal, running her fingers through his black hair, tugging at it, gripping it in fistfuls. She wrapped her legs all the way around him, and settled her heels on his buttocks, digging into him, kicking lightly from time to time. "Ah, your passion stings tonight," she observed from time to time with a wondrous, open-mouthed grin.

"Do you like it?" he asked roughly.

"Yes, I do." She could feel his pelvis knocking against her, slapping her, making her turn pink. She could feel the length of his manhood piercing her insides, rubbing her into excitement, forcing her into moistness.

"Are you going to moan?" he asked. "Because when you do, I hope it will be loud."

She met his crisp blue eyes.

"Do you understand?"

"Yes," she whispered, squeezing him in a cuddly embrace, trying to rub her breasts against his chest hair, for they so longed to be touched. "Mmmm. Marques, I'll moan as loud as you want me to. Just hurry and . . . and get me there."

He couldn't help grinning, for as badly as he was behaving tonight, he still had the habits of a womanizer. Nothing pleased him more than hearing a lady beg to climax. Much of his life had been spent in trying to reach this moment, and as often as possible. "Only if you're good," he said, for that created another one of his favorite moments.

"Mmmm," she begged, tickling her breasts against him, "just hurry."

Music to his ears. He cast a quick, thankful glance toward the heavens, then turned his attention back to the lady. "Will you suck on this?" he smiled, moving a finger to her mouth. Isabella was eager to wrap her lips around it. "Not too hard," he warned, snatching it away. He put it back in her mouth and watched her suckle it softly like a babe. "Mmmm," he moaned, the joy of making her do something so strange, and having her dive so eagerly, gave him a rush like none other. "That's good," he smiled, opening her mouth wide with two fingers. "Now just stay still while I kiss you." He dove in to her defenseless mouth with a forceful and curious tongue.

"Marques," she begged, when he came up for air. "Please." She took her own breasts in her hands and pinched them.

His smile was so bright that his angry eyes began to twinkle with their old life again. "I understand, sweet thing," he said, brushing his callused knuckles against her pink cheek. "A promise is a promise, after all. And you have been very good."

Isabella knew she was being teased, but she could not bring herself to defy him. He could have his game. She wanted only one thing. If she got that, she would punish him later for his torture.

"All right," he relented. "Let's see if we can put you out of your misery." He slid a hand between their two bodies and touched her swollen, rosy, neglected womanly pearl. This felt so good to her that she nearly broke instantly. He felt the beginnings of her shudder, and stopped short. "Not so fast," he grinned, slapping the fleshy side of her hip. "Wait until I say."

"Marques!" she growled.

"Mmmm," he sighed. "I like the way you say my name when you're desperate. Say it again."

She grabbed his ear and twisted it until it hurt.

"Ouch," he winced.

"Now, you listen to me," she instructed, her eyes wide and wild. "You're going to give it to me right now, or you're not going to have an ear! Do you understand me!"

She was yelling so loud that the volume hurt him as much as the ear twisting did. "Yes, all right!" he cried. "Yes, fine. I promise."

"Yes, madam!" she demanded, giving his ear another tug.

"Yes, madam." His ear was freed, and he touched it to make sure it was still attached to his head. It was. "Phew," he said, returning his hand to the place she wanted it. "Never knew how dangerous it could be to tease a lady."

"Hurry!" she cried.

"Yes, madam." He was nearly chuckling as he returned to his thrusting. His fingers stroked her while the length of him found an easy glide in and out of her. His eyes sparkled as he watched her close her eyes and concentrate on finding that place of perfect fulfillment. He adored her, he admitted to himself. What a woman. So exciting, so free, so . . . so very much like himself.

Her face contorted before his very eyes. She wrinkled her nose and her forehead, opened her mouth as though in some sort of ragged pain. And then, she broke into a smile and began to free her voice. She sounded like a kitten. Marques let her reach up and bring him down for a kiss. She needed to feel him there, needed to thank him for doing this, and he understood that. He did his best to tell her that he loved her, to tell her it was all right to let go, as best he could without speaking a word. Then his own body gave way to the feelings she'd been stirring in him. He'd had to hear her meow, had to watch her melt and soften beneath him, had to feel her tremble without control. And he couldn't take anymore. He exploded inside her, filling her with something soft and very private. Isabella didn't want him to pull away from her. She wanted to lie there and just feel him resting inside her body. But he slid out with a kiss, leaving her empty and lonely.

"Marques . . ." She turned her light head to the side and flopped out an arm, expecting to catch him on its way down. But there was nothing there. "Marques?"

He was getting dressed.

Isabella sat upright on her elbows, watching, but not believing what she saw. He was just going to leave. She did not speak, but begged him to stay with every silent plea her soul could muster.

He was completely unreceptive to her telepathy. He felt rejuvenated by their joining. Still confused, still lost, still grief stricken by the real possibility of having lost his way of life. But he now had the energy to work on his problem, and the self-absorption to cast Isabella aside as tomorrow's problem. "I shall visit you again," he promised, bending over her naked body, planting a dry kiss upon her liquid lips. "I love you. Remember the gold I've just given you. And the gown. I'd rather you didn't work, but we'll discuss it later, all right? Another time."

Isabella was fading, becoming invisible before his very eyes. There was very little color left in her flesh when she whispered, "Stay with me, Marques." But what she'd meant to say was "Don't go."

To Marques, "stay with me," meant "let's talk." And this was something he felt he shouldn't do. Not right now. He needed to think before he talked any more. He was captain of a doomed ship, lover of an impossible woman, and he felt he was long overdue for a good thinking. Until he'd gotten himself back on his feet, decided how to steer his course, he'd better not speak to anyone. "I'm sorry, my love," he replied, fastening a cufflink while he bent down for another heartless kiss. "I don't have time to stay tonight. In my self-pity, I'm afraid I've neglected my duties longer than I should have," he admitted with a smile that was not shared. "Besides, Luisa will return soon, and we mustn't leave her with nowhere to sleep, eh? But I promise I shall return. Good night, my strange angel. I shall return." This time, he noticed that his kiss was not received.

In fact, Isabella's eyes were rather solid all of the sudden, rather steely. But he did not have time to analyze this. ''Good night,'' he repeated, grabbing his cloak. He turned and stared at her one last time. She was still naked, and had done nothing to cover herself. That seemed odd. And while she was looking at him, her mind seemed quite far away. Strange woman. Unreadable, beautiful creature of air. He would never understand her. He turned and walked away, closing the door behind him with a gentle bump that shook Isabella's bones.

She did not weep, and she did put on her bed gown. She fell asleep rather quickly, even before Luisa had returned to the room. But during the night, her temperature went up. And in the morning, there was no doubt. She had caught fever.

Chapter Forty

"Isabella? Are you all right?" Luisa looked prettier than usual. She was wearing a gown of white cotton, which looked milky beside her black hair. She looked soft, kittenish, and just a little bit in love.

"Hmm? Yes, I'm fine, Luisa." Was it morning already? Isabella's throat felt raw, and it seemed too cold to get out of bed, though the sun was shining. She clasped her blankets to her chin and shivered. Every time she swallowed, her ears clicked.

"You were sleeping restlessly," said Luisa, trying not to embarrass her friend by stating the truth of it. In fact, Isabella had been moaning the whole night through. "I thought you were just having bad dreams, but your forehead was so moist, and you've slept so terribly late."

Isabella blinked curiously. "What time is it?"

"Nearly midday."

This was depressing news. It wasn't that Isabella had anything important to do, but knowing that she had missed most of the day made her feel even groggier. She tried to remember her dreams last night. There had been something in them, something important, and she feared that the moment she rose from her bed, the night's images would be lost forever. She tried to remember.

"Shall I get a doctor?" asked Luisa, pressing her palm against a hot forehead.

"No," said Isabella, wiggling away from the touch. "No, I'm fine."

"You're awfully hot," said Luisa worriedly.

Isabella wanted to be left alone. Not only was the sight of Luisa's pretty dress and fresh face depressing in the midst of her own ugly illness, but Isabella felt that she wanted to be alone with her ailing body. The fever was a private feud between herself and herself. She felt she must face it alone. "It's just a little cold," she lied. "Really, I'll be fine. Why don't you go get some lunch with Samir? I'm sure I'll be up by the time you return."

Luisa looked skeptical. "I'm not sure you should be getting up today."

"No, no, it's the best thing," promised Isabella. "I'm sure of it. A little fresh air, some exercise, a good meal. I'm sure it will help me improve." She felt a cough coming on, and did everything she could to keep it from surfacing. The strain caused a nervous smile to cross her lips.

"Well, if you say so," relented Luisa, "but wouldn't you like to join Samir and me for lunch?"

The last thing Isabella wanted in her current state was the burden of company. "No thank you," she replied as kindly as she could. "I . . . I have some important things to do."

It was clear that Luisa would have liked to remain by her friend's side, for she did have motherly tendencies. But she was also a pirate, and understood independence. "Well, I hope you'll feel better," she said at last. "Please don't go to work tonight if your fever hasn't gone down."

Work tonight. Isabella had nearly forgotten. How could she possibly survive a night of work when she felt like this? She couldn't let herself think about it. She could never get out of bed if she had to think about facing a five-hour shift on her feet, being shouted at. When Luisa was gone, she closed her eyes one last time. She needed energy. She needed to fight this aggravating illness that was pinning her to the bed. She didn't want to be sick! She didn't want to be. She pushed herself to her feet, crossed her arms against what felt like cold air, and immediately felt dizzy. "Ahh," she moaned, dropping her forehead into her palm. She had just noticed that her head hurt. It felt as though her brain were throbbing. And the forehead that reached her palm felt dangerously hot.

She staggered toward the package that Marques had left for her. She needed a new dress. All she could think as she opened it was that she hoped it would be warm. When she saw velvet, she sniffed her relief. *Thank goodness the sleeves are long!* She barely took notice of the gown's beauty. It was a striking sapphire, which brightened the yellow of her pale hair. Stones of golden topaz lined the low, square neckline, which exaggerated her modest bust and emphasized the milky white skin of her chest and throat. The fabric was strong enough to be warm, but thin enough to sway and lilt when she moved, like waves of water behind her. None of this mattered as she worked frantically to cover her icy skin with its warmth. She had never been in such a hurry to get dressed in all her life.

She steadied herself against the wall as she felt another dizzy spell coming on. *Don't faint,* she scolded herself. *Don't faint.* And then, she remembered a part of her dream. The memory hit her suddenly, almost as though it had arisen from her dizziness. Her mother. Her golden-haired mother had been smiling at her. She was laughing, no . . . maybe just smiling. And there was something about her face. Something eerie. It had not been a good dream at all, had it? No, it had been frightening. But why? Was it something about her face? Her face had been . . . her face had been . . . melting off in flames. Isabella gasped and ran to the door. She would get away from this illness, she swore to herself. She would not give in to the fever.

She took a table alone at the restaurant downstairs. Though she looked beautiful, no one approached her, nor even laid eyes upon her for more than a moment. She was ghostly white and shivering. Instinct told everyone to stay away. The angel of death hung near. "Garlic soup," she told the daytime waitress, whom she did not know. "Just garlic in hot water. Thank you." She brought a handkerchief to her nose. What good would garlic soup do her now? She knew it was a futile gesture, this weak attempt to take care of her health. Her fever was far beyond the helpful reach of garlic soup, and she knew it. But she would not give in.

A wig caught her eye, and made her heart drop and then pound, as though she had jumped from a great height and barely caught herself in time. It was a gentleman's wig, a silver wig. It was exactly the one her father had worn. Every curl was in exactly the right place. The pigtail in back was precisely the same length. Even the bow was the same bright yellow. Her father. How long it had been since she'd thought of him! She squinted in the distance, slouching against her chills, sniffing in her body's hot water. She was getting dizzy again. Had she really once been a child? A child with two parents? Right now, it seemed that she had been born about a week ago. It seemed she had always been what she was now. It'd been so long since she'd looked back.

The man in the wig turned, and he was, in fact, her father. Isabella's heart leaped. Then it settled. No. It had been an illusion. She had only thought it was her father. Her vision was blurry today. Her head was still throbbing. It was just a man. Just another stranger. "Here's your soup," said the waitress. "You all right? Don't look like you're feeling well."

Why did everyone have to keep reminding her of that? Did they think it was helping? Did they think her illness would disappear if only they mentioned it enough times? "It's just a little cold," she said, wondering from where her irritable thoughts had sprung. "I'm fine. Thank you."

As she watched the waitress disappear, she suddenly heard

a voice. It made her grab her heart. She looked over each shoulder, and then all around the room, but she couldn't find the speaker. She heard the voice again. It was low and echoing, like the voice of someone speaking through a horn. She looked around. "Who is that?" she whispered. "Where are you?" It was fortunate for her that no one saw her speak, for she was, of course, talking to herself.

"I see you."

That was the first time Isabella had understood the words. She looked under the table, up at the ceiling, and outside of the window. Crowds were gathering out in the streets for some reason. People were running and yelling, but she didn't care about that right now. She was scared, and she found herself whispering desperately, "Leave me be. Why are you haunting me?"

There was no reply. But there was a loud ringing in Isabella's ears. Her head was nearly on fire. "You left me," the voice said at last.

"No, spirit. I waited for you. I waited until the despair your negligence caused me nearly took my life." Unfortunately, a few people heard her say that, and were now staring rather frightened.

Isabella knew what her ghost would say next, even before she heard the next gust of wind which carried his voice. She was thinking about Marques. His face shone in her mind like a bolt of electrifying color that she was too weak right now to look at. Tears flooded down her already feverishly moist cheeks. "Disappointing, isn't it?" spoke the cruel voice, "You left me for him, and he doesn't even love you. Why did you lose faith?"

Isabella's face was contorted; her eyes were melting from her face. "Stop it," she begged, tasting the salt of her own tears.

"Is he the best you could do, Isabella? He'll never marry you. He's only been using you."

"No. It's not true. It's just his father—"

"And you believe that?"

A customer had caught the waitress's attention. She now hurried toward Isabella, panic all over her face. "Madam," she said. "Madam, I think I'd better help you to your room. You're staying upstairs. Isn't that right?"

Isabella wracked out a horrible sob. "Help me."

"I will, honey," said the frantic waitress. "Just let me help you up. Here."

Isabella was too ill to feel embarrassed. She let the kind woman help her to her feet, and then she saw the crowds outside the window again. Why were there crowds? Hadn't this town been nearly empty yesterday? And why did everyone look so angry? Some of them were running. Some of them were yelling. Oh no, she thought. A lynching. Mobs of people. They were worse than packs of wolves. They would kill someone, she just knew it. They loved to kill. They had always loved to kill— for sport, for diversion, for . . . she saw the faces of her screaming parents in their last moments of life.

Isabella collapsed, and her head hit the floor with such force that the boards were stained red.

Chapter Forty-one

Word had gotten out. The antipiracy laws were passed, and something much worse. "They've killed Roberts!" Moans of sorrow, wails of despair, and shouts of anger echoed throughout the streets of Madeira. For if pirates had a playground, it was New Providence. But if they had a home, it was here. "It can't be true! Roberts could never die!"

Marques, who stood proudly away from the crowd, heard that particular remark and chuckled. Roberts could never die, indeed. Hadn't piracy taught these men anything? Hadn't they learned to stop worshipping mortals?

He watched in bitter amusement as seemingly sturdy pirates rampaged the streets, shouting curses to all kings. The ones who wept earned his respect. They were doing the right thing. They were honoring the memory of a great man. But those who yelled obscenities and smashed random windows in protest were behaving like school children, and he could see that. He hoped he had not been as bad when he first learned of the tragedy. He feared he had been worse. It was this thought which caused him to move away from the crowd. Arms crossed sternly, he sauntered toward home. He could see it all around him. He could see what was needed. Everywhere, children in men's bodies were running amuck, swearing revenge against kings and lawmen who were no more grown up than they. The world had a shortage of true men.

He did not go directly home, but took a sharp left turn in the forest. A turn he had never taken before. His thoughts were moving so rapidly, he scarcely observed his own legs walking. *A man is not a man without a woman,* he reflected. If there were no women, there would be no word for "man." Today, he would stop being a child. The pirates needed bravery, needed leadership, needed someone to step forward among the chaos and be strong. This was his destiny, and he was prepared to face it, though first, he had to make an important stop.

The tombstone was small and ugly, and it was hard to think of something to say to a piece of rock. It was even harder to think of something to say to a man he'd never known and never liked. Marques felt he should say something respectful, if not in honor of the deceased, then at least in honor of the graveyard where so many struggling souls had finally found peace. He knelt before his father's stone, one knee down and the other up, not so much a humble posture as a gallant one. He thought it was a little sad how weeds and simple wildflowers had overtaken the graves. It seemed that few people ever visited this little plot, perhaps because the old nearby church had burned down, and burials here were now a thing of the past. Still, it seemed sad that his father had been so abandoned, so forgotten. He was aware of a vague hope that he himself would not be left alone and unloved after death.

He opened his mouth several times, prepared to say something respectful. Perhaps, he thought, he should say the Lord's Prayer. That was impersonal enough, yet certainly appropriate. *Oh, blast it.* He couldn't remember the words. He should have paid more attention in church. He took a deep breath, and let it out roughly. He crossed himself in three places, then bowed his head. He almost began to speak, but at the last moment, just couldn't do it. He shook his head at the stone, as though blaming it for all he had suffered. And the only words which surfaced were, "You son of a bitch." He smiled darkly at his own irreverence. "I came here to make my peace with you, and I can't even do that much. I can't even say a kind word to your bloody tombstone. That's how much I hate you." His head dropped.

He picked at the grass for a few minutes, twirling it in his hands and ripping it from the ground. He looked up when a gust of wind caught his hair. "You know?" he said with an incredulous grin. "I don't even feel right kneeling here in a place of God. I feel evil, as though my very presence were an insult to this graveyard." The strong wind was making his eyes tear. "And I know that it's not the hordes of law-abiding pirate haters who make me feel this way. I know that it's you. You've always made me feel as though I were unworthy of manhood, unworthy of God. You pretended it was because of all the ways I misbehaved, but that wasn't it. In fact, you *hoped* that I would never become worthy. In fact, you beat me down every time I showed signs of blossoming." He shook his head scoldingly at the stone.

"But I'm going to disappoint you. I'm going to be more than what you wanted me to be. I'm going to be something you never were—a man." He bit his lip painfully, and let a tear ride down his cheek without interruption. "I'm not going to be the criminal that you and the rest of the world would have me be. I'm going to do something noble." He nodded decisively. "And I know that I can never be a man without a woman at my side. You never understood that. You never valued my mother, but beat her like a disruptive animal." His head shook instinctively, warningly. "I won't be the fool you were. I will treasure that which I need. And I will protect my lady from men like you." The mischievous sparkle in his eye took on new maturity, but lost none of its playfulness. "Sorry to disappoint you, old man. But I won't let the fear of becoming you prevent me from outrunning you. Goodbye." He stood up, and awkwardly crossed himself again. "Sleep well. I'll . . . I'll have Maria put some flowers out here or something." He kicked up a patch of grass. "Or I don't know. Maybe I'll just let you rot." He spun around and sauntered away.

Within minutes, he had decided on flowers.

Chapter Forty-two

Marques called a meeting of all the pirate captains on the island. Some arrived at the burned down church wearing full plumage—elegant hats and rich velvet trimmed in the finest gold. But some merely arrived in street clothes, too frantic about the dire news to bother with a change of attire. Marques had made a compromise. He wore an elegant suit of black velvet to symbolize that he was, despite the tragedy, still a pirate king. But he wore no fancy hat or expensive jewels, for he wished also to demonstrate that they were all here on business, and not to show off their wealth and status. He was the only captain who looked calm. His callused fingers were entwined, his chair tilted back, his eyes steady and observant. He watched as the other pirates ranted.

"We can't let them get away with this! They are killing our people! They are slandering us! They are telling lies!"

"I agree! This is an outrage, and if ever there were a time for us to unite our power of weaponry, it is now. Thank you, Captain Santana, for calling this meeting."

Marques nodded courteously, but continued to watch from a distance, and to strum his fingers together.

"I say we go on a rampage," said another. "Let's put the fear of God in them. If once we robbed only for gold, let us now rob for pleasure and for bloodshed. Make them think twice about waging this war."

"How long will it be before they attack Madeira? That's what I want to know. They know that hundreds of us are here. How long before they make a go of this island?"

"They'll probably save the tough battles for last. First, they're picking off the easy targets—lone ships traveling near their shores."

"But the bodies are hanging from cages off the coasts by the thousands! Where are they finding all those pirates? They must have raided some of our regular resting stops. How else could they be murdering us in such numbers?"

"They won't touch Madeira. Not yet. I'm sure of it."

"But what happens when we pull away from port? Surely, they're just waiting for us to set sail so they can attack. I fear we may be stranded on this island."

"Which countries are after us? Is it mainly England? If it's England, they've got a lot of sea power."

"I heard it's all of them. I've heard they've all banned together to finish us off once and for all."

"Then let's fight back! We'll never join them! We'll never become part of any of their corrupt kingdoms!"

"If pirates die, all that is free and majestic will die with us! We must fight!"

Suddenly, someone turned to Marques. And when one person did, everyone else followed. "You haven't said anything," said a burly armed captain, "and you're the one who called this meeting. So why don't you tell us what you think?"

Marques had been waiting for them to ask. But now that the moment was upon him, he hesitated. What he had to say would not be popular. And saying it in the face of all this rage and anxiety would be next to dangerous. But this was what he had come here to do. He was the only one who saw—the only one who knew what must be done. "It's over," he said boldly, his voice low and steady, his posture unflinching. "We are finished. Piracy as we have known it came to an end when those new laws were passed."

A hush came over the room, and many angry eyes were directed at Marques. "That doesn't mean we should give in," he added. "We just need to admit where we stand."

"But we can fight them!" one man cried.

"No we can't!" he shouted back. Then he relaxed his jaw and steadied his tone. "We don't have enough firepower to take on a whole army. Not to mention dozens of armies sailing in from every powerful country in the world. We are strong, but not that strong. There aren't enough of us, and not all of us will help. You all know as well as I do that there are two breeds of pirates. Gentlemen pirates like ourselves, and . . . the other kind. They will not join us."

The thought of admitting defeat rested so painfully in their throats, that many a pirate captain turned red. "Then what do you propose we do? Roll over?"

Marques knew this would happen. He knew that tempers were raging, and that he was volunteering himself as a target. But he remained calm and stern. "A pirate never rolls over," he announced, to all of their relief, "but a dead pirate is no use. We mustn't all set sail on personal missions of vengeance. They'll win, and we'll die."

"Then what do you propose we do? Become farmers?" Some much-needed laughter broke the room's tension. It was the first time some of the captains had breathed since Marques first opened his mouth.

Marques himself let a spark of laughter reach his eyes. Then he said, "No. I propose that we flee."

This caused grunts of annoyance from all corners of the room. People murmured to one another, "Flee where?" and "He's lost it" and "Let's just go on without him." But an older pirate captain leaned forward in all of his silver-haired glory and asked, "What do you mean, Captain?"

"I mean that if they wipe us out, then they win," said Marques, suddenly gaining the respect and attention of the rest of the rowdy crowd. "If we fight them and die, they win. They've eliminated us forever. Also, if we change our ways and become men of dry land, then they win. If we want to preserve our freedom, then we have no choice but to flee."

"But where?"

"We'll have to give up our nests, our ports, our security. That part of our lives is gone. There will be no more safe havens for us, for we are hunted as never before. But there are still places yet untouched by dry civilization. There are still waters they do not know, still islands they have not discovered."

"But how will we live?" asked someone with a half-laugh. "If we travel uncharted waters, if we never encounter other ships, then who will we rob?" He looked around in hopes that others would join in his snickering. But they were all looking at Marques.

"That is another part of our lives that will have to end," he explained soberly. "It is our dependence on their wealth that has kept us close to them—close enough to be caught. We must sever that tie."

"*What?*" several people shouted at once. "But pirates who don't rob aren't pirates! What are you talking about?"

But the older captain was still listening intently. "No, I think he may be right," he said slowly. "I think this may be a good time to rethink our position."

Marques showed his appreciation with a twinkle of the eye. "A pirate is more than a robber," he argued boldly. "Robbing has been our way to make a living, because it was the only way we could support ourselves on the outskirts of civilization. But if gold is all you want, then you're with the wrong band of pirates. Go join the riffraff. A true pirate craves only freedom, and will do whatever it takes to win that freedom. Even if it means poverty. Even if it means permanent banishment to a part of the world where gold will buy him nothing.''

Some bowed their heads reverently. They were ashamed that they had nearly forgotten his sentiment, that they'd had to be reminded. ''But how will we escape?'' asked the elderly captain. ''The minute any of us set sail, we'll likely be attacked.''

''That's the difficult part,'' admitted Marques. ''It is true that reaching uncharted waters will be nearly impossible with half the world's naval resources at our backs. So we will need a decoy.''

''What?'' someone laughed. ''A decoy? Someone to sail ahead and be followed while the rest escape? Oh, that sounds like fun. Who's going to volunteer for that job?''

''I am,'' said Marques, causing another hush.

''What?'' someone asked at last.

Marques rose to his feet. ''What is most important is that some of our kind escape. It doesn't matter who. We cannot tolerate a world in which every baby is born into an obedience he never pledged. There must be an alternative. There must be somewhere for those who will not swear allegiance to roam. I am willing to give anything to that cause. Including my life.''

At first, the men's faces were blank. And then they were sorrowful. And then, at last, their eyes were filled with respect. Many of them had heard noble things about Captain Santana, but none had expected this. They were all trying to meet his eyes now, and nod their approval and awe. But the elderly Captain Aguilar broke in. ''Nay, it isn't right for the job to go to such a young man. I will do it.''

The captains looked at one another guiltily, feeling that perhaps one of them should have volunteered, rather than be bested by an old man. Marques met his eyes fiercely. ''I would never ask you to volunteer. It is a suicide mission.''

''I know, son. And you didn't ask. And I appreciate that you didn't ask. But my years ahead are few, and I would like to end them in glory.''

Marques nodded, his eyes cool and respectful. ''Then do as

your conscience bids you. I shall do everything I can to devise a plan that will bring you to safety."

Captain Aguilar met his eyes. They both knew that there would be no safe return from this mission. But he appreciated the sentiment. "I know you shall do a fine job, Marques."

"Captain Santana should be the leader of our mission eastward!" cried someone from the crowd. "He should lead our convoy to uncharted waters."

Marques blinked soberly. "I'm afraid I cannot do that," he announced, managing to shock his colleagues one last time. A mild smile crossed his lips as he explained the new twist to his plans. "I'm afraid I won't be going with you at all."

"What?" came a universal gasp.

Marques shrugged and settled into a chair. "I had a backup plan," he confessed, "in case my blood was not needed at sea." He hadn't planned to tell them all of this, but as he looked around the room, it became clear to him that he would have to explain. "I plan to take a bride," he said, causing many men to sigh and say, "Ohhhh," as if that would explain any man's irrational behavior. "Uncharted sea is too dangerous for a woman who doesn't pirate. We could starve; we could find out the hard way that sea monsters really exist. It's no place to bring a young lady. I shall remain in Madeira," he said with resolve. "I shall miss you all, and pray for my children that they grow to be pirates."

"Need a ship's captain to marry you?" asked one man in jest. Many chuckled at that, but Marques gave the matter some thought.

It was true, of course, that the law would scarcely recognize a pirate captain as a legitimate instigator of marriage. But he himself thought it rather appropriate. "I shall consult my bride," he replied in all earnest. "We'll see how she feels about a pirate wedding."

Some of the men chuckled, and yet, they were clearly flattered by the notion that he would even consider them worthy of such a task. "Hey, not so fast," teased one. "How do you know the lady is even going to marry a swarthy pirate like yourself?"

Marques smiled, a little light flickering in his eye. "I think I'm going to get it right this time," he said. "I think I know what to say."

But of course, he forgot his lines the moment he saw Isabella lying on the bed, drenched in sweat, contorted in fever, and about half an inch from Heaven.

Chapter Forty-three

Marques turned accusing eyes on Luisa, as though she herself had allowed Isabella to become ill in his absence. "Why didn't you summon me?"

Luisa shivered. To be scolded by a man she respected so much was nothing short of torment. "It happened only a few hours ago," she explained meekly, "and I didn't know that . . ." She lowered her eyelids. "I thought you were . . . that the two of you were . . . well, not speaking."

"You thought I wouldn't care?" he bellowed.

Luisa flinched, as though expecting to be struck. "I'm sorry, Marques," she nearly wept. "It just happened so suddenly. And I had to fetch the doctor."

"Well, never mind," he said sharply. "Just tell me what happened. When did she collapse?"

"The owner says it was downstairs. The waitress saw her, and said she looked like she was hallucinating."

"Hallucinating?" He knelt by his lover's bedside, and raised her hot hand to his face. She looked to be in pain. Her skin was so red, her hair so moist against her forehead and neck, her mind shut down. He couldn't bear to see her so sad, so tortured. He could only imagine what horrific images her mind was pressing upon her closed eyes. "What did the doctor say?"

"He said she has a fever. He charged me all the gold I had in my purse, and then left."

Marques scowled. "Didn't he say anything else?"

"Yes, he said he would return tomorrow. And if she was still alive, he'd give her a leech treatment, but it would cost me double."

"Couldn't you find a pirate doctor?" he demanded.

"All of the pirates are rioting today. I could only find a land doctor. Marques . . ." She could wait no longer to ask this question. "Is it true what they're saying? Is it true that Roberts is dead?"

"How could you ask me such a thing at a time like this?" he scolded, lowering his head over Isabella's tormented body. "Have you more concern for a stranger than a friend?"

Luisa thought she would cry. It was the second time he'd scolded her, and she had done her best. She had done everything she could think to do in the short time since she'd discovered her friend's ailment. "Marques, I . . ." She couldn't bring herself to speak. She bowed her head and wept shamelessly before her captain.

"Oh, now stop that," he pleaded when he saw her puckered face. He rubbed his hair, and collected his temper. As distraught as he was, he could not just kneel there and let Luisa cry. So he stood up and took her in his arms. "Come now," he said, stroking her fine, black hair, "it isn't your fault. Please stop your weeping."

Luisa couldn't believe she was in Marques's embrace. His chest was so hard against her; his arms were so comforting. She admitted to herself that she had always wanted this. She had always loved her captain, both as a warrior and as a man. She had envied Isabella for winning his affections, and now, she could see that for the sin it was. Isabella was her friend. And though Luisa had never acted upon her jealousy, her heart had been troubled by the sadness of seeing Marques's heart going freely to someone he had known for such a short time. When Luisa had been there all along. She rested her face against his shoulder and accepted his comfort. He was a very comforting man, as she had always guessed he would be. And she wondered whether there might be room in his heart for a second love. "Marques?" her voice squeaked.

"Yes, Luisa?" He tightened his reassuring squeeze.

"You really love Isabella, don't you?"

"Aye, I do." He dropped his head on top of hers, as though asking for comfort of his own.

"It isn't just because of her beauty, is it, Marques?"

"No, it's not," he whispered coarsely. "I bedded her for her beauty, but I learned to love her for her wild soul."

Luisa had hoped as much, and a smile lightened her mouth. "I love that about her too," she replied. "I imagine a lot of people have mistreated her. She's such an easy target—so puzzled by the world around her."

"I fear you're right," he muttered into her hair.

"I love her too, Marques."

"I know."

"But I love you as well."

He stiffened. His eyes opened wide, and he continued to listen cautiously, concerned.

Luisa broke into a grin against his warm chest. "Don't worry," she promised him. "I know that your heart belongs to Isabella. And in truth, I have become interested in Samir. But I realized at this moment that while I love Samir, I could never live without you in my life. I need you both, for different reasons. I wonder whether you could ever feel the same." She wiggled out of his embrace, and looked up at his puzzled expression. "I wonder if there's room for another lady in your life, Marques. A friend? Sort of a surrogate sister perhaps?"

Marques, like everyone else, could not resist the way Luisa's face scrunched up when she smiled. He broke into a smile of his own and said, "I would be honored to call you my friend. I would be honored to call you 'family.' "

"Thank you," she said. "I have always longed to be more to you than a crew member."

He offered her another crooked smile before kneeling once again beside Isabella. "I never knew you cared, Luisa."

"I know," she sniffed. "It's not your fault. Men are dense."

Marques laughed outright at that, his eyes sparkling even as he took his ailing lover's hand. "I fear I can offer no defense. Now, come, let us see if we can do something to bring Isabella to health. Otherwise, you'll have the unsavory task of committing your new brother to an asylum in his grief. Hand me that cup of water."

Luisa lifted the cup with some reluctance. "I tried to get her to drink, Captain." She carried the water cautiously across the room, watching it shake in her slightly nervous hands. "But she can't seem to understand anything that is said. She only turns her head away when I put the cup to her lips."

"Then we'll try it another way," he grumbled, dipping his fingers in the water. "And if we're going to be friends, Luisa, you'd better start calling me Marques."

"But Captain!"

"Which do you want, Luisa? To love me as a symbol of the ship? Or to know me as a human being. I make my crew use my title so that their service to me is symbolic rather than personal. But my friends use my first name, accepting all the shortcomings that accompany a man, rather than a symbol. So what will it be?" He pressed his moistened fingers against Isabella's lips, smoothing out their dryness.

"Yes, Marques," she gave in with a shy smile. "I suppose you're right. Though it will take some getting used to."

"Get me another blanket," he ordered. "I'm not sure what she has is enough." He patted the layers of covering, wondering how warm they would feel to a person suffering fever.

"Might we have to bathe her in ice?" asked Luisa worriedly. She handed Marques the requested blanket, and looked sadly

down at her ailing friend. Ice baths were torturous, especially
to those who needed them most. But if it meant saving her
life . . .

Marques pressed a hand upon Isabella's burning forehead.
He placed one on his own for comparison. "No," he sighed,
though there was clearly some doubt. "Not unless she gets any
hotter. Let's try everything else first."

Luisa bowed her head. She knew how he must feel, especially
since he was the one who would have to restrain her under the
ice water while she begged and howled. Secretly, she hoped
he wasn't being too softhearted. She hoped he wasn't letting
mercy cloud his judgment. But then she remembered of whom
she was thinking. Marques was a pirate captain. He would
never endanger someone's life by being soft. Confidently, she
decided that if Marques said Isabella didn't need ice yet, she
probably didn't. "Shall I fetch something to eat from downstairs?" she asked, "In case she . . . wakes up?"

Marques shook his head. He looked down at his shivering
love with eyes that longed to weep. "I don't think she's going
to wake up very soon," he said bravely. "I don't think . . ." He
jerked his head up. "But why don't you get something for
us?" he suggested. "It may be a long night."

Luisa curtsied courteously. "All right. Anything in particular
you'd like?"

"No," he grumbled. "Just . . . just get me something that
will keep until I'm ready to eat it."

Luisa departed obediently, and Marques dropped his head
upon Isabella's breast. "Oh God," he whispered into the blankets. "Oh God, don't leave me, Isabella. I've been waiting for
you all my life. Don't leave me now."

Marques and Luisa were going to take turns staying up in
the night. But Marques found that giving up his shift was
impossible. "Just go back to bed," he told Luisa, giving her
hand a firm squeeze. "I think I'll stay up a bit more."

"But Marques, you need your sleep too," she protested.

"I can't sleep," he confessed. "Now go back to bed. I'll wake you if there's any change."

Isabella remained motionless much of the time; her eyes closed, her face pink and wet, her teeth chattering from imagined cold. During the long stillness, Marques would try to warm her, try to lend his own heat by holding her or pressing the blankets more firmly about her chin. Sometimes, he would rub water on her white lips, hoping to revive them, hoping that a little moisture would keep her from completely dehydrating. Then sometimes, Isabella would have short fits of movement. Moaning in pain, she would flip from side to side, grasping her blankets as though they were her life. In some ways, these fits were the most difficult for Marques. For during them, her misty eyes would open, and in them, he could see nothing. No sign of Isabella. Her eyes were only a vacant fog, aimed at nothing. He could put his hand right in front of her, and she would not see it. He would do his best to console her during these outbursts, to calm her without restraining her. But they scared him. For only when she was releasing hollow moans and gazing outward with empty eyes did it really feel possible to him that she might never fully return. That even if she came back to life, she might not be the same.

It was either very late at night or early in the morning, Marques could not tell which. Isabella had just stopped one of her wild feverish fits, and was now resting peacefully. Well, no, he decided, not peacefully. She wore an expression of pain. She looked as though she had trapped herself in an imaginary world which tormented her. Yet she was not trying to emerge. Perhaps no world she could dream up would ever be as bad as the one she really lived in. Marques knew instinctively that he now understood her illness, for he was beginning to understand Isabella. And while that was no easy task, he felt he had taken great strides in achieving it.

He moved away from the window, where he'd been staring at the stars. He knelt beside her once more and took her hand, as he had done a thousand times today. But this time, he looked right at her vacant face, and spoke to her as though she were still there. "Isabella," he said, just above a whisper so that Luisa would not be awakened. "Isabella, I believe you can hear me." He did not search for a response. He had faith that what he said was true, and did not need confirmation. "I know you can hear me, because if I have ever known someone who lived a fuller life in her unconscious than in her conscious, it was you." He smiled. "There is a piece of you which does not need to see or hear or perhaps even breathe, in order to live. And it's that part that I know can hear me."

The moonlight cut through the darkness and caught him in a moment of poetry, when his face was aglow with youth and his eyes alight with unfounded faith. "Isabella, I know that . . ." He stopped speaking, and wiped his own tears with her limp hand. He pressed his lips into her palm and nearly broke into a sob, but stopped himself. He looked up again, met her inattentive face, and said, "I know that your life has . . ." Again, he couldn't finish, and closed his eyes. "I know that your life has been a terrible disappointment to you. I know it has." He squeezed her hand with all his might, until he feared he would break it if he didn't ease up. "And I can't think of anything to tell you, to persuade you that it would be worth coming back." He thought hard, chewed on his cheek, and let the blackness grow thick around his kneeling body.

"I know what you're doing," he whispered pensively. "You're trying to leave us. You're trying to go where you've always wanted to go. Somewhere without mobs or murder, or groping sailors, or orphaned children, or public executions or . . . or good-for-nothing pirates who make love to you and then walk out." He bowed his head guiltily. But guilt would not help, so he lifted his chin once more. "And what's worse, Isabella . . ." He shook his head slowly, defeatedly. "I can't give you one good reason why you shouldn't just slip away. I have nothing to offer you. Nothing at all. This world is worse than any priest's hell." He reached out and grabbed her jaw, cupping it in his hand, forcing her empty face to look directly at him. "All I can say is this. We need you here, Isabella. We need you. There is nothing this world can give you, but God, there is so much you can give to *it*. We need more people like you, Isabella. We're suffering in our monotony. We need more women who believe in magic." He thumped a clenched fist against his chest. "I need you, Isabella. You can rest later. You can leave us later. First, have mercy enough to come back for a while. Forgive the world its betrayal of your hopes, just long enough to have mercy on one man who happens to live here." He planted a tender kiss upon her forehead. "I know you, Isabella. I know you'll come back. You're too kind not to." He fell asleep, still kneeling, and still touching her hot cheek.

Chapter Forty-four

In a room which seemed destined for an eternal night, morning did miraculously come. Sunlight broke in, as it had every morning for as long as anyone could remember. And it worked first to cast strangely colored shadows around three sleeping bodies. Next, it touched Isabella's pale hand and, gradually, awoke Marques with a kiss upon the cheek. He opened his eyes, disbelieving that the sun could have found its way into this room. Everything looked so beautiful in the chilly morning light. Even Isabella looked suddenly peaceful, as though her nightmares had ended and she was finally at rest. With alarm, he reached out and touched her forehead, panicked that she might be dead. He found warmth in her skin and breath on her lips. Then, his relief gave way to something stronger. It was joy. For Isabella's forehead was warm, but no longer hot.

"Marques," she whispered, struggling to open her eyes.

Marques could not speak.

Her face was worn, her hair tangled and plastered to her head. But Marques thought he had never seen anyone so beautiful in all of his life. "Marques," she grinned, her face alive and blessed with streaks of sunlight. She struggled to sit up, and Marques was too stunned to stop her. "Oh Marques," she smiled wildly, taking his face in both her hands.

Marques emerged from his stupor and wrapped his arms around her, squeezing her until she could scarcely breathe. "Isabella, let me say this quickly," he wept. "I want you to marry me. And it isn't like before. I will not settle for anything less than having you for my bride. I will take you back no other way. You are my destiny, and I am not a man without you. Please be my wife. Please say you will."

"Oh Marques," she grinned into his shoulder. Her face showed more wisdom than it had before her illness. There was something strange in her, a new light, something that made her feel that everything would be all right. "Oh Marques," she repeated.

"And don't worry," he continued to ramble. "We'll not live at sea. We'll stay here on Madeira and make an honest living. I'll build a house and—"

Isabella was already shaking her head, the troubles of a thousand years of life gleaming kindly from her gray eyes. "No, Marques," she said, holding his cheek in her own strong palm. "No."

Marques blanched. "You won't marry me?"

She laughed with delight. "No, of course I'll marry you!" she cried, "But you are a pirate, and a pirate you shall stay. When do we set sail?"

He protested. "No, you don't understand. Some things have happened. The antipiracy laws. Well, I told you about that, but . . . you see, we're going to sail out of European waters and stay away. That is, *they* are going to sail out of European waters. It's very dangerous, and—"

"When do we leave?" she asked, her rosy cheeks aglow.

"But—"

"When do we leave?" she repeated firmly.

Marques didn't know what to say. He had never dreamed she would want to travel to the ends of the earth with him.

Hope swelled in his heart. He missed the saltwater splashing against his face on deck. But still, he felt he should dissuade her. "Isabella, it's . . . it's too dangerous. I—"

She replied with a loving smile in her eyes. "Marques," she gently scolded, "if you wanted an ordinary life, you should have proposed to an ordinary woman. Now, when do we leave?"

He opened his mouth to speak, but hesitated. His face broke into a grin. Then he reached out and kissed her full on the lips, with passion such as no pirate had ever known before.

Chapter Forty-five

There was gaiety in the little Santana house as Maria knelt behind Isabella, pins in her mouth, pulling a corset closed with all her might. "How did you get so skinny?" she griped. "I've never seen a corset this small in all my life."

Isabella was beaming so brightly that she did not even mind the pinching pain. Today was her wedding day, and all was glorious. "I've always been thin," she replied apologetically, "but I would rather be strong like you."

"Well, you're lucky I'm so strong," said Maria, pulling, "because this thing is as stiff as iron. Mmph."

Catalina hobbled upstairs to visit the young girls in their fuss and fun. "What a lovely dress," she said, admiring the white lace that hung before an open window. "Very good embroidery," she commented, as one who knew good embroidery when she saw it. "And I like the slight pinkish tone. It will look lovely with Isabella's skin, don't you think, Maria?"

"Mmmph!" She gave the corset another sturdy tug. "Yes, I'm sure Isabella will look wonderful," she replied, panting.

"Ahh," the old woman sighed, "I remember my bridal gown."

"I hope it was black," scowled Maria.

"Why no, of course not," said her mother in surprise. "Why would it be?"

"No reason." She tied and untied some of the bows, making sure they were smooth enough not to poke through the dress.

"You're such a lovely girl," said Catalina, pinching Isabella's rosy cheek. "It's too bad your parents can't be here to see you now."

"Oh, that's good, Mother," said Maria. "Why don't you go get a knife and some salt. I'm sure Isabella would appreciate that too. Hold still," she ordered, then yanked the last fastening closed.

Isabella winced. Her undergarments must have been properly fastened, because she could no longer breathe a single gasp. "I wish they could be here also," said Isabella with a kind smile.

Catalina shook her head. "Now if only I could get that son of mine to wear a wig for his wedding. It's so improper, wandering around like that with his hair uncovered! Wouldn't you think he could wear one just this once, Maria?"

Maria was hardly listening, she was taking her task so seriously. It was now time to fix Isabella's blond hair, and that was going to be a challenge. The strange girl seemed to take terrible care of her lovely, soft waves. Pinning them up properly and getting a few strands to curl at her temples would be no easy task. "If I had hair like yours, I'd put a little more work into keeping it," she couldn't help mentioning.

"Maria!" snapped Catalina. "Don't be insulting. And answer my question. Don't you think we should tell Marques to wear a wig?"

"Uhhhhh." She pulled a hairpin from her teeth. "I'd think you'd be more worried about the plumed hat, Mother. But if you want him to wear a wig, just tell him. Hold still, Isabella. You have a knot in your hair."

"He won't listen to me," griped Catalina.

"Then why suffer? Just forget about it."

"Hmph," she grumbled. "You'd think a mother could count on her son to listen."

"If it makes you feel better, your daughter doesn't listen either. Pass me that flower. I want to see if it matches her hair."

Catalina picked up the lovely daisy. "Oh, what a pretty flower," she grinned. "Yes, the yellow center will be perfect against her hair."

"Let me see," said Maria, stretching out her hand demandingly. "Hmmm. Yes, I think that's acceptable."

"Ouch," said Isabella, as Maria began to wind her hair into a painfully tight knot.

Maria had no mercy. "Do you want to be comfortable or do you want to be pretty?" she asked. "No, don't answer that question. I'm afraid I know what you'll say. We're going with pretty, and that's that. Hold still."

"Maria, dear. Shouldn't you get yourself dressed? It's nearly time."

She gave Isabella's hair a few merciless whacks with the brush. "I don't need much time. It doesn't matter what the maid of honor looks like, but I'm going to make sure my brother's bride looks sensational. Necklace, please." She held out her palm. "Hmm, this is no good," she said, wrapping it about Isabella's long throat. "The stone on here doesn't bring out anything in her face. Mother, go get my jewelry box. I think there might be something in there that will work. Hurry!"

When the jewelry box was retrieved, Maria snatched out a golden necklace. "Ahh, here we go." She wrapped the thick chain around her model's neck. "Perfect," she said, hands on hips, eyes scrutinizing. "And you can keep that, because it looks better on you than on me."

Isabella touched the aquamarine stone at her throat. "Oh, Maria, no. I couldn't."

"No, I want you to keep it," she said casually. "Call it a gift from your new sister-in-law. Besides, I need to do something to thank you for making me maid of honor. I know I was hard on you at first.''

"You weren't mean," Isabella assured her.

"Sure I was. A little, anyway." She took the lacy dress down from the window. "I hope you know I didn't mean anything by it. I didn't know that Marques really loved you. I thought you were just . . . well . . .''

"I know what you thought," smiled Isabella. "It's all right. Truth be told, I . . . I sometimes wondered the same thing. If I were just one of the others.''

Maria cast her a crooked smile. "Well, thanks for getting over it and making me the maid of honor.''

"I wouldn't have it any other way. Marques loves you, and so I love you too.''

Maria clucked her tongue, preferring to ignore such a sentimental remark. "I hope this lace won't itch," she said, rubbing it between her fingers. "If it does, you'd better just grin and bear it. No scratching, understand?''

Isabella knew that Maria had heard what she said about loving her. She did not press the point, did not force the strong-minded woman to express an emotion with which she was uncomfortable. Instead, she brought up something much heavier, and much more practical. "Maria," she implored.

"Yes?''

Isabella swallowed. "You know, Marques would greatly prefer it if you quit your job.''

"So he tells me. Turn around.''

Isabella obeyed, allowing Maria to begin the slow process of fastening the wedding gown. "Maria, I don't mean to pry . . .''

Maria snorted, but let the bride continue.

"I don't mean to pry," she repeated, "but it would mean so much to Marques if you would let him support you instead of your working at such a vulgar establishment.''

"How's he going to support me? He's sailing off the edge of the earth.''

"Which means you could keep all of his money," Isabella explained.

"No, thanks," said Maria, adjusting the dress frame. "That is to say, I'm happy to take his money. But I'm still keeping my job."

"But I thought you hated it."

"And I thought you didn't want to pry."

"I'm sorry," said Isabella with head hung low. "It's just that Marques would be so much happier setting sail if he knew that you would give all of that up."

"Give up what? The job or the opium?"

"Both, I imagine."

"Well, he's out of luck. I'm his sister, not his daughter."

"But Maria—"

"Look." Maria spun Isabella around and showed her the fierceness of her wide, sapphire eyes. "Let me explain something to you."

Isabella listened patiently, not at all troubled by her rash temper.

"Nobody takes care of Maria but Maria. Do you understand that? It isn't because I wanted it that way. It's because it has always been that way, whether I wanted it or not. Some little girls have a daddy to rescue them whenever things get bad. But I wasn't one of them. I learned that people are going to walk all over me unless I defend myself. *Me.* Nobody else will do it. Do you understand that?"

"Actually, I do."

Maria wasn't listening. "So when someone comes along and tells me I'm not living right, do you know what I say? I say, 'Are you going to take care of me? Are you going to fix all my problems? Are you going protect me at every turn? No? Then don't tell me I'm doing a bad job of it.' "

Isabella laughed. "You sound just like a pirate."

"Yeah, well, I guess it must run in the family. Oh, this gown's looking nice." She continued fastening the pearl buttons.

"Then why don't you join us?" Isabella suggested.

Maria chuckled, but when the women locked eyes, she realized Isabella was not joking. "Are you serious?"

"Very serious. I think you'd make a fine pirate."

"Hmm." An excited flutter shot down her spine. This was a thought which had never occurred to her before. "No, I couldn't. I couldn't take orders from my own brother."

"You wouldn't have to. I promise. As long as you weren't disrespectful, I guarantee he wouldn't expect you to call him 'captain' or bow."

Maria couldn't help grinning in her excitement. Could she? Could she leave today? Set sail and never return to that filthy brothel? "What about the opium?" she asked.

"You'd have to give it up. Marques doesn't allow smoking of any kind with all those explosives in the hold. But I know you could do it, Maria. You said yourself that the reason you smoke it is because you have so little joy in life. At sea, you would find so much joy, I promise you'd not miss it for more than a week or so. And we would all help you through that time. I swear it."

"Hmm. I don't know. It's such a big change. Just set sail with you? Just go? Now?"

"Yes! Won't it be exciting?"

"What if we get caught and killed?"

Isabella shrugged. "Life is short."

"I can't believe I'm even thinking about this," said Maria. "What about Mother? We can't leave her here all alone, without any children."

"Then she can come too."

"What? Oh, now I know you're joking. You think my mother will join a pirate ship?"

Isabella raised an eyebrow. "What pirate ship? She'll think it's a fishing vessel, won't she? And since we're not going to rob anyone, that's almost the truth."

"No, she'll never agree to it. Mother's never even been on a boat!"

"Well, then, at her age, she'd better hurry up and get on one or else she'll never know the joy of sailing."

"I can't believe this," said Maria, biting her fist. "This is the stupidest plan I have ever heard. And yet, it's flawless! Mother will be much happier sailing around with her children than she ever was sitting alone in this house. And I . . . I think I would like to be a pirate." She straightened her back and flexed an arm. "I'll bet I'd be pretty good with a sword."

"Marques will be an excellent teacher," she promised. "I myself have never fought, but Marques can show you how."

Maria laughed joyfully. "Oh, Isabella. Can you believe this? I'm going with you!" She screeched as she picked Isabella up in her sturdy arms, and nearly squeezed the breath out of her. "Thank you for being such a free-spirited nut!"

It was a beautiful day for a wedding. The sun was light, but not blinding. A gentle breeze was blowing, and the sky overhead was a perfect baby blue. Isabella had instructed her bridesmaids to wear their favorite colors. So Maria stood tall in her simple navy blue velvet, her thick, brown hair coiled on top of her proud head. Saada wore the brightest of yellows, her hair worked into fifty tiny braids and then locked together with a red rose. Luisa wore emerald lace that flared at her elbows and made whispering noises around her ankles. Everyone was gathered on board Marques's deck. The ship swayed as it struggled to free itself from anchor, but the pirate guests were steady on their feet and did not stumble.

"Isn't the ship supposed to be at sea before a captain can perform the ceremony?" asked one curious guest.

"Yes," replied another, "and the captain's also not supposed to be a pirate, so relax, will you?"

Marques stood respectfully beside Captain Aguilar. The elderly captain was touched to have been asked to perform the wedding. He knew it might very well be the last thing he ever did. He knew this voyage might be his last. He and Marques

chatted lightly as the guests arrived, and both managed to appear
chipper, even on the brink of this most crucial and dangerous
of journeys. Many guests were looking at Marques, expecting
to see him wince or grow anxious as the moment of marital
vows neared. But he remained stoic and formal, unwilling to
display any juvenile anxiety. He had worn not his second best,
but his very best suit. It was black velvet and trimmed with all
of his most expensive gold buttons, cuffs, and pins. He even
wore the black plumed hat which was traditional among pirates,
though it had gone out of fashion on dry land many years ago.
He stood respectfully before his audience in a wide stance with
hands clasped behind his back. Occasionally, he whispered
something to Captain Aguilar, and the two of them chuckled.

Gabriel, who stood as best man, was dressed in pirate rags—
loose-fitting, undyed breeches, an oversized shirt tied with a
red sash, and no shoes at all. He was too old, he'd told his
captain, to pretend to be a civilized man. Marques had agreed
that he should wear what felt comfortable, and not feel obliged
to ''play along'' with the ceremony. Other guests had taken
care in making this choice as well. The few guests from dry
land wore expensive and appropriate attire, including Marques's own mother, who dabbed her tearful eyes with a lacy
blue handkerchief to match her gown. But the pirates had been
torn. Some wore their finest garb, in honor of their captain.
Others had forgotten how one dresses for a ceremony such as
this, and were now embarrassed by their sloppiness. The women
fighters were, for the most part, finely attired. But not in wom-
en's clothes—in the most expensive of men's clothes. For it
was tradition that pirate women dress as men at all times, their
hair tucked under plumed hats.

The ship's fiddler played a song, causing all of the guests
to hush. He was a talented musician, normally confined to the
playing of fast, drunken tunes. But today, he got to demonstrate
his talent at playing something soulful. Everyone was
impressed, until something more impressive caught their collec-
tive eye. It was Isabella, dressed in heavy white lace and car-

rying a bouquet of white roses. The gown's cut was low and wide, emphasizing and exaggerating her tender white breasts. She was cinched so tightly at the waist that she seemed to disappear and then manifest again, just at the plump sway of her hip. From there, the skirt flared into a thousand moving layers of thick lace that were white, yet seemed to take on a pinkish hue in the sunlight. Isabella's hair was tied tightly to her head, save for a few perfectly waving wisps down her forehead and along her temples. Her wonderfully sculpted face was blushing a pretty pink. Her soft lips were curved into a frightened smile. And her gray eyes looked like pure liquid.

Marques could not help letting his eyes wander up and down her appreciatively. But as soon as he caught himself doing it, he stopped. It was a bad habit, and there would be plenty of time to look later. "Ladies and gentlemen," said Captain Aguilar, raising a hand to stop the commotion caused by Isabella's entrance. He had never performed a marriage ceremony in his life, and had only seen it done once. He hoped he wouldn't say anything wrong. "I uh ... well, we've come here, or *gathered* here to uh ... to honor one of our own who has decided to take a bride." He cleared his throat, recovering from his initial stage fright. "Now, I know that some people think that taking a bride isn't very piratelike." Some men in the crowd chuckled uneasily. "I know that some still think that a woman has no place on board a ship." Some of the female pirates let out loud boos. "Some even think that a woman is bad luck at sea. But I'll tell you the opinion of this old pirate," he grinned. "If finding yourself at sea with a hundred sweaty men and no woman within a month's journey isn't bad luck, I don't know what is. How can your luck get any worse than that?" he cried, causing many cheers and much laughter.

Once again, he raised a hand to silence the crowd. "So I, for one, commend Captain Santana for breaking tradition, and not only marrying, but bringing his bride to sea. We mustn't let men of dry land tell us what it means to be a pirate! If we say a pirate can be a family man, and a free spirit, then so be it!'' This caused a ruckus of cheers and applause, and Marque couldn't help grinning proudly. ''So let us get to the point, then. Marques? Do you take this lady to be your wife, to honor and cherish from this day forth, not even at death shall ye part?''

''Aye,'' he said with a respectful nod.

''Isabella, do you take this man to be your husband, to honor and cherish from this day forth, not even at death shall ye part?''

''Aye,'' she smiled nervously.

''No, don't do it!'' joked someone in the crowd. ''He's no good, Isabella.''

''Too late,'' Marques winked at him. ''She already said it.''

Isabella laughed, not disturbed in the least by the interruption. She felt for the first time in her life that she was surrounded by family.

''Then you may kiss the bride,'' said Captain Aguilar.

Marques pulled her into a tasteful embrace, and delivered a kiss that was respectful of the ceremony. This took a great deal of willpower, but he had sworn to himself that he would be a proper gentleman at his own wedding, and not deprive Isabella of her romantic ceremony. So his kiss was restrained, though filled with affection. Many a pirate cheered and howled over watching his captain caress a woman, but Marques did not respond to that. He let Isabella fall quickly from his embrace, and left only a courteous hand upon her waist. The couple strolled away, hand in hand to much excitement and joyful fiddling. ''I'm sorry my men were a bit boisterous,'' Marques whispered to her.

''Oh no,'' she nearly wept, dabbing her eyes with the back of her hand. ''It was the most beautiful wedding I could ever have hoped for.''

Marques grinned joyfully, and led her to the cake. Saada and Luisa had baked it together, and each blamed the other for its lopsided posture. Thanks to Catalina's help, it was adorned with a beautiful cascade of fresh red roses. But Saada and Luisa held hands nervously as Marques sliced into its white center. "Wait!" cried Luisa, rushing through the crowd to stop him. "Wait, Marques! I . . . it's all Saada's fault, but . . ."

After handing Isabella a slice, Marques had just put a piece in his mouth, and was now waiting anxiously to hear whether he'd been poisoned.

"It isn't my fault," said Saada with a fist upon her hip, "I'm no baker. Besides, I was just in charge of stirring."

"You were not! You know perfectly well that I told you to put it in. Don't deny it, Saada! It was your fault!"

"My fault was volunteering to help with your haphazard cake in the first place! You told me you knew how to bake!"

Isabella broke in. "What is it, Luisa? What's the matter with it?"

"No sugar."

Marques had just come to observe this for himself, and now finished chewing with some trepidation. "Ah," he said at last, washing down the flavor with a hearty gulp of port. "A nice, healthy cake. Good for you. Isabella? Shall I, uh, relieve you of yours?"

"Yes, please," she laughed, handing it to him so he could toss it overboard.

"Very well," he remarked. "Now, we shall have the pleasure of seeing how long it takes the guests to discover it, and whether they eat it anyway."

All four of them laughed, then moved into the crowd. "Captain!" a crewman greeted, patting Marques on the back. "Congratulations! Now, how'd you get this pretty lady to marry you? Can't you see she's too good for you?"

Marques cast him a friendly scowl. "I see you want bilge pump duty when we set sail."

The crewman, who'd probably already had too much punch, laughed much too loud. "No, sir. I'll appeal to your bride for mercy. She'll get me out of it."

"You think I'll let my wife override my orders?" asked Marques.

"No, sir. I just think she'll do it anyway. Welcome to married life, sir!" he bellowed out another laugh, patting his captain's shoulder once again in departure.

"Captain!" one of his women crew greeted.

"Joana," he bowed.

The manly dressed woman held out a package. "The lady fighters all got together and bought this for Isabella," she announced with a mischievous twinkle in her eye.

Marques grinned with savvy. "Let me see this." He tore open the wrapping and found a beautiful, silver cutlass in his hand. "This is exquisite," he marveled, temporarily forgetting it had been a joke gift. He ran his thumb reverently along the sharp blade.

"We thought we'd try to convince her to become one of us fighters," said Joana. "And besides, with you in her bed, she's going to need some protection."

Marques laughed and scowled at the same time. "Thank you, Joana. Tell the women I'll not forget this," he warned with a wink.

Isabella reached over. "Let me see it, Marques."

"Be careful with the blade," he warned, showing her how to grip the handle.

"Ah!" She nearly dropped it, but Marques made a quick catch. "I had no idea swords were so heavy!" she said, shaking her strained wrist. "How can you worry about aiming, when just lifting them off the ground is such a chore?"

Marques didn't want to tell her that his female fighters had no trouble lifting even the heaviest of swords, that they would laugh at her inability to wield this relatively slim one. "Just takes practice," he said.

A myriad of guests and well-wishers who were not invited continued to greet the captain and his new bride. Isabella was blushing fiercely throughout all the fuss, for she had often dreamed of her wedding day. And while this is not at all what she had imagined, it was better. For she could not have predicted how lovely it would be to marry on a boat, with ocean waves lapping all around her. She could not have thought how warm it would feel to marry among a crowd of friends, for she'd never had any before. And she never could have dreamed that her groom would be someone like Marques—as graceful as he was deadly, as courteous as he was savage, as comforting as he was enticing. She couldn't help wondering about tonight, about their wedding bed. And every time she looked at him, imagining how it might be, her stomach positively fluttered.

"Uh, Isabella," he remarked at last, when most of the guests had been properly acknowledged. "May I ask why my mother is carrying a trunk?"

Isabella feigned ignorance. "Why, I don't know. Perhaps no one has offered to carry it for her."

"That's not what I mean," he said calmly, sipping from a goblet of port. "And I suspect you know that."

"Hmm." She tapped thoughtfully on her chin. "Oh yes!" she cried at last. "That's right. I invited her to voyage with us."

Marques captured her with a piercing stare. "You what?" he spat.

"I asked her to join us. Well, actually, I asked Maria. And Maria wouldn't come without Catalina, so I invited them both." She took a casual swig from her own goblet.

"You're joking, right?"

She shook her head.

"What were you thinking?" he cried angrily.

"No, what were *you* thinking," she countered boldly. "Were you just going to leave your mother and sister? Never see them again? Let your mother finish out her old age all alone with no children about? Let your sister return to that miserable life?"

"Maria does what she wishes," he announced bitterly, but with more calm. "I cannot persuade her."

"Obviously not," she smiled, her eyes twinkling proudly. "But I did."

Marques studied his bride with something between awe and annoyance. "How?"

She shrugged. "I just have a gift, I suppose."

"Well, what about my mother?" he demanded. "This is too dangerous a journey for such an old woman."

"Better to leave her alone?"

"Better alone than killed, yes."

Isabella put one fist on her hip, a posture she had learned from Saada. "Well, obviously, your mother didn't agree with you. She chose to come."

"It's too dangerous!"

"Ah, Marques," she sighed, reaching up to take his twitching jaw in her loving palm. "You know, there just aren't enough princes out there. The women in your life have learned independence, and you'll just have to let them be their own saviors."

"But—"

Isabella silenced him with a shake of her head. "They've made up their minds. And besides," she giggled, "I'd think you'd be proud of me. My first day as cocaptain of this vessel, and I've already got two new recruits."

"Cocaptain?" he scowled, "Now, wait a minute. If you think—"

"The Great Cabin could really use some renovation. There'd be more room for dancing if we pushed the dining table nearer the stern. And the food has got to go, Marques. All we need is a fishing net, and we could have fresh fish every night. Fortunately, I had one brought on board yesterday, with a little help from Gabriel."

Marques's face was blank, save an underglow of love. "I think we're going to have to have a little talk," he warned. "No one takes command of this vessel without dueling me for it."

Isabella wrapped her arms around his waist, and looked up at him sweetly. "I've been dueling you for months now, haven't I?"

He brushed her cheek with his knuckles and smiled. "Yes, I suppose you have."

"And haven't I already won?"

He smiled complacently, and brushed her cheek. "We both won." He offered her a soft kiss.

"Still," she added, pulling away, "if you insist on the other kind of duel, well, you'd better be careful. I've got my own sword now, you know, and I hear it's a good one." She proudly patted her new sparkling blade.

"Very true," he admitted pleasantly. "I shall have to watch my step."

The party wound down around sunset. It was a beautiful early night sky that blessed the coming of their most dangerous, final voyage. Streaks of magnetic orange cut through a lavender sky. On one side of the anchored boat, there was a man-made village. But on the other side, as far as the eye could see, there was nothing but vast, strangely painted sky and frightening ocean, which went on for endless miles before dropping off at what appeared to be the edge of the earth. The waves were changing from blue to pale black, from serene to active. And when Marques caught sight of the first evening star, he squeezed Isabella around the waist and whispered, "Do you have everything? All of your gowns? Everything you need?"

"Yes," she whispered. "Is it time?" Her heart was pounding with fire.

"Yes," he told her, kissing her hair. "It's time. Let us say goodbye."

The hardest person to whom they had to bid farewell was Saada. "Captain," she said, head held high, lips trembling nervously, "this is Omari." She gestured to the handsome African gentleman at her side.

Marques bowed. "It is a pleasure to meet the man who has stolen the heart of my finest navigator."

Omari returned the bow. "I would like to thank you, Captain, for keeping her safe all of these years."

Marques nodded his understanding. "She has been invaluable to me."

"Captain," said Saada, straightening her back uncomfortably, "we will not be going with you."

Marques eyed her soberly. "I have heard this. And I am deeply sorry."

"Sir," she tried to explain, "I . . . it has been my pleasure to serve your ship. But . . ." She looked anxiously at Omari. "But we would like to settle down. We would like to marry and raise children here in Madeira."

"I understand," said Marques, "and I wish happiness for you both."

Saada broke down and wrapped her arms around her captain. "I shall never forget you, Marques," she wept, as though he were a dying man. "I shall never forget how you saved me."

He returned her hug with an affectionate squeeze. "Be happy, Saada," was all he said. "Be happy and raise many fine children."

Still in tears, she flung herself at Isabella. "I shall miss you too," she wept. "You are strange, and you are the only woman I would ever have given to my captain."

Isabella shed tears of her own. "I shall never forget you, Saada."

Saada planted a kiss on her cheek, and then disappeared without looking back. She looked only into the eyes of her love as they stepped away from the unruly waters and onto solid land.

Luisa was next to approach them. "Don't tell me you're abandoning me too," said Marques.

"Oh no!" she cried, hauling Samir by the elbow. "We're all packed and ready to set sail, aren't we, Samir?"

"I hate sea travel," he moaned. "I've always hated it."

"I told you I wouldn't marry you unless I could stay a pirate!" she griped. "Now, we're going with Marques and Isabella, and that's that."

"Just so long as I don't have to fight," he replied. "I hate blood. It's not so bad when it's someone else's, but when it's mine—"

"Believe me," Marques assured him, "you won't be asked

to fight." He tried not to laugh. He would sooner send Luisa into battle than Samir.

"Thank you, sir," he replied. "Now if only you could convince my bride-to-be that a pirate's life is too reckless for a man of my intelligence."

"Oh, stop that," griped Luisa. "You're just complaining to drive me crazy. Now, let's get below deck. Marques is giving us one of the private cabins. Isabella, I'll see you at supper, all right? And I promise to leave you-know-who behind if he's still griping."

"I'm not griping," he griped. "Just given the choice between hanging from a noose and not, I choose not!"

"Oh, Samir. How would you rather earn a living?"

"I don't know. I'd always hoped to have wives work for me. Hey, don't go! I'm joking! Just joking! Of course I want to be a pirate! I was just kidding. See my smile? Hey, wait for me!"

At last, everyone who was planning to stay was on board, and everyone else waved from the rocky shore. It was a later start than Marques had wanted, for the formalities of saying goodbye had taken too long. But just as the sky darkened to the same shade of deep gray as the sea, the ship sped off to mighty, hopeful cheers. Aguilar's ship was a half hour ahead, and no one knew what had become of it. But they prayed that it had paved a clear path for this ship and the rest of the convoy to slip through the Mediterranean, past the Red Sea, into the Indian Ocean, and eventually, into the dangerous waters of the Northern Pacific.

Isabella watched Madeira disappear, wondering whether she would ever see dry land again. She was scared. The wind seemed chillier than it had been. With Maria's help, she changed out of her wedding dress and into a comfortable pink sack gown, among the many that Marques had bought on the island. She let her hair fall past her shoulders and blow in the wind. She stood on deck and looked out at the endless dark waters. Night was nearing and, with it, would come spookiness, especially in her fragile, worried frame of mind. She had never been so scared of the ocean before. It was so wild, she believed it could tear this little ship apart if it chose to. And everything was so dark. Her knees were shaking.

But then, she heard fiddling downstairs, conquering the eerie sound of wind whirling about her. She heard laughter and was sure that there was dancing. A smile warmed her face. And then an arm squeezed her tender waist. "Come," Marques whispered in her ear. "Don't be afraid. Whatever happens, I'm here." He brushed a strand of lemon hair from her cheek. "We've got fresh meat on the table tonight. Shall we go downstairs?"

Isabella gulped and threw her arms about her captain. "Oh, Marques. I feel so frightened, but so happy!"

He returned her embrace with tenderness. "I love you, Isabella. And you're home now."

She smiled into his shoulder. "Yes. I believe I am home."

A smile lit up his handsome face as the wind blew back his hair. He took her by the hand and led her from the dangers of the deck, to the warmth of a Great Cabin filled with friends.

Chapter Forty-six

After a night of magic and revelry, in which Isabella smiled almost nonstop, Marques finally caught her eye from the far side of the Great Cabin. It was time to go to bed, and Isabella bowed her head nervously in reply to Marques's silent demand. "I think I must go," she told Luisa. "I think Marques is ready to retire."

"Very well," beamed her friend. "I'll see you in the morning then. Don't stay up too late," she giggled devilishly.

Isabella flushed.

Marques appeared behind her, squeezing her shoulders in both hands. "Luisa," he nodded courteously, "I'm afraid I must deprive you of my bride, for it is getting late."

The squeezes to her shoulders felt good, and Isabella closed her eyes at the loosening of her muscles. There were some crude hollers as Marques helped her up by the hand and shouted, "Gabriel! See the lanterns are out in an hour!"

"Yes, sir," replied Gabriel, a strange, sentimental glint in his eye.

Marques silenced his men's jeering with one stern, captainly look. They fell silent at once, but still grinned. It was marvelous fun to tease their captain as he led his new bride to their wedding chamber. But Gabriel was rather somber as he watched the couple trot down the hall. This whole day had made him think and wonder. What would it have been like if he himself had chosen a different path? What if he had not broken the heart of that romantic little flower so many years ago? What if he had learned that he could love only one, and still be a man? He watched them go with envy.

Isabella felt shy as Marques shooed Pedro from his cabin for the night, and closed the door behind them. "You know, I've really come to like that dog," he said. "I don't think I'd ever really paid him much attention before I saw how much he meant to you."

Isabella smiled. "I'm glad I taught you to hear the voices of animals."

"You've taught me many things." He gave her a look that was so loving, it seemed demanding.

Isabella found herself being nervous. Her arms were crossed, her face beet red, and her eyes downcast. Marques observed this with amusement. After lighting candles around the room, and making sure the door was securely latched, he planted a kiss upon his lady's delicate forehead, causing her to look up. "What is it?" he smiled, pulling her gently against him in a strong, but loose embrace.

Isabella was trembling. "I don't know," she replied, her voice somewhere between a whisper and a squeak.

"We've done this before," he reminded her, a finger lifting her chin so she could see his unthreatening face.

"I know," she said, feeling utterly ridiculous, "but I just . . ." She swallowed uncomfortably. "It just feels different this time."

"Because you're my wife and my property?" he goaded her.

This caused her eyes to flash in rage. "I am not your property!"

He laughed. He'd only said it to lighten her mood. Now, he squeezed her with all of his might, and rocked her gently side to side. "Oh, Isabella. What was I doing before I knew you?"

"Sleeping with everyone on the planet, from what I hear."

He didn't laugh, because her joke had been too near the truth, and he was no longer proud of his conquests. He felt ashamed that he had been a man with the mentality of an adolescent boy. He kissed her hungrily, possessiveness in his force, and tenderness in his skillful execution. "Never again," he swore to her in a breath. "You are all women to me now. And I honor them by honoring you."

Isabella smiled, but she was still shaking. Her trembling worsened when he picked her up and carried her to the bed. "Marques," she giggled, red-faced, "please." She reached up from the cot and touched his lightly bearded face. "Don't go too fast. I feel so . . ."

His face lit up in a smile. "I've never seen you so timid about this before," he marveled, offering a soothing stroke against her cheek with the back of his hand.

"I'm sorry," she said.

"Don't be," he chuckled. "I think it's rather adorable."

She flushed as his hot hands moved gently beneath her gown, and rested on her bare skin.

"It's all right," he said firmly, giving her thigh a squeeze. "You know it's all right, don't you?"

She met his eyes and broke into an uneasy smile. He looked so tender, so sure of himself, so sure that everything was all right. "Yes, I know."

"And you know I won't hurt you, right?" he asked, holding her in his confident gaze, not letting his hands venture further until she'd answered.

Shakily, Isabella nodded.

"All right then," he whispered, bending down to kiss her sweet lips, "then let's see if we can get you over these jitters."

He warmed her with his hands, stroking and grappling every inch of her except the places that would arouse her fears. He brought goosebumps to her thighs, her hips, and then her waist, kissing her all the while, awakening her with the heat of his breath. Gradually, he felt her respond. Her arms wrapped around his neck, her mouth opened for him. Slowly, her eyes fell shut.

"Mmmm, Marques. I . . . I love you so much."

"I love you too," he whispered into her neck.

"Marques, if we are caught—"

"Don't speak of that." He tried to silence her with a halting kiss, but it was no use.

"No, I must," she demanded breathlessly. "I must say this."

"Then speak," he relented, letting his hands venture to the cushion of her breasts. He folded their softness in his broad palms, squeezing them, watching them return to perfect shape upon his release.

Isabella was arching into his fondling, trying to control herself long enough to speak, but finding it difficult. "Marques," she managed to get out, "if we are caught . . ."

"Yes?" he asked disinterestedly, or perhaps even with some agitation.

"If we are caught, I want you to . . ."

He met her eyes with a startle. He didn't know how, but he was sure he knew what she was about to say. "You want me to what?" he asked, taking her face in his hand.

Isabella's eyes were as impenetrable as smoke. "Marques," she whispered, "if they kill you, I don't want to face them."

His look was stern. "If they capture this ship, you will pretend to be a victim of piracy," he ordered. "You will pretend to be an innocent captive."

"No," she replied firmly, "that is what I'm trying to say. I will not stand trial before the men who see fit to kill you. I will not be at their mercy. I will not beg them for my life. I won't."

"Then what . . ."

She told him the answer with a distant and ethereal gaze.

He frowned, and dotted her chin with his finger. "The first time we met," he recalled, "you asked me to cut your throat. I thought it was a joke, a way to ward off my advances. An effective one too," he chuckled uncomfortably.

Isabella shared his smile.

"Little did I know," he mused, entwining a strand of pale hair in his fingers, "that I would be lying here, all these months later, wed to you, and promising to do just that."

Isabella grabbed hold of the back of his head. "We shall live together or die together," she swore.

And to her relief and surprise, Marques slowly nodded. "Yes," he answered, blue eyes alight with courage, "I'll not send you back to that world alone. If it is your wish . . ."

"My demand."

Again, he nodded. "Then I won't let them bring you to trial, Isabella." That was the only way he could bear to phrase it.

She smiled her gratitude. "Now take me, Marques," she pleaded. "Take me in case they come. Take me before it's too late."

"We've spied no enemy ships yet," he assured her. "It may be that we are safe."

"Just in case," she argued, tearing off what was left of her gown, "ravish me while you have the chance. I want them to find me in your arms, with my legs spread wide before you, with my heart freely surrendered to your outlaw's soul."

Marques nearly smiled. "M'lady, I believe you are excited by danger."

"Oh, Marques, I'm excited by everything. Now, get over here." She pulled him by the collar to her face, and into a demanding kiss.

"You are the wildest woman I have ever met," he said for not the first time since they'd met. "I'm glad to see you're over your wedding jitters."

Isabella lifted her face to the moonlight, which streamed in from a porthole. Her eyes were closed, and her spirit was already fleeing far ahead of him. "Make love to me, Marques,

Let the ocean receive our souls while we are on the brink of madness, while we are oblivious to our fate."

"How could I ever be afraid of anything," he asked, "when you have taught me to see such beauty where there is none? Even in death and defeat, you see magic."

"I do."

And so he took her, as rhythmically as the ocean's waves, as tenderly as a man in love, and as desperately as a man who didn't know how much time he had left. They met each other's eyes and gazed, strong blue eyes penetrating watery gray. Their movements were as one, their passion was softened and strengthened by a deep acceptance of all that they were. At last, she burst open into a wave a shudders. Her whispering, high-pitched cries sounded as helpless as they were passionate. And he could not keep himself from offering the final thrust which would send him flying over the edge after her. His own moans were just as helpless, his own body just as shaky. He collapsed on top of her, his heart pounding, his breath heavy, his aching muscles limp. It took him a minute before he was able to grant her the courtesy of removing his weight from her breast. With several thankful kisses, he rolled to her side and wrapped his arm around her tender white shoulder.

"Come here, my princess," he said, squeezing her gently to his side, and lowering her head to his hard chest. "Are you all right?"

"Yes," she sighed, "I am more than all right." Her eyes were heavy, and she seemed ready for sleep as she curled up against him, prepared to face anything from within his embrace.

"I love you," he said, stroking her lemon-colored locks. "I will be a good husband to you, Isabella. At least, I will try."

"Thank you," she said. There was a long pause before she ventured to ask, "But do you think we are safe?"

He chewed pensively on his lip. "I think we have a good crew. And I think this ship will not go down easily."

"But do you think they are after us?"

"Someone is," he assured her. "Someone will always be

after us. Even if we have escaped the law for now, there will be danger ahead. The danger won't ever stop.''

"Then will we never find a safe haven?''

"Of course not,'' he said, stroking her shoulder with care. "There are no safe havens—no permanent ones anyway. Death finds everyone in the end.''

"Mightn't we find peace for just a little while?'' she asked hopefully.

He looked her steadily in the eye, his blue eyes sparkling with temporary life and eternal devotion. "We just did.''

Isabella smiled back, and for just that moment, they both knew that they would make it to the Northern Pacific. They knew that fate had not spared their lives this long only to have them forfeit now. For nature knew no right and wrong, only balance. There would always be a need for outlaws. And saving them in pairs was the only way nature could ensure that their wild spirits lived on, forever causing trouble and creating havoc in the lives of obedient men. So long as there were those who would cooperate with anything, there must also be those who would cooperate with nothing.

Isabella fell asleep to the comforting sound of the ocean rocking her ark to safety, and the steady motions of Marques' chest beneath her head. The ship was quiet. All she could hear was wood creaking and water pounding. It was so deliciousl dangerous, this life at sea. And yet, come morning, there would be friendship and food and a day's routine ahead. Stillnes balanced with motion. Routine balanced with constant adventure. She buried her face in Marques's strong, warm chest, and sighed as his arm flopped around her shoulder. Thrill balance with peace. It was not the eternal bliss she had always sought in a happy ending. But it was real, and it was alive, and would always be hers.

Thrilling Romance from
Meryl Sawyer

The Queen of Romance
Cassie Edwards